Toms, Coons, Mulattoes, Mammies, and Bucks

TOMS, COONS, MULATTOES, MAMMIES, AND BUCKS

*An Interpretive History of
Blacks in American Films*

DONALD BOGLE

The Viking Press | *New York*

First published in 1973 by The Viking Press, Inc.
625 Madison Avenue, New York, N.Y. 10022
Published simultaneously in Canada by
The Macmillan Company of Canada Limited
SBN 670–71935–8
Library of Congress catalog card number: 72–76776
Published by arrangement with Bantam Books, Inc.
Printed in U.S.A.

Second Printing October 1973

Acknowledgment is made as follows for the use of photographs:

The Bettmann Archive, Inc.: page 58, bottom; page 91; page 153, bottom. *Alfred "Slick" Chester:* page 106, bottom. *Cinema 5, Ltd.:* page 203, top. *Copyright by Columbia Pictures Industries, Inc.:* page 163; page 173, bottom; page 177, bottom; page 197, bottom. *Copyright © 1967 by Columbia Pictures Corporation:* page 218. *Copyright © 1970 by Columbia Pictures Corporation:* page 228, bottom. *Ken Freeman:* page 106, top; page 112, bottom. *Hal Roach Productions, Inc.:* page 22. *Louis de Rochemont:* page 149. *Metro-Goldwyn-Mayer, Inc.:* page 32, top; page 87, top; page 130, top; page 177, top; page 221. *Copyright © 1969 Theatre Guild Films:* page 228, top. *Lorenzo Tucker:* page 104; page 112, top; page 112, top and bottom. *Twentieth Century-Fox Film Corporation:* page 40, bottom; page 49, top and bottom; page 51; page 87, bottom; page 120; page 130, bottom; page 153, top; page 167; page 170, top and bottom; page 233, top. *Universal Pictures:* page 5; page 58, top. *Melvin Van Peebles and Friedman-Abeles:* page 233, bottom.

Frontispiece: Louise Beavers in *Imitation of Life* (courtesy Universal Pictures).

To my mother

to papa g.
to jeanne & janet & bettina
&
to dodson & dawson

PREFACE

In 1954, when I was a wide-eyed, pint-sized six-year-old growing up in Pennsylvania and still believing in ideals and dreams, I decided one gloomy rainy afternoon to run away from home and go to live at the movies. By chance, the movie I went to "live at" was something called *Carmen Jones*. In no conceivable way has my life been the same since.

Carmen Jones was the first black film I had seen, and as I sat intoxicated by Dorothy Dandridge's lush beauty and invigorated by the dazzling enthusiasm the cast displayed for its work, I realized the film and the actors were unlike any I had ever viewed before. It was more than the fact that these were black faces on the silver screen. I was also affected and moved because these were immensely talented and dynamic people, more colorful, more unpredictable, and more outrageous than most other actors appearing in American films. *Carmen Jones* proved to be a source of inspiration. Thereafter for the duration of my childhood in the 1950s and throughout adolescence in the 1960s, I found myself always on the look-out in movies and on television for black faces. From the old films on the tube, I caught glimpses of a variety of performers with such "bizarre" names as Stepin, Hattie, Butterfly, Bojangles, Rochester, and Lena. At the local movie houses, I had brief introductions to Sidney Poitier, Ruby Dee, and Ossie Davis. As I silently watched, I compared and contrasted the black actors not only with white performers but with one another. To my surprise and delight, the old-timers came off best. They seemed outfitted with a charm, a spontaneity, and an individuality the modern performers lacked. As my interest in the old-timers mounted, I longed for more information about them. How many pictures had Stepin Fetchit made? Had Hattie McDaniel ever played a *submissive* servant? Was there a movie in which Bojangles did not dance?

Seldom was I able to find answers to my questions. There was not one reference work in the library that I could go to for information. But perhaps more disappointing was the apathy of others about all black actors, old and new. Among my schoolmates, there was hardly any concern about a black face—other than Sidney Poitier's—and if one dared mention a Fetchit or a Rochester, he was soon informed that these people were "villains," "betrayers," nothing more than toms and handkerchief heads. Eventually in this age of great conformity, I learned to keep my mouth shut about any black actor I really did care about. But when alone I still responded to and ultimately came to love the performances of certain black actors.

That love continued through high school, through college, through graduate school, right on up to the beginning of my professional life. Subconsciously, I think I was writing a history of movie blacks in my head. Then two "traumatic" experiences not only heightened my interest in blacks in American movies but served better than anything else as catalysts for the writing of this book.

The first occurred in the late 1960s at the office of film director Otto Preminger, where I was employed as a story editor. One day in the middle of an interoffice debate, I was asked who had played the character Sam in the 1942 movie *Casablanca*. Preminger was certain a black actor had performed the role. But I self-righteously declared that Hoagy Carmichael had played the part. To my everlasting chagrin, I learned that Dooley Wilson, an obscure black actor, was the performer in the picture. Afterward I felt pitifully inadequate for not knowing something that was a part of my own cultural heritage.

My second traumatic experience occurred a year later in 1969 while I was a staff writer for *Ebony* in Chicago. Having recently seen the reissued *Gone with the Wind*, I suggested to the managing editors of the magazine that we do a feature story on Butterfly McQueen, who portrayed Prissy. There was a renewed interest in her career because of the film and also her comeback on the stage in *Curley McDimple*. She was a nostalgic favorite for older readers, I assumed, and I had hoped that an article on McQueen might serve as a kick-off for a series on other forgotten black performers. To my surprise, I heard the *Ebony* editors sounding off like my former grade-school classmates. They dismissed the old-time actors· as toms and mammies and spoke of them with boredom, disgust, contempt, and even condescension—as if our bright new movies of the 1960s with their bright new black actors had arrived at something called cinematic integrity!

The attitude of the *Ebony* editors, however, simply pointed out the sad state of black film history in America. There was no history. And it seemed to me that a number of talented people were dismissed or ignored or even vilified because no one knew anything about the nature of their work and the conditions under which they performed. No, I thought. The past had to be contended with. It had to be defined, recorded, reasoned with, and interpreted. And I felt it my task to do so.

Once I decided to write the book, I returned to New York City, where I began an intense and alternately gratifying and frustrating period of research. I watched film after film at almost any place I could—at the Museum of Modern Art, at the Jewish Museum, at the Studio Museum in Harlem, at the Library of Congress, at the homes of friends, at rundown theaters on Forty-second Street, and often in my apartment in front of the friendly tube. My great ambition was to see every motion picture in which a black had ever worked. But that obviously proved impossible. Those black films I was unable to see I read about, going through albums of pictures and clippings at the Schomberg Library, through personal scrapbooks of black personalities at their homes, and through reams of old yellowed newspaper movie reviews. At one point, I seated myself at the library and went through every copy of *Ebony* ever published to track down information on films and actors.

When I checked into what had been written on the subject, I found only one formal piece of work, by an Englishman, Peter Noble. Written in the 1940s, Noble's *The Negro in Films* proved disappointing because it was so much the typical, unintentionally patronizing, white liberal "tasteful" approach. He deplored—rightfully—the stereotyping of Negroes in American movies. But what he clearly failed to see was what certain black actors accomplished with even demeaning stereotyped roles. Noble was ready to dismiss Hattie McDaniel and Butterfly McQueen as mere mammy and pickaninny. But anyone who had seen them in *Gone with the Wind* and left the theater with no more than that impression really missed or ignored the strength of the performances, and at the same time denied black America a certain cultural heritage. In the opening sections of the book, I have had to cover much of the same historical territory as Noble. But what we have each gotten from the experience of blacks in American cinema has been vastly different. From my point of view, the history of blacks in American films is one in which actors have elevated *kitsch* or trash and brought to it arty qualities if not pure art itself. Indeed, the thesis of my book is that all black actors—from Stepin Fetchit to Rex Ingram to Lena Horne to Sidney Poitier and Jim Brown—have played stereotyped roles. But the essence of black film history is not found in the stereotyped role but in what certain talented actors have done with the stereotype.

My final source of information was the personal interview. Many black actors refused to talk to me, perhaps out of some fear that I might demean them even more than their old films had. Some of the newer ones were remote and difficult. One older actress, a particular favorite, promised an interview only if I paid her a thousand dollars. Another prominent actor/singer refused to see me but requested that I send him galleys of my book before publication. However, those who consented to interviews, formal or informal, were most helpful. In Hollywood Mantan Moreland was lively and full of fun as he reminisced on his early movie roles. Clarence Muse proved a bit cantankerous when I visited him at his California ranch, but he was nonetheless informative as he discussed his career in the 1930s and 1940s. Sidney Poitier, standing tall and sleek at Kennedy Airport, was so gracious, polite, and charming during the few minutes that I talked with him, that I was ready to forgive him for all his recent bad movies. Behind his massive marble desk in Manhattan, Otto Preminger sat like a monarch as he casually discussed his two all-black films and provided capsule analyses of black actors he had worked with. At a Manhattan restaurant Robert Hooks was first guarded, then thoroughly at ease as he reviewed his roles in *Hurry Sundown* and *Last of the Mobile Hot Shots*. King Vidor was extremely helpful as we talked in his office in Beverly Hills and later as we lunched at Farmer's Market. An enormous treat for me was a special cocktail party arranged by Lorenzo Tucker, once an important leading man who had been called "the black Valentino." At Tucker's party, I came face to face with "the sepia Mae West," "the colored Cagney," and many others. And I learned not only about their careers but about those of others who had worked in American films. One important black actor ended his days as a redcap. Another became a notorious Harlem pool-shark. Some became hustlers of all sorts. At least two vivacious leading ladies ended up as domestic workers. Other black luminaries drifted into alcoholism, drugs, suicide, or bitter self-recrimination.

For me, the most exciting and at the same time depressing interview was a startling, delirious eight-hour chat with Vivian Dandridge, the sister of Dorothy. From Vivian, there emerged the clearest, most articulate definition of black movie stardom (and its differences from white stardom) that I had ever heard. The embarrassments, the humiliations, the affronts her sister endured were distressing. Dorothy's final self-destructive bent was clearly an outgrowth of her experiences as a black woman in a white movie colony.

Once the research was completed, I gathered my material and tried fitting it into some order. As I did so, I saw emerging something more than history. Having come of age at a time when it has been almost impossible to keep politics and aesthetics apart, I felt compelled to interpret the past from my own point of view, that of a black looking at other blacks in motion pictures, that of a black under twenty-five reviewing the work of his cultural ancestors. When I watched *Stormy Weather* with an all-black audience that openly mocked the stereotypes on screen, or when I saw *The Birth of a Nation* with a black audience that openly cheered for the black villains to defeat the white heroes, or when I viewed *The Emperor Jones* with a young black audience that openly admitted it was there simply to "understand" the legendary Robeson whom their parents had worshiped, I knew I was seeing reactions far different from those that initially greeted these three films and other black movies. I was also aware, while sitting in a Times Square theater one afternoon and listening to black teen-agers howling and deriding Juano Hernandez's toothless janitor character in *They Call Me MISTER Tibbs,* that somehow or other I had to make them understand what this man had been like in the early 1950s. These teen-agers had to see that without an actor like Hernandez in the 1950s, there might never have been a *They Call Me MISTER Tibbs.* What I have tried to do is put black films and black personalities in their proper historical perspective, at the same time trying to say what these films and actors mean to us today.

Another problem for me in writing the book was deciding whom to include or exclude. Had it not been that the critics of their time were so impressed by performers Hazel Scott and Clarence Muse, I might have referred to them only in passing. Instead I included them and am now glad I did. At the same time, I would have preferred spending more time discussing Hernandez and James Edwards and less on Sidney Poitier. But it was obvious to me that Poitier is such an important figure in the history of black films and black performers that he demanded extensive coverage. In short, I have forced myself to be objective on certain historical matters. I should say also that this book deals primarily with blacks in Hollywood films. There is one general chapter on the independent film companies (operating outside of Hollywood) which produced all-black movies exclusively for ghetto theaters in the 1930s and 1940s, but because information on the independents is still in such disarray, I have limited my comments on the independents and have not always given dates for the films. But I felt it essential that something be said about this vast area of film history that has gone for years without any recognition.

A third problem centered on the personal lives of certain actors. One cannot discuss the careers of Fetchit or Dandridge without some reference to their off-screen lives. For the most part, I have dealt with the lives of the early black performers because theirs usually ended up so tragically, or so desperately unfulfilled, with Hollywood often contributing to their tragedies. In dealing with many latter-day actors, however, I have not gone into their personal lives. The work of such professionals as Ruby Dee or Ivan Dixon or Diana Sands is clearly less closely linked to their private lives.

A final problem was simply one of language. Certain performers such as the Lena Horne of the 1940s or the Hazel Scott of the 1940s were clearly bourgeois *Negro* creations. Others, like the tough and uncompromising Hattie McDaniel, were always outspokenly *black* personalities. Generally, I have used *colored, Negro,* and *black* discriminately and in their proper historical context.

All the problems connected with writing the book weighed on me heavily, but as I worked I saw my perspective changing. Ultimately, my study of blacks in American movies has become not only a discussion of actors and pictures but a statement on the development of my own consciousness. The energies, the tensions, the study and analysis, the concerns, and then the summation that I poured into this book occurred during a clearly circumscribed time in my life. I was not much out of my teens, and I wrote on problems and difficulties as well as pleasures that certain films and personalities raised for me. At this point, I can say with candor and relief that the book has succeeded for me. I see blacks in films differently, with a new awareness and an altered sensitivity. I have been liberated, and I think some kind of general position on blacks in the movies has taken shape at a time when it is badly needed.

Of course, no book is ever written without the help of others. Along the way to completing any manuscript, almost every author encounters friends and adversaries who motivate or discourage him, who inspire or deflate him, who tell him their problems or listen to his. In the end, these people all influence his work, even if it is just the fact that they delay his getting it done.

Nevertheless it is a pleasure to thank those who helped me in this venture. My thanks go to Arlene Donovan of Creative Management Associates who encouraged me to pursue this project at the very beginning. Later during the research period and for three-quarters of the writing span, Eileen Lottman was most considerate, helpful, and a great ego booster. During the editing and rewriting process, Bob Silverstein stood by with astounding degrees of patience and insight to offer pertinent comments on my work. My gratitude is also extended to Nora Sutton and Vivienne Seraqué of Bantam Books, to Regina Cornwell and Melinda Ward of the Museum of Modern Art, to Pearl Bowser during her stint at the Jewish Museum, to Patrick Sheehan of the Library of Congress, to Douglas Barone and Jeffrey Conrad of Doubleday and Company, and to Alice West, Mary Sampson, Reubenia Frazier, and dear Octavia Glasgow. Final special thanks go to Steven Morris of *Ebony*, Daniel Dawson of the Studio Museum, Vivien Dandridge, and last, the most patient of all, Marc Jaffe of Bantam Books.

CONTENTS

Preface   vii

1   Black Beginnings: from Uncle Tom's Cabin *to*
The Birth of a Nation   *3*

    The Tom   4
    The Coon   7
    The Tragic Mulatto   9
    The Mammy   9
    The Brutal Black Buck and *The Birth of a Nation*   10

2   Into the 1920s: the Jesters   19

3   The 1930s: the Servants   35

    High-Steppin' Sir Stepin   38
    Waiting on West and Serving Shirley   45
    Mr. Bojangles: the Cool-Eyed Tom   47
    Clarence Muse: the Inhibited, Humanized Tom Standing in a
       Corner by Himself   53
    Imitation of Life: Mother Knows Best   57
    Iridescent Fredi: Black Girl in Search of a Black Role   60
    Louise Beavers: the Black Guardian Angel   62
    The Green Pastures   67
    Rex Ingram: First of the Freed Black Men   69
    Stepin's Step-Chillun   71
    Rochester: the Gentleman's Gentleman   77
    Hi-Hat Hattie   82
    Gone with the Wind: Black Realities and the End of a Tradition   86
    Paul Robeson: the Black Colossus   94

4   *The Interlude: Black-Market Cinema* *101*

      Oscar Micheaux 109

5   *The 1940s: the Entertainers, the New Negroes, and the Problem People* *117*

      THE ENTERTAINERS 118
      Hazel Scott: Miss Proper Middle-Class Lady 122
      Lena Horne: Black Beauty in Residence 125
      Cabin in the Sky 128
      Stormy Weather 131
      Bits and Pieces of Black Action 132
      Song of the South 135

      THE NEW NEGROES: AN INTERIM 136

      THE PROBLEM PEOPLE 143
      Home of the Brave and the Postwar Good Sensitive Negro 144
      Lost Boundaries' Tragic Mulattoes 147
      Pinky's Tragic Mulatto and Its Strong Black Woman 150
      Intruder in the Dust and the Defiantly Proud Black Man 154

6   *The 1950s: Black Stars* *159*

      Ethel Waters: Earth Mother for an Alienated Age 161
      Dorothy Dandridge: Apotheosis of the Mulatto 166
      Sidney Poitier: Hero for an Integrationist Age 175
      Black Odds and Ends 183

7   *The 1960s: Problem People into Militants* *194*

      Steps Forward 196
      Black Art Films 200
      A Step Backward: Ossie Davis and *Gone Are the Days* 204
      Along the Road, in Harlem, and on the Subway 206
      Way Down in de New Ole South with Tom-Tom, Miss Bronze Barbie Doll, and Ms. Militant Mammy 208
      A Man Called Adam and the Son of Sunshine Sammy 213
      Super Sidney of the 1960s 215
      Jim Brown: Black Buck Hero for a Separatist Age 220
      The New-Style Black Film 223

  Epilogue: 1970 Onward *230*

  Index *245*

ILLUSTRATIONS

page

James B. Lowe in *Uncle Tom's Cabin*   5
Scenes from *The Birth of a Nation*   11
Farina   22
Daniel Haynes and Nina Mae McKinney in *Hallelujah*   32
Nina Mae McKinney   32
Stepin Fetchit   40
Stepin Fetchit and Will Rogers   40
Shirley Temple and Bill Robinson in *The Littlest Rebel*   49
Bill Robinson and Willie Best in *The Littlest Rebel*   51
Clarence Muse   55
Louise Beavers in *Imitation of Life*   58
Louise Beavers and Fredi Washington in *Imitation of Life*   58
Fredi Washington   61
Louise Beavers   65
Willie Best and Arthur Treacher in *Thank You, Jeeves*   73
Mantan Moreland   73
Louis Armstrong and Bing Crosby   76
Eddie "Rochester" Anderson   78
Hattie McDaniel and Vivien Leigh in *Gone with the Wind*   87
Hattie McDaniel and Ben Carter in *Maryland*   87
Butterfly McQueen, Clark Gable, and Vivien Leigh in
     Gone with the Wind   91
Paul Robeson and Nina Mae McKinney   96
Page from an Ideal Pictures Catalogue   104
Scenes from *Miracle in Harlem*   106
Lorenzo Tucker   112
Bee Freeman and Oscar Polk in *Underworld*   112
Scene from *Daughter of the Congo*   113
Ethel Moses   113
"Aunt Jemima" in *Stand Up and Cheer*   120
Hazel Scott   123
Lena Horne   126

Lena Horne, Eddie Anderson, and Ethel Waters in
    Cabin in the Sky   130
Lena Horne and Fats Waller in *Stormy Weather*   130
The Nicholas Brothers   133
Mel Ferrer and Beatrice Pearson in *Lost Boundaries*   149
Ethel Waters and Jeanne Crain in *Pinky*   153
Juano Hernandez and David Brian in *Intruder in the Dust*   153
Ethel Waters and Julie Harris in *The Member of the Wedding*   163
Dorothy Dandridge   167
Joe Adams, Dorothy Dandridge, and Harry Belafonte in
    Carmen Jones   170
Pearl Bailey, Dorothy Dandridge, and Diahann Carroll in
    Carmen Jones   170
Dorothy Dandridge and Curt Jurgens in *Tamango*   173
Sammy Davis, Jr.; Dorothy Dandridge; and Sidney Poitier in
    Porgy and Bess   173
Sidney Poitier and John Cassavetes in *Edge of the City*   177
Sidney Poitier and Tony Curtis in *The Defiant Ones*   177
Jackie Robinson and Ruby Dee in *The Jackie Robinson Story*   197
Sidney Poitier, Ruby Dee, Claudia McNeil, and Diana Sands in
    A Raisin in the Sun   197
Barbara Barrie and Bernie Hamilton in *One Potato, Two Potato*   203
Brock Peters   203
Sidney Poitier, Katharine Hepburn, and Katharine Houghton in
    Guess Who's Coming to Dinner   218
Jim Brown   221
Ossie Davis, Dionne Warwick, and Stephen Boyd in *Slaves*   228
Lola Falana and Roscoe Lee Browne in *The Liberation of
    L. B. Jones*   228
James Earl Jones and Jane Alexander in *The Great White Hope*   233
Melvin Van Peebles   233

Toms, Coons, Mulattoes, Mammies, and Bucks

Black Beginnings:
from Uncle Tom's Cabin *to* The Birth of a Nation

1

In the beginning, there was an Uncle Tom. A former mechanic photographed him in a motion picture that ran no longer than twelve minutes. And a new dimension was added to American movies.

The year was 1903. The mechanic-turned-movie-director was Edwin S. Porter. The twelve-minute motion picture was *Uncle Tom's Cabin*. And the new dimension was Uncle Tom himself. He was the American movies' first black character. The great paradox was that in actuality Tom was not black at all. Instead he was portrayed by a nameless, slightly overweight white actor made up in blackface. But the use of whites in black roles was then a common practice, a tradition carried over from the stage and maintained during the early days of silent films. Still, the first Negro character had arrived in films, and he had done so at a time when the motion-picture industry itself was virtually nonexistent. The movies were without stars or studios or sound. There were no great directors or writers. And the community of Hollywood had not yet come into being.

After the tom's debut, there appeared a variety of black presences bearing the fanciful names of the coon, the tragic mulatto, the mammy, and the brutal black buck. All were character types used for the same effect: to entertain by stressing Negro inferiority. Fun was poked at the American Negro by presenting him as either a nitwit or a childlike lackey. None of the types was meant to do great harm, although at various times individual ones did. All were merely filmic reproductions of black stereotypes that had existed since the days of slavery and were already popularized in American life and arts. The movies, which catered to public tastes, borrowed profusely from all the other popular art forms. Whenever dealing with black characters, they simply adapted the old familiar stereotypes, often further distorting them beyond recognition.

In the early days when all the black characters were still portrayed by white actors in blackface, there was nothing but the old character types. They sat like square boxes on a shelf. A white actor walked by, selected a box, and used it as a base for a very square, rigidly defined performance. Later, when real black actors played the roles and found themselves wedged into these categories, the history became one of actors battling against the types to create rich, stimulating, diverse characters. At various points the tom, the coon, the tragic mulatto, the mammy, and the brutal black buck were brought to life respectively by Bill "Bojangles" Robinson, Stepin Fetchit, Nina Mae McKinney, Hattie McDaniel, and Walter Long (actually a white actor who portrayed a black villain in *The Birth of a Nation*), and later "modernized" by such performers as Sidney Poitier, Sammy Davis, Jr., Dorothy Dandridge, Ethel Waters, and Jim Brown. Often it seemed as if the mark of the actor was the manner in which he individualized the mythic type or towered above it. The types were to prove deadly for some actors and inconsequential for others. But try as any actor may to forget the typecasting, the familiar types have most always been present in American black movies. The early silent period of motion pictures remains important, not because there were any great black performances—there weren't—but because the five basic types—the boxes sitting on the shelf—that were to dominate black characters for the next half century were first introduced then.

The Tom

Porter's tom was the first in a long line of socially acceptable Good Negro characters. Always as toms are chased, harassed, hounded, flogged, enslaved, and insulted, they keep the faith, n'er

James B. Lowe, the star of 1927's *Uncle Tom's Cabin* and the first black actor to be ballyhooed by his studio.

turn against their white massas, and remain hearty, submissive, stoic, generous, selfless, and oh-so-very kind. Thus they endear themselves to white audiences and emerge as heroes of sorts.

Two early toms appeared in the shorts *Confederate Spy* (c. 1910) and *For Massa's Sake* (1911). In the former, dear old Uncle Daniel is a Negro spy for the South. He dies before a Northern firing squad, but he is content, happy that he "did it for massa's sake and little massa." In *For Massa's Sake* a former slave is so attached to his erstwhile master that he sells himself back into slavery to help the master through a period of financial difficulties.

During the silent period, there were also remakes of the Harriet Beecher Stowe novel in which the tale of the good Christian slave was again made the meat of melodrama. The first remakes in 1909 and 1913 had little in style or treatment to distinguish them. But a fourth version, directed by William Robert Daly in 1914, distinguished itself and the tom tradition by starring the Negro stage actor Sam Lucas in the title role. Lucas became the first black man to play a leading role in a movie. Later in 1927, when Universal Pictures filmed *Uncle Tom's Cabin,* the handsome Negro actor James B. Lowe was signed for the leading role. Harry Pollard directed the Universal feature. Twelve years earlier, Pollard had filmed a version of the Stowe classic in which he portrayed the Christian slave in blackface. But for this new venture Negro Lowe was selected to fit in with the "realistic" demands of the times. Congratulating itself on its liberalism, Universal sent out press releases about its good colored star:

> James B. Lowe has made history. A history that reflects only credit to the Negro race, not only because he has given the "Uncle Tom" character a new slant, but because of his exemplary conduct with the Universal company. They look upon Lowe at the Universal Studio as a living black god. . . . Of the directors, critics, artists, and actors who have seen James Lowe work at the studio there are none who will not say he is the most suited of all men for the part of "Tom." Those who are religious say that a heavenly power brought him to Universal and all predict a most marvelous future and worldwide reputation for James B. Lowe.

Although a "heavenly power" may have been with actor Lowe, it had little effect on his interpretation of the role. Tom still came off as a genial darky, furnished with new color but no new sentiments. Yet to Lowe's credit, he did his tomming with such an arresting effectiveness that he was sent to England on a promotional tour to ballyhoo the picture, thus becoming the first black actor to be publicized by his studio. The film also introduced the massive baptism scene, which later became a Hollywood favorite. Curiously, in 1958 this version of *Uncle Tom's Cabin*, although silent, was reissued with an added prologue by Raymond Massey. Because it arrived just when the sit-ins were erupting in the South, many wondered if by reissuing this film Universal Studios hoped to remind the restless black masses of an earlier, less turbulent period, when obeying one's master was the answer to every black man's problems.

The Coon

Although tom was to outdistance every other type and dominate American hearth and home, he had serious competition from a group of coons. They appeared in a series of black films presenting the Negro as amusement object and black buffoon. They lacked the single-mindedness of tom. There were the pure coon and two variants of his type: the pickaninny and the uncle remus.

The pickaninny was the first of the coon types to make its screen debut. It gave the Negro child actor his place in the black pantheon. Generally, he was a harmless, little screwball creation whose eyes popped, whose hair stood on end with the least excitement, and whose antics were pleasant and diverting. Thomas Alva Edison proved to be a pioneer in the exploitation and exploration of this type when he presented *Ten Pickaninnies* in 1904, a forerunner of the Hal Roach *Our Gang* series. During his camera experiments in 1893, Edison had photographed some blacks as "interesting side effects." In *Ten Pickaninnies*, the side effects moved to the forefront of the action as a group of nameless Negro children romped and ran about while being referred to as snowballs, cherubs, coons, bad chillun, inky kids, smoky kids, black lambs, cute ebonies, and chubbie ebonies. In due time, the pickaninnies were to be called by other names. In the 1920s and the 1930s, such child actors as Sunshine Sammy, Farina, Stymie, and Buckwheat picked up the pickaninny mantle and carried it to new summits. In all the versions of *Uncle Tom's Cabin*, the slave child Topsy was presented as a lively pickaninny, used solely for comic relief. When the 1927 version of *Uncle Tom's Cabin* opened, the character was singled out by one critic who wrote: "Topsy is played by Mona Ray, a wonderfully bright youngster who seems to have the comedy of her part in extraordinary fashion . . . her eyes roll back and forth in alarm. She also evinces no liking for her plight when she is found by Miss Ophelia while dabbing powder on her ebony countenance." In her day, the character Topsy was clownish and droll and became such a film favorite that she starred in *Topsy and Eva* (1927), in which her far-fetched meanderings and her pickaninnying won mass audience approval.

Shortly after Edison introduced the pickaninny in 1904, the pure coon made its way onto the screen in *Wooing and Wedding of a Coon* (1905). This short depicted a honeymooning black couple as stumbling and stuttering idiots. Later the coon appeared in *The Masher* (1907), which was about a self-styled white ladies' man who is rebuffed by all the women he pursues. When he meets a mysterious veiled woman who responds to his passes, the hero thinks he has arrived at his blue heaven. And so finding success, he removes the veil only to discover that his mystery lady love is *colored!* Without further ado, he takes off. He may have been looking for a blue heaven, but he certainly did not want a black one.

Before its death, the coon developed into the most blatantly degrading of all black stereotypes. The pure coons emerged as no-account niggers, those unreliable, crazy, lazy, subhuman creatures good for nothing more than eating watermelons, stealing chickens, shooting crap, or butchering the English language. A character named Rastus was just such a figure.

How Rastus Got His Turkey (c. 1910) was the first of a series of slapstick comedies centering on the antics of a Negro called Rastus. Here Rastus tries to steal a turkey for his Thanksgiving dinner. Next came *Rastus in Zululand*, about a darky who dreams of going to Zululand in the heart of Africa. There he wins the affections of the chief's daughter. He is willing to flirt with the girl, but when asked to marry her, in true unreliable, no-account nigger fashion, he refuses, expressing a wish for death rather than matrimony. The savage chief (from the beginning, all Africans are savages) nearly grants that wish, too. *Rastus and Chicken, Pickaninnies and Watermelon,* and *Chicken Thief* were other shorts in the series, all appearing during 1910 and 1911. In some respects, this series and its central character simply paved the way for the greatest coon of all time, Stepin Fetchit.

The final member of the coon triumvirate is the uncle remus. Harmless and congenial, he is a first cousin to the tom, yet he distinguishes himself by his quaint, naïve, and comic philosophizing. During the silent period he was only hinted at. He did not come into full flower until the 1930s and 1940s with films such as *The Green Pastures* (1936) and *Song of the South* (1946). Remus's mirth, like tom's contentment and the coon's antics, has always been used to indicate the black man's satisfaction with the system and his place in it.

The Tragic Mulatto

The third figure of the black pantheon and the one that proved itself a moviemaker's darling is the tragic mulatto. One of the type's earliest appearances was in *The Debt* (1912), a two-reeler about the Old South. A white man's wife and his black mistress bear him children at the same time. Growing up together, the white son and the mulatto daughter fall in love and decide to marry, only to have their relationship revealed to them at the crucial moment. Their lives are thus ruined not only because they are brother and sister but also—and here was the catch—because the girl has a drop of black blood!

In Humanity's Cause, In Slavery Days, and *The Octoroon*, all made around 1913, explored the plight of a fair-skinned mulatto attempting to pass for white. Usually the mulatto is made likable —even sympathetic (because of her white blood, no doubt)—and the audience believes that the girl's life could have been productive and happy had she not been a "victim of divided racial inheritance."

The Mammy

Mammy, the fourth black type, is so closely related to the comic coons that she is usually relegated to their ranks. Mammy is distinguished, however, by her sex and her fierce independence. She is usually big, fat, and cantankerous. She made her debut around 1914 when audiences were treated to a blackface version of *Lysistrata*. The comedy, titled *Coon Town Suffragettes*, dealt with a group of bossy mammy washerwomen who organize a militant movement to keep their good-for-nothing husbands at home. Aristophanes would no doubt have risen from his grave with righteous indignation. But the militancy of the washerwomen served as a primer for the mammy roles Hattie McDaniel was to perfect in the 1930s.

Mammy's offshoot is the aunt jemima, sometimes derogatorily referred to as a "handkerchief head." Often aunt jemimas are toms blessed with religion or mammies who wedge themselves into the dominant white culture. Generally they are sweet, jolly, and good-tempered—a bit more polite than mammy and certainly never as headstrong. The maids in the Mae West films of the 1930s fit snugly into this category.

The Brutal Black Buck and *The Birth of a Nation*

D. W. Griffith's *The Birth of a Nation* (1915) was the motion picture to introduce the final mythic type, the brutal black buck. This extraordinary, multidimensional movie was also the first feature film to deal with a black theme and at the same time to articulate fully the entire pantheon of black gods and goddesses. Griffith presented all the types with such force and power that his film touched off a wave of controversy and was denounced as the most slanderous anti-Negro movie ever released.

In almost every way, *The Birth of a Nation* was a stupendous undertaking, unlike any film that had preceded it. Up to then American movies had been two- or three-reel affairs, shorts running no longer than ten or fifteen minutes, crudely and casually filmed. But *The Birth of a Nation* was rehearsed for six weeks, filmed in nine, later edited in three months, and finally released as a record-breaking hundred-thousand-dollar spectacle, twelve reels in length and over three hours in running time. It altered the entire course and concept of American moviemaking, developing the close-up, cross-cutting, rapid-fire editing, the iris, the split-screen shot, and realistic and impressionistic lighting. Creating sequences and images yet to be surpassed, the film's magnitude and epic grandeur swept audiences off their feet. At a private White House screening President Woodrow Wilson exclaimed, "It's like writing history with lightning!" *The Birth of a Nation*, however, not only vividly re-created history, but revealed its director's philosophical concept of the universe and his personal racial bigotry. For D. W. Griffith there was a moral order at work in the universe. If that order were ever thrown out of whack, he believed chaos would ensue. Griffith's thesis was sound, relatively exciting, and even classic in a purely Shakespearean sense. But in articulating his thesis, Griffith seemed to be saying that things were in order only when whites were in control and when the American Negro was kept in his place. In the end, Griffith's "lofty" statement—and the film's subject matter—transformed *The Birth of a Nation* into a hotly debated and bitterly cursed motion picture.

It told the story of the Old South, the Civil War, the Reconstruction period, and the emergence of the Ku Klux Klan. Basing his film on Thomas Dixon's novel *The Clansman* (also the original title of the film), Griffith focused on a good, decent "little" family, the Camerons of Piedmont, South Carolina. Before the war, the family lives in an idyllic "quaintly way that is to be no more." Dr. Cameron and his sons are gentle, benevolent "fathers" to their child-

Scenes from D. W. Griffith's *The Birth of a Nation*, the most controversial Civil War drama ever released in America. ABOVE: the blacks take over the voting polls from the defeated Southern whites. BELOW: white actors in blackface portray Mammy and the "uppity nigger from de No'" (1915).

like servants. The slaves themselves could be no happier. In the fields they contentedly pick cotton. In their quarters they dance and sing for their master. In the Big House Mammy joyously goes about her chores. All is in order. Everyone knows his place. Then the Civil War breaks out, and the old order cracks.

The war years take their toll. In Piedmont, the Cameron family is terrorized by a troop of Negro raiders, and all the South undergoes "ruin, devastation, rapine, and pillage." Then comes Reconstruction. Carpetbaggers and uppity niggers from the North move into Piedmont, exploiting and corrupting the former slaves, unleashing the sadism and bestiality innate in the Negro, turning the once congenial darkies into renegades, and using them to "crush the white South under the heel of the black South." "Lawlessness runs riot!" says one title card. The old slaves have quit work to dance. They roam the streets, shoving whites off sidewalks. They take over the political polls and disenfranchise the whites. A black political victory culminates in an orgiastic street celebration. Blacks dance, sing, drink, rejoice. Later they conduct a black Congressional session, itself a mockery of Old South ideals, in which the freed Negro legislators are depicted as lustful, arrogant, and idiotic. They bite on chicken legs and drink whiskey from bottles while sprawling with bare feet upon their desks. During the Congressional meeting, the stench created by the barefoot Congressmen becomes so great that they pass as their first act a ruling that every member must keep his shoes on during legislative meetings! Matters in *The Birth of a Nation* reach a heady climax later when the renegade black Gus sets out to rape the younger Cameron daughter. Rather than submit, the Pet Sister flees from him and throws herself from a cliff—into the "opal gates of death." Then the mulatto Silas Lynch attempts to force the white Elsie Stoneman to marry him. Finally, when all looks hopelessly lost, there emerges a group of good, upright Southern white men, members of an "invisible empire," who, while wearing white sheets and hoods, battle the blacks in a direct confrontation. Led by Ben Cameron in a rousing stampede, they magnificently defeat the black rebels! Defenders of white womanhood, white honor, and white glory, they restore to the South everything it has lost, including its white supremacy. Thus we have the birth of a nation. And the birth of the Ku Klux Klan.

The plot machinations of the Griffith epic may today resound with melodramatic absurdities, but the action, the actors, and the direction did not. The final ride of the Klan was an impressive piece of film propaganda, superbly lit and brilliantly edited. Indeed it was so stirring that audiences screamed in delight, cheering for the white heroes and booing, hissing, and cursing the black militants. *The Birth of a Nation* remains significant not only because of its artistry but also because of its wide-ranging influence. One can detect in this single film the trends and sentiments that were to run through almost every black film made for a long time afterward. Later film makers were to pick up Griffith's ideas—his very images—but were to keep them "nicely" toned down in order not to offend audiences.

Griffith used three varieties of blacks. The first were the "faithful souls," a mammy and an uncle tom, who remain with the Cameron family throughout and stanchly defend them from the rebels. By means of these characters, as well as the pickaninny slaves seen dancing, singing, and clowning in their quarters, director Griffith propagated the myth of slave contentment and made it appear as if slavery had elevated the Negro from his bestial instincts. At heart, Griffith's "faithful souls" were shamelessly naïve representations of the Negro as Child or the Negro as Watered-Down Noble Savage. But these characters were to make their way through scores of other Civil War epics, and they were to leave their mark on the characterizations of Clarence Muse in *Huckleberry Finn* (1931) and *Broadway Bill* (1934) and of Bill Robinson in *The Little Colonel* (1935) and *The Littlest Rebel* (1935).

Griffith's second variety were the brutal black bucks. Just as the coon stereotype could be broken into subgroups, the brutal black buck type could likewise be divided into two categories: the black brutes and the black bucks. Differences between the two are minimal. The black brute was a barbaric black out to raise havoc. Audiences could assume that his physical violence served as an outlet for a man who was sexually repressed. In *The Birth of a Nation*, the black brutes, subhuman and feral, are the nameless characters setting out on a rampage full of black rage. They flog the Camerons' faithful servant. They shove and assault white men of the town. They flaunt placards demanding "equal marriage." These characters figured prominently in the Black Congress sequence, and their film descendants were to appear years later as the rebellious slaves of *So Red the Rose* (1935), as the revolutionaries of *Uptight* (1969), and as the militants of *Putney Swope* (1969).

But it was the pure black bucks that were Griffith's really great archetypal figures. Bucks are always big, baadddd niggers, oversexed and savage, violent and frenzied as they lust for white flesh. No greater sin hath any black man. Both Lynch, the mulatto, and Gus, the renegade, fall into this category. Among other things, these two characters revealed the tie between sex and racism in America. Griffith played on the myth of the Negro's high-powered sexuality, then articulated the great white fear that every black man longs for a white woman. Underlying the fear was the assumption that the white woman was the ultimate in female desirability, herself a symbol of white pride, power, and beauty. Consequently, when Lillian Gish, the frailest, purest of all screen heroines, was attacked by the character Lynch—when he put his big black arms around this pale blond beauty—audiences literally panicked. Here was the classic battle of good and evil, innocence and corruption. It was a master stroke and a brilliant use of contrast, one that drew its audience into the film emotionally.* But in uncovering the attraction of black to white, Griffith failed to reveal the political implications. Traditionally, certain black males have been drawn to white women because these women are power symbols, an ideal of the oppressor. But Griffith attributed the attraction to an animalism innate in the Negro male. Thus the black bucks of the film are psychopaths, one always panting and salivating, the other forever stiffening his body as if the mere presence of a white woman in the same room could bring him to a sexual climax. Griffith played hard on the bestiality of his black villainous bucks and used it to arouse hatred.

Closely aligned to the bucks and brutes of *The Birth of a Nation* is the mulatto character, Lydia. She is presented as the mistress of the white abolitionist carpetbagger, Senator Stoneman. Through Lydia, Griffith explored the possibilities of the dark, sinister halfbreed as a tragic leading lady. Although merely a supporting character, Lydia is the only black role to suggest even remotely genuine mental anguish. She hates whites. She refuses to be treated as an inferior. She wants power. Throughout, she anguishes over her predicament as a black woman in a hostile white world.

Lydia is also the film's only passionate female. Griffith was the first important movie director to divide his black women into categories based on their individual colors. Both Lydia and Mammy are played by white actresses in blackface. But Mammy is darker. She is representative of the all-black woman, overweight, middle-aged, and so dark, so thoroughly black, that it is preposterous even to suggest that she be a sex object. Instead she

*Lillian Gish's comments in the January 1937, issue of *Stage* verify the fact that Griffith was well aware of this contrast and that he used it to arouse his audience. Said Gish: "At first I was not cast to play in *The Clansman*. My sister and I had been the last to join the company and we naturally supposed . . . that the main assignments would go to the older members. But one day while we were rehearsing the scene where the colored man picks up the Northern girl gorilla-fashion, my hair, which was very blond, fell far below my waist and Griffith, seeing the contrast in the two figures, assigned me to play Elsie Stoneman (who was to have been Mae Marsh)."

was desexed. This tradition of the desexed, overweight, dowdy *dark* black woman was continued in films throughout the 1930s and 1940s. Vestiges of it popped up as late as the 1960s with Claudia McNeil in *A Raisin in the Sun* (1961) and Beah Richards in *Hurry Sundown* (1967). A dark black actress was considered for no role but that of a mammy or an aunt jemima. On the other hand, the part-black woman—the light-skinned Negress—was given a chance at lead parts and was graced with a modicum of sex appeal. Every sexy black woman who appeared afterward in movies was to be a "cinnamon-colored gal" with Caucasian features. The mulatto came closest to the white ideal. Whether conscious or not, Griffith's division of the black woman into color categories survived in movies the way many set values continue long after they are discredited. In fact, it was said in 1958 and 1970 that one reason why such actresses as Eartha Kitt in *Anna Lucasta* and Lola Falana in *The Liberation of L. B. Jones* failed to emerge as important screen love goddesses was that they were too dark.

Influential and detrimental as the Griffith blacks were to be for later generations, they were not meekly accepted in 1915. *The Birth of a Nation's* blackfaced baddies aroused a rash of hostilities. At the film's New York première, the NAACP picketed the theater, calling the movie racist propaganda. Later the Chicago and Boston branches of the NAACP led massive demonstrations against its presentation. Other civil rights and religious organizations were quick to protest. Race riots broke out in a number of cities. Newspaper editorials and speeches censured the film. Black critics such as Laurence Reddick said it glorified the Ku Klux Klan, and Reddick added that the film's immense success was at least one factor contributing to the great and growing popularity the organization enjoyed during this period. In the South, the film was often advertised as calculated to "work audiences into a frenzy . . . it will make you hate." In some regions, the ad campaign may have been effective, for in 1915 lynchings in the United States reached their highest peak since 1908. Ultimately, *The Birth of a Nation* was banned in five states and nineteen cities.

The anger and fury did not die in 1915 either. The film was reissued at regular intervals in later years. At each reopening, outraged moviegoers, both black and white, vehemently opposed its showing. In 1921, *The Birth of a Nation* was attacked as a part of a "Southern campaign to stimulate the Ku Klux Klan"—which it had already done. The Museum of Modern Art temporarily shelved the picture in 1946. Because of "the potency of its anti-Negro bias . . . " read the Museum's press announcement, "exhibiting it at this time of heightened social tensions cannot be justified."

The 1947 revival of the movie by the Dixie Film Exchange was blasted by the Civil Rights Congress, and the NAACP picketed New York's Republic Theatre where it was to be shown. "It brings race hatred to New York City," said NAACP Secretary Walter White, "and we don't want it here." The Progressive Labor Party led demonstrations against the film during the following year. In 1950, there were renewed outcries when word leaked out that a Hollywood company was to remake the movie in sound. The remake plans were quickly aborted, as were the 1959 proposals to present it on television.

Throughout the years, D. W. Griffith defended himself as a mere filmmaker with no political or ideological view in mind. Surprised and apparently genuinely hurt when called a racist, Griffith made speeches across the country, wrote letters to the press, accused the NAACP and its supporters of trying to bring about screen censorship, and even went so far as to issue a pamphlet titled "The Rise and Fall of Free Speech in America," all in an effort to squelch the controversy. As late as 1947, one year before his death and some thirty-two years after the movie's release, D. W. Griffith still maintained that his film was not an attack on the American Negro.

The Birth of a Nation has become one of the highest grossing movies of all time. (The amount it has earned has never been fully tabulated.) Eyeing its profits, a number of Hollywood producers undertook projects with similar anti-Negro themes. *Broken Chains* (c. 1916) and *Free and Equal* (filmed in 1915 but not released until 1925) were prominent imitations. The former failed miserably. The latter's release was held up for some ten years while the producer waited for the furor to cool down. For one thing was certain after *The Birth of a Nation:* never again could the Negro be depicted in the guise of an out-and-out villain. This treatment was too touchy and too controversial. Griffith's film had succeeded because of its director's artistry and technical virtuosity, but no studio dared risk it again. Consequently, blacks in Hollywood films were cast almost exclusively in comic roles. And thus even the great comic tradition of the Negro in the American film has its roots in the Griffith spectacle. Finally, many of Hollywood's hang-ups and hesitations in presenting sensual black men on screen resulted, in part, from the reactions to the Griffith spectacle. So strong was his presentation, and so controversial its reception, that movie companies ignored and avoided such a type of black character for fear of raising new hostilities. Not until more than a half century later, when Melvin Van Peebles' *Sweet Sweetback's Baadasssss Song* (1971) appeared, did sexually assertive black males make their way back to the screen. Afterward, when the box-office success of that film indicated that audiences could at long last accept such a type, the screen was bombarded with an array of buck heroes in such films as *Shaft* (1971), *Super Fly* (1972), *Slaughter* (1972), and *Melinda* (1972).

With *The Birth of a Nation* in 1915, all the major black screen types had been introduced. Literal and unimaginative as some types might now appear, the naïve and cinematically untutored audiences of the early part of the century responded to the character types as if they were the real thing.

As far as the audiences were concerned, the toms, the coons, the mulattoes, the mammies, and the bucks embodied all the aspects and facets of the black experience itself. The audience's deep-set prejudice against any "foreigners" accounts for the typing of all minorities in all American films. But no minority was so relentlessly or fiercely typed as the black man. Audiences rejected even subtle modifications of the black caricatures. When Jack Johnson became the first black heavyweight champion of the world in 1908, filmed sequences of him knocking out white Tommy Burns so disturbed the "racial pride" of white America that they were banned for fear of race riots. Thereafter, black boxers in films were invariably defeated by their white opponents. Similarly, when the first film versions of *Uncle Tom's Cabin* were released in the South, advertisements announced that the black characters were portrayed by white actors. Even at this stage, the evolving film industry feared offending its dominant white audience.

Once the basic mythic types were introduced, a number of things occurred. Specific black themes soon emerged. (The Old South theme proved to be a great favorite.) And the basic types came and went in various guises. Guises long confused many movie viewers. They were (and remain) deceptive, and they have traditionally been used by the film industry to camouflage the familiar types. If a black appeared as a butler, audiences thought of him as merely a servant. What they failed to note was the variety of servants. There were tom servants (faithful and submissive), coon servants (lazy and unreliable), and mammy servants, just to name a few. What has to be remembered is that the servant's uniform was the guise certain types wore during a given period. That way Hollywood could give its audience the same product (the types themselves) but with new packaging (the guise).

With the Griffith spectacle, audiences saw the first of the guises. The brutes, the bucks, and the tragic mulatto all wore the guise of villains. Afterward, during the 1920s, audiences saw their toms and coons dressed in the guise of plantation jesters. In the 1930s, all the types were dressed in servants' uniforms. In the early 1940s, they sported entertainers' costumes. In the late 1940s and the 1950s, they donned the gear of troubled problem people. In the 1960s, they appeared as angry militants. Because the guises were always changing, audiences were sometimes tricked into believing the depictions of the American Negro were altered, too. But at heart beneath the various guises, there lurked the familiar types.

Into the 1920s: the Jesters

2

An engaging Negro child actor brings authentic black humor to the screen . . . . A Jewish singer made up in blackface to look like a darky minstrel of old proves the movies can talk . . . . At Fox Pictures, a gregarious group of perpetually happy-go-lucky plantation hands whoop it up in the screen's first all-singing, all-talking, all-Negro musical . . . . At MGM, a troupe of contented cotton pickers laugh and cry to the heavens above in the screen's second all-singing, all-talking, all-Negro musical . . . . And a black love goddess and a black blues singer shake their asses and roll their stomachs, burning holes in movie screens with their raunchy sexuality.

By 1918, the villains had come and gone. And the jester was about to be enshrined. Hollywood's postwar films reflected its postwar spirit of artistic aggressiveness and programmed levity. Its production having more than tripled during the war years, Hollywood emerged as the unchallenged film capital of the world. Energetic, frivolous, audacious, and determined to maintain its position, it set out to captivate audiences the world over. Throughout the era and into the 1920s, the black figure that dominated— replacing Griffith's villains—was the black jester. High-stepping and high-falutin' and crazy as all get-out, the comic Negro was ushered in. But the movies of the period, like the post–World War I era itself, started with a slight identity crisis before it saw the comic light. Consequently, the era began—in 1918—with a whimper and ended—in 1929—with both a crash and a bang.

The whimper was *The Greatest Thing in Life*, a film so far removed from the mainstream that it was hard to believe it was directed by one so much a part of the mainstream as D. W. Griffith. It represented a curious departure from the sentiments expressed in *The Birth of a Nation*. Released in 1918, its theme, says Lillian Gish, was its director's favorite—"the brotherhood of man." In its climactic scene, a white racist Southern officer finds himself sharing a shell hole with a black private. At first there is great hostility. But war makes strange bedfellows—and evidently compatible ones. For when the white officer is hit by an enemy shell, the black soldier rescues him. In doing so, he saves the life of the officer but is critically wounded himself. Dying, he calls for his mother, requesting a last kiss. The injured officer grants that request. He pretends to be the black man's mother and kisses the soldier—on the lips. According to Miss Gish, "It was a dramatic and touching sceen, during which audiences sat tense and quiet."

As tense and quiet as audiences may have sat, *The Greatest Thing in Life* was a financial failure. Yet it was one of the few early films to depict blacks heroically. Or even sympathetically. At the same time, the Creel Committee issued a film called *Our Colored Fighters* as an endeavor to reveal the contributions of the American Negro to the war crisis. *Our Hell Fighters*, a one-reeler about the 367th all-Negro Regiment, was also filmed and released for the same purpose. These films, like Griffith's, were government propaganda vehicles, produced at a time when the country was promoting all-inclusive solidarity and brotherhood. Made to rally support for the war effort, they reveal the obvious fact that in critical times the use of movies as propaganda becomes intentional and overt. (During noncritical periods, motion pictures still function as propaganda but in more subtle ways.) The great paradox was that after the war was over the country and the motion picture industry appeared washed of their racial sins and reverted to their old ways. For black actors, the old way was soon indicated when a call was issued to "Make Way for the Jesters!"

During 1922 the first of the *Our Gang* comedy shorts was released. Produced by Hal Roach and dealing with "comedies of child life," the series was one of its studio's most successful creations. It ran into the talkie period and was known for a time as *The Little Rascals*. Featured through its run were a motley collection of black schoolchildren with the cornball names of Farina, Stymie, and Buckwheat.

The careers of all three followed in the wake of Sunshine Sammy, an energetic tot, described as a "lovable little pickaninny" and noted for his ability to widen his eyes to the size of ping-pong balls. Sunshine Sammy costarred with comedian Harold Lloyd in early two-reel comedies. He proved such a popular success that he became one of the highest paid juveniles in early silents. As motion pictures grew up, however, so did this "lovable little pickaninny" —so much so that by 1921 his employer, Hal Roach, was on the lookout for a playmate for Sammy. The playmate eventually became a replacement.

After a talent hunt was initiated to find a "colored boy with hair long enough to play either a boy or a girl," a studio representative announced he had discovered just such a child, an eighteen-month-old boy named Allen Clayton Hoskins. Once he was signed to a contract, there was a problem of an image and a name. When one executive thought the child so "chubby and agreeable" that he was reminded of breakfast "mush"—hot cereal—the problem was solved. Shortly thereafter the name was lifted from the cereal box and bestowed on the little fellow. Thus was born the one and only Farina!

A first assignment for Farina was to feed pearls to a flock of geese in a Roach short! Each time the geese came near him, the child burst into tears, ruining his director's setups. Later, when viewing the rushes, the director realized what a natural-born crier little Farina was, and henceforth the child was relegated to crying parts in shorts.

In *Our Gang*, Farina's face soon became familiar. Typically dressed up with tightly twisted pickaninny pigtails (they stood straight up whenever he was frightened) and old patched gingham clothes, both of which were to become his trademarks, Farina had a success that paved the way for other young black actors. His sister, Mango, made her movie debut at the age of three months in a 1927 *Our Gang* short. Her career was short-lived, however.

Like Farina, the black children who followed him also had their props. Stymie Beard sported a derby, had a head shaved completely bald, and was occasionally decked out in colorful zoot suits. Buckwheat had the pigtails and the gingham clothes of his predecessor. He also resembled Farina in that no one was sure whether he was a boy or a girl. The sexual ambiguity of the pair remains puzzling.

While all the children were admittedly made up as backwoods

At the height of his career as the late 1920s' best-known pickaninny, Farina takes time out for some soul food.

pickaninnies, each individualized his performances through his own unique personality. With his husky voice and an arrogantly pleasant way about him, Farina was noted for his common sense and a certain heroic demeanor. Often he came to the rescue of little white damsels in distress. In one episode, he attempts to help a little white girl who has fallen into a puddle of mud, only to be accused by the girl's mother of having pushed her in. Farina, however, has the last laugh when the mother herself tumbles into the mud. While Farina was given to heroics (except when there were ghosts about—at which time he was quick to head for the hills), Stymie was noted for his nonchalance and detached shrewdness. Usually, he saw straight through any sham. One *Our Gang* short centers on a pair of midgets who disguise themselves as infants and set out to rob a charity party being given for the neighborhood children by a group of ritzy society matrons. As the disguised midgets rob the society guests, it is Stymie alone who realizes that somethin' ain't right with dem dere chillun. No one pays any heed to Stymie's warnings, but at the end of the short the jewel thieves are unmasked and Stymie's cool perceptiveness has helped save the day. Possibly Stymie's chief charm was that he always spoke as if his mouth were full of food. He was, too, a master of the double take. Little Buckwheat was the last but certainly not the least of the important black children appearing in the series. With a round chocolate moon face and enormous eyes, Buckwheat always came across as a quiet, odd-ball type, the perfect little dum-dum tag-along.

The *Our Gang* series revolved around a group of lower-middle-class American youngsters making their way through childhood in entertaining ups and downs, ins and outs, as black and white together tried figuring out life and play. Throughout the series the black children spoke in a dialect of the familiar *dats* and *deres* as well as the *I is's, you is's,* and *we was's.* On more than one occasion, Farina was seen banqueting on a colored man's favorite dishes—fried chicken and watermelon. In these respects, the adventures and life styles of the black children conformed to accepted notions and attitudes of the day. But for the most part the approach to the relationships of the black children with the whites was almost as if there were no such thing as race at all. Indeed, the charming sense of *Our Gang* was that all the children were buffoons, forever in scraps and scrapes, forever plagued by setbacks and sidetracks as they set out to have fun, and everyone had his turn at being outwitted.

The "liberal" treatment of the pint-sized jesters in Roach's *Our Gang* was more an exception than the rule of the day. Black comic characters in other features or series did not fare as well. D. W. Griffith's *One Exciting Night* (1922) featured a ludicrous Negro character named Romeo Washington who finds himself trapped in a haunted house way down in ole Kentucky. Cloaked figures wander about. Arms extend from secret hidden passages. Women scream out in the night. Murders are mysteriously committed. Throughout, Romeo and another darky run through the house like scared chickens. Played by white actor Porter Strong in outrageous blackface, Romeo Washington was pure coon, a crude and racially self-demeaning character. But he delighted audiences, and the Griffith film was a great success. In another Hal Roach series featuring Charlie Chase, one could readily spot a colored maid or butler or bystander whose eyes popped or who ran off scared out of his wits by some Chase antic.

In the Buster Keaton film *Seven Chances* (1925), Keaton will inherit millions if he can find a wife within seven hours. When word spreads of the millionaire-to-be in need of a spouse, practically every eligible female in town pursues him, including a rough-and-ready black mammy. Featured in the same film is a slow-as-molasses colored messenger. Although there were still few roles for blacks in movies, whenever they were used in this period, it was usually in this sort of demeaning manner. What degraded the black comic figures of the day even further and made them appear more grotesque and less individualized was that whites still played the Negro roles. The acting was always grossly overdone. This tradition, however, fell into decline during the mid-1920s, just about the time of the release of Thomas Ince's *Free and Equal.*

Free and Equal, made in 1915, as we have already seen, was as much an example of a producer's miscalculation as it was a demonstration of how prejudice leads to lunacy. It was removed from the jester tradition of the day in that its black characters were literally that of another period. The film's release was held up by its producer, Thomas Ince, who was waiting for the adverse criticism against *The Birth of a Nation* to simmer down. As it turned out, that cooling-off period took ten years.

Free and Equal finally had its premiere in New York in 1925. Its themes were social equality and intermarriage. A Northern liberal, Judge Lowell, having waged a bet with a Southern colonel that blacks are equal to whites, takes young Alexander Marshall, a Negro, into his home. Once ensconced in the good Northern liberal's house, Marshall hotly pursues the white man's daughter. When it appears as if he has failed to seduce her, he succeeds in raping and strangling the family maid! Marshall is brought to trial and convicted. At the same time, he is exposed as not only having married the judge's daughter but as also having a Negro wife. The judge, who has been writing a lengthy treatise on intermarriage, tosses his document into the fireplace. And in the end, the "perfect" Negro has been revealed as the perfect rogue.

Obviously, *Free and Equal* portrayed the black man again as a villain, and the character Marshall was the familiar brutal black buck type. Vicious as the film was, it bore the defects and absurdities of movies made in 1915. Consequently, in 1925 it was a prodigious failure. "A dramatic catastrophe," said *The New York World*, while *The New York Amsterdam News* called it a "dramatic dud." *The New York Times* added: "The dramatic sequences last night caused outbursts of loud laughter. . . . No wonder old Judge Lowell chucked his precious book advocating full equality into the fire. It might have been well if Mr. Ince had done the same thing with the film."

Better than any other film of the period, *Free and Equal* demonstrated that the old racial themes and thought patterns would no longer stand up. What was denounced as its gravest anachronism was its use of white actor Jack Richardson in blackface to portray Marshall. "Richardson as a Negro is hopelessly out of date and fails to stir a single spark of conviction," *The New York Amsterdam News* commented, pointing out the success and excitement of Eugene O'Neill's play *All God's Chillun Got Wings*, in which a genuine Negro—Paul Robeson—appeared opposite a white actress. When would the cinema reflect such realism? At this time the film industry found itself face to face with a question it had always evaded.

The blackface tradition had hung on after its "effectiveness" had worn thin. The practice had originated in the days of slavery, when Negroes were not permitted to appear on stage. Troupes of white minstrels blackened themselves with burnt cork better to mock and caricature the plantation slaves they imitated. After the Civil War, freed slaves could form their own minstrel companies, but they too were required to darken themselves with burnt cork. Vaudeville upheld the same tradition. In the early 1900s, the popular Negro comedian Bert Williams appeared and almost always had to darken his already dark face. Even Sammy Davis, Jr., has said that he recalls as a vivid childhood memory standing in the wings of a vaudeville theater and being warned by his father not to touch his face—for fear he would smear the burnt cork. The tradition was ridiculous and unnecessary certainly, but it was merely one of any number of ways in which the entertainment world bowed to prejudice.

When the blackface tradition had popped up in early movies, no one gave it a second thought. After *The Birth of a Nation* appeared, the protests against Griffith's use of whites for the important black roles alarmed the film industry. Later, Hollywood countered the continued protests of the newly formed NAACP and other civil rights organizations by gradually casting Negro actors in small roles. Noble Johnson, Rex Ingram, and Carolyn Snowden were among the early bit players in such silent films as *The Ten Commandments* (1923), *The Thief of Bagdad* (1924), *Little Robinson Crusoe* (1924), *The Navigator* (1924), *The Big Parade* (1925), *The First Year* (1926), *Topsy and Eva* (1927), *King of Kings* (1927), and *In Old Kentucky* (1927). Sometimes they portrayed Mexicans and Spaniards or other "foreigners." By the 1920s, the absurdity of the blackface tradition was apparent. What finally killed the practice and simultaneously opened the door for a new realism that virtually demanded real Negroes in Negro roles was the advent of sound. Ironically, the film that at once revealed the power and popularity of the talking motion picture was also the one in which the blackface tradition attained its crowning achievement and its final success. That film was *The Jazz Singer.*

Released by Warner Brothers in 1927, *The Jazz Singer* revolutionized the motion-picture industry. Its routine generations-conflict plot offered little to stir audiences, but when its star, the legendary Jewish entertainer Al Jolson, appeared in burnt cork and belted out a passionate rendition of "Mammy," moviegoers were thrilled actually to hear their idol's voice. Jolson's ever-crooning-swooning darky jester was a classic example of the minstrel tradition at its sentimentalized, corrupt best. But it was a great moment for the movies. The picture launched Jolson's film career, and ever afterward he seemed to pay homage to it by including at least one blackface number in subsequent features. But more important, *The Jazz Singer* launched the talking-motion-picture era. The film was an enormous success. As a result, the movie industry experienced a great expansion and underwent a period of profound transition.

For blacks in films, the talkie era proved to be a major breakthrough. In the period 1927 to 1940, the number of Negro parts greatly increased. From the start, Hollywood was aware that talking movies needed sounds—music, rhythm, pizzazz, singing, dancing, clowning. And who, according to American myth, were more rhythmic or more musical than Negroes? No sooner had the talkies come into vogue than two major studios, Fox Pictures and MGM, operating on just such a premise, set out to put all that ole-time natchel rhythm on dazzling display. The end results of their labors were *Hearts in Dixie* and *Hallelujah.*

Hearts in Dixie (1929) was released first. It had originally been conceived as a short vehicle for offering spirituals and some minstrel men highjinks, but had been expanded into a feature. On a Southern plantation, pickaninnies romped and ran. Toms worshiped their master, labored in the fields during the day, and then played during the night. There were scenes of the steamboat *Nellie Bly* going down the river while slaves sang in the fields nearby. There was the mournful collection of darkies crooning "Massa's in the cold, cold ground." Throughout all the picturesque episodes, the blacks of *Hearts in Dixie* were mindlessly contented. Here were characters living in shacks and working from sunrise to sunset, and always, instead of suffering or misery, they seemed to be floating on some euphoric high brought on, one would assume, by cotton fields and spirituals. "The spirit of the Southern Negro a year or so after the Civil War is cleverly captured," wrote the *New York Times* film critic. "It is something restful, a talking and singing picture that is gentle in mood and truthful in its reflection of black men of those days down yonder in the cornfields." One would like to say the *Times* review was written with tongue in cheek, but it wasn't. Once again the perpetually happy-go-lucky Negro was presented to movie audiences—stamped with a seal of Establishment approval!

For the most part, the actors played their roles according to the script. Dressed in rags and tatters and grotesquely made up as simple, unaffected rurals, the performers, mostly recruited from the New York stage, often revealed the art of their theatrical experiences a bit too well. Too broad and emphatic, they tended to overplay. In the film they portrayed plantation workers, but without being aware of it they came across as a group of black-faced jesters rather than as valid representations of black folk culture. In the end, as the first all-Negro musical, *Hearts in Dixie* pinpointed the problem that was to haunt certain black actors for the next half century: the *blackface fixation*. Directed by whites in scripts authored by whites and then photographed, dressed, and made up by whites, the Negro actor, like the slaves he portrayed, aimed (and still does aim) always to please the master figure. To do so, he gives not a performance of his own, not one in which he interprets black life, but one in which he presents for mass consumption black life as seen through the eyes of white artists. The actor becomes a black man in blackface. In almost every all-black spectacle to follow, from the 1936 *Green Pastures* to the 1959 *Porgy and Bess*, most of the actors suffered from the blackface fixation. Only the very gifted, very talented have overcome it.

Hearts in Dixie may not have been the best of all possible movies, but its group of unknowns was the first all-black cast ever seen on the screen. They introduced an exuberance and vitality that eventually came to be associated with the American movie musical. Most of the dancing sequences were exceptionally good. No doubt the performers were given full reign in these sequences, and many looked as if they were ready to jump from the screen into the lap of the audience, so abundant were their energy and eagerness to please. But the dancers' lack of restraint added excitement to their work, and many of the dance steps themselves were derivative of African tribal dances. Without the benefit of a fussy white choreographer, the blacks in *Hearts in Dixie* were able to bring a part of the black cultural experience to American movie screens.

Prominent among the cast were Clarence Muse and Mildred Washington. Muse portrayed the good-hearted grandfather Napus. He displayed a rich and stimulating voice, and it was obvious he knew how to use it rhythmically. But his Napus was too submissive, disciplined, and stagey to cause much excitement among movie patrons. Neither Muse nor Washington was able to startle or delight audiences as did a walking, talking, dancing, prancing piece of coon dynamite called Stepin Fetchit. This was one of Fetchit's first important roles. Although he was not quite at the height of his powers, he was still the strongest performer in the picture, and the second half of the movie revolved completely around him. In fact, *Hearts in Dixie* was expanded because Fetchit's work in the first half had proved so good. As the roustabout slave Gummy, Fetchit was an outlandish plantation coon. Many may have objected to his self-demeaning absurdities, but it had to be admitted that this disoriented, baffled clown picked up a slow-moving and patronizing film and carried it to new summits with his free-wheeling nuttiness. *Hearts in Dixie* provided Fetchit with the first in a series of coon jesters and coon servants that he was to develop to enormous popularity in the 1930s.

Hallelujah (1929) was the second of the big spectacles. Director King Vidor had long been interested in filming a story of "real Negro folk culture." Not until the sound period, however, did such a project seem commercially feasible. Even then, Vidor was able to get his picture past certain MGM executives only after he invested his own money in it. Vidor meticulously gathered a cast of New York performers, then shot his movie on location in the swamps and forests of Tennessee and Arkansas. When released, *Hallelujah* ranked well above the films of the period. It remains a landmark in sound films.

Hallelujah took as its theme the age-old problem of a Good

Colored Boy going bad and the battle within him between callings of the spirit and temptations of the flesh. The film opens on the idyllic little Johnson farm, where the family—Pappy Johnson, Mammy, their adopted daughter, Missy Rose, their eldest son, Zeke, and their younger boys—energetically gather the cotton harvest. Nearing the last rows, the group bursts into song, singing to the heavens. In the evening, when away from the fields, the family entertains itself with spirituals and lively gospels. Good, gentle folk, the Johnsons are pictured as serene and uncomplicated—as long as baser instincts are kept in check. When these are unleashed, however, trouble's a-brewin'!

In this case, trouble proves to be firmly embodied in a full-bosomed, spicy cabaret dancer, Chick. When the eldest son, Zeke, journeys to town with brother Spunk to collect the family's earnings for their reapings, he takes one look at Chick, and family and finances are forgotten.

"Yo' is jest what I's got on my mind," he tells her.

"Git outta my way, small change," she replies. "You don't look like Big Money to me!"

So begins their evening. When it ends, Zeke has not only lost the family's money, but has accidently killed his brother Spunk during a barroom brawl.

Repenting for his sins, Zeke becomes an itinerant preacher, only to meet up again with Chick. Intrigued by his conversion, she too repents, and in one of the most explicit scenes ever to link the bonds of religious ecstasy with sexual fervor, she is baptized by Zeke. During a revival meeting, the religious-sexual fervor builds until Zeke finally deserts his congregation to chase Chick through the woods.

Chick leads Zeke down a path of degradation and tragedy. In a fit of jealous rage he kills her and her lover. The story ends with a repentant Zeke returning home to the serene, uncomplicated family plantation. There he finds his faithful Mammy and Pappy and Missy Rose, the girl he has always loved. Rejoicing, the quartet sings a spiritual. And thus a Good Colored Boy Gone Bad becomes good again, and life is once more idyllic.

Hallelujah's plot may border on operatic absurdity, but director Vidor was able to capture in music a whole emotional aura. In its best moments, *Hallelujah* proved to be the finest record of black grief and passion to reach a movie screen. Although at times the spirituals of the Dixie Jubilee Choir appeared too slicked up—and geared too much toward the mass audience—they supported demanding and difficult scenes and were quite effective. They managed, as do all great spirituals, to touch some psychic cord in their audience and to communicate not only discontent and disillusionment but also a sense of the supernatural and the sublime.

Hallelujah's view of black life was enthusiastically greeted by the white press. The *New York Times* critic Mordaunt Hall, charmed by the reality Vidor had imparted in his treatment of the Negro, said the film succeeded in presenting the "peculiarly typical religious hysteria of the darkies and their gullibility . . . their hankering after salvation, the dread of water in the baptism." *Variety* commended Vidor's direction: "Apparently in the massed ensemble groups, Vidor had a mighty tough job holding that bunch down, yet he held them under remarkable restraint and still brought out the effects desired." Much of the Negro press, however, was less charitable. When *Hallelujah* had simultaneous premières at the Lafayette Theatre in Harlem and the Embassy in the downtown white area, the black press denounced the racism inherent in the dual opening. Black patrons viewed it as a tactical move by MGM to spare the feelings of "swanky whites" who might not object to watching a screenful of darkies but who most certainly did not want to sit next to any in a theater. Of greater concern to some black critics, though, were the spiritual-singing, crap-shooting characters who were old types even in 1929.

In due time, *Hallelujah* became not only an American classic but the precursor of all-Negro musicals, setting the tone for the treatment of Negro casts and themes. Vidor, himself an idealist, had presented his Negroes in an idealized, isolated world. By having his blacks battle it out among themselves rather than with any white antagonists, he created an unreal universe and consequently divorced himself from real issues confronting blacks and whites in America. Vidor's theme of the good colored boy who meets up with the bad black girl while leaving back home the ever-patient, all-submissive Christian Negress came to serve as the basic plot outline for a number of black spectacles. Indeed individual scenes and sequences from *Hallelujah* have popped up repeatedly in other films. The action in the scene of Chick dying in the arms of Zeke was used almost exactly by Otto Preminger some twenty years later in *Carmen Jones* when Dorothy Dandridge died in the arms of Harry Belafonte. Vidor's directorial approach, that of the white visitor rather than the black inhabitant, survived too. His blacks were often pawns, used for an expression of his own lyrical view of realism and his own feeling for mood and atmosphere rather than for any comment of their own. *Hallelujah* remains the first of Hollywood's attempts to deal with the black family, and is directly related to subsequent black family dramas such as *The Learning Tree* (1969) and *Sounder* (1972).

In most respects, the characters of *Hallelujah* were indeed stereotypes, blacks depicted as either sentimental idealists or highly emotional animals. But it should be said that to the credit of the actors, although many suffered from the blackface fixation, they still invested their characters with energy and a raw urgency. Although the film's vision (its view of life) was firmly controlled by Vidor, the director had the sense and sensitivity to let his actors do certain things their way. Often the actors improvised splendidly. Daniel Haynes played Zeke. Originally, Vidor had wanted Paul Robeson for the lead; the picture was written with him in mind. But when Robeson was unavailable, Vidor selected Haynes, then an understudy in *Show Boat*. Haynes often seemed too saintly to be shooting crap or romping through the woods, but he had a voice large enough to move an entire theater, and it added depth and texture to his performance. William Fountaine portrayed the no-account gambler, Hot Shot. Sporting zoot suits and a derby, Fountaine remains the screen model for Sammy Davis, Jr.'s Sportin' Life in *Porgy and Bess*. A ninety-year-old employee of *The New York Amsterdam News* (and a former slave), Harry Gray, made an impressive screen debut as Pappy, while Victoria Spivey interjected a somber, mystical quality as the sad-eyed, sensitive girl-back-home, Missy Rose. Fannie Belle DeKnight played Mammy. Everett McGarrity presented a very poignant Spunk. For most of the cast, *Hallelujah* was the beginning and ending of their screen careers. Hollywood had not yet found a place for the black performer. Of all the actors in the film, the one to meet with the greatest "success"—and heartache—was its energetic leading lady, Nina Mae McKinney.

Executing sensuous bumps and grinds in the famous cabaret scene in *Hallelujah*, Nina Mae McKinney was the movies' first black whore. Almost every black leading lady in motion pictures, from Lena Horne in *Cabin in the Sky* to Lola Falana in *The Liberation of L. B. Jones*, owes a debt to the gyrations and groans of McKinney's character Chick.

Born in 1912 in Lancaster, South Carolina, Nina Mae McKinney had come with her family to New York and had just won a role in Lew Leslie's famous *Blackbirds* revue when word leaked out that King Vidor was auditioning performers for *Hallelujah*. Vidor had originally considered Ethel Waters for the role of Chick, and had she played the part her career might have run an entirely different course, but when McKinney was spotted—she was seventeen at the time—Vidor virtually lifted her from the chorus and starred her in the vamp role.

In McKinney's hands and hips, Chick represented the black

ABOVE: "Yo'se jest what I'se got on my mind," Daniel Haynes (right) exclaims as he catches sight of Nina Mae McKinney in *Hallelujah* (1929), one of the first all-talking, all-singing, all-colored musicals.
LEFT: Nina Mae McKinney, the screen's first black love goddess—and its first black victim as well (1929).

RIGHT: McKinney during the later years of her career when she appeared in independently produced all-black movies.

woman as an exotic sex object, half woman, half child. She was the black woman out of control of her emotions, split in two by her loyalties and her own vulnerabilities. Implied throughout the battle with self was the tragic mulatto theme. Chick was always referred to as "that cinnamon-colored gal" or "high yeller." The white half of her represented the spiritual; the black half, the animalistic.

Nina Mae McKinney emerged as the first recognized black actress of the silver screen. She was the first, too, in the tradition of light-skinned black leading ladies. In *The New York Post*, Richard Watts, Jr., called her "assuredly one of the most beautiful women of our time." King Vidor added that it was McKinney's performance more than any other actor's that helped carry *Hallelujah*. "She's sensational," he said. Even Irving Thalberg proclaimed her one of the greatest discoveries of the age. MGM was so impressed that she was signed to a five-year contract. But in the end, her phenomenal success in *Hallelujah* lead her nowhere. Instead of the screen stardom McKinney had expected, and rightfully so, she was the first black actress to learn (as Dorothy Dandridge discovered thirty years later) that there were no leading roles for black leading ladies. All *Hallelujah* secured for her were minor film roles and a handful of appearances in obscure shorts.

Barely five years after *Hallelujah*, Nina Mae McKinney was forgotten in America. But from Greece, Richard Watts, Jr., reported on a spectacular cabaret performer billed as the Black Garbo. The Black Garbo was none other than McKinney, who was touring Europe, singing in cafés and nightclubs in Paris, London, Budapest, and Dublin. Like Josephine Baker before her, she found European audiences more receptive to her talents. While in England in 1935, she appeared opposite Paul Robeson in Zoltan Korda's *Sanders of the River*. Later she returned to the United States and appeared in a number of independent all-black films. Her last important role was as a razor-totin', high-strung, high-yeller girl in *Pinky* (1949). Though she was effective, the part did little for her career, and it was hard to believe that the stocky, bleary-eyed harridan on screen had once been the bright-eyed, carefree Chick.

Nina Mae McKinney's later film work obviously did not live up to her early promise, but much that she experimented with in *Hallelujah*—the hands on the hips, the hard-as-nails brassy voice —became stock in trade for black leading ladies. One merely has to view Dandridge's cafeteria entrance in *Carmen Jones* with her particular type of sensual swagger and her hands-on-hips arrogance to realize that McKinney's techniques were picked up by other actresses. At times even Jean Harlow appeared as if she had learned something about rough nightlife heroines from her. Nina Mae McKinney's final contribution to the movies now lay in those she influenced.

St. Louis Blues (1929) was the final black film of the 1920s. It, too, featured a tempestuous female performer. This short, directed by Dudley Murphy and financed by Warner Brothers, starred the legendary Bessie Smith, affording her a one and only chance to sing her blues and sway her hips on film. The Murphy venture spotlighted the anguish and misery the major musicals had avoided. It centers on Bessie as Bessie, a blues singer done wrong by her Man, Jimmy the pimp. Bessie fights for Jimmy and runs rampant on a girl who has an eye for him. But ultimately she finds herself deserted and unhappy. *St. Louis Blues* was marred by its white director's overstatement, but it was distinguished by Bessie Smith's extraordinary ability to express black pain. The film swayed and resounded to her great ache. She remains as well the most sensual black woman ever to have been turned loose in an American movie.

Hearts in Dixie, Hallelujah, and *St. Louis Blues* brought the roaring 1920s to a close. None was successful at the box office. *Hallelujah* was banned by the Southern Theatre Federation. American movie audiences were still unprepared to accept blacks in important leading roles. The commercial failure of these films accounts for the long eight-year interval between them and the next big black spectacle, *The Green Pastures.*

Regardless of the failure of this trio, they showed triumphantly the contributions the black performer could make to the sound era. Each film helped open the door wider. In the next decade, a diverse group of household servants, led by Stepin Fetchit, ripped the door from its hinges and proved that in spite of the stock-market crash, a little black humor and a lot of black magic never hurt—at least in the movies. The 1920s may have ended on a crash, but they led the way to the 1930s with a bang.

The 1930s: the Servants

3

Sir Stepin Fetchit is a much maligned handyman, flamboyantly shufflin' and stammerin'. . . . Bill "Bojangles" Robinson is a smooth-as-silk butler, calm, cool, and lighthearted as he dances up a staircase with Shirley Temple. . . . Louise Beavers is a jolly but submissive cook, forever on the verge of heartfelt tears as she whips up a batch of pancakes. . . . Eddie "Rochester" Anderson is a bright, brisk, and clever manservant without whom Jack Benny would be lost. . . . Hi-Hat Hattie McDaniel is a big, black, bossy, and beautiful maid who continually forgets her place. . . . Butterfly McQueen is a nervous and panicky housegirl, lettin' it all hang out as she confesses, "Gee, Miss Scarlett, I don't knows nothin' 'bout birthin' babies." . . . Willie "Sleep 'n' Eat" Best is a dim-witted hireling, terr'fied of ghosts. . . . And Paul Robeson is a lordly Pullman car porter, towering above it all.

They were all there. Everybody's favorites. All those strange, neurotically engrossing personalities who were thought of fondly despite the fact that they tommed or jemimaed their ways through scores of bad movies. But it was the 1930s. The toms, coons, mulattoes, mammies, and bucks were no longer dressed as old-style jesters. Instead they had become respectable domestics. Hollywood had found a new place for the Negro—in the kitchens, the laundry rooms, and the pantries. And thus was born the Age of the Negro Servant.

No other period in motion-picture history could boast of more black faces carrying mops and pails or lifting pots and pans than the Depression years. In the movies, as in the streets, it was a time when the only people without job worries were the maids, the butlers, the bootblacks, the bus boys, the elevator men, the cooks, and the custodians. In almost any film of the period, from breezy, light-hearted comedies like *It Happened One Night* (1934) or *Twentieth Century* (1934) to super-deluxe spectacles such as *Gone with the Wind* (1939), a black face was bound to appear. And whether that face was seen for two minutes or three and a half hours, it was invariably there to tidy up the house, cook a meal, or watch over the livery stables.

The black servants of the Hollywood films of the 1930s met the demands of their times. They were used for a number of reasons. With their incredible antics, their unbelievable dialects, and their amazing absurdities, the black servants provided a down-hearted Depression age with buoyancy and jocularity. As they delivered their wisecracks or acted the fool, the servants were a marvelous relief from the harsh financial realities of the day. Not only their joy and zest but their loyalty, too, demonstrated that nothing in life was ever completely hopeless. The servants were always around when the boss needed them. They were always ready to lend a helping hand when times were tough. It was many a down-and-out movie hero or heroine who realized his Negro servant was his only real friend. During this period of bread lines, of fireside chats from President Roosevelt over the radio, of labor problems, of intellectual Leftist activities, and of WPA programs, blacks in films were used to reaffirm for a socially chaotic age a belief in life and the American way of living itself. Indeed, the black servants of the 1930s proved that human beings could and should endure. They seemed to say that even during the worst of times everything could be straightened out as long as people kept their chins up.

With its servant syndrome, or perhaps in spite of it, the 1930s was for individual black performers a Golden Age. Admittedly, the black servants were repeatedly exploited and mistreated, and the black servant performers themselves were often criticized by civil rights organizations for accepting such demeaning roles. But through their black characters, the actors accomplished the almost impossible: they proved single-handedly that the mythic types could be individualized and made, if not into things of beauty, then at least into things of joy. Almost every black actor of the period approached his role with a *joie de vivre* the movies were never to see again. Indeed, the enthusiasm the actors poured into their characters seemed often to parallel their own gratitude that at long last blacks were working in films. Perhaps most significantly, because there were but three important black films in this decade, the era was distinguished by personalties rather than pictures. It was in many respects a crucial, exasperating period because the emphasis fell so squarely on the shoulders of the black actors themselves. Without scripts to aid them and generally without even sympathetic directors or important roles, black actors in American films were compelled to rely on their own ingenuity to create memorable characters.

One can detect among the personalities of the 1930s a world order, a microcosm, in which each black performer had his speciality. Traditionally, American whites have felt one Negro looks like another. That attitude was prevalent in the early years of this decade. But each major black actor of the day managed to reveal some unique quality of voice or personality that audiences immediately responded to. Who could forget Bojangles' urbanity? Or Rochester's cement-mixer voice? Or Louise Beavers' jollity? Or Hattie McDaniel's haughtiness? Eventually, audiences came to hold these personalities in such affectionate regard that they were readily identifiable by their nicknames. The very best black performers played their types but played against them. They built and molded themselves into what film critic Andrew Sarris might call nondirectorial *auteurs*. With their own brand of outrageousness, the blacks created comic worlds all their own in which the servant often outshone the master.

But the distinctive black servants were not the first to arrive. In the early 1930s, once black servants were acceptable, countless black faces roamed in and out of movies. They would enter, say or mumble their bit, then quickly fade from the scene. Langston Hughes once described the standard direction for the Negro actor: "Upon opening the car door for one's white employer in any film, the director would command, 'Jump to ground. . . . Remove cap. . . . Open again. . . . Step back and bow. . . . Come up smiling. . . . Now bow again. . . . Now straighten up and grin!'" And at the beginning of the decade many actors went through just these mechanics without trying to individualize their roles. Their appearances, however brief, were always overblown, flashy, far-out, and farcical. Invariably, just the sight of a black face on screen guaranteed laughs from the audience. In the Marx Brothers' feature *Animal Crackers* (1930), Groucho made a spectacular entrance into a Los Angeles ballroom borne on a stretcher by four

African natives. "What! From Africa to here on a dollar eighty-five?" he exclaims, chuckling quizzically. In the Al Jolson starrer *Hallelujah, I'm a Bum* (1933), black actor Edgar Connor portrayed a simple-minded character called Acorn. As two noboes, Acorn and the white character Bumper finally give up their life of leisure to go to work. Upon receiving their first pay check, Bumper is ecstatic about having money in his pockets. Acorn agrees that having cash is fine; his only complaint is that one has to waste so much time to get it. In *Mississippi* (1935), a Negro coachman, made to look ludicrous in top hat and frock-coat two sizes too large for him, became the butt of a classic W.C. Fields joke: "Get along, you Senegambian!" Al Jolson, in and out of blackface in *Wonder Bar* (1934), visited a black heaven where a sepia Saint Peter and some ebony angels transformed God's paradise into an elaborate Pullman-porter playground. In *Go into Your Dance* (1935), Jolson, again in and out of black drag, was waited on by a knuckle-headed valet called Snowflake. Jolson often rubbed the servant's head—playing on an old Southern superstition: touch a nigger's head for luck! The actor who portrayed Snowflake in this film was also billed as such when he portrayed grotesque mugging domestics in *Twentieth Century, Lady by Choice* (1934), and *The Biscuit Eater* (1940).

To catalogue other movies in the early and middle 1930s in which the Snowflake type of black servant appeared without any significance would result in a plethora of titles. The change and the individualization of the servant came about gradually. In the films of the decade, one can trace a haphazard progression of the black character from field jester to house servant to domesticated servant to humanized servant to posthumanized eccentric. Stepin Fetchit was the actor whose roles marked the first transition from field clown to house handyman. He was as well the movies' first distinctive black personality.

High-Steppin' Sir Stepin

One newspaper carried the following item:

> [He] has been missing appointments for 32 years . . . is the world's champion job-loser. Because of his intolerable memory, he has been thrown out of all the best American race meetings, lost several distinguished positions as a shoe-black and forfeited one of the biggest starring contracts Hollywood had to offer—they could never find him.

Columnist Sidney Skolsky commented:

Fox has re-signed Stepin Fetchit. The colored performer who had such a promising movie career will be given another chance. They hesitated about signing Fetchit again. According to Helen Gwynn, they first called him in and told him that they were going to let him make a short.

He was told that if he behaved during the making of the short he would be given features. He was reminded that he was Hollywood's bad boy.

"You don't have to worry about me any more," said Fetchit. "You're not taking any chances at all. I've been reading history, and I've noticed that they all became big guys after they were 32. Napoleon, Washington, and Abe Lincoln. You don't have to worry about me any more. I'm 32 today."

In the year 1934—at the age of thirty-two—Stepin Fetchit was already a legend and one of movieland's few authentic oddities. Only a few years earlier, no one could have predicted that this actor who gave the appearance of being a lanky, slow-witted, simple-minded, obtuse, synthetic, confused humbug would take an entire nation and an era by storm. But Stepin Fetchit went far beyond anyone's predictions or expectations, and in his own inspired way he did so brilliantly. In the early 1930s he was the best known and most successful black actor working in Hollywood. At a time when contracts for black players were unheard of, Fetchit was signed, then dropped, then spectacularly re-signed by Fox Pictures. From 1929 to 1935, he appeared in some twenty-six films. Often working in as many as four movies at a time, Fetchit was the first Negro to receive featured billing, and special scenes were often written into pictures for him. He popularized the dim-witted, tongue-tied stammer and the phenomenal slow-lazyman shuffle. So successful was he with his slow gait that for years audiences thought Stepin Fetchit actually could not run. Negro bootblacks and bus boys were said to have imitated his notorious walk on the streets.

Fox Pictures, in promoting their first black star, did much to exploit his private life. What with Fetchit's own startling capacity for generating news, stories circulated of his flamboyant high style of life: his six houses, his sixteen Chinese servants, his two-thousand-dollar cashmere suits imported from India, his lavish parties, his twelve cars. (One was a champagne-pink Cadillac with his name emblazoned on the side in neon lights.) Whenever High-Steppin' Step came to town, so the stories went, two chauffeured limousines followed. The off-screen flamboyance and super-nigger highjinks whetted the public's appetite and at the same time often overshadowed the actual screen performances of a rather gifted personality.

Fetchit came to Hollywood in the late 1920s. Named after four

LEFT: The 1930s' archetypal coon, Stepin Fetchit, avoids work by hiding in a hayloft. BELOW: Abused and demeaned in picture after picture, Fetchit here takes orders from Will Rogers, an actor he was closely associated with in the 1930s.

Presidents, he was born Lincoln Theodore Monroe Andrew Perry in Key West, Florida, in 1902. He had first hoped (or so the press releases indicated) to enter the ministry, but before long he turned to vaudeville. With comic Ed Lee, he had an act called "Step and Fetch It." When a Fox talent scout spotted him, he was tested successfully for films, and his career began.

From the outset, Fetchit displayed an instinctive awareness of public tastes. No doubt he noted the popularity of toms, but he must have realized, too, that toms were not much fun. Coons, however—those lazy, no-account, good-for-nothing, forever-in-hot-water, natural-born comedians—were loved by everyone. Consequently, Stepin Fetchit developed into the arch-coon, and as such he had no equal, introducing to audiences of the 1930s all the antics and tomfoolery every later black comedian was to draw from. His very name fitted his image, for it conjured up a portrait of the plantation darky who must *step in* (the Big House), *fetch it*, and then go his way. His appearance, too, added to the caricature. He was tall and skinny and always had his head shaved completely bald. He invariably wore clothes that were too large for him and that looked as if they had been passed down from his white master. His grin was always very wide, his teeth very white, his eyes very widened, his feet very large, his walk very slow, his dialect very broken. But Fetchit was able to tie together all the disparate elements to create a stylized character. As if aware of his own effect, he gave performances that were often a series of extravagant poses. When he sang and danced in films, it was hard for audiences not to respond to the precise control of his body. "Mr. Fetchit's feet are like chained lightning as he performs," wrote one critic. Even when his characters were flamboyantly exaggerated, the master Fetchit was economic and in command of his movements. Never was there a false footstep. Never was there excessive excessiveness.

In his early films, as the lackey in *In Old Kentucky* (1927), as Christopher C. Lee in *The Ghost Talks* (1929), as Pilot Joe in *Show Boat* (1929), and as the call-boy in *Fox Movietone Follies* (1929), he was the embodiment of the nitwit colored man. Stepin Fetchit was always forgetful. Stepin Fetchit could never pronounce a word with more than one syllable. Stepin Fetchit seldom seemed to have his senses about him. In *Stand Up and Cheer* (1934), he was tricked into thinking a "talking" penguin was actually a shrunken Jimmy Durante. In *The World Moves On* (1934), he found himself a recruit in the French army! Whining and scratching his head in disbelief, he wondered how he of all people could be mistaken for a Frenchman! In *David Harum* (1934) Stepin nonchalantly soaked his aching feet in a tubful of hot water. When his wife berated him for using the hot water she was boiling to wash her dishes in, Fetchit calmly informed her that she had nothing to worry about. He had killed two birds with one stone, he said, as he lifted from the tub the family's dishes, which had been soaking right along with his feet. For movie audiences it was a classic comic moment.

Perhaps the most typical of the Fetchit features were *David Harum* and the other three in which he costarred with Will Rogers: *The County Chairman* (1935) and two movies directed by John Ford, *Judge Priest* (1934) and *Steamboat 'Round the Bend* (1935). In these four films, Fetchit was cast as the triflin', inarticulate, backward handyman who was there to do odd jobs for master Will Rogers. Throughout these films the black actor cowered, shuffled, or stammered, rendering himself almost unintelligible. Usually, he was demeaned and racially degraded. In *David Harum* he was traded to Will Rogers along with a horse in a shady horse deal. Afterwards, Rogers traded the same horse and Fetchit to another man. Later Fetchit and the bum horse were traded back again. Clearly, Stepin Fetchit's character was considered less than human. As Jeff in *Judge Priest,* the actor often found himself pushed, shoved, and yelled at by Will Rogers to the sheer joy of movie patrons. "Hey, boy, wake up there!" Rogers commanded him. In the film's finale, Fetchit led a notorious street parade, dressed in a mile-high top hat and an enormous fur coat, to the tune of "Dixie." Here, though, the actor triumphed over the role. Traditionally, movie audiences responded to spectacles and extravaganzas, and as Stepin Fetchit's character marched down the street, stepping high and caring less, he became a one-man carnival, an aesthetic happening for humdrum 1930s audiences. "That cloudy streak of greased lightning, Stepin Fetchit, is riotous as the judge's man of all or no work, and he is always threatening to drop the auditors into the Music Hall's plush aisles," wrote *The New York Times* when *Judge Priest* opened at Radio City.

Fetchit's antics eventually destroyed him, but in the early years they made him a star. Fetchit himself took pains to ensure his characters' "respectability." He shrewdly perceived that his coons, although extravagant and outlandish, must never be a threat to the white master, and, most important, they must be servants who could be reformed. Thus he created and popularized what he himself termed the "lazy man with a soul." He has been quoted as saying that he was the first to portray Negro characters who were acceptable to polite Jim Crow society. By the time Fetchit appeared in *Carolina* (1934) and *Steamboat 'Round the*

Bend (1935), his characters had become integral parts of the household, involved in the affairs and troubles of the ruling families. They were still used for crude comic relief but at heart they were harmless creatures who, during crucial moments, would "come through." What Fetchit's "lazy man with a soul" ultimately did was to place the black character in the mainstream of filmic action and to remove him from the false idealization of the all-Negro movie. Between Fetchit's master and himself there were a spirit of good will and much mutual affection. These traits figured prominently in later Depression movies and were at the core of the developing master-servant syndrome.

Fetchit's heyday in films came to an end in the late 1930s. The self-demeaning tomfoolery he went through in film after film, as well as the superstitious chicken thieves or clownish show-offs or menial good-for-nothings he invariably portrayed, alienated him from black audiences. Whites had already viewed him as a representative of the American Negro. But black audiences knew better, and civil rights organizations were quick to criticize him. In films such as *Helldorado* (1935), *One More Spring* (1935), *36 Hours to Kill* (1936), *Dimples* (1936), *On the Avenue* (1937), and *Zenobia* (1939), even Fetchit began showing signs of disillusionment with his coon characters, and the quality of his work gradually declined.

Generally, though, there was a complex contradictory element to all Fetchit's appearances that was usually glossed over or ignored. Evidently, at least on a subconscious level, no one knew better than Fetchit the injustices and cruelties of the "benevolent" white masters in his films. Fetchit's great gift was in rendering his coons as such thoroughly illiterate figures that they did not have to respond when demeaned because they were always unaware of what was being done. When he was kicked in one film, Fetchit merely winked to his audience. When he was shoved in another, he merely moaned "Yessir" and went on his way. By removing his characters' intellects—indeed their psyches—from the real world, Stepin Fetchit's dimwits never had to acknowledge the inhumanity that surrounded them. They were inhabitants of detached, ironic, artistically controlled worlds. The ambiguity in Fetchit's work was so strong that audiences often asked, "Can he be serious?" That was something never asked of later black comics, and it was this aspect of Fetchit's work that distinguished him and made him more than just a stereotype figure. There was about him a sad, much-maligned, whining quality. Though he was a great comic figure, he seemed a bruised creature, and always his withdrawal within self—his retreat into a self-protective shell—

indicated an overriding, often excruciating nihilism. This nihilistic aspect might explain in part his popularity in a disillusioned age. Yet it was not enough to save him, and when he became a target for the civil rights advocates, his career came to an abrupt end.

What no doubt helped to finish him was his own immaturity. With his penchant for high living, he reportedly went bankrupt, having run up debts of four million dollars with but $144 in the bank. Fetchit left Hollywood at the end of the 1930s and fell into obscurity. During the lean obscure years, he worked in a number of underground independently produced all-black features. Although removed from the Hollywood system that had always typed him, he continued playing the same coon character. In 1952, Fetchit appeared with James Stewart in a major studio film, *Bend of the River.* His comeback was casually dismissed. "We are sorry to note that Stepin Fetchit is back to play a clownish stereotype," wrote Bosley Crowther in *The New York Times.* Afterward, Fetchit made an appearance in John Ford's *The Sun Shines Bright* (1954). He had worked under Ford not only in his important films *Judge Priest* and *Steamboat 'Round the Bend* but in *Salute* (1929) and *The World Moves On* as well. This fifth feature with Ford, however, sadly did little to revive Fetchit's film career. Fetchit was not to be heard from again until the late 1960s, when he denounced a television series on black history for "taking me, a Negro hero, and converting me into a villain." "It was Step," he said, "who elevated the Negro to the dignity of a Hollywood star. I made the Negro a first-class citizen all over the world . . . somebody it was all right to associate with. I opened all the theaters."

To many, Stepin Fetchit may have sounded as if he were a man suffering from delusions. But his place in black film history remains significant, for indeed he did open studio doors to blacks in Hollywood. Today because his films are seldom shown and often neglected—to the point where his scenes are even cut when shown on television—the credit due him is generally denied. In recent years, he has appeared with the Muhammad Ali entourage and done stand-up comedy appearances in nightclubs. But new audiences seeing a somewhat stale Fetchit have no idea what he was like when his routines were fresh. Fetchit's early characters remain the first of the house servants, the first of the white master's darling pets. After he arrived on the scene, a servant is a servant is a servant is a servant was no longer the case. When Fetchit ripped the door from its hinges a slew of domesticated servants came romping through, most significantly in the films of two blond leading ladies.

Waiting on West and Serving Shirley

Mae West and Shirley Temple were worlds apart, but their servants were not. For both actresses, blacks became confidantes and playmates, and like the Stepin Fetchit of *Judge Priest* and *Steamboat 'Round the Bend*, they were also important plot fixtures.

Depression audiences viewing such prime Mae West features as *I'm No Angel* (1933), *She Done Him Wrong* (1933), and *Belle of the Nineties* (1934) could not help noticing the black maids who clustered about the platinum-blond heroine. The domestics were always overweight, middle-aged, and made up as jolly aunt jemimas. They wore patch-work dresses and colorful kerchiefs tied about their heads, and they had the usual names: Pearl, Beulah, and Jasmine. Their naïve blackness generally was used as a contrast to Mae West's sophisticated whiteness. Inevitably set against white carpeting, white furniture, white decor—not to mention the white Miss West—the stout black figures hustling and bustling about served to heighten the hot white sexuality of their bawdy mistress.

Seldom did the black maids have lives of their own. Instead they were comments on their mistress. Hardly any moviegoer of the 1930s has forgotten how in *I'm No Angel* Mae West, after having bounced from her apartment a socialite who has snubbed her, quickly recovered her cool by giving the most famous instructions any movie maid ever received. "Beulah," she commanded, "peel me a grape!" Beulah (portrayed by Gertrude Howard) scurried into the room. Once again Mae West was in complete control of a situation. In the same film, Mae West, when trying on a new gown or testing her latest quip, gathered her chubby, affable servant gals around her to see their reactions. Often giggling and gaping or even literally kneeling before her as they checked a hemline, the Negro maids appeared to be paying homage to the supreme power of their white mistress. As she rattled off her sophisticated banter, the maids became her foils. "I wouldn't want no policeman to catch me without a petticoat," said maid Pearl in *She Done Him Wrong*. "How about a fireman?" cracked West.

Most important, Mae West's black maids were taken into her confidence and were pictured as knowing her better than any of her men. In *She Done Him Wrong*, maid Pearl (played by Louise Beavers) realized it was Cary Grant who had caught her mistress's eye. It was she who informed Miss West that Grant (portraying a Salvation Army officer) would be evicted from his mission settlement. The possible eviction proved crucial to the plot—and Mae West's romantic inclinations. Consequently, servant Pearl saved the day and proved herself the most dependable of loyal servants. In *I'm No Angel*, Gertrude Howard as Beulah performed the same function by testifying in her mistress's behalf during a hilarious courtroom sequence. In *Belle of the Nineties*, it was Libby Taylor as Jasmine who, upon learning her mistress had a date with a gentleman of dubious character, felt she knew her well enough to say, "Well, I'm surprised at you goin'," to which Miss West replied, "I'm surprised *you'd* think I was."

The implications throughout the films were that black women could not possibly be rivals to Mae West's femininity and that only black women were fit to wait on whores. Because both blacks and whores were at the bottom of the social scale, Mae West could rely on her colored maids and enjoy a livelier camaraderie with them than she might with whites. Some of this camaraderie must have existed off-screen, too, for Libby Taylor, who portrayed Miss West's servant, had actually been her domestic. When she left New York to go to Hollywood, maid Taylor went with her.

What the blacks in the Mae West films represented was the second step in servant evolution—the domestic servant as trusted good friend. In some of the Shirley Temple features, audiences witnessed the first signs of the humanization of the black domestic.

Shirley Temple herself occupied a unique position in relation to Negroes in films. Of all leading ladies to be waited on by colored help, none was ever more dutifully attended to than little Miss Curlytop. Blacks appeared so often in her important films that there was an inside industry joke that a Temple picture was incomplete without at least one darky. In *Stand Up and Cheer* (1934), the elaborate musical that made Shirley Temple a star, a blues singer—incredibly billed as "Aunt Jemima"—led a spiritual revival session. Stepin Fetchit was featured in this film as well as in *Dimples* (1936). In *Little Miss Marker* (1934) and *The Littlest Rebel* (1935), long, lean Willie Best was but one in a bevy of black actors. In *The Little Colonel* (1935), Hattie McDaniel, usually a tough and no-nonsense maid, was the picture of modesty as she portrayed Shirley's mammy. Later she was just as uncharacteristically subdued when she portrayed the faithful family maid to an adolescent Shirley in *Since You Went Away* (1944).

As a genuine Depression heroine who was as much a victim of hard times as anyone else, Shirley Temple often associated with the low-lifers in her movies. But among Shirley and these low-lifers, particularly these black low-lifers—the livery keepers, the faithful old butlers, the big bossy maids, the doormen, the cooks —there was always a sense of community and an abiding feeling of order, as if everyone knew his place, accepted it, and therefore managed to make life bearable. With most adults, she was overbearing, outspoken, and forever in charge of the situation. Her common sense outranked theirs. But in her dealings with her black servants, there was occasionally some condescension or manipulation. Thus in *The Little Colonel,* audiences saw Shirley give commands to her crusty old grandfather, Lionel Barrymore, or offer advice to her distraught mother, or bring comfort to her desperately ill father. But with the hired help, Bill Robinson and Hattie McDaniel, Shirley Temple relaxed. She learned to pick up her heels and have some good clean fun. Robinson became the master in their relationship when he taught her the staircase dance routines.

Throughout her films, Shirley and her black servants were obvious buddies. The servants' vitality, spontaneity, and childlike qualities equaled her own. From them she learned to maintain good spirits in the face of adversity. As they danced and sang and laughed together, Shirley and her subservients gave Depression audiences their greatest gift; the impression that if everyone were kind to one another, the bad times would soon be over. Finally, to her, the black servants represented fellow children with whom she could sympathize more readily than with real (white) grownups or even with real children. When Shirley encountered her peers, especially the pickaninnies in *The Little Colonel* and *The Littlest Rebel,* she could be a real tyrant!

Mr. Bojangles: the Cool-Eyed Tom

Of all the black servants in the Shirley Temple films none was more closely associated with her than Bill "Bojangles" Robinson, who costarred with her in no less than four features. Theirs was the perfect interracial love match. For surely nothing would come of it. Indeed audiences so readily accepted them as a pair that in their biggest hit together, *The Littlest Rebel,* Robinson played her guardian, certainly the first time in the history of motion pictures that a black servant was made responsible for a white life. As Shirley's "Uncle Billy," Robinson reaped many condescending smiles and quaint compliments from nice little old ladies who were given to such comments as, "My, isn't he a sweet colored man." "Uncle Billy" was the perfect—perhaps the quintessential —tom role. But by then, 1936, that type of characterization was to be expected from Bill "Bojangles" Robinson.

Robinson had come to films only a few years earlier after a varied and legendary career as a tap dancer. The grandson of a slave, he was said to have never had a dancing lesson in his life, to have run away from his home in Richmond, Virginia, at the age of eight, and to have soon earned his living by dancing for pennies in saloons and on streets. He formally entered show business with a vaudeville act and in 1928 proved a smashing success in the *Blackbirds* revue. The hit *Brown Buddies* followed, and then spectacular appearances at the Palace Theatre in New York. Robinson coined the word "copasetic" which seemed to mean everything was just fine and dandy or better than okay. He originated the staircase tap dance. And Fred Astaire called him the greatest dancer of all time. Robinson's first film appearance was in *Dixiana* (1930) with Bebe Daniels and the comedians Wheeler and Woolsey. When he tapped away, his act was greeted by rounds of applause in theaters throughout the country. But it was when he returned to Hollywood in the mid-1930s that his movie performances climaxed his spectacular career.

"Now, honey, all you gotta do is listen with your feet," he told Shirley Temple in their first feature, *The Little Colonel,* and as he glided up the stairs with her, a star tom was born. In this film, Robinson proved himself a well-behaved, mannerly Negro attendant. When the old Southern colonel, Lionel Barrymore, cursed and cussed and fussed at him, good old Bill stood by patiently. He knew de ole massa didn't mean no harm. His respect won him audience approval, and he was rewarded for his "gentlemanliness" with more film work. From *The Little Colonel,* he went to *Hooray for Love* (1935), in which he not only sang "Got a Snap to My Finger" but was formally crowned the Mayor of Harlem. Later there were appearances as a genial servant to Will Rogers in *In Old Kentucky* (1935), a dancing sequence in *The Big Broadcast of 1936,* and finally what remains the definitive Robinson tom performance in David Butler's *The Littlest Rebel.*

The Littlest Rebel was Shirley Temple's big Old South vehicle. As it began, she was the happiest of pint-sized Southern belles. An elaborate birthday party was being given for her, and Shirley was surrounded by her fair-haired mother, her tall, stalwart father, her tot friends, and the household slaves, of whom Uncle Billy was her favorite. Her chief delight was having Uncle Billy dance for her. When called upon, the good-natured servant always complied, and at this birthday party the highlight of the day's events was Uncle Billy's performance. But in the middle of the immense celebration, the ideal way of the Old South was interrupted by the war call. The party scattered. Yankees invaded the plantation. Shirley made up in bootblack, pretending to be a harmless pickaninny. When the ruse failed, she turned to Uncle Billy. Now he must protect her from the Yankees. And he did just that. When

ABOVE: Shirley Temple seeks aid from Bill "Bojangles" Robinson and the black community in *The Littlest Rebel* (1935).
RIGHT: The screen's first interracial couple: Temple and Robinson.

Shirley's mother took ill and died and her father was captured by Union troops and hauled off to a Northern prison camp, Uncle Billy became her guardian-companion. Here his dancing ability again proved useful. Determined to finance a trip North for Shirley to visit her father, but low on cash, he decided to tap up the deficit. Near a railroad station, he and Shirley performed energetically for all who passed by while another servant, portrayed by sleepy Willie Best, passed the cap to "help the cause." Thus the pair earned their fare to Washington. Together they visited President Lincoln and pleaded for the release of the girl's father. Lincoln pardoned him, and Uncle Billy and little Shirley lived happily ever after.

The actual performance by Bill Robinson in this feature as well as in the others was generally superficial and terribly unvaried. Indeed he often recited his lines as if reading from a blackboard. When he danced, however, audiences could not have cared less what he had to say. Robinson's greatest gift as a dancer in the movies was that his sense of rhythm, his physical dexterity, and his easy-going naturalness all combined to convey an optimistic—a copasetic—air. As he tapped across the room his sheer joy made audiences think that life after all was what you made of it. The real significance of a Bill Robinson performance was therefore never as much in what he had to say as in what he came to represent. His work in *The Littlest Rebel* was successful because he provided a reassuring framework for the film. Shirley Temple fans, forever anxious because of the plights and perils of their favorite heroine, could rest at ease as soon as Bojangles' name flashed in the credits. For it was obvious that if all the others in the movie lost their heads, Bill would be sure to keep his. He patiently listened to Shirley's chatter, understood her problems, sympathized with them, and ultimately made a decisive move to aid her—something no one else in the movie was capable of doing. "Uncle Billy can do anything. He can sing. He can dance. He can climb trees," said little Miss Curlytop. Audiences agreed. *The New York Times* wrote of Robinson: "As Uncle Billy, the faithful family butler, Bill Robinson is excellent and some of the best moments . . . are those in which he breaks into song and dances with Mistress Temple."

The Robinson figure was obviously the familiar contented slave, distinguished, however, because he was congenial, confident, and very, very *cool*. Unlike Stepin Fetchit, he was articulate too, and, more important, consistently reliable. His reliability and his detached urbane cool perhaps explain why there were seldom complaints about Bill Robinson's performances as there were against Fetchit's or even those of Willie Best.

Tom and coon at odds with one another: Bill Robinson and Willie Best in *The Littlest Rebel*.

Interestingly, Best made one of his typically somnambulistic appearances in *The Littlest Rebel*. Known for his outrageous coon portrayals, he served as a contrasting figure to point up the trustworthiness of Robinson. During the approach of Union soldiers fighting to free all the slaves, Best trembled. Robinson, still at ease, asked why he was so frightened, and Best replied that his mind told him not to worry but "my body don't pay no mind." In this scene, Best was the typical terrified darky, *scared of his own shadow*, whereas Bill Robinson came across even more than usual as the sensible and responsible Good Negro because of the contrast. Ironically, though, despite Robinson's earnest sobriety, it has to be admitted that of the two, Willie Best now certainly seems the funnier.

Bill Robinson's characters were all part of the humanized servant tradition. Humanization was nothing more than a softening or refinement of black characters. Perhaps it would be more appropriate to say that certain black actors by individualizing their servants through their own unique and winning personalities had proven that these black faces were not just escapist creations on the screen but realistic human ones, too. The humanized servants ushered in black dignity, and generally they escaped the self-demeaning antics that weighed other black servants down. Robinson was the most prominent of the male humanized figures.

Until the late 1930s, Bill Robinson's career was flourishing. Then the cracks in his screen popularity began to appear. Although he was to be loved by fans throughout his career, his courteous, humanized tom spirits gave way to more ribald, iconoclastic presences. After *The Littlest Rebel*, Robinson appeared in a serious role in *One Mile from Heaven* (1937), then as Aloysius in *Rebecca of Sunnybrook Farm* (1938—again with Shirley Temple), then later in 1938 in *Road Demon, Up the River,* and *Just Around the Corner*. In the last, as Corporal Jones, the doorman at Shirley Temple's hotel, he danced and sang "This Is a Happy Little Ditty." But the role was far from impressive and gone was much of his spontaneous effervescence. As his movie career ebbed, he wisely returned to the theater, making a successful comeback in 1939 in Mike Todd's *Hot Mikado*. After that success, he returned to Hollywood in 1943 to star in *Stormy Weather*. The movie had great entertainment segments, but, sadly, the cool *savoir-faire* of the old master Bojangles proved not half as interesting as the perfect beauty of the up-and-coming Lena Horne. Robinson died in 1949.

Clarence Muse: the Inhibited, Humanized Tom
Standing in a Corner by Himself

An actor whose presence also distinguished his characters but who was virtually ignored during the 1930s was Clarence Muse. He was a short, stocky man with a large resonant voice, more inhibited than any other black performer of the period. Perhaps unable to produce the high-style flamboyance his fellow players so exuberantly displayed, he was instead very skillful at presenting mild-mannered docile manservants.

Muse's educational and theatrical background may in part explain why he was often so inhibited and restrained an actor. Born in Baltimore in 1889, he was a graduate of the Dickinson School of Law in Pennsylvania. He had worked for many years in the South with black acting troupes, and in New York he first appeared with the Lincoln Players and later the Lafayette Players. His training was generally in a more serious vein than that of most black performers, and he was not accustomed to working only for laughs.

When he first arrived in Hollywood, he was handled with a bit of care. In *Hearts in Dixie* he portrayed the old man, Uncle Napus. Here his tom character served as a dignified contrast to the broad foolery of Stepin Fetchit. Ironically, in *A Royal Romance* (1930), Muse found himself going through some of the same foolery. As the razor-totin' right-hand coon friend of a white detective, he helped look for spooks in an old deserted house. His befuddled antics were used for routine comic relief.

By 1931, Muse was back in top tom form when he appeared in *Huckleberry Finn* as the archetypal tom, the kindly Nigger Jim who sets out on the raft with Huck. Although he did not figure prominently in the film, Muse's Jim was still the congenial confidant and amiable alter ego of the adolescent Huck. What was most intriguing was that Muse seemed miscast because his slave was too intelligent. His dialect was obviously faked and forced, and during excruciatingly harsh close-ups used solely for laughs, audiences must have felt pained to see such a dignified and decent presence demeaned so. No other black performer of the period ever had quite such an effect, perhaps because most were able to forget themselves and become lost in the part. Muse always seemed to be standing at a great distance looking on with his large questioning eyes and sadly shaking his head.

Frank Capra's *Broadway Bill* (1934) was one of Muse's most important features. Muse had previously worked for Capra in

Rain or Shine (1930) and *Dirigible* (1931), and the director, who affectionately called Muse his "pet actor," handled him sensitively. Cast opposite white actor Warner Baxter, Muse again played the amiable alter ego. The film is about a race horse, Broadway Bill, that Baxter and Muse hope to enter in the Kentucky Derby. Both are short on cash, and when Baxter discovers Muse's savings in the latter's boots, he persuades his black friend to pour them into their investment. Throughout the film the two men are true compatriots. They sleep under the same roof. They share whatever food they can get. Still Muse's role called for much tommery and even some racking instances of Jim Crowism. In one scene, the film's producers upheld their self-imposed color bar by having Muse eat his food standing while Baxter remained seated. It would have been unheard of to have a black and white sit at the same table. Yet again Muse managed to strike at consciences through the depth of his own personality. Even the manner in which he walked—with head lifted, body erect, eyes straight ahead—indicated a self-respect and black self-awareness that other actors of the period lacked.

By 1935, Muse had appeared in an array of films including *Last Parade* (1931), *Secret Witness* (1931), *Woman from Monte Carlo* (1932), *Cabin in the Cotton* (1932), *Winner Take All* (1933), *Washington Merry-Go-Round* (1933), *From Hell to Heaven* (1933), and *The Count of Monte Cristo* (1934). Midway in the decade, he devastatingly went against the grain of the toms he proved so good at portraying when he appeared as a resurrected old mythic type, the black brute, in King Vidor's *So Red the Rose*. The film was a perfect example of the Old South (or Old South-oriented) pictures that were popular in the 1930s and very early 1940s. Others were *Carolina, In Old Kentucky, Steamboat 'Round the Bend, The Littlest Rebel, Jezebel* (1938), *Virginia* (1941), *The Vanishing Virginian* (1941), and, of course, *Gone with the Wind.* Romanticized and quasi-historical, *So Red the Rose* starred Margaret Sullavan as a Southern belle who is left stranded in the Big House with her dying father. Almost all the men are off fighting in the Civil War. When a rebellion erupts among her faithful slaves, the impetuous, headstrong, and ever-so-valiant Sullavan marches to the slave quarters to quench the rebellious fires. But who should be playing Cato, the renegade, rebel-rousing leader of the incendiaries but Clarence Muse! Muse played his upstart with an insolent conviction and anger that was perhaps *too* good. During the shooting of the film, the actor evidently was carried away by the rough-tough character he portrayed. In a climactic sequence when his Cato was to be slapped by the film's heroine, the actor refused to do the

Clarence Muse, the dignified, humanized tom.

scene. Things were resolved by having actress Sullavan strike another black actor instead. Today it is obvious that Muse's performance lacked control, but it does reveal what can happen to a tom performer who is finally let loose.

Afterward Muse returned to tomming in *Show Boat* (1936), *Follow Your Heart* (1936), *Spirit of Youth* (1937), and *Way Down South* (1939). In this last film, Muse expanded his accomplishments. With Langston Hughes, he wrote eleven spirituals to be sung by the Hall Johnson Choir, as well as some original music for Bobby Breen. More important, Muse co-authored the screenplay of the picture with Langston Hughes. Essentially an Old South melodrama, *Way Down South* told the story of an orphaned white Southern lad (Bobby Breen) and his devotion to the slaves his deceased father had treated so humanely. When a Simon Legree-ish character mistreats the slaves, young Bobby undertakes to save them, particularly his favorite, dear old Uncle Caton. This role was played by none other than Muse, who realized in 1935 that perhaps the most effective way for a black actor to come up with a solid role was to write that role for himself. In 1940, he also wrote the script for *Broken Strings*, an independently produced film in which he starred as a concert violinist. Here the hint of dignity was brought to the forefront and made an integral part of the character. The role remains Muse's finest. In 1940, Muse played a coon minister in *Maryland*. This picture was a bad one not only for him but also for his black co-stars, Hattie McDaniel and Ben Carter. All three were abominable and fraudulently cute and homey. Thereafter, Clarence Muse was stuck with the tom character in films such as *Zanzibar* (1940), *Tales of Manhattan, Shadow of a Doubt* (1943), *Heaven Can Wait* (1943), *Watch on the Rhine* (1943), *Two Smart People* (1946), *Joe Palooka in the Knockout* (1947), and *An Act of Murder* (1948). In 1950, Muse returned to work under Frank Capra's direction in *Riding High* with Bing Crosby. The movie was a remake of *Broadway Bill,* and Muse re-created his role of the faithful servant. Nine years later he appeared in *Porgy and Bess,* and once again he had to soar from beneath the dialect and farm clothes of his character to prove that here was a most knowledgeable and eminent man. Afterward Muse went into semi-retirement, but he returned to films in 1972 in the role of Cudjo in *Buck and the Preacher.* Muse's roles—indeed his very performances—were neither great nor heroic, and taken out of their historical context they might seem far from impressive. They lacked the flashiness most black performances of the day were noted for. But they appeared at a time when being black and human in the movies was neither easy nor expected.

Imitation of Life: Mother Knows Best

The humanization of the Negro servant was carried to new and highly publicized heights with the appearance of the first important "black film" of the 1930s, *Imitation of Life.* It arrived in 1934, at a time when a new social consciousness had infiltrated the motion picture industry. Already Roosevelt's election, the New Deal, the growing liberalism of the country, and the Depression itself had brought to American films a new world view and a new social order whereby many of the old racial proprieties were starting to be discarded. *Imitation of Life* was an outgrowth of this new conscious liberal spirit. It prided itself on its portrait of the modern black woman, still a servant but now imbued with dignity and a character that were an integral part of the American way of life.

Based on Fannie Hurst's best-selling novel, Universal's *Imitation of Life* was directed by John Stahl and starred the black actresses Louise Beavers and Fredi Washington as well as Claudette Colbert, Rochelle Hudson, Ned Sparks, and Warren William. The film traced the lives of two widows, one white, the other black, who meet by chance and decide to throw their lots together. Both women are left with daughters to raise. The black widow, Aunt Delilah, will care for the house and Miss Bea's child, Jesse, while the white Miss Bea will work at a career and be the breadwinner. The early days are hard. The two suffer from the Depression realities of hunger and poverty. But fortune comes their way in the form of a pancake recipe. Passed down to Aunt Delilah for generations as a family secret, the pancake flour has such a wonderful flavor that Miss Bea decides to market it. In an act of magnanimity, she offers Aunt Delilah a twenty-per-cent interest in the concern.

"Now, Delilah, you're going to be rich. You'll be able to move away and buy yourself a nice house," Miss Bea tells her. "My own house?" the servant asks incredulously. "You gonna send me away? Don't do that to me. How I gonna take care of you and Miss Jesse if I's away? I's yo' cook. You kin have it. I makes you a present of it."

And so the two women remain lifelong friends and successful business partners. Aunt Delilah's mix, as marketed by Miss Bea, is a phenomenal success, reaping prosperity for both. But ultimately the prosperity is coupled with heartache, then despair, brought on by the widows' respective daughters. Miss Bea's Jesse becomes her rival in a love affair. At an early age, Aunt Delilah's light-skinned daughter, Peola, becomes annoyed whenever her efforts to mingle

ABOVE: Service with a smile! Louise Beavers as the jolly, good-hearted, submissive cook in *Imitation of Life* (1934).

RIGHT: Beavers as the stoic Aunt Delilah and Fredi Washington as her wayward daughter Peola "passing" for white in *Imitation of Life*.

with whites as a white are frustrated by the appearance of her very dark mother. Ultimately, she rejects her mother, leaves home, and attempts to cross the color line. Aunt Delilah's heart is broken.

The story is resolved with the death of the good Aunt Delilah, who is laid to rest with the one thing she wanted most: "the biggest funeral Harlem ever did see." As directed by Stahl, it was super-deluxe Hollywood at its most extravagant, complete with white horses, a white hearse, and a full-sized band. The highlight of this orgiastically tearful funeral was the returning repentant daughter, Peola.

Because of its racial theme and some inspired casting, *Imitation of Life* turned itself into the slickest and possibly the best made tear-jerker of all time. On the surface, the film was a simple tale of motherly love and motherly woes. In the relationship between Beavers and Colbert, audiences were assured that differences between white and black, like differences between the rich and poor, could easily be done away with if everybody worked together. Beneath the surface, though, *Imitation of Life* was a conscious apotheosis of the tom spirit and an unconsciously bitter comment on race relations in America.

Louise Beavers' Delilah was a combination of tom and aunt jemima magnified and glorified in full-blown Hollywood fashion. But she introduced to the 1930s audience the idea of black Christian stoicism. "Bow your head," she tells daughter Peola. "You got to learn to take it. Your pappy kept beating his fists against life all his days until it eat him through." In its historical perspective, this Christian stoicism—particularly because Beavers was able to make movie patrons believe that she herself believed it—"elevated" the Negro character in films by endowing him with Christian goodness far exceeding that of any other character. This same doctrine of Christian stoicism as first displayed by Beavers was later to inform the work of Ethel Waters, Sidney Poitier, Ruby Dee, and Ossie Davis. Indeed, Beavers' bow-your-head scene with Peola was later magnificently re-created by Ethel Waters in *Pinky*. Of course, the irony of this stoicism was that it made the Negro character more self-effacing than ever and even more resolutely resigned to accepting his fate of inferiority.

Imitation of Life's great contradiction, its single subversive element, was the character Peola. For the most part, her story was submerged. Originally, Peola had been conceived as a tragic mulatto type, the beautiful girl doomed because she has a "drop of Negra blood." But as played by Fredi Washington, Peola became a character in search of a movie. With eyes light and liquid and almost haunted, Miss Washington made Peola a password for non-passive resistance. "Mama," she cried, "I want the same things in life other people enjoy." The line was the film's great one, its simplest, its most heartfelt. To obtain the equality she wants, Peola has to rebel against the system. Peola was the New Negro demanding a real New Deal. But as *The New York Times* pointed out in its review of the film: "The photoplay was content to suggest that the sensitive daughter of the Negro woman is bound to be unhappy if she happens to be able to pass for white." The explanation for Peola's rebellion is simply that she wants to be white, not that she wants white opportunities. Her weeping by her mother's casket was Hollywood's slick way of finally humiliating her, its way of finally making the character who had run away with herself conform to the remorseful mulatto type.

Regardless of its shortcomings, *Imitation of Life* was a solid box-office success. So responsive were audiences to its story that the film was revived in the 1940s and then remade in the 1950s. Louise Beavers and Fredi Washington became respected black actresses, although neither was to receive the recognition due her.

Iridescent Fredi: Black Girl in Search of a Black Role

For black Americans, Fredi Washington was for a time the great black hope. They saw in her a sophisticated and talented black actress with the range and the beauty to win leading roles. But in the end, she fell a victim to the times and her own peculiar looks.

Born in Savannah, Georgia, in 1903, Fredi Washington began her career as an entertainer in nightclubs and cafés. In Harlem society in the 1920s and 1930s, she and her sister, Isabelle, were legendary beauties, hotly pursued and discussed. After a brief career on the stage, Isabelle married Adam Clayton Powell. For Fredi, there was moderate success in a touring company of *Shuffle Along* and later on the stage in *Singin' the Blues* and *Porgy*. It was always a problem casting her, for, like Peola, Fredi Washington was a black girl who looked white. Her features were sharply defined, her hair long, dark, and straight, and her eyes a vibrant green. Press releases described her as looking French or Italian. Columnists were quick to relate the problems she had because of her white looks.

When she was cast opposite Paul Robeson in the play *Black Boy*, Fredi Washington portrayed a black girl passing for white. Therein her type was discovered. But in the film capital, it took some time before directors could decide on how best to use her. In *The Emperor Jones* (1933), opposite Paul Robeson, she played a light-skinned Harlem slut, but she proved too sophisticated and

The melancholy and iridescent Fredi Washington.

intelligent in the role. It also looked as if she had been heavily darkened with make-up to look more Negroid. In the relaxed musical shorts she did with Duke Ellington and Cab Calloway in the 1930s, she seemed more at home. But it was as Peola in *Imitation of Life* that she emerged as the archetypal tragic mulatto for the Depression era. Her other films were *Drums of the Jungle* (1935) and *One Mile from Heaven*. In the former, she portrayed a villainous half-breed island girl. In *One Mile from Heaven*, she appeared opposite Bill Robinson as the radiant beauty who discovers a white foundling and wants to raise the child as her own.

Fredi Washington's characters were never happy ones, but for a while it looked as if her provocative and promising performances would make her a star. The newspaper *Afro-American* even asked in a feature article: ". . . who would her leading man be if Hollywood really let her go romantic?" Of course, there was to be no black leading lady. The movies were not ready for idealized tragic black heroines. Audiences preferred mammies and jemimas who could be laughed at or enjoyed or pitied but who would not strike at their consciences. Fredi Washington discovered that the spectacular looks that had opened the door for an important film role ultimately closed that door in her face.

In 1939 Fredi Washington returned to her stage career, making an impressive appearance in *Mamba's Daughters* as Ethel Waters' rebellious child. In the late 1940s, rumors spread that she would play the postwar mulatto heroine, Pinky, a perfect role for her. But by then she was too old for the part, and her name meant nothing at the box office.

Louise Beavers: the Black Guardian Angel

Louise Beavers, however, prevailed. Because of her humanized domesticity, she was for a time the most important black actress working in films. Even before she appeared in *Imitation of Life,* she had played an assortment of maid roles in Hollywood pictures, and she had been carefully groomed by herself and the studios to fit into the mammy–aunt jemima category. Before her there had been no distinctive mammy figure. And the studios realized Beavers was a perfect foil and background flavor for such Depression heroines as Jean Harlow, Mae West, and Claudette Colbert— women forced by the times to be on their own, yet needing someone in their corner to cheer them up when things looked too rough, to advise them when personal problems overwhelmed them.

Louise Beavers was a big-boned, robust woman with skin that

was described as smooth as chocolate velvet, and eyes bright, large, and wondrously naïve. In the late 1920s, when she was spotted by a studio agent in an amateur show, she was considered for a mammy role in Universal's *Uncle Tom's Cabin* because of her size and color. She was eventually assigned the role of a cook, however, because of her youthful appearance. She was heavy and hearty but not heavy and hearty enough. Thereafter she went on force-feed diets, compelling herself to eat beyond her normal appetite. Generally, she weighed close to two hundred pounds, but it was a steady battle for her to stay overweight. During filming, due to pressures, she often lost weight and then had to be padded to look more like a full-bosomed domestic who was capable of carrying the world on her shoulders. Another problem was her accent. Born in Cincinnati, she came to Los Angeles in 1913 and studied at Pasadena High. Consequently, her voice had no trace of a dialect or Southern patois. When the talkies came in, she schooled herself in the slow-and-easy backwoods accent compulsory for every black servant.

Another problem for Louise Beavers, certainly the least important but surely the most ironic, was that although she invariably was cast as a cook, she detested kitchen work and abhorred pancakes. During filming, professional white cooks had to prepare the food. Then Beavers was situated at the stove, smile intact and pancake flipper in her hand; thus the image of the jolly black cook was completely manufactured and presented for mass consumption. Once the contours of her screen personality were physically established, Beavers supplied the good-natured affability to round out the characters. She was always happy, always kind, always intricately involved in the private lives of her employers, so much so that she usually completely lacked a private life of her own.

Her early screen performances were in the 1931 films *Annabelle's Affairs*, *Girls Around Town*, and *Sundown Trail*. In 1932 she made some ten films, including George Cukor's *What Price Hollywood* and *Divorce in the Family*. The following year she came into her own as the cheerful, hopelessly naïve servant Pearl in Mae West's *She Done Him Wrong* and again as a similar cheerful, naïve servant Loretta in Jean Harlow's *Bombshell*. By 1933, during which year she appeared in seven other films, Louise Beavers was a standard fixture on the movie screen. Then came *Imitation of Life*.

Stories still circulate of the humiliation Louise Beavers endured once she had successfully tested for the role. During the filming a young white girl, Dorothy Howard, portrayed Peola at the age of ten. As the cast gathered to rehearse, Dorothy learned that Miss

Beavers was to portray her mother, whereupon the child screamed that she did not want her. "She's black!" Later when Beavers requested that the word "nigger" be removed from the script, she won her case with the help of the NAACP. But when she was called afterward into the front office and made to pronounce "Negro" repeatedly as a means of punishment, she may have wondered if she had really won after all. Nevertheless, *Imitation of Life* was her great triumph. She was consistently singled out by the critics, and when the Academy failed to nominate her for an Oscar, columnist Jimmy Fiddler complained:

> I also lament the fact that the motion picture industry has not set aside racial prejudice in naming actresses. I don't see how it is possible to overlook the magnificent portrayal of the Negro actress, Louise Beavers, who played the mother in *Imitation of Life*. If the industry chooses to ignore Miss Beavers' performance, please let this reporter, born and bred in the South, tender a special award of praise to Louise Beavers for the finest performance of 1934.

Not long after her triumph, Louise Beavers appeared in another submissive and sympathetic role. Previously, she had made a mark by taking the black woman off the plantation. In *Rainbow on the River* she found herself right back there. In this Reconstruction days tale, she was cast as a former slave, Toinette, who raises and comes to love dearly a white child orphaned after the Civil War. When it is discovered that the boy has Yankee kinfolk, Toinette's heart is broken. But her Christian stoicism will not allow her to hold on to the child selfishly. As before, the performance went beyond the tom-mammy-jemima type because Louise Beavers played it with simplicity and sincerity. The most shameless thing, however (and something for which she might never be forgiven), was her intimation that during the Civil War she never wanted freedom anyway. Her masters had been so kind to her. To her credit or her chagrin, Louise Beavers played the scene beautifully and, worst of all, convincingly.

During the latter part of the decade, she made more than her share of mediocre films, and often she was required to do nothing more than giggle happily or smile knowingly. *Make Way for Tomorrow* (1937), *Wings over Honolulu* (1937), *Love in a Bungalow* (1937), *The Last Gangster* (1937), *Scandal Street* (1938), *Life Goes On* (1938), *Peck's Bad Boy with the Circus* (1938), and *The Lady's from Kentucky* (1938) were some of the movies she made toward the end of the decade.

One of Louise Beavers' better roles was in David O. Selznick's *Made for Each Other* (1939). Selznick believed in American hearth and home, and to him this meant nothing less than two cars in the

The screen's favorite domestic or its biggest phony? Check Louise Beavers' sly smile and take one look at those beautifully polished nails. Those hands never touched a dish in their life.

garage, a chicken in the oven, and a black cook in the kitchen. His *Gone with the Wind* and later his *Since You Went Away* featured Beavers' rival, Hattie McDaniel. His *Duel in the Sun* (1947) had Butterfly McQueen. But for *Made for Each Other* he selected Louise Beavers to portray dewy-eyed, devoted Lily, the servant to the Depression victims Carole Lombard and James Stewart. When Lily realizes Lombard does not have enough money to maintain her services, she saves her white mistress the embarrassment of having to let her go by saying, "Ah, never you mind, honey. I's a luxury." Before she leaves, she not only elevates Lombard's down-and-out spirits but offers the white woman some classic words of advice. "Lily's a whole lot older than you, honey, and she's learned one thing. Never let the seeds stop you from enjoying the water-melon. . . . Spit out those seeds before they stop you from enjoying the melon." Here, with even the tritest of lines, Louise Beavers remained the essence of Christian unselfishness. When seen today, her eyes do not convey any kind of grand sought-after truth. But they do evoke heartfelt kindness to the point where Louise Beavers is, as press releases liked to say, "a black angel."

In the 1940s, Beavers added her touch to *Shadow of the Thin Man* (1941), *Reap the Wild Wind* (1942), *DuBarry Was a Lady* (1943), and *Jack London* (1943). When it looked as if her career was just about finished, she appeared in *Mr. Blandings Builds His Dream House* (1948). Here she portrayed the family maid who supplies her employer, Cary Grant, with a winning slogan for baked ham. "Not ham! WHAM! If you ain't eating WHAM, you ain't eatin' ham!" she exclaims with a laugh. "Darling, give Gussie a ten-dollar raise," responds Grant. Thus the young advertising executive about to lose his job because he couldn't come up with the right slogan for a ham account has been saved from ruin! For Louise Beavers it was a small but important role. Again she was the black nourishing the white family.

When the "enlightened" post–World War II spirit virtually obliterated the servant figures, Louise Beavers made a slight image change to play Jackie Robinson's mother in *The Jackie Robinson Story* (1950). Moon-faced, still mellow, and marvelously meek, she was a touching presence. Her last important appearance was as the maid Beulah on the television series. Hattie McDaniel originated the part on radio. After her death, Ethel Waters took over. Then Beavers. It remains one of the great perversities of the motion-picture industry that the three greatest mammies of the movies should ultimately portray the same jolly, docile cook. Afterward Beavers appeared as the maid in Mae West's nightclub act in Las Vegas. Before her death in the early 1960s, she made her final film appearances in *Teen-Age Rebel* (1956), *Tammy and the Bachelor* (1957), *The Goddess* (1958), *All the Fine Young Cannibals* (1960), and *The Facts of Life* (1961).

The Green Pastures

"Gangway! Gangway! For de Lawd God Jehovah!" cried the black archangel Gabriel, and the screen was bombarded with the liveliest collection of agreeable toms, uncle remuses, aunt jemimas, and corn-patch pickaninnies ever assembled in one motion picture. It was *The Green Pastures*, the second of the important black films of the decade. In 1936, the year of its release, it brought the humanized servant tradition to an early apex.

The Green Pastures was an adaptation of Marc Connelly's enormously successful Broadway play. Directed by Connelly and William Keighley and released by Warner Brothers, it was the first major studio all-black spectacle since 1929. Because of the financial disappointment of the early all-black features, the major studios had steered clear of them. But a number of factors indicated the time might be ripe for another try. The box-office success of *Imitation of Life* had proved that blacks in important character roles could woo and affect audiences. At the same time the increase in ghetto theaters and the success of a number of independently produced all-Negro features had revealed that there was a growing Negro audience eager for any product even remotely touching on their own experiences. Finally, the long run of *The Green Pastures* on Broadway indicated that this was a property with meaning to many audiences. Warner Brothers decided to take a chance on it. That chance resulted in one of their biggest hits and one of the most successful Negro movies of all time.

The Green Pastures was a very *likable* motion picture. Its simple theology, its naïve philosophizing, and its "acceptable" portrait of black America as quaint and charming made it a gratifying experience. The story it told was simple. At a Sunday school class in Louisiana, a kindly Negro teacher, the good Mr. Deshee, visualizes the wonders of the Good Book so that his young pupils might better understand their meaning. Thus the biblical characters of old are transformed into contemporary Louisiana Negroes—in attire, in vernacular, and in customs. Adam and Eve are presented as a muscular bronze man and his vain coquettish mate. Cain the Sixth is a rough-and-ready no-account, and his high-yaller gal, Zeba, a high-strung strumpet. Moses becomes a clever conjurer. And Noah is a gregarious tom, complete with top hat and raincoat.

In heaven the angels, seraphim, and cherubim are also contemporary Negroes, strutting about with straw hats or uttering quaint Negro colloquialisms. "Being de Lawd ain't no bed of roses," moans the heavenly host. "Now you heared me. You want me to fly up there and slap you down?" belts out a mammy angel to her little no-account cherub son who rides a friendly cloud. In this heaven, de Lawd proudly passes out his most prized possessions: ten-cent seegars for everybody! Thus the heaven of *The Green Pastures* ultimately becomes a perpetual Negro holiday, one everlasting weekend fish fry. Harmony and good spirits reign supreme as the Hall Johnson Choir's resonant rendition of spirituals reminds everyone that there is no heaven like a black one.

A lively amalgam of sugar and subservience, *The Green Pastures* opened at Radio City Music Hall to unanimous praise from the white press and much of the black. *The New York World Telegram* called it "a beautiful film—the screen version of the tender, gently pathetic, curiously touching Negro miracle play." *The New York Times* commented:

> That disturbance in and around the Music Hall yesterday was the noise of shuffling queues in Sixth Avenue and the sound of motion picture critics dancing in the street. The occasion was the coming at last to the screen of Marc Connelly's naïve, ludicrous, sublime and heartbreaking masterpiece of American folk drama. . . . It still has the rough beauty of homespun, the irresistible compulsion of simple faith.

In the *Afro-American,* however, one perceptive black reviewer wrote that the movie's characterization of the religion of the Negro was *only* caricature and that there was nothing in it except childlike faith. "Let *The Green Pastures* go for what it is: an interesting and entertaining spectacle with a cast of underpaid colored actors portraying Connelly's conception of . . . unlearned earlier-day beliefs of heaven and the Bible. Any other viewpoint is outrageous."

Contemporary audiences tend to share the dissenter's viewpoint. It is now evident that *The Green Pastures* rested on a cruel assumption: that nothing could be more ludicrous than transporting the lowly language and folkways of the early-twentieth-century Negro back to the high stately world before the Flood. The movie played hard at exploiting the incongruity of angels with dirty faces. And in this juxtaposition of low with high, there were implied Negro ignorance and inferiority. All this went under the guise of a "Negro miracle play." Nothing could have been more absurd. For Negroes of the period never pictured historical or biblical events in terms of their own experience. Indeed, the problem was that they always dreamt of a white heaven and a white heavenly host.

But in 1936 few movie patrons linked sociology with films. Consequently, audiences found *The Green Pastures* a great cinematic treat. What transcended the shortcomings of the script, too, was the brilliance of the performances. Few film casts have ever equaled the sheer dynamics and unabashed delight that these actors showed. Among this crew of celestial lights, there was not one disagreeable or even remotely unpleasant type of performer. All put on a magnificent show of talent and spontaneous humor. Edna Mae Harris attacked the role of Zeba with great sly, vixenish relish, the kind audiences saw only when an actress was giving her once-in-a-lifetime performance—and knew it. The same was true of Frank Wilson's fine, ironic Moses. Oscar Polk portrayed the long, lean Gabriel with a surprisingly appropriate nonchalance and understatement. In this film, as in most of his others, Polk seems emasculated, but here it adds to the diversity of this black heaven. Eddie Anderson was a charming Noah. Also included in the cast were Clinton Rosemond, George Reed, Myrtle Anderson, and Ernest Whitman. Reed portrayed the kindly Reverend Deshee. Whitman appeared as a cantankerous loud-mouthing pharoah. He was a coon in ancient Egypt. Both Reed and Whitman were skilled performers and worked in a number of Hollywood films afterward. Whitman's later pictures included *White Hunter* (1936), *Daughter of Shanghai* (1937), *Congo Maisie* (1940), *Maryland* (1940), *Return of Frank James* (1940), *Drums of the Congo* (1942), *Cabin in the Sky*, and *Stormy Weather*. Whitman and Reed, however, were more fortunate than many of the other actors in *The Green Pastures*. After the movie was completed, a number of the performers returned to jobs as porters, cooks, and maids. Their holiday in Hollywood had come to an abrupt end.

Rex Ingram: First of the Freed Black Men

Of all the actors in *The Green Pastures*, Rex Ingram won the greatest recognition. As De Lawd, Ingram soared above all the sequences, all the characters, all the pageantry. He was a physically impressive actor. Tall, solid, yet athletically trim, with piercing eyes, skin that gleamed, and silver hair that gave him an ageless quality, he was the quintessence of Hollywood handsome. He was also an intelligent performer, the first black man to earn a Phi Beta Kappa key at Northwestern University and a graduate of that university's medical school in 1919. His early work included bit parts in silent movies and appearances on the stage in *Stevedore*, *Porgy*, and *Once in a Lifetime*. Among his first talking films were *Trader Horn* (1931), *Sign of the Cross* (1932), *King Kong*

(1933), and *The Emperor Jones* (1933). *The Green Pastures* was a big opportunity, and with his stentorian voice that could in one moment be raised triumphantly in anger and in the next lowered in sympathy or remorse, Ingram made the most of that opportunity and proved a most befitting Lawd. His heavenly host was, as the script dictated, a backwoods preacher, but one ironically detached enough from himself so that he could play the role with moderation. He also portrayed Adam and Hedzrel.

Other important roles followed for Rex Ingram in *The Adventures of Huckleberry Finn* (1939), *The Thief of Bagdad* (1940), *Talk of the Town* (1942), *Cabin in the Sky* (1943), *Sahara* (1943), *Fired Wife* (1943), *A Thousand and One Nights* (1948), and *Moonrise* (1948). In all his movies, Ingram escaped the rigid typing most black actors had to endure. True, he was cast as a servant, but in none of his films was he required to tom or coon. In *The Green Pastures* he was an Uncle Remus of sorts, full of comic homespun wisdom. But generally, like Paul Robeson, Rex Ingram played men who seemed essentially free, slightly heroic, and removed from typical American life. In *The Adventures of Huckleberry Finn*, Ingram's character withdrew from conventional society by taking to the raft with the adolescent Huck. Rex Ingram's Nigger Jim was never servile like that of Clarence Muse in the earlier version or Archie Moore in the 1960 one. Instead, his Jim was a heroic guide leading Huck to manhood. And with his large chest and thick biceps Ingram seemed so powerful that audiences knew there were no chains strong enough to hold him down. *The Thief of Bagdad* and its remake, *A Thousand and One Nights,* cast him in the fantasy world of the Arabian Nights. As a towering genie finally released by Sabu from a bottle in which he had been trapped for centuries, Ingram screamed, "Free! I'm free at last!" And his call of freedom rang out far beyond the motion-picture screen.

Rex Ingram was frequently compared to Paul Robeson. Both men presented immensely dignified and self-contained black male characters. Yet there were differences. Although Ingram was not as good an actor as Robeson, nor as heroic a presence, he was able to express the one thing Robeson lacked: a gentleness, an overriding interest and sympathy in all of mankind. No matter how much producers tried to make Robeson a symbol of black humanity, he always came across as a man more interested in himself than anyone else. (It was precisely for this reason that he fared so well as the crafty, determined-to-survive-and-triumph egomaniac Emperor Jones.) Ingram's gentleness, coupled with his physical strength, made him more than appropriate as De Lawd and much later in his career as the Sudanese soldier who sacrificed his life for the troops in *Sahara*. These same qualities added depth to his performance in *Moonrise*, too, when he portrayed a kindly old Negro outcast who befriended a rebellious white boy. And, of course, the strength, the dignity, the gentleness, and the good spirits of his characters were what made them stand at the heart of the humanized tradition.

After 1948, Rex Ingram's career rapidly ran downhill. When he pleaded guilty to having transported a fifteen-year-old white Kansas girl to New York for immoral purposes, an abrupt end came to the grand performances. He still worked in movies—although not as consistently—but the spark was gone from his work. Eventually it appeared as if he had stopped acting altogether and that he was merely relying on the force of his voice and his physical presence to get him through his roles, so much so that by the time he did *Anna Lucasta* in 1958, he seemed nothing more than the perfect wreck the script called for. Before his death in 1968, Ingram appeared in *God's Little Acre* (1958), *Elmer Gantry* (1960), *Your Cheating Heart* (1964), and (in the bit role of the professor) *Hurry Sundown* (1967).

Stepin's Step-Chillun

In contrast to Rex Ingram's vigorous and humanized free black male characters were the highjinks of a lively set of coon figures who picked up Fetchit's mantle and by borrowing, stealing, or elaborating on his techniques were able to find employment at a time when he was on his way out. Although they had none of the master's ambivalent nihilism, they attained great popularity. The most prominent of Stepin's step-chillun were Willie Best, Mantan Moreland, and Louis Armstrong.

The first of the imitators and certainly the closest in style, technique, and physical appearance to the master was Willie Best. Best was born in Mississippi and came to Hollywood in the late 1920s. In films such as *Up Pops the Devil* (1931), *The Monster Walks* (1931), *Kentucky Kernals* (1934), *West of the Pecos* (1934), and *Murder on a Honeymoon* (1935), he was known as Sleep 'n' Eat, a name that, like Fetchit's, conjured up a darky image: the coon is content as long as he has enough to eat and a place to sleep. Also like Fetchit, Best was tall and thin, and he specialized in dense, dim-witted characters who walked about half awake, half asleep. He was usually treated shamelessly or acted shamelessly of his own accord. "Why is a shoe called a shoe?" he asks in *The Littlest Rebel*. "I spent all yesterday wondering why a horse is called a horse." In a typical Best film such as *The Ghost Breakers* (1940), he was the butt of crude racial jokes. During an electrical black-out in this film, Best trembles in fear of ghosts, but is soon reprimanded by his employer, Bob Hope, who tells the film's heroine, Paulette Goddard, "He always sees the darkest side of everything. He was born during an eclipse." Later Hope says to Best, "You look like a black-out in a black-out. If this keeps up, I'm going to have to paint you white."

Best's characters seemed even more self-demeaning than Fetchit's, for he lacked the latter's great style. Yet he endowed his characters with more warmth and humanity. They were not aesthetically perfect automatons, and although they were without complexities or ambiguities, they seemed more intensely alive. Best had the familiar dialect, but audiences could understand him. Moreover, he made his characters fit in to the whole conception of the film rather than rendering them as isolated happenings. Finally, Best was easier for the studios to manipulate. Consequently, when Fetchit's various scrapes with the law alienated him from audiences and when he had begun repeating himself in a deadly mechanized manner, Best inherited his coon crown and was steadily employed. In the 1930s alone, he worked in some twenty-five motion pictures, including *Two in Revolt* (1936)—in which he was billed as Willie Best for the first time—*Murder on a Bridle Path* (1936), *General Spanky* (1936), *Breezing Home* (1937), *Racing Lady* (1937), *Super Sleuth* (1937), *Merrily We Live* (1938), *Vivacious Lady* (1938), and *Nancy Drew, Trouble Shooter* (1939). In the 1940s he appeared in thirty-five movies, including *I Take This Woman* (1940), *The Smiling Ghost* (1941), *Whispering Ghosts* (1942), *A–Haunting We Will Go* (1942), *The Hidden Hands* (1943), *Cabin in the Sky* (1943), *Thank Your Lucky Stars* (1943), *Pillow to Post* (1945), and *Red Stallion* (1947).

Mantan Moreland was the second of the prominent Fetchit step-chillun. A round-faced, wide-eyed, cherubic coon, he did not come into his own until the late 1930s. But he endured throughout the beginning years of the 1940s, and as late as the early 1970s he was still making cameo appearances in films. In the 1930s Moreland was one of the few pure coons to attain popularity at a time when the humanized toms had taken over.

Mantan Moreland was born in Monroe, Louisiana, in 1902. By the time he was twelve he had run away from home and begun an informal career as a dancer. Later he met and toured in a comedy act with Tim Moore, a former prize fighter who later won fame as Kingfish on the television series "Amos 'n' Andy." After

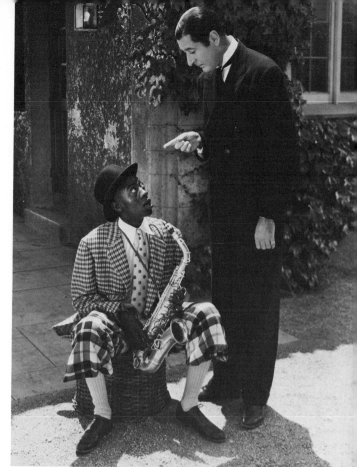

RIGHT: Ready for action but not for work, Willie Best gets a dressing down by Arthur Treacher in *Thank You, Jeeves* (1936).
BELOW: Mantan Moreland: the man with the fastest eyes in the West!

playing the black café-nightclub circuit for a number of years, Mantan Moreland finally caught the moviegoing public's fancy in 1938 with appearances in *Next Time I Marry, Frontier Scout,* and *Irish Luck.* Always cast as the faithful right-hand man, he added a perverse twist to the tradition. Generally, Mantan was always there *until* his white friend needed him. Then he took off for the hills. He was a fantastic cowardly lion with an uncanny command of stagecraft. In those films in which he was terr'fied of de ghosts, Moreland displayed an arsenal of gestures and grimaces that actors had traditionally used to steal scenes and develop characters. He was forever tripping over his own feet as he tried to make a hasty departure. He was notorious for his perfectly timed double-takes. No other actor could widen his eyes like Moreland. Nor could any other manage his trick of running without actually moving at all. When he appeared in the Charlie Chan mysteries as the dubiously reliable chauffeur, Birmingham Brown, Moreland captivated audiences with his rapid, high-pitched, squeaky-voiced banter. Previously, Fetchit had appeared as Chan's servant in *Charlie Chan in Egypt* (1935) and even Willie Best had a stint in the Chan thriller *The Red Dragon* (1942). But neither lit up the screen with their terror as did Moreland. To such Chan features as *The Chinese Cat* (1944), *The Scarlet Clue* (1945), *The Jade Mask* (1945), *Shadow over Chinatown* (1946), *The Chinese Ring* (1947), and a host of others, Moreland brought demented energy to his chauffeur, and it was Moreland himself who thought up his own great exit lines: "Feets! Do your stuff."

In the 1940s, Moreland was admittedly already an anachronism. Still, he was kept busy with the Chan series and such features as *Cabin in the Sky, Sarong Girl* (1943), *Revenge of the Zombies* (1943), *Melody Parade* (1943), *South of Dixie* (1944). Doubtless a reason for his durability was his great charm and his small stature. Because he was invariably shorter than the leading men of his films, audiences could accept his cowardice, his befuddled fumblings and mishaps. Sometimes his size elevated him from mere coon to a symbol of the universal little man. An independently produced all-black film, *One Dark Night* (1939), made excellent use of Moreland as a perpetually jobless black father. When one of his far-out schemes finally works out, the comic-pathetic little man assumes his role as the big man of the house and heroically saves his daughter from the clutches of a villain. Here Mantan Moreland broke away from his formula roles to create a sensitive character. The actor considered this role his best. Much later in his career, Moreland ventured out into new types of drama. In 1957 he appeared off-Broadway in an all-black version of *Waiting for*

Godot. As the tragic-comic Estragon, he received favorable reviews. Finally, when he returned to films in minor roles in *The Comic* (1969) and *Watermelon Man* (1970), Moreland finally escaped the humiliating antics that made him such a popular servant in the 1930s and 1940s, and at long last his characters were funny because of their human idiosyncrasies rather than their stereotyped racial shortcomings.

Louis Armstrong was the third of the important Fetchit imitators. His career on screen spanned four decades and two syndromes. Not only was he a reliable-servant figure in the 1930s, but in the 1940s and 1950s he was also the perfect entertainer. Armstrong first worked in films with his band in *Ex-Flame* (1931). He made his acting debut in Bing Crosby's *Pennies from Heaven* (1936), portraying the leader of a band appearing at Crosby's Haunted House Café. He sang a number that derived from the old racial stereotype of Negro fear and superstition titled "Skeleton in My Closet." Armstrong mugged and grinned his way through the song in the antics for which he later became famous. He was the perfect foil for Crosby. In *Artists and Models* (1937) Armstrong performed similar antics with Jack Benny and Martha Raye. In 1938 Armstrong teamed again with Bing Crosby in *Doctor Rhythm.* In a movie called *Going Places* (1939) his high-flung mugging madness just about stole the show. The *New York Times* film critic wrote of "a trumpet-tooting groom known to the jitterbugs as Louis (Satchel-Mouth) Armstrong. Satchel-Mo' caught the Strand's [theater] audience going and coming. . . . Satchel-Mo' blows a mean horn; better still he's a solid man for comedy."

When Armstrong made later appearances in such films as *Cabin in the Sky, Jam Session* (1944), *Atlantic City* (1945), *Pillow to Post* (1945), *Young Man with a Horn* (1950), *Glory Alley* (1952), *High Society* (1956), and *Paris Blues* (1961), his work was neatly covered with a new veneer. Armstrong learned early that a layer of gregarious charm could make even cooning appeal to everyone, and, although in films he often sold himself down the river, everyone loved seeing him sail away with his high-styled exhibitionism. When he attempted more serious roles after World War II, his charm proved vaporous. Without his music, it was obvious that here was a coon and a tom all rolled into one. In the end, the only thing that distinguished his film work was his music. When Satchmo played his horn—as when Bojangles danced—no one cared what he represented in the movie. He was a musician par excellence. His last film appearance was in *Hello, Dolly* (1968).

Louis Armstrong gives Bing Crosby a lesson in "natchel rhythm" in one of their early movies together.

All in all, the step-chillun were throwbacks to the earlier part of the 1930s. They represented a delayed crystallization of the prehumanized servant just as the congenial, uncomplicated creatures of *The Green Pastures* represented the ultimate distillation of the humanized servant tradition. The next and final stage in the evolution of the Negro servant in films was the posthumanized period. In the earlier period the acceptable, humanized black domestic was often forced to have a superhuman humaneness, a superhuman tolerance merely to point up his fitness for racial justice and to win audience sympathy. Thus Bill Robinson stood by stoically while the master bawled him out. Thus Louise Beavers sacrificed her own life and chances for fulfillment in order to serve better her white mistress. Here the Good Negro Servant's goodness was used to assert his equality. He *proved* his worth. But in the posthumanized servant tradition, no character ever gave a second thought to proving anything to anybody. This new set of eccentrics, led by Eddie "Rochester" Anderson, Hattie McDaniel, and Butterfly McQueen, lived in their own screwball worlds, did exactly as they pleased, and took little time to weigh the pros and cons of racial protocol. Seldom were they called upon to perform demeaning antics, and on those rare occasions when they were, they triumphed over the antics. Ultimately, this group brought an end to the servant syndrome as we think of it today.

Rochester: the Gentleman's Gentleman

There are two stories about how Eddie "Rochester" Anderson began his career. The first is that he sold newspapers as a child in Oakland, California, and while competing with other leather-lunged newspaper carriers, each outshouting the news of the other, the boy strained his vocal cords, eventually "ruining" his voice but in turn acquiring the inimitable gravelly quality.

The second story says that in 1937 comedian Jack Benny, on a trip West with his radio troupe, spotted a lively colored porter in a railroad car. The porter, Benny thought, was a natural-born philosopher-comedian, and soon afterward his radio-show writers decided to put such a character on the show. A search for candidates was begun. When a stocky, balloon-faced comic with a cement mixer of a voice appeared, they decided he was perfect for the role and thereafter christened him Rochester.

Both stories could be the fabrications of a press agent. But it is certain that Eddie Anderson's most distinct attribute was his gravelly voice and that he had his greatest success once he teamed with Jack Benny. In the late 1930s and into the 1940s, Anderson's alac-

The gentleman's gentleman: Eddie "Rochester" Anderson.

rity and coherent tomfoolery as the agreeable valet Rochester made him the most popular black comedian in the movies.

Eddie Anderson started working in films in the early 1930s, but it was a long time before he clicked. He had comic and chaotic moments in *What Price Hollywood* and *Rainbow on the River* but nothing earthshaking. As Noah in *The Green Pastures,* he had a rare opportunity to play a character both comic and pathetic, a role he handled well. In 1937 he appeared in *Three Men on a Horse, Melody for Two, Bill Cracks Down, On Such a Night, White Bondage,* and *One Mile from Heaven.* In some of the pre-Benny features he was surprisingly subdued. In William Wyler's Old South epic *Jezebel* (1938) he played Bette Davis's loyal servant, stoically leading her through a disease-infested swamp so that she could be reunited with Henry Fonda. Although he performed well, the role consisted of little more than "yessims." In W. C. Fields's *You Can't Cheat an Honest Man* (1939), Anderson was more at home as a clever but minor circus roustabout named Cheerful. The role now proves arch Anderson. When he warns Fields that detectives are about to close in after one of bumble-nose's master plots has backfired, Anderson is ignored. Consequently, when the police do close in and arrest Fields, Anderson, shaking his head as the bossman is taken off, has the last laugh. The privilege of enjoying a joke at the boss's expense soon became an Anderson trademark. *Man About Town* (1939) established this trait beyond a doubt.

Man About Town was vintage late-1930s Paramount fluff. Directed by Mark Sandrich, it starred Jack Benny, Dorothy Lamour, and Phil Harris and featured Anderson as Rochester, the character he had by then already popularized on the radio. The plot was straightforward but contained enough mishaps to keep audiences confused and happy. Benny woos two wealthy socialites, unaware that their hot-tempered husbands are out to do away with him. Throughout the film, Rochester warns him of the consequences of "foolin' round." Benny pays no heed. But at the film's conclusion, it is Rochester who untangles all the entanglements and saves the boss's neck. In this film, he brought new dimensions to the servant figure. Fetchit had taken him indoors. Robinson had domesticated him. Now Rochester gave him full run of the house. When he first appears, he is found in typical coon position. He sleeps comfortably in the boss's chair, unaware that Benny has entered the apartment. Soon he is on his feet, the clever, manipulative servant who under the guise of working for the boss accomplishes much for himself. Later one merely has to see him with his feet propped casually on top of the table as he uses the boss's telephone, smokes the boss's cigars, and takes over the boss's apartment to realize that here was a servant who considered himself more a weekend guest than a subservient domestic.

In his second Benny feature, *Buck Benny Rides Again* (1940), Rochester again played a free uninhibited spirit. In his first scene, he has an important date with his girl friend and uses every excuse to get out of Benny's apartment. Finally, he says that the stork has presented his aunt with twins this very afternoon, and he must visit her. "If I remember correctly," says Benny, "the stork visited your aunt two months ago." "He sure gets around," replies Rochester. Finally the servant outwits the boss. Benny is going to a party and plans to wear his full-dress suit. Rochester tells him the suit is inappropriate and advises him to wear something else. Benny complies, wears another set of clothing, and then takes off. In the next cut, whom do audiences see driving up to his girl friend's apartment in the boss's car wearing the boss's top hat and the boss's dress suit but crafty old Rochester!

Some critics thought that in the first two films and the later Benny-Rochester features, *Love Thy Neighbor* (1940) and *The Meanest Man in the World* (1943), there was a father-son relationship between the two. Obviously, this was but one way of simplifying their camaraderie to fit into the great-white-father-poor-black-slave-son category. But for such a relationship to exist, one man must control or overshadow the other. That was never the case with the Benny-Rochester films. Rather one sensed that Rochester was far too independent to be completely subservient to anyone. In fact, judging by the number of times Benny was extricated from tight situations by the wit and resourcefulness of his valet, the master-servant relationship was close to being reversed. As an indication of his equal footing with his employer, Rochester addressed Benny as "Boss" or "Boss, Sir" rather than the traditional lone "Sir." Today such a privilege may seem grossly patronizing, but in the 1930s it was a step forward.

Ultimately, Rochester fused the tom and coon types into a gregarious eccentric presence. In a feature such as *Topper Returns* (1941), in which he portrays a chauffeur-turned-detective, he is the typical coon-in-the-haunted-house, terrified when he sees cigarettes floating in the air and scared out of his wits when he falls through a trick chair into a lake. Although he performed such antics, Rochester also rose above the old tradition because at heart his humor—along with the warmth and affection he engendered in his audience—was based more on his wisecracks and his shrewdness than on his color. When in film after film he warned Benny of dire consequences, audiences laughed not because of any racial jokes but because Rochester was a very bright little fellow who was bound to be proved right in the end.

Rochester's name was wedded to Benny's throughout his career. Indeed, it has always been said that Jack Benny owned the rights to the name "Rochester" and that he could have replaced Anderson and given the name to another actor any time he wanted. But Anderson-Rochester was such a distinct personality and such an instant radio success that this fate never befell him. In fact, many of the Benny-Rochester movies seemed more the valet's than the master's. "If Hollywood's other comedians are on their toes," wrote *The New York Times* in 1939, "the West Coast's domestic employment agencies may expect to be swamped any day now with requests for valets, preferably saddle-colored and answering to the name Rochester. For in Paramount's *Man About Town*, a sly little gentleman's gentleman—or comedian's comedian—called Rochester has restored Jack Benny to the comic map and cleared a sizable place there for himself." When Rochester and Benny appeared in *Love Thy Neighbor* the same newspaper commented: "Rochester is still putting Mr. Benny very much behind the eight ball and stealing as much of the show as he can get his hands upon. But enough, unfortunately, is not stolen. . . ."

In some of his movies, Rochester was granted a privilege usually denied black actors, namely some cinematic love life. Black actors in movies were generally denied black women, which was one way of making them sexless—therefore harmless—creatures. But Rochester's love life rounded out his creations. Theresa Harris, a beautiful dark-skinned actress who was to lose a chance at leading roles because of her darkness, first appeared with Rochester in *Jezebel*. The two had no romantic scenes together. Harris portrayed Bette Davis's scatterbrained maid, one of Hollywood's most excruciatingly demeaned characters. But later things went better for her when she appeared as Rochester's girl friend Josephine in two of the Benny features and also in *What's Buzzin' Cousin* (1943).

The most obvious testament to Rochester's uniqueness as a personality and his ability to carry a picture alone came in the 1940s with *Cabin in the Sky*. The critics unanimously commended him for his performance. Under the sensitive direction of Vincente Minnelli, Anderson hit at an area his predecessors never approached: he touched his audience. As the forever scheming-dreaming Little Joe Jackson, he was at first engaging as he shot craps or wooed the sultry Lena Horne. But when his plots failed and particularly when his good wife, Petunia, was about to leave him for good, audiences did not feel embarrassed by wanting to comfort him. They were drawn to Rochester's charming, funny, and sad diminutive hero. Had he been given an opportunity to explore his wondrous admixture of the comic and the pathetic in other roles, there is no telling how great his contributions to American screen comedy might have been.

In the 1940s Anderson remained a great favorite, appearing in a long line of important productions such as *Kiss the Boys Good-Bye* (1941), *Birth of the Blues* (1941), *Tales of Manhattan, Star-Spangled Rhythm* (1942), *Broadway Rhythm* (1944), *Brewster's Millions* (1945), *The Sailor Takes a Wife* (1945), and *The Show-Off* (1946). In *I Love a Bandleader* (1945), he was touted as the highest paid black actor in Hollywood. His film appearances—except for a cameo in *It's a Mad, Mad, Mad, Mad World* (1963)—ended just after World War II.

Hi-Hat Hattie

Rochester's female counterpart was Hattie McDaniel, a massive, high-strung mammy figure. Often criticized because of her stereotype characters, she answered her critics just as tartly as she might have answered an employer in one of her movies, "Why should I complain about making seven thousand dollars a week playing a maid? If I didn't, I'd be making seven dollars a week actually being one!" McDaniel's statement gives a true picture of the options available to black performers of the 1930s. She played the fussy, boisterous, big-bosomed maid time and time again, using the stereotyped figure to display her remarkable talent and affinity for pure broad comedy. With her fiercely and distinctively American aggressiveness and her stupendous sonic boom of a voice, Hattie created rich, dazzling characterizations. Audiences of the 1930s responded to her excessive showmanship, her effrontery, and her audacity. She emerged as the one servant of the era to speak her mind fully, and the world of her eccentric characters was a helter-skelter, topsy-turvy one in which the servant became the social equal, the mammy became the literal mother figure, the put-on was carried to the forefront of the action, and the style of the servant overpowered the content of the script.

Hattie McDaniel came to Hollywood in the late 1920s. Born in Wichita, Kansas, in 1898, the thirteenth child of a Baptist minister, Hattie mastered her gospels and religious, self-righteous sauciness at an early age. Afterward she struggled upward from roles in road companies—billed as everything from the "colored Sophie Tucker" to the "female Bert Williams"—to appearances on radio and then finally parts in the movies. Once ensconced in the film capital, she was typed as a mammy. A powerfully built woman, she weighed close to three hundred pounds, was very dark, and had typically Negro features. With her enormous mouth, wonderfully expressive eyes, "pearly white teeth," and mammoth rounded face, Hattie McDaniel was one of the screen's greatest presences, a pre-Fellini-esque figure of the absurd and a marvel of energetic verve and enthusiasm.

In her early films, *The Gold West* (1932) and *The Story of Temple Drake* (1933), her mammies were loyal, unobtrusive figures. One detects in Josef von Sternberg's *Blonde Venus* (1932) an attempt at first to pass her off as a humorless, less jolly version of Louise Beavers. The film stars Marlene Dietrich as a Depression heroine driven to shame by her poverty. Fleeing her husband who fights for custody of their young son and carrying the boy with her, Dietrich hides out in a small Southern town where she is befriended by a congenial local mammy. Not only does mammy McDaniel supply provisions and moral support, but she also serves as a lookout, quick to warn Dietrich before the detectives close in. The down-and-out heroine has come to rely on the servant as her last friend, and once again the prehumanized black domestic is the true and trusted companion out to aid the white world, not harm it. Hattie McDaniel seemed slightly miscast in even this minor role. For one thing, her distinctive booming voice did not seem right for a character the script says is submissive. Even nicely toned down by von Sternberg, Hattie's voice sounded as if it were meant to give commands, not take them.

Judge Priest (1934) cast McDaniel as a cheerful aunt jemima with Will Rogers and Stepin Fetchit. In her scenes with Fetchit, audiences could see evolving the great McDaniel rebellious spirit. Fetchit portrayed the arch no-account, Hattie the industrious domestic, fiercely interested in her work and unable to abide any niggerish foolery. "Cut that monkeyshine," she cries out when Fetchit dares to lounge and play his harmonica in the kitchen of the house. "Come on in here when I holler at you," she belts out to him at another point. Here she was the quick-tempered, outspoken black woman, not about to take any nonsense. Some of that same spirit was evident in her 1934 films, *Operator 13, Lost in the Stratosphere, Little Men;* and in her 1935 *Music Is Magic, Another Face,* and *The Little Colonel.* Then came the first of the classic roles in George Stevens' *Alice Adams* (1935).

In the careers of most important actors, there is a moment—in some play or movie or scene—in which they realize their own uniqueness and in which an observant director encourages them to reveal, or even revel in, that quality. The actor finally gives a super-deluxe, grand-slam, all-or-nothing performance. Great careers are made on such moments, and director George Stevens gave McDaniel hers. *Alice Adams* is about a small-town social climber, played by Katharine Hepburn, a poor girl actually brighter and more sophisticated than those higher up on the social ladder. She wants desperately to fit in. When she meets a handsome rich boy (Fred MacMurray), she leads him into believing that she too comes from a wealthy background. Her mother invites him to dinner. To impress their guest and ensure the evening's success, the Adamses hire a Negro cook to prepare and serve the meal. Well aware of the low status of the Adams family, she feels she is lowering herself by serving the dinner.

Hattie McDaniel plays her in a formidable and unorthodox fashion. From her entrance, she says things—amid some rambunctious gum chewing—that no other maid in the movies would ever have dared. When the mistress of the house tells her to serve the dinner soup, McDaniel counters, "But don't you think it's getting pretty hot for soup?" The weather does prove too hot for soup, and later when she is asked airily by Alice to "Please take this dreadful soup away," McDaniel merely stops dead in her tracks and stares at the girl imperially, indeed contemptuously, as if to say, "I done tol' you so!" Used by director Stevens not only for comic relief but to point up the pretenses of the Adamses, McDaniel's maid repeatedly makes fun of the family's foolish attempts to put on airs. She makes her dining-room entrances and exits lethargically, as if she could not care less. Why should she hurry for these no-'count white folks? She carries her tray in the most off-hand fashion. When Alice speaks French to impress her guest, McDaniel is there to undercut the girl's airs with a monosyllabic grunt.

After *Alice Adams*'s opening, one newspaper critic wrote: "The recital would be incomplete if it neglected to applaud Hattie McDaniel for her hilarious bit as hired maid during the classic dinner scene." Thus was fixed, in this film, the nature of Hattie McDaniel's relations with her white masters. Through her uproarious conduct, she puts them in *their* place without overtly offending them. Nor does she, as some might wish, pick up a gun to blow out their brains. Instead she struts about looking down on them, all the while pretending to be the model servant. But even the 1930s audiences knew Hattie McDaniel was putting them on.

In 1936, Hattie McDaniel appeared in eleven films: *Gentle Julia, The First Baby, Show Boat, Hearts Divided, High Tension, Star for the Night, Postal Inspector, The Bride Walks Out, Valiant Is the Word for Carrie, Reunion,* and *Can This Be Dixie?* Of these, *Show*

Boat remains one of her better pictures. When she is first seen, it is evident that the toughness and assurance she carried with her in *Alice Adams* is still firmly intact. "Outta my way," an arrogant white dock worker tells her. "Who wants to get in your way!" she answers back. Later when he tries prying information from her on the doings of the showboat's leading lady, Julie, McDaniel answers with a sly, mischievous smile, "Ask me no questions, and I'll tell you no lies." Here Hattie McDaniel was talking back to Whitey, and there was nothing subtle about it.

In 1937 McDaniel appeared in seven films. Her most interesting role was as the maid in *Saratoga*, which starred Clark Gable and Jean Harlow. There was such a fine rapport between Gable and McDaniel that audiences lost sight of their master-servant roles. Never was McDaniel seen kowtowing. On those rare occasions when she attempted a "yes sir" or "no sir" with appropriate sub-missiveness, she came across as hopelessly fraudulent. *Saratoga* incorporated special scenes, too, to play on McDaniel's rich humor and infectious charm. In one scene, she joined in with other members of the starving proletariat to sing a let's-be-jolly-despite-the-Depression melody. Here she asserted herself as a social equal. Most important, in this film Hattie McDaniel's mammy emerged as a mother figure to Jean Harlow. McDaniel and Harlow had previously worked together in *China Seas* (1935). In that film Harlow's highflung legendary temperament had found its match. McDaniel had not screamed back at Harlow; she just did what she pleased in the film, disregarding her mistress. She knew better than any other actor in the movies—except for Gable, perhaps—just how to handle the irascible blonde beauty. In *Saratoga* she portrayed Harlow's fastidious maid. McDaniel was quick to note her mistress's quirks and kinks. She was adviser, protectress, and a source of nourishment. "You got a pencil smudge on your chin, honey," she tells Harlow just before Gable enters to pay a call. "Don't you want to fix up?" Harlow, as a true rebellious daughter, pretends to ignore her mammy maid's advice. But later she does clean off the smudge. When Harlow needs motherly comfort, particularly after a battle with Gable, Hattie is there to dry her tears. "Oh, Miss Carol. Why, honey, baby," she croons, taking her to her shoulder. But, like a dutiful mother, McDaniel refuses to take any nonsense. When a letter arrives from Gable for Harlow, she asks Harlow if she wants it read. Harlow screams no, but Hattie realizes the letter's import and reads it aloud anyway, oblivious to the blonde's outbursts.

One year and seven movies later when she appeared with Barbara Stanwyck in *The Mad Miss Manton* (1938), the mother-surrogate, social-equal aspects of McDaniel's personality were already familiar to audiences and roles were being tailor-made for her. Stanwyck portrayed a flighty society girl forever involved in pranks with a group of young socialite friends. McDaniel, as her maid, Hilda, has to pick up behind the society girls, but from the moment of her entrance, the audience knows that Hilda is not about to take anything from anybody. A solid mass of cantankerous confidence and vitality, she hurls verbal barbs with the speed and accuracy of an ace pitcher. At one point, she nonchalantly informs one of Stanwyck's young society friends that there is a telephone call for her. "Sounds like my date," says the giggling girl as she runs to answer the phone. "Sounds more like a pipsqueak to me!" counters McDaniel offhandedly.

Later, as Stanwyck begs Hattie not to be so rough on one of her society friends because "She's our guest, Hilda," McDaniel haughtily replies, "Umh! I didn't ask her up!" Obviously, if Stanwyck says "our guest," the apartment is as much the maid's as the mistress's. Just talking back was a triumph of sorts, and Hattie McDaniel was doing what every black maid in America must have wanted to do at one time or another. Throughout *The Mad Miss Manton*, as she orders Stanwyck and her friends about, criticizing their beaux, dissecting their schoolgirl chatter, and reprimanding them for their bad manners, Hattie McDaniel stands as an iconoclastic arbiter of taste. She also expresses a strong maternal concern for Stanwyck. Hattie demands approval of Stanwyck's boy friends, and she does not hesitate to listen in on phone conversations. Finally, as the true protective mother figure, she saves the heroine's life, mainly through her maternal interference.

McDaniel.s flamboyant bossiness often can be read as a cover-up for deep hostility. Indeed, she seemed to time her lines to give her black audience that impression. In *The Mad Miss Manton*, as in all her best movies, Hattie McDaniel refused to accept typical domesticity, to yield to the meek brand of Christianity that characterized Louise Beavers. Only one year and one film separates the Hilda of *The Mad Miss Manton* from the Mammy of *Gone with the Wind*. In that film, McDaniel fused the elements of all her earlier screen performances to give what certainly was her finest characterization.

Gone with the Wind: Black Realities and the End of a Tradition

David O. Selznick's *Gone with the Wind* was the third and final feature of the 1930s spotlighting blacks. Based on Margaret Mitchell's novel, the story took more than two years to film and cost

ABOVE: Hattie McDaniel, the most outspoken servant figure in the 1930s, fastens Vivien Leigh's corset in *Gone with the Wind* (1939). At the same time, Hattie lets her mistress know she's not about to take any nonsense.
BELOW: Life couldn't be better! So Hattie McDaniel and Ben Carter seem to think in *Maryland* (1940).

almost four million dollars. At heart, the film was nothing more than an elaborate romance, centering on the rebellious spirits of Scarlett O'Hara and her iconoclastic lover, Rhett Butler. The two were removed from politics and sociology, but in their own ways both saw through the sham and shame of their Old South world. Strangely enough, amid all the romantic unreality of this spectacular film, the black-white relationships were probably closer to the real ones of ante-bellum America than any ever before presented in the movies.

The problem with Civil War spectacles has never been that they presented Negroes as slaves—for how else could they be depicted? —but that the films have humiliated and debased them far beyond the callings of the script. *Gone with the Wind* was often criticized because the slaves were not shown taking up rifles against their former masters. But the really beautiful aspect of this film was not what was omitted but what was ultimately accomplished by the black actors who transformed their slaves into complex human beings.

Hattie McDaniel portrayed the O'Hara family's faithful Mammy. Boasting that she diapered three generations of O'Hara women, Mammy is proud of the mutual affection between master and servant. During the war years it is she who keeps Tara, the family plantation, going. Like earlier film slaves, Hattie McDaniel's character is motivated almost solely out of concern for the master family, but her Mammy also feels confident enough to express anger toward her masters. She berates and hounds anyone who goes against *her* conception of right and wrong, whether it be Mrs. O'Hara or Scarlett and Rhett. Not once does she bite her tongue.

But most significantly, Scarlett and Mammy maintain a complex mother-daughter relationship, much like those which actually existed in the old South, the kind of relationship that was either glossed over or treated condescendingly in other films. In *Gone with the Wind*, McDaniel's Mammy becomes an all-seeing, all-hearing, all-knowing commentator and observer. She remarks. She annotates. She makes asides. She always opinionizes. Shortly after the movie opens, Mammy is seen helping Scarlett into a corset, at the same time commanding her young mistress to eat before departing for a barbecue. It has already been revealed that Scarlett is upset because Ashley Wilkes, the man she loves, will marry someone else. Scarlett pines and moans, but only Mammy is aware of her feelings. When Scarlett refuses to eat the meal, Mammy does not hesitate to threaten her: "I ain't notice Mr. Ashley askin' for to marry you," she says, slyly smiling to let Scarlett know that she knows all about the infatuation. Her eyes widening in disbelief at being discovered, Scarlett, like the obedient, terrified daughter, eats! In her compliance, she becomes just as much a testament to Mammy's power as the giggling maids were to Mae West's.

It is Mammy who knows—and keeps secret—Scarlett's every plot. It is she who criticizes or advises, counsels or warns, protects or defends, but always understands. When Scarlett, just widowed, privately models a flashy new hat, it is Mammy who spies the action and promptly reprimands her. When Scarlett decides to return to Atlanta to request a loan from Rhett Butler, Mammy insists upon accompanying her. "No proper young lady is going there alone!" she snaps. She even makes a dress for Scarlett from the green drapes that once adorned Tara. As Scarlett walks the streets of Reconstruction Atlanta, Mammy literally clears the way, pushing aside the renegade blacks who line the sidwalks. Later, when Butler comes to pay a call after Scarlett is widowed a second time, Mammy, aware that Scarlett is not grieving at all (instead she's been hitting the bottle), informs Scarlett in the haughtiest manner, "I done tol' him you was prostrate with grief!" Delivered by McDaniel, it was the most perfectly timed, the funniest, indeed the most satiric line in the film.

Certainly *Gone with the Wind*'s script had much to do with presenting such an inspired Mammy. It has always been said that once Selznick had tested McDaniel for the role, he decided that only she could play Mammy and made script changes to meet with the special brand of McDaniel humor. Yet through the force of her own personality, McDaniel's character became free of the greatest burden that slavery—on screen and off—inflicted on blacks: a sense of innate inferiority. Her Mammy has a self-righteous grandeur that glows. Even audiences unaware of what a fine performer McDaniel was sensed by her mammoth presence and her strong, hearty voice that here was an actress larger than her lines, bigger than her role. "Best of all," wrote *The New York Times*, "perhaps next to Miss Leigh, is Hattie McDaniel's Mammy." For her performance, Hattie McDaniel became the first Negro to win an Academy Award as Best Supporting Actress.

No two black actresses of the 1930s differed so widely as did Hattie McDaniel and Butterfly McQueen. Yet in an equally exciting and perhaps even subtler way, McQueen built up the comedy interludes of the character Prissy in *Gone with the Wind*, capping them with her own masterful bit of madness. McDaniel was tough and resilient and could take a small incident and magnify it into a mountain. Butterfly, however, could take a big scene and condense it into the tiniest of lyrical poems. Her performance was marked by fragility, hysteria, and absurdity.

McQueen's Prissy is a servant girl for the O'Hara family. When the townspeople are deserting Atlanta in fear of Sherman's oncoming siege, Scarlett agrees to stay on to help Melanie through a difficult pregnancy *only* after Prissy has assured her that she can help with the delivery of the baby. "I'se knows all 'bout birthin' babies," Prissy declares, smiling with head lowered. But the day of the actual arrival, Prissy is nowhere in sight. When finally found by a panic-stricken Scarlett and told to take over, the girl stares into Scarlett's eyes, first in astonishment, then in absolute fright. "Gee, Miss Scarlett," she cries in her high, tense, fluttery voice, "I'se don't knows nothin' 'bout birthin' babies!" As Melanie moans in agony, Prissy nervously suggests, "Miss Scarlett, my mammy always said to put a knife under the bed. 'Cause it cuts the pain." Throughout, McQueen delivered her lines with a sobriety that made them seem twice as funny.

Later, when Scarlett is about to flee Atlanta, Prissy gathers essentials. Packing chinaware amid thunderous cannon roars, she drops the dishes, screams in terror, and runs from corner to corner of the room. Finally, as the wagon, driven by Rhett Butler, departs from the city with Prissy, Melanie, and the newborn baby in the back, McQueen pops her head up every other frame or so, glimpses the flames of the city, and screams hysterically.

Some observers saw Butterfly as the stock darky figure. But there was much more to her performance. Had she been a mere pickaninny, she might have engendered hostility or embarrassed audiences. Instead she seemed to provide an outlet for the repressed fears of the audience. That perhaps explains why everyone laughed hysterically at her hysterics. For during the crisis sequences, the film built beautifully, and there was a need for release. Mere comic relief of the old type would have been vulgar. But because of her artistic mayhem, her controlled fright, and her heightened awareness and articulation of the emotions of the audiences, Butterfly McQueen seemed to flow wonderfully with the rest of the film. She had a pleasant waiflike quality, too, not in the patronizing style of *The Green Pastures,* in which the grown-up people behaved like rambunctious idiot children, but in a special, purely personal way. Tiny and delicate, Butterfly McQueen seemed to ask for protection and was a unique combination of the comic and the pathetic.

Usually little is said of the male servants in *Gone with the Wind,* particularly Oscar Polk, who played the emasculated Pork. His

Butterfly McQueen as Prissy, the girl who knows all 'bout birthin' babies, with Clark Gable and Vivien Leigh in *Gone with the Wind*.

important scene occurs during the second half of the film when Scarlett presents him with a watch once owned by her father. Pork wants it desperately, but as a man who has had his brain, his soul, his individuality sapped from him during long years of servitude he cannot accept it at first. Here Oscar Polk expressed accurately that aspect of slavery that Hattie McDaniel soared above, the sense of inferiority. His was written on him in his stumped, bent-over posture and in his hesitant manner of speaking. He is a man fighting to hold himself together. Polk's Pork was a valid comment on the slave system. But unfortunately in presenting something so real, the film made the character the focus of humor rather than pity.

Everett Brown appeared as the noble Big Sam, the former slave who rescues Scarlett from her attackers in Shantytown, and he did well in a minor role. *Gone with the Wind*'s most rigidly typed black character, and perhaps the one unredeemable black stereotype in the entire picture, was Uncle Peter, the clownish backwoods dolt who works for Aunt Pittypat. Surprisingly, the part was played by Eddie Anderson, and the only thing that saved him was that he was so buried under layers of make-up that audiences failed to realize their favorite was being used for the crudest comic relief.

Because they had carried the servant tradition to its highest point, the black characters of *Gone with the Wind* brought that tradition to a fitting close. In the 1940s, although the servants still appeared in films, the enthusiasm and creativity that distinguished figures such as Hattie McDaniel and Butterfly McQueen were gone. In the next decade, McDaniel appeared in some twenty-one features. Her presence still provided rich ribald humor, but her impact was not as great. In *Gone with the Wind*, her Mammy had brought to light a fact that white audiences had long ignored or suppressed: here was a black maid who not only was capable of running the Big House but proclaimed in her own contorted way her brand of black power. McDaniel scared her audience. Indeed, in the South there were complaints that she had been too familiar with her white employers. (There were similar Southern complaints against Rochester in the Benny movies.) In the 1940 film *Maryland* Hattie McDaniel was made too jolly and sweet. In films such as *Janie* (1944), *Since You Went Away* (1944), and *Margie* (1946), she was made too doggedly faithful. And perhaps worst of all, in *Song of the South* (1946), as she was seen merrily baking pies and singing cheerful darky songs, Hattie McDaniel displayed a newfound Christian domesticity that was the exact antithesis of her haughty grandeur in the late 1930s. Before her death in the early 1950s, McDaniel left the movies to play the wild and witty maid Beulah on radio.

Butterfly McQueen's screen personality was not as drastically altered as McDaniel's, but she, too, was stripped of some of her individuality in the next era. Her later films included *The Women* (1939), *Affectionately Yours* (1941), *I Dood It* (1943), *Cabin in the Sky, Since You Went Away* (her role was left on the cutting-room floor), *Mildred Pierce* (1945), and *Duel in the Sun* (1947). Her talents were often misused or misunderstood by directors and writers. In *Affectionately Yours*, she had to deliver what might be the most demeaning line ever uttered by a black in the movies. "Who dat say who dat when you say dat," she crooned. "I never thought I would have to say a line like that," the actress later said, obviously embarrassed. "I had imagined that since I was an intelligent woman, I could play any kind of role." Perhaps the final irony of that line and the best tribute to Butterfly McQueen's comic talent was that her performance in *Affectionately Yours* was thoroughly disarming and considered by some critics the best in the movie. "[The] only glints of brightness . . . are contributed by a hair-spring brownie called Butterfly McQueen, as a maid. Her frequent dissolves into tears upon the slightest provocation are ludicrous," wrote *The New York Times*.

McQueen's real problem, however, was that she had to be handled as a surreal creature rather than as the stock comic servant. Her comedic gifts were too special and delicate, too unique a blending of the comic and the pathetic, to be effective in ordinary dumb niggery roles. With her large expressive eyes, her bewildered and perplexed stare, and her quivering tremor of a voice, she seemed almost otherworldly. Surely, producer David O. Selznick and director King Vidor understood the peculiar nature of the McQueen personality. In their film *Duel in the Sun*, she was wisely cast as the mysterious Vashti, a mystifying character wandering in and out of the picture.

Butterfly McQueen's career took a disastrous turn in the late 1940s. There was little or no work. In the 1950s, when servants in the movies had all but vanished, she found herself in New York City struggling to survive as a sales clerk at Macy's, a waitress, a factory worker, a dishwasher, and as a companion to a Long Island white woman. In the early 1960s, when blacks were used in television commercials, many had hoped to see McQueen and other old servant figures pop up on the home screens. But network advertisers feared presenting a black as a maid in this new era of boycotts, protests, and militancy. (To cast McQueen as anything other than a maid also seemed out of the question.) Butterfly McQueen's story does have a somewhat happy ending. In the very late 1960s, she was rediscovered by a whole new generation when she appeared in the off-Broadway play *Curley McDimple. Gone with the Wind* was reissued. And she was a name again. She still was not overrun with offers, but at least she was out of the kitchen and back before the lights.

Before leaving the 1930s, a final word should be said about the one black actor who stood apart from the rest of the servant figures, who seemed to tower above the era itself. He still has a special place in the history of American entertainment and politics.

Paul Robeson: the Black Colossus

By the Depression era, Paul Robeson was already an authentic legendary figure in twentieth-century America. The son of a former slave, he had a rare intellect and athletic ability that enabled him to reach out for all the best white America could offer. Born in Princeton, New Jersey, in 1898, by the time of high school he was an academic *cause célèbre.* An honor student, he won a scholarship to Rutgers University at a time when they were virtually unheard-of for black students. At Rutgers he distinguished himself as an athlete of astounding skill, a four-letter man and a terror on the football field. When he was named to the All-American football team in 1918, he was called "the greatest defensive end who had ever trod the gridiron." Robeson's academic record was equally impressive. He was elected to Phi Beta Kappa in his junior year, graduated with honors the next, then went on to Columbia University's law school. Always proud and quick-tempered, he attained new triumphs as an actor and concert singer. Eugene O'Neill's plays *The Emperor Jones* and *All God's Chillun Got Wings* took on new dimensions with Robeson as their star. The plays *Stevedore, Taboo,* and *Black Boy* are recalled today simply because he appeared in them. Later his *Othello* had the longest run of any Shakespeare play to appear on Broadway. Robeson seemed to have achieved all that a man can hope for, but ultimately his life mingled irony with heartache, idealism with disillusionment, a love for his people with an eventual rejection by them. He became a victim.

It is one of the less pleasant aspects of the American way that when a black artist is successful and silent, he remains a national favorite. But when a black artist becomes important enough to want better roles (usually those with more dignity and less racism inherent in them) or when the artist makes some comment against the social-political climate of the country, he becomes a doomed man. When Robeson became associated with the Communist Party in the mid-1930s, when he spoke out against American discrimination and segregation, when he began making trips to the Soviet Union, he was singled out and finally silenced. Eventually the concert halls were closed to him. Negroes on the streets whispered his name in fear or shame. Reportedly, the State Department refused to let him leave the country. At another time, they did not want to let him back in. And Paul Robeson became the first of the controversial black political prisoners, the first of our great black artists to have his art denied him because of his political beliefs.

Because Robeson was denied a platform on which to display his art, the legend about him was to grow. Was he really the greatest baritone of all time? Was he actually America's greatest actor? Was he really so incredibly handsome? Was he actually too much of an assertive black male in his plays and films for white America to permit him to continue? Was his smile the key to understanding his enigmatic personality? The questions about Robeson had really begun as early as the 1920s, and they continued with rapacious fervor throughout subsequent decades. If there ever have been any answers, they were found in his movies, and audiences of the 1930s, like those today, went to see his pictures to learn more about the myth and the man, the mask and the mystique.

Most of the important Paul Robeson features were made abroad. He was the only black star of the 1930s to work in foreign pictures, where he could escape typing—or so he thought. But like his Hollywood features the foreign films seldom met with his approval. Always Robeson went into a motion picture with the hope that it would elevate the state of his people. But after completing a role Robeson would discover that if anything his talents had been exploited and used to demean the black man's struggle for equality and full independence. His first foreign film, the silent *Borderline* (1928), starred him opposite his wife Eslanda and the poet Hilda Doolittle and had little to offend anyone. But his second, *Sanders of the River* (1935), an African drama that he agreed to star in for British producer Zoltan Korda out of a "passionate concern with African culture," was transformed into a glorification of British colonial rule. Scenes in which he did not appear had been rewritten without the actor's knowledge, and at a special preview an irate Robeson stormed out of the movie house in protest.

In most of his other European motion pictures—*Song of Free-*

Paul Robeson and Nina Mae McKinney in *Sanders of the River*.

dom (1938), *Dark Sands* (1938), *King Solomon's Mines* (1937), and *The Proud Valley* (1941)—Robeson was cast as an "undercover servant," exploited in much the same way Sidney Poitier was to be some twenty-five years later. He was always at the service of some white friend in the films—but the friend was little more than the old white massa figure. Robeson's films were the first to use this technique. In *Sanders of the River* he was Bosambo, the trusty right-hand man of Sanders, the white "man of iron" who rules the dark, backward tribes of Africa. Robeson provided not only physical strength for his master but some comic and romantic interludes for the mass audience. In *King Solomon's Mines*, Robeson was Umbopa, the Mashona chief who aids the white Sir Cedric Hardwicke in his search for the legendary mines. In *Proud Valley*, the film Robeson felt proudest of, he was again the black servant, a strong, heroic coal miner who sacrifices his life so that his white brothers may live. The servant proceedings were slightly altered in *Song of Freedom;* here Robeson portrayed a successful concert singer in England who suddenly discovers he is a descendant of a West African queen whose tribe is now in need of a leader. As the archetypal modern black man, Robeson was also depicted as still having the jungle blood running through his veins. That he can never escape. The classic aspect of *Song of Freedom* was its fascinating but unconscious homage to colonial rule. As an industrious British black man, Robeson was the epitome of black middle-class sobriety. He has been trained by whites and adheres to their value system. His wife is a fair-skinned, straight-haired, proper mulatto. And he has a dark-skinned coon servant. When he journeys to deep dark Africa, he takes his British manners and mores and civilizes the savage natives. Great Britain could not have asked for a more loyal subject.

In a way, these films were dishonest. Audiences may have deplored the master-servant antics of even so enlightened a pair as Benny and Rochester, but at least with them patrons knew where they stood. There was no attempt to trick the audience into believing they were viewing something modern and significant. In contrast, the Robeson films were meant to reflect the liberal and even radical attitudes of the day. Yet they now seem dated and false.

What was impressive about the Robeson films, however, was Robeson himself. In all his movies, audiences were aware of his great bulk and presence. His eyes gleamed. His smile was brilliant and infectious, oten revealing the complete joy of the actor as he sang, sometimes masking an ambivalent, ironic side of his personality. But always Paul Robeson used his smile to draw his audience to him. Physically, Robeson was such a towering figure, a colossus actually, that he immediately suggested strength. One could never imagine him portraying a weakling. He was made for heroic parts in the classical sense. He seemed a man of instinct and intuition, and seldom played characters of intellect. Robeson was all heart or all guts or all bombast or all passion or all fury, elemental and pure. His lack of intellectual control added to the excitement and theatricality of each performance.

Robeson's greatest contribution to black film history—and the aspect of his work that most disturbed American white moviegoers—was his proud, defiant portrait of the black man. In his best known film, *The Emperor Jones* (1933), Robeson portrays O'Neill's black man who refuses to kowtow to anyone—Brutus Jones, an arrogant, strong-willed braggart, who rises from Pullman porter to autocrat. In one particularly interesting scene on a railroad car, Robeson goes through the stock "yes sirs" and "no sirs" to his white employers, but is so full of energy and self-mockery that his behavior is not self-demeaning. Later when he attempts to blackmail his employer (and afterward when he mocks the employer for the benefit of his black woman), he is a black man consciously asserting himself, consciously cutting The Man down to size.

The Emperor Jones made Paul Robeson a symbol of black confidence and self-fulfillment. When he argues with a friend in a crap game, he kills him, then is sent to a chain gang. When a sadistic guard there whips Jones, he kills the guard, escapes, and sets off for Jamaica. There he works for a white trader, maneuvers (and eventually forces) his way into a partnership, and then usurps the throne of the island's black king. For the next two and a half years, he struts through his palace in his high patent leather boots. He gazes at himself in his corridor of mirrors. "King Brutus!" he proclaims. "Somehow that don't make enough noise." He pauses. "The Emperor Jones!" And thus a ruler is born.

Surely, as Robeson was seen standing by his throne with a crown on his head and a scepter in his hand, as he ordered his old white partner about, black audiences must have felt immensely proud and fond of that badd nigger up there on the screen, telling them white folks to get outta his way to give him room to breathe. Despite the fact that at the end, in punishment for his iniquities (and we might assume his self-assertion), Robeson's Brutus is hunted in the jungle and killed, and despite the fact that in the jungle sequences Robeson, with his chest bare and a terrified expression on his face, was often a black brute figure, black audiences still saw a black male completely unlike the servile characters of most American movies.

The Emperor Jones gave Robeson his finest screen role. One of his few American projects, it was independently produced by John Krimsky and Gifford Cochran and directed by Dudley Murphy. Yet it was thought tainted (by Robeson himself on occasion) because it presented the Negro as a murderer and a rogue.

Robeson did not fare as well in his three other American pictures. His first, *Body and Soul* (1924), was a silent independently produced by Oscar Micheaux. The plot was badly jumbled, and Robeson without his voice was merely beautiful and mysterious. *Show Boat* was a film Robeson might not have cared for, but, curiously, today he seems more relaxed and less stagey in this movie than in any other. The picture itself had an interracial theme, which was handled melodramatically but nonetheless well. Among the traveling troupe of entertainers who perform on the showboat there is a somber, good-hearted beauty named Julie. She becomes a victim of racism when it is discovered that she has "Negro blood." When word reaches the showboat company, Julie's white husband swiftly cuts her hand with a knife and sucks her blood. Miscegenation is a crime in the South. The husband performs this ritual because "One drop of Negro blood makes you a Negro in these parts." Afterward Julie and her now-mulatto husband slowly depart from the showboat hand in hand. Later the tragic Julie becomes an alcoholic. The white blues singer Helen Morgan played Julie in the film. Robeson and Hattie McDaniel portrayed the comic servants, Captain Joe and Queenie. Both went through stereotype routines, but Robeson never fully demeaned himself, and when he sang "Ole Man River" and "Ah Still Suits Me" (with Hattie McDaniel), he lifted the entire movie onto his massive shoulders and carried it to moments of eloquence and greatness.

In *Tales of Manhattan* (1942), which also featured Ethel Waters and Eddie Anderson, Paul Robeson played his last American film role. Unfortunately, the movie was a personal disaster. Robeson portrays a backwoods Southern coon who discovers a satchel of money that has been dropped into his cotton field from an airplane. Immediately, he and Waters thank de almighty Gawd in de hebben above. Throughout the film the blacks sing in the fields, dance in the churches, clap their hands in joy, and stand tremblin' 'fore de power and de glory above. Again superstition had been substituted for the genuine intensity of the black religious experience, and the Negro sequence of this all-star film alienated black audiences and aroused great controversy. Surprisingly, NAACP Secretary Walter White defended the film. But other civil rights groups picketed it, and publications such as *PM* and *The Daily*

Worker criticized it vehemently. Star Robeson joined in the protests. "I wouldn't blame any Negro for picketing this film," he announced after having seen a completed version. Thereafter he picketed the film *and* Hollywood. He narrated the movie *Native Land* (1942), but he never accepted another motion-picture role.

Paul Robeson was the last major personality in the 1930s gallery of black artists. All the actors distinguished themselves not so much through characters as through their interpretations. Ultimately, they just about exhausted themselves. They used up their supply of ingenuity. Indeed, their servant characters had become so rich, so dazzling, so individualized—in short, so real, significant, and perhaps even threatening—that the servant syndrome could be developed no further. The greatest black character actors in the history of American movies had invigorated the era with their idiosyncrasies and style. In later eras, although the black actor was to be given bigger and better roles and more prominence in films, the actors themselves were never again able to take their audiences to such luminous and wacky heights. But the servants ended by serving themselves better than the masters, and they provided American movies of the Depression with some of their most sublime and absurd moments.

Because he was one of the few black actors to triumph in an independently produced black film, Paul Robeson now serves as a lead-in for the next great phase of blacks in films—the period of the black moviemakers, when independent directors and producers made movies to tell the world what being black was really about.

The Interlude:
Black-Market Cinema

4

*Bert Williams mugs and clowns, and a new era in motion-picture
history has its genesis. . . . The scholarly secretary of Booker T.
Washington sets out to make a Negro-accomplishment movie,
ends up by turning out a prodigious flop, yet fathers a movement. . . . In Nebraska, Kansas City, Chicago, New York, and other
cities and states independent filmmakers set up shop to supply
ghetto theaters with relevant all-black movies. . . . Stepin, Mantan,
Nina, and a score of other old-timers and newcomers find employment in movies made outside of Hollywood. . . . And an oversized,
overweight man named Oscar Micheaux becomes America's first
legendary black filmmaker.*

After *The Birth of a Nation* was released in 1915, there came the
great public furor against its racism. At the time, a standard reply
to protests about how Negroes were depicted in American films
was that blacks should develop their own crop of filmmakers. To
some extent that standard reply prevails today. The truth is that
black Americans have made their own films for many years. While
the mainstream of Hollywood filmmakers demeaned and ridi-
culed the American Negro, an underground movement gave rise
to a group of independent black filmmakers who flourished in the

late 1920s and the 1930s. They tried to present realistic portraits of black Americans, but more often than not were trapped by the same stereotype conceptions as their white competitors. And always they were plagued by financial, technical, and distributing problems. Yet some came up with remarkable achievements that survive today. A host of black writers, directors, producers, and technicians gained valuable experience from working on these films. In fact, had it not been for such underground features, many blacks would never have worked in films at all.

The films also offered employment for a great number of actors. Paul Robeson, as we have seen, started his movie career in a film directed by Oscar Micheaux. The only surviving recorded performance of the legendary black stage actor Charles Gilpin was in an independently produced black film. During the late 1930s and early 1940s these films offered exposure and experience to Lena Horne, Eddie Anderson, Spencer Williams (who later starred as Andy on the television series "Amos 'n' Andy"), Nina Mae McKinney, Mantan Moreland, Louise Beavers, Herbert Jeffery, comics Moms Mabley and Pigmeat Markham, and even Stepin Fetchit. All in all the underground black film movement provided film history with an exciting interlude, perhaps now of greater interest for sociological rather than artistic reasons.

In this period of the independents, producers explored and experimented with black themes. Films were made exclusively to please black audiences, and on occasion revealed black fantasies. The era had opened rather inauspiciously in 1914, when a lanky and limber black comedian dressed himself outrageously in a zoot suit and top hat for his motion-picture debut. The comedian was the legendary Bert Williams. The film was *Darktown Jubilee.* When it opened in Brooklyn, the picture was greeted with howls and bellows. When it closed, it did so amid race riots. In other areas, the film was met with undercover boycotts.

Darktown Jubilee was the first attempt of an independent film company to star a black actor in a movie. But in 1914 white audiences refused to accept a black in a leading role, unless, of course, he played a tom. The attempt became the first catastrophe, and with very little left for anyone to jubilate about, *Darktown Jubilee* was lifted out of circulation before it had ever really been in it.

The real father of the movement was a most unlikely candidate, a mild-mannered scholarly man named Emmet J. Scott, who was a secretary for Booker T. Washington. After the release of *The Birth of a Nation* a number of American blacks hoped to produce a short film to cite the accomplishments of colored America as a counterattack to Griffith's alleged racist propaganda. The NAACP toyed with the idea but eventually decided to fight the Griffith feature through the courts and picket lines. As the NAACP shied away, the scholarly Scott strolled to the foreground. He enlisted the aid of the black bourgeoisie, which furnished him with the capital for *Lincoln's Dream.* Initially, Scott hoped to tack this Negro-achievement short onto *The Birth of a Nation* as a prologue. But later Scott's modest proposals stretched to larger proportions. Scriptwriter Elaine Sterne expanded the short project into a feature. The script was submitted to Universal but rejected. Finally, the movie was shot in Chicago and Florida, where the company was haunted by bad weather, poorly designed and constructed sets, an inexperienced cast and crew, and inadequate lighting facilities. When the production ran into dire financial difficulties, Scott had to seek support from white backers, who altered his film's theme and sentiments. After three long hard years, *Lincoln's Dream* was some twelve reels long, ran three hours, and was retitled *The Birth of a Race.* Publicity posters promoted it as "The Greatest and Most Daring of Photoplays . . . The Story of Sin . . . A Master Picture Conceived in the Spirit of Truth and Dedicated to All of the Races of the World." It opened at Chicago's Blackstone Theater in 1918 and was a disaster artistically and financially. Yet it served as an impetus for others.

The organization to pick up where Scott had left off, the first of the black company pioneers, was the Lincoln Motion Picture Company. Incorporated in 1916 (before Scott's film was even completed) and based in Nebraska, the organization was the brainchild of black actor Noble P. Johnson and his brother George. *The Realization of the Negro's Dream* was one of the company's first products. Like Scott's, this film extolled Negro achievements. Another release, *Trooper K*, was about the massacre of Negro troops of the famous Tenth Cavalry and the historic rescue of Captain Lewis S. Morey by the "unknown and unhonored" Trooper K. Both films were distributed to ghetto theaters. George Johnson had shrewdly noted that because of segregation in the South and de facto segregation in the North, a number of all-black theaters were opening. A growing black audience was anxious for black merchandise. The Lincoln Motion Picture Corporation made movies for the black market until the early 1920s, turning out approximately ten films, each no longer than three reels.

The Reol Motion Picture Corporation, headed by Robert Levy, emerged after World War I. *The Call of His People* was an early project. This film, made in Irvington-on-the-Hudson, New York (the estate of the Negro millionairess Leila Walker), was an adaptation of the novel *The Man Who Would Be White* by the black

Moon Over Harlem

All-Negro Cast Films

BIG TIMERS
Stepin Fetchit in a mix-up with a chamber maid.
44 minutes $10

THE BLOOD OF JESUS
Undoubtedly the most powerful All-Negro motion picture ever produced. A great religious epic.
60 minutes $15

BROKEN STRINGS
Clarence Muse appears as a famous violinist who overcomes adversity with his son's help.
70 minutes $15

BRONZE BUCKAROO
Herbert Jeffrey and the Four Tones Another fine Western with an all-star cast.
60 minutes $15

DARK MANHATTAN
Ralph Cooper stars in this smashing underworld drama.
66 minutes $15

THE DEVIL'S DAUGHTER
Nina Mae McKinney, Hamtree Harrington A burning drama of love and hate in the tropics.
70 minutes $15

DOUBLE DEAL
Monte Hawley, Jeni Legon.
Florence (Sulumai) O'Brien
His best pal gives him a double deal.
70 minutes $15

THE EXILE
Stanley Murrell and an all-star cast.
70 minutes $15

GANG WAR
Ralph Cooper
See this machine gun thriller.
70 minutes $15

GO DOWN DEATH
Saturday sinners and Sunday saints clash in the battle of Good against Evil.
70 minutes $15

HARLEM BIG SHOT
A. B. Comethiere and Lorenzo Tucker, "the Negro Valentino."
70 minutes $15

HARLEM IS HEAVEN
Bill Robinson
A fun-fest of joy, with Eubie Blake's Orchestra.
70 minutes $15

GOD'S STEPCHILDREN
From the story "Naomi, Negress," of a baby that looks white.
70 minutes $15

IT HAPPENED IN HARLEM
The owner of the Paradise Cafe finds a new singing star at the drug store.
30 minutes $7.50

LYING LIPS
Edna Mae Harris and an all-star cast.
70 minutes $15

A page from the 1958 Ideal Pictures catalogue listing all-Negro films available for rental. Unfortunately, most of the movies made by the independents have been destroyed or remain undiscovered.

writer Aubrey Browser. Its theme—the Negro light enough to pass for white—later developed into a favorite among the independents. More often than not, these "passing" films seemed to be wish-fulfillment yearnings of their producers. But the theme revealed the preoccupation of black America at the time: how to come as close as possible to the great White American Norm. Other Reol films included *The Jazz Hound, The Burden of Race* (the best title of the lot), *Easy Money, The Spitfire, Secret Sorrow,* and *Sport of the Gods,* the last based on a work by black poet Paul Laurence Dunbar. Reol was one of the first companies to make film versions of black classics. The company also boasted of a circuit of three hundred theaters throughout sections of the South and in many of the Northern big-city ghettos. Finally, Reol titillated the black mass imagination by launching the first colored movie star! Edna Morton was billed as the "colored Mary Pickford" and was described as a "teasing brown" torrid dancer "with the grace and abandon of her race."

Whereas Reol had its "colored Mary Pickford," another black company soon boasted of its "black Sherlock Holmes." This was the title of the film with which the Chicago-based Ebony Film Corporation formally opened. The company specialized in a series of one-reel comedies, mostly parodies on popular white vehicles, as the Holmes title suggests.

According to film historian Thomas Cripps in an article in *Negro Digest*, a rash of film companies grew to supply the seven hundred or so ghetto movie houses that had sprouted up by the late 1920s. In the years to come, more than one hundred firms and corporations were founded to produce Negro films. Among them were the Foster Photoplay in Chicago; the Gate City Film Corporation in Kansas City; Constellation Films, formed in 1921 in New York; the Renaissance Company, which produced all-Negro newsreels and was headed by black actor Leigh Whipper in New York in 1922; and Dunbar Pictures and Roseland Pictures and Recording Laboratories, both based in New York in 1928 and 1929. From Jamaica, Long Island, Buddy Holman headed Paragon Pictures in 1932. The company released the films *The Dusky Village* and *Crimson Fog.*

During this period a number of whites moved in and began making all-black films for ghetto audiences. White backers organized the Famous Artists Company in 1927. Octavus Roy Cohen produced a series of all-colored shorts in the mid-1920s. Usually his films made fun of Negro lawyers and doctors by depicting them as familiar coons. Often Cohen required his black actors to go in blackface. Much later the Cohen viewpoint—depicting Negro

LEFT: Scene from Herald Pictures Incorporated's *Miracle in Harlem* (1947). The picture, a mystery melodrama, was considered a technical landmark in the history of ghetto cinema.

BELOW: Three spade detectives in *Miracle in Harlem.*

professionals as just as idiotic as the servant figures of the Holly-wood films—was to be popularized on radio's and television's "Amos 'n' Andy" series. The Cohen shorts no doubt represented the underground movement at its worst, but in some cases a few curiously valid products were made. Whites were behind the Colored Players of Philadelphia, yet this company produced two remarkable films: *Ten Nights in a Barroom* with Charles Gilpin in 1926 and *Scar of Shame* in 1929. The latter remains an effective piece of work. Slow-moving and melancholy, *Scar of Shame* tells the story of an ill-matched marriage between a black concert pianist and a poor lower-class black girl. Secretly ashamed of his wife, the young man keeps her hidden from his socially prominent middle-class mother. At the same time, the girl's derelict drunken father plans to kidnap her, in hopes of having her sing at the nightclub of one of his racketeer friends. During a confrontation between the girl (who is about to leave her husband when she learns he is embarrassed by her), the racketeer (who is about to take her off for his nightclub), and the husband (who pleads with her to stay with him), the husband accidentally shoots and disfigures the wife. He is sent to prison but later escapes. He begins life anew and falls in love with another woman, only—through circumstances beyond his control—to meet up with the wife again. She still loves him but knows she can never be his equal. Socially—despite the fact that both are black—they are of different worlds. Despondent, the wife commits suicide. Afterward the husband marries the new girl of his dreams—who is his social equal. Melodramatic but effective, *Scar of Shame* was an eloquent statement on the color caste system and the divisions that exist among black Americans. (The girl's father is very dark; so, too, is the racketeer. Almost all the other characters are fair-skinned. The girl is clearly a victim of her "dark" biological background.) This movie was possibly the finest product of the entire independent movement.

Despite the rapid growth of the new black audience, particularly between 1915 and 1923, a number of unfortunate events halted the burgeoning black industry. A flu epidemic in 1923 had a devastating effect, closing many ghetto theaters and amplifying the problem of distribution. When talkies came in, many companies lacked the capital to keep up production and to acquire the sound equipment the new era demanded. The release of the big studio productions *Hearts in Dixie* and *Hallelujah* spelled disaster for the small independents. Finally, the Depression finished off all but the sturdiest.

During the Depression, independent black films for black audiences were being made almost entirely by white moviemakers; thus, the underground movement then went into a bizarre second phase. The new films concentrated on major Hollywood genres: mystery, melodrama, boy-meets-girl love story, musical, western. White writers and directors, using pseudonyms, constructed the vehicles. In the late 1930s, producer Jed Buell filmed *Harlem on the Prairie*, touted as the first Negro western. Buell also filmed *Lucky Ghost*, which featured an eye-rolling coon hero, and a series of successful films with Mantan Moreland.

During this second phase, there were films that treated blacks sensitively, among which *The Emperor Jones* was probably the best of the lot. The Southland Pictures Corporation released Bud Pollard's *The Black King* in 1932. Filmed in Fort Lee, New Jersey, the movie centered on a back-to-Africa movement reminiscent of Marcus Garvey's endeavors. In 1937 National Pictures released *The Spirit of Youth*, dramatizing the meteoric rise of a black boxer. Joe Louis played the central character, a figure closely related to the champ himself. As might be expected, Louis's acting was wooden. Also featured in *Spirit of Youth* were Clarence Muse, Mantan Moreland, and Clarence Brooks. Afterward, in 1940, Muse was able to write and star in *Broken Strings*, technically one of the better-made features of the period. Spencer Williams, too, with white backers, wrote, directed, and co-starred in *Go Down Death* in 1944. Williams also directed *The Blood of Jesus*. Both films were serious but unsuccessful attempts to analyze the black religious tradition.

Some of the more prominent white-backed film corporations were Astor Pictures, Herald Pictures Incorporated, and Million Dollar Pictures. Astor, headed by the white Southern-born Robert M. Savini, turned out comedies such as *Tall, Tan, and Terrific* in 1946 with Mantan Moreland and *Big Timers* in 1946 with Stepin Fetchit. It also released black musicals such as *Beware*, directed by Bud Pollard in 1946 (a forty-five-minute feature starring the jazz musician Louis Jordan) and *Ebony Parade* in 1947. Two energetic brothers, Jack and Dave Goldberg, organized Herald Pictures, Incorporated. The company released shorts starring the black blues singer Mamie Smith as well as such features as *Harlem Is Heaven* with Bill Robinson and *Miracle in Harlem* in 1947 with Stepin Fetchit. The latter, a combination mystery-gangster melodrama, was considered a technical landmark in the history of the all-black film. The Goldbergs' 1938 western *Bronze Buckeroo* is another of their films that remains interesting because of its "color design." Light-skinned performers Herbert Jeffrey and Artie Young played the leads and were actually white figures. As a singing cowboy, Jeffrey went through the expected Tex Ritter–Gene Autry heroics and exploits. Jeffrey, out to find the murderer of the heroine's father, was always immaculatley dressed in tight riding clothes and fancy silver spurs and guns. At the movie's conclusion he captures the murderous culprit, and then he and his light-skinned, ever-so-polished middle-class heroine ride off into the sunset. Jeffrey's light skin classified him as a hero for ghetto audiences. Conversely, the supporting players, the comic, eye-rolling Dusty and the sinister villain, were played by the dark actors Lucius Brooks and Spencer Williams.

Million Dollar Pictures was organized by the handsome black actor Ralph Cooper and a group of white associates. The company turned out a healthy series of hits in the late 1930s and the early 1940s. One of the company's first big hits was a black gangster movie, *Dark Manhattan,* in 1937. *One Dark Night* featured Mantan Moreland in a serious role. In *Reform School* Louise Beavers undid her kerchief for one of the few times in her career. This film was so successful that Million Dollar Pictures later made a sequel to it. The company also released *Bargain with Bullets* and *Life Goes On.* Still noteworthy today is Million Dollar's *The Duke Is Tops* which starred Ralph Cooper opposite a pretty little "bronze colored gal" then making her movie debut. That gal was Lena Horne, who afterward returned periodically to star in other independent all-black productions.

From phase one to phase two, the black independents supplied ghetto theaters with an array of entertaining black products. Even when blacks could view films at white theaters, most still preferred the ghetto movie houses, where they could "give full rein to their feelings and impulses." The sociologist E. Franklin Frazier has said that it was in these ghetto theaters, some battered and broken down, others poorly heated or ventilated, that black audiences felt most comfortable because they were with their own people. In this respect, the black market cinema was a triumph of sorts. The films today might appear dated or naïve, but they were a source of pride to black America. And the independent underground black film movement did provide American film history with at least one astounding presence.

Oscar Micheaux

The one filmmaker who survived the flu epidemic, the competition from the Hollywood studios, and even the financial pinch of the Depression was Oscar Micheaux. This fiendishly aggressive young entrepreneur started his Oscar Micheaux Corporation in

1918 with short features, then produced full-length films. In 1931, when most black independents were closing up shop, he released *The Exile*, the first all-talking motion picture made by a black company. For almost thirty years, Micheaux wrote, directed, and produced thirty-four pictures. His last film, *The Betrayal*, released in 1948, was promoted as the "Greatest Negro photoplay of all time."

Mystery and myths have long surrounded the corporation and the man Micheaux. His widow, Alice B. Russell, an actress who appeared in a number of his films, lived for years in virtual seclusion in New York City, refusing to comment on her husband's life or work. Through her silence, the aura enveloping her husband merely heightened and intensified. Where Micheaux came from or how he learned anything about films remains part of the mystery. But it is certain that Micheaux began his professional career as a novelist.

In a ten-year period Oscar Micheaux manufactured ten melodramatic novels, having formed his own company to publish them. *The Homesteader, The Wind from Nowhere, Masquerade*, and *The Case of Mrs. Wingate* were some. The novels might easily have sat unread had it not been for their author's ingenuity. Micheaux well understood the mass imagination, and by catering to its wants and needs he was able to survive and become successful. His philosophy on literature later extended to his films: Learn from the masses; then teach them. And teach he did.

Once a novel was completed, Micheaux arranged aggressive promotional tours to launch it. During these tours, Micheaux traveled by car from New York City through all sections of the country, making sure to hit the black belts. Meeting with leaders of the black communities—doctors, lawyers, businessmen, and schoolteachers—as well as with black laborers, domestics, and farmers, he lectured in schools, in churches, even in homes, promoting himself and his work. Gradually he acquired a certain following and established a name for himself that quickly circulated through the black grapevine.

Indeed, so widespread had the Micheaux reputation become that soon after the formation of the Lincoln Motion Picture Company, Micheaux was approached by the Johnson brothers for the screen rights to his novel *The Homesteader*. He accepted an invitation to come West to confer on the project but traveled a roundabout route, stopping in Oklahoma and other states to promote his latest novel. During this trip, Micheaux, already fascinated by films and determined to make his own, decided to sell the rights to the novel *only* if he was able to direct the film version. When his bid was rejected, Micheaux headed east again, resolved more than ever to make movies. Taking a similar roundabout route back, he enlisted on the way the support of a group of Oklahoma farmers to whom he had previously sold his novels. Who gave what or how much is still unknown, but Oscar Micheaux rounded up enough capital to get his project off the ground. His first movie was *The Homesteader* in 1919. Soon afterward a host of others appeared: *Within Our Gates, The Brute, Symbol of the Unconquered* in 1920; *Gonzales Mystery* and *Deceit* in 1921; *The Dungeon, The Virgin of the Seminole,* and *Son of Satan* in 1922; *Jasper Landry's Will* in 1923; *Birthright* and *Body and Soul* in 1924; *The Spider's Web* in 1926; *Millionaire* in 1927; *When Men Betray* and *Easy Street* in 1928; *Wages of Sin* in 1929; *Daughter of the Congo* in 1930; *The Exile* and *Darktown Revue* in 1931; *Veiled Aristocrats, Black Magic,* and *Ten Minutes to Live* in 1932; *The Girl from Chicago* and *Ten Minutes to Kill* in 1933; *Harlem after Midnight* in 1934; *Lem Hawkin's Confession* in 1935; *Temptation* and *Underworld* in 1936; *God's Stepchildren* in 1937; *Betrayal* in 1948.

Micheaux used the same techniques in promoting and financing his films that he had used with his books. But he had a new dash and flair, befitting a motion-picture director. A hefty six-footer, given to wearing long Russian coats and extravagant wide-brimmed hats, Micheaux is said to have toured the country, stepping out of cars and into meeting halls as if "he were God about to deliver a sermon." "Why, he was so impressive and so charming," said Lorenzo Tucker, one of the most important of Micheaux's leading men, "that he could talk the shirt off your back." Just this sort of charm enabled Micheaux to persuade Southern theater owners to show his films. On his tours, Micheaux approached white Southerners and told them of the new black audience. At first they shied away, but when he spoke of the cash register, theater managers listened. It was soon arranged to have Micheaux features shown at special matinee performances held for black audiences. His movies were also sometimes shown at midnight performances for white audiences eager for black camp. Well aware of the mystique of black bars and nightclubs, he cleverly inserted into almost all his films raunchy cabaret scenes that he knew would appeal to whites.

As for his actors, Micheaux generally gathered them from black acting companies such as the Lafayette Players in New York. But he came across some of his stars under bizarre circumstances. Legend has it that Micheaux would spot a figure or note a gesture or be struck by the way the light fell across a face and would immediately sign the person up. Lorenzo Tucker said he was first

LEFT: Lorenzo Tucker, the "black Valentino."
BELOW: The "sepia Mae West," Bee Freeman, with Oscar Polk in Oscar Micheaux's gangster thriller, *Underworld* (1936).

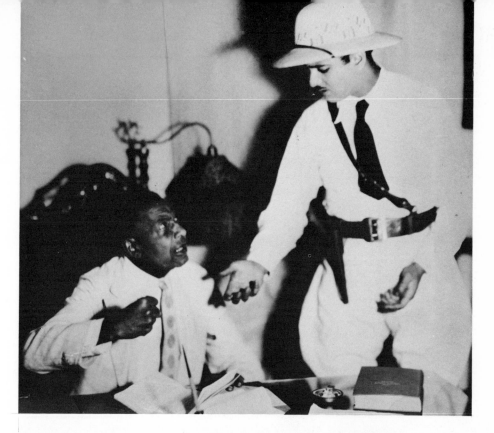

ABOVE: The stalwart good colored fellow goes to savage Africa to rescue a pretty Negro girl in Micheaux's *Daughter of the Congo* (1930).

RIGHT: One of Micheaux's favorite leading ladies, the fair-skinned Ethel Moses, seems to be losing her scarf.

spotted by Micheaux in Philadelphia. Having gone there to audition for a show, he was sitting in the lobby of the Dunbar Hotel when crafty Micheaux, whom he did not know, approached him and asked if he was an actor. "You're one of them who *thinks* they are," Micheaux added. Afterward, Tucker went to see Micheaux in New York. He was given a part, and all in all worked in some fourteen Micheaux productions.

Micheaux cast his actors on the basis of type. He modeled his stars after white Hollywood personalities and publicized them as black versions. Handsome and smooth Lorenzo Tucker was first referred to as the "black Valentino." Later when talkies came in, he was the "colored William Powell." Sexy and insolent Bee Freeman, a vamp figure, was the "sepia Mae West." Slick Chester, a character actor who played gangster roles, was the "colored Cagney." Lovely Ethel Moses was sometimes touted as the "Negro Harlow." The leads in Micheaux pictures were usually played by light-colored Negro actors, and in later years Micheaux was to be severely criticized by more militant black audiences for selecting "light-brights."

Once Micheaux had completed a film, he carried stills from it to theater managers. "Here's my black Valentino. The girls love him," he would boast. "If I can get the right backing, I'll star him in my next film, too." In this way he was often able to solicit financing for his *next* picture. He also sent his stars on personal-appearance junkets to Northern ghetto theaters. By these vigorous promotion tactics he established himself as the most successful black moviemaker of the period.

Despite clever campaigns, Micheaux was repeatedly dogged by financial problems. The little money he gathered was still far from what was needed to see a film through production, and he was compelled to work on the tightest of budgets. A picture was usually completed within six weeks. When shooting in New York, he worked with a minimum crew, all union workers. Usually he hired his cameraman for one day at a time. Often a scene was made in a single take as the camera followed an actor through a door or down a hallway. Since he was forced to shoot scenes so rapidly, he seldom was able to do retakes. Consequently, audiences often saw an actor flub his lines and then just pick up the pieces of his sentence and keep on going. Likewise, most of the action in his films centered around one set. In *God's Stepchildren*, almost every crisis occurred in front of a staircase. Filming in the home of a friend, Micheaux discovered that the staircase area offered the best lighting angles, and thus worked all his big scenes around it.

Filming on location at actual homes or offices was almost standard procedure for the Micheaux Company. It saved money and time. Micheaux might be visiting friends when he would nonchalantly pan the room, noting a particularly photogenic style of furniture or decor. He rarely had any difficulty charming his hostess into permitting him to film scenes for his next movie there.

In most cases the Micheaux feature was similar to the Hollywood product, only technically inferior. His films resembled the best B pictures of the time. Lighting and editing were usually poor, and the acting could be dreadful. Still, the standards of the Micheaux feature were far above those of the other black independents. Intertwined in all his films was the race theme. Just as Negro newspapers and magazines took major news stories and reported on them from a black angle, Micheaux took the typical Hollywood script and gave it a racial slant. *Underworld* was a gangster film with black gangsters and a black gun moll. *Daughter of the Congo* was an African adventure story with a colored cavalry officer bent on rescuing a young rich Negro girl lost in the savage tropics. *The Deceit* and *The Dungeon* were conventional melodramas. *Temptation* was a sophisticated sex drama in the De Mille vein.

There were exceptions and oddities. *Birthright* was an out-and-out race-achievement film. A young black Harvard graduate returns to his home town in Tennessee bent upon founding a colored college "to uplift the race." Naturally, he encounters opposition; but, surprisingly, it comes not only from the white community but from blacks, too, who agree with white Southerners that education ruins a Negro. In its own silly and sly way, *Birthright* made a definite plea for black unity while seriously satirizing the old-style toms. On the other hand, Micheaux's 1937 melodrama *God's Step-Children* zeroed in on the problem of the light-skinned black attempting to "pass" for white. The movie seems corny today, but better than any other of its period it captured the entire racial philosophy of the black middle classes in the 1930s and 1940s.

What remains Oscar Micheaux's greatest contribution (and something revealed explicitly in *God's Stepchildren*) is often viewed by contemporary black audiences as his severest shortcoming. That his films reflected the interests and outlooks of the black bourgeoisie will no doubt always be held against him. His films never centered on the ghetto; they seldom dealt with racial misery and decay. Instead they concentrated on the problems of "passing" or the difficulties facing "professional people." But to appreciate Micheaux's films one must understand that he was moving as far as possible away from Hollywood's jesters and servants. He wanted to give his audience something "to further the race, not hinder it." Often he sacrificed plausibility to do so. He created a fantasy world where blacks were just as affluent, just as educated, just as "cultured," just as well-mannered—in short, just as white—as white America. Though Micheaux's films—with their shameless promotion of the world of hair-straighteners and skin-lighteners—might embarrass many people today, they represent an important part of black film and social history.

Eventually, Micheaux and the few other companies that hung on into the 1940s were killed off after World War II. Ironically, Micheaux's last movie, *The Betrayal*, opened in 1948 in the downtown New York area at a white theater. It received major review attention, but the movie was received poorly and was a failure. Afterward there were no others, and Micheaux died in 1951 in relative obscurity. What ultimately killed off the efforts of even the sturdiest of the independents, however, were the problem pictures which took up racial themes. The independents could not compete with these Hollywood-made features. Soon their products were no longer distinct. But the independent black filmmakers, whose body of work deserves close attention, kept the faith for as long as they could and for a long time before it was fashionable.

The 1940s: the Entertainers, the New Negroes, and the Problem People

Lena Horne stands, pinned to a pillar, singing of love and loneliness. . . . A black G.I. lies in a hospital, yet to recover from a wartime racial incident that has left him paralyzed and amnesiac. . . . Hazel Scott, seated at a piano and spectacular in a formfitting, low-cut gown, plays Gershwin in her inimitable style. . . . A light-skinned Negro girl called Pinky returns south to a life of racial agony after having passed for white in the North. . . . Duke Ellington, Count Basie, Lionel Hampton, and Louis Armstrong perform their swing music to the delight of a war-fatigued nation. . . . A prosperous New England family confesses to their staid community—and themselves—that they are Negroes and have been passing for the last twenty years. . . . Ethel Waters and Rochester sing a lively duet and turn Cabin in the Sky *into a hit movie fantasy. . . . A proud Mississippi Negro maintains his dignity—and his manhood—as his Southern neighbors set out to lynch him.*

These were the black film people of the 1940s. The villains were forgotten. The jesters had had their day. And the servants, now that the great financial slump had ended, exchanged their mops and pails for zoot suits and sequined gowns. The new era began enthusiastically by presenting a lively set of Negro entertainers. Singers, dancers, musicians, acrobats, and clowns abounded, and the ring and roar of the cash register reflected their ability to entertain. For a time, it appeared as if the era would be exclusively theirs. But before its end the entertainers were to be virtually shoved aside as a puzzling set of people appeared and revealed that in America there was such a thing as a race problem.

For the film industry the 1930s had been consistently frivolous, spirited, and screwballish, but the next era was not so clearly defined. Its identity was split in two by a war abroad and then the emergence of one at home. Before the 1940s ended, the decade proved to be the most bizarre and certainly broke the most ground of all for blacks in American films.

THE ENTERTAINERS

Although it flowered in the early 1940s, reached its apex with two important all-black musicals, and was to be used throughout the war years as the standard procedure for handling black personalities, the Negro Entertainment Syndrome was not really new. The servants dominated the important movies of the 1930s, but the entertainment aspect was never ignored. Indeed, in almost every American movie in which a black had appeared, filmmakers had been trying to maintain the myth that Negroes were naturally rhythmic and natural-born entertainers. With their cast of darkies singing and dancing, *Hearts in Dixie* and *Hallelujah* had obviously presented blacks not only as jesters but as uninhibited entertainers too. Even as Bessie Smith cried the blues in *St. Louis Blues*, she was at heart the entertainer.

Ethel Waters sang "Am I Blue" in her first film, *On with the Show* (1929), and in an early short of the 1930s, *Rufus Jones for President*, she held a tot named Sammy Davis, Jr., on her lap as she rocked him to sleep with a lullaby. Sometimes the entertainment aspect was implied in the servants' performances, even though there was no singing or dancing. The actor seemed to express himself in a musical or rhythmic way. At other times the entertainer aspect was more explicit. Hattie McDaniel sang an extemporaneous homecoming celebration number in *The Little Colonel*. In *Judge Priest* she sang "In My Old Kentucky Home" in one episode, and in another she performed a merry work song. "I got to take down the clothes and take 'em in the house . . . yes, lawd," she crooned, glorifying her servitude in song. In the same film, Stepin Fetchit led the "Dixie" street parade. Rochester sang and danced in *Man About Town*. Bill Robinson had at least one tap-dancing number in all his films.

Often clusters of blacks would perform exaggerated revival sessions, as in *Belle of the Nineties* and *Stand Up and Cheer*. On rare occasions individual black entertainers were able to move audiences with their song. Paul Robeson's mighty voice poured over from the screen to fill theaters as he sang, and even in his great, serious movies such as *The Emperor Jones* or *Song of Freedom* there was at least one musical selection by the handsome baritone. In *Gold Diggers of 1933*, the lovely Etta Moten became the Negro girl of every Depression man's dream as she crooned the sentimentally charged "Remember My Forgotten Man."

In the mid-1930s, as the swing era reached its zenith, blacks were employed even more as musical entertainers in Hollywood films. Duke Ellington—elegantly dressed in white—not only was featured with his band in Mae West's *Belle of the Nineties* but also starred in a number of musical shorts and *The Hit Parade of 1937*. Cab Calloway, who had appeared in talkie shorts, also performed "Reefer Man" (dressed in white) in the W. C. Fields feature *International House* (1933). Before the decade ended, Calloway was cast in *The Singing Kid* (1936) with Al Jolson and in *Manhattan Merry-Go-Round* (1937). Louis Armstrong was one more talented musical performer imported to the West Coast to be featured in films. Such shorts as *Rhapsody in Black and Blue* (1932), *Bundle of Blues* (1933), *Jitterbug Party* (c. 1933), *Symphony in Black* (1935), and *Hi-De-Ho* (1935) were only a few in a long array at the beginning of the swing era that featured one or another of these three musicians.

Gradually, as the Negro performers grew in popularity, there evolved a special platform for displaying the entertainer to his best advantage. Rather than include him in the regular plot of the movie and have to stop in the middle of the serving scene while a Negro sang his song, producers introduced specific musical interludes in which the entertainer could perform unhampered by a story line. Frequently a nightclub scene was introduced into the movie so that the performer would have a natural setting. The interludes were casually inserted in the films. The central characters might be planning a big event—such as a political rally (as in *Every Day's a Holiday*, 1938), a stage show (*Belle of the Nineties*, 1934), or the launching of a swanky new café (*Pennies from*

The entertainer billed as "Aunt Jemima" livens up a revival session in *Stand Up and Cheer* (1934).

Heaven, 1936)—and would need a spectacular show-stopping routine to attract attention. Luckily Louis Armstrong or Duke Ellington or Cab Calloway was never far away! The entertainer would provide a dazzling interlude and then fade from the scene, leaving the plot to continue without him.

It was not long before the entertainers became so successful in this format that there was hardly a *Big Broadcast* or a *Broadway Melody* or a *Hit Parade* in which there was not at least one number by a black personality. Even as late as the 1950s, remnants of the entertainer syndrome were present in films such as Fritz Lang's *The Blue Gardenia* (1953) and Jean Negulesco's *A Certain Smile* (1958), in which Nat "King" Cole and Johnny Mathis sang in nightclub interludes. But in the 1940s the tradition had its heyday.

The gregariousness and energy of the entertainers were used in the 1940s to ease the tensions of a war-depressed nation. It was during the war years, more than ever before, that the great gift of the movies, that of allowing people to escape to other worlds where blues, bad times, and heartaches could be forgotten, was most consciously employed. In part, they were used to boost the nation's morale and to promote patriotism. USO troupes were entertaining the boys overseas while at home the black entertainers stated through their song and dance that America was indeed a good and decent country full of joy and unity, a place well worth fighting for. Like the servants of the 1930s, the entertainers, too, set out to delight and please without at all changing anyone's life. Yet unlike the servants, whose familiarity with the stars of the 1930s films had irritated some patrons, the entertainers syndrome was clearly a safe device. Because musical numbers were not integrated into the script, the scenes featuring the blacks could be cut from the films without spoiling them should local (or Southern) theater owners feel their audiences would object to seeing a Negro. The whole procedure now seems ridiculous and archaic; it was but another way in which motion pictures catered to audience prejudices.

Two Negro personalities who prospered and perished because of this built-in cutting procedure were among the era's big favorites as well as two of its big rebels and the 1940s' most prominent and handsome black creations. One was always strategically seated at a piano, the other conspicuously draped around a column. One was Hazel Scott, the other Lena Horne. Each entertainer—a remarkable pianist and a sultry song stylist—brought to the movies her own concept of black pride and steadfastly adhered to it.

Hazel Scott: Miss Proper Middle-Class Lady

Hazel Scott remained important in later decades mainly because she was considered so important by her own generation. In the early 1940s she was an immensely popular performer, acclaimed for her successful nightclub appearances and noted for her fiery temperament. A proud and demanding performer, who never tried to conceal either her color or her anger, Hazel Scott was one of the first black artists to refuse to appear before segregated audiences. In the end, her militancy may have put a damper on her career and brought a halt to her meteoric rise in the 1940s. But for a brief spell she was an important personality in Hollywood films.

Hazel Scott, born in 1920 in Port of Spain, Trinidad, came to the movies in 1943 after a legendary childhood. She was the daughter of two creative parents. Her father, R. Thomas Scott, was a well-known Negro scholar; her mother, Alma Long Scott, a musician and a Trinidad aristocrat. When the Scotts migrated to Harlem in 1924, their young daughter was already a child prodigy. She read at three. It was found that she had perfect pitch at three and a half. She played the piano at four. She had mastered the classics—and was improvising—at five. Afterward she studied privately with a professor from the Juilliard School of Music. At the age of twenty Hazel Scott made her professional nightclub debut at a Greenwich Village club, Café Society Downtown. She was an overnight sensation and soon became the rage of New York City. Two years later, director Gregory Ratoff filmed sequences of her at the piano to be inserted in Columbia Pictures' *Something to Shout About* (1943). When the Columbia executives viewed the sequences, they were so impressed they wrote in a part for Scott and asked her to come to Hollywood.

Hazel Scott immediately distinguished herself from the blacks who had previously worked in the movies. She had developed into a shrewd and articulate young woman and a very self-assured one as well. She had no doubts about either her talents or her superiority. And she did not hesitate to make demands. Thus she refused to play a role in a film, well aware, as she informed *Ebony* in 1944, that black women were too often cast as whores or maids. Instead she always appeared in movies as herself, seated at the piano just as she would be in a nightclub.

The Scott specialty—the aspect of her musicianship which made her a star—was a unique and daring blending of the classics and swing music. *Time* magazine described her technique:

Hazel Scott.

Where others murder the classics, Hazel Scott merely commits arson.
. . . She seems coolly determined to play legitimately, and, for a brief
while, triumphs. But gradually it becomes apparent that evil forces are
struggling within her for expression. Strange notes and rhythms creep
in, the melody is tortured with hints of boogie-woogie, until finally,
happily, Hazel Scott surrenders to her worst nature and beats the
keyboard into a rack of bones. The reverse is also true: into "Tea for
Two" may creep a few bars of Debussy's "Clair de Lune."

The Scott technique was on display in a number of 1940s products: *I Dood It* (1943), *The Heat's On* (1943), and *Broadway
Rhythm* (1944). Perhaps her typical performance—the one her
devotees called the "quintessential Scott"—was in Warner Brothers' *Rhapsody in Blue* (1945), a schmaltzy biography of George
Gershwin directed by Irving Rapper. She made an unforgettable
appearance at a Paris nightclub singing Gershwin's "The Man I
Love." Stirring as this five-minute sequence was, it was cut from
the film by Southern censors. But *Rhapsody in Blue* best revealed
Hazel Scott's ability to invest her characters with "refinement"
and "taste." She sits upright at the piano, back perfectly erect until
the "evil forces" get to her. She is immaculately gowned and
coifed. She lifts her chin in subdued condescension. Surely in 1945
it must have been marvelous for black audiences to see a black
woman so supremely confident. Yet one of the perverse ironies of
Hazel Scott's work is that younger audiences seeing her today find
her appallingly bourgeois and terribly affected. She suffered from
the great black fixation of the 1940s and 1950s: she had to *prove*
something, perhaps how good she was, for the sake of her race.
Consequently, her performances were often forced. Paradoxically, too, she frequently slipped, without even realizing it herself,
into just the stereotypes she fought to escape. During the "Jeri-
cho" sequence of Red Skelton's *I Dood It*, Scott rehearses a backstage routine with a group of Negro singers. As they perform they
work themselves into a frenzy and soon transform the rehearsal
hall into an orgiastic revival session, evoking all the religious
fanaticism typically associated with the American Negro. Although Scott glided through the sequence on the strength of her
great style, even she had battle scars. American audiences con-
gratulated themselves for appreciating this "cultured" black
woman who knew the classics so well. But in restrospect those
audiences were just like the blue-haired ladies in the 1950s who
watched Harry Belafonte in his tight pants and open shirts and left
the theater raving about the "anthropological research" that enriched his folk tunes. Either the ladies had not seen straight or they
were not saying what they really did enjoy about a Belafonte

performance. With Hazel Scott, "culture" was the cover-up explanation for what her presence actually represented. At heart the very proper, middle-class Hazel Scott was a new variation of the age-old "exotic black woman" who is a sex object rather than a sex symbol. Certainly critic James Agee realized it when he criticized Scott for exploiting her breasts and armpits. There sat Hazel Scott on display. Her style was the come-on. And even in her smile there was a lewd suggestiveness that remains intriguing. Hazel Scott, who refused to play the whore roles, may have given Hollywood even more than they had originally bargained for. Her movie career came to a halt in the mid-1940s. Afterward she appeared in only one feature, *The Night Affair*, in 1961. Still, she made herself a permanent footnote in black political history when in 1945 she became the second wife of the foremost black politician of her time, Adam Clayton Powell. The marriage ended in 1961.

Lena Horne: Black Beauty in Residence

Hazel Scott's greatest rival during the period was Lena Horne. Actually, it would be better to say that the nearest thing Lena Horne had to a rival was Hazel Scott. For Lena Horne was unquestionably the 1940s' biggest Negro attraction.

By now one of the entertainment world's legendary figures, Lena Horne was born in 1917 in a small Brooklyn hospital. Stories are still told of how the nurses excitedly carried the newborn infant through the corridors and the wards, raving about her unusual "copper color." That was but the first in a long line of such exhibits throughout Lena Horne's career, and, as she herself admitted, most of her successes came from exhibiting that extraordinary copper skin tone.

Lena Horne was already a star by the time she migrated to Hollywood in the early 1940s. She had appeared at the Cotton Club at age sixteen, had successfully performed in Lew Leslie's *Blackbirds*, and had spectacularly worked her way up to appearances at most of the smart New York night spots. *Time* and *Life* magazines had done articles on her, and everywhere she was touted as the *café au lait* Hedy Lamarr. In Hollywood, everyone waited eagerly to see what roles she would be assigned in films. NAACP Secretary Walter White took a personal interest in her career. He was convinced that Lena Horne could alter the trend of Negroes in American movies.

Lena Horne's first Hollywood film was *Panama Hattie* (1942) starring Red Skelton and Ann Sothern. In an episode directed by Vincente Minnelli, Lena Horne came on sumptuously gowned,

Lena Horne.

sang a Latin song, danced with the Berry Brothers, then exited. Brief as the appearance was, her presence had impact. Shortly thereafter MGM received a number of letters from whites asking who their new *Latin American* discovery was. At the same time, MGM was accused by some irate Negroes of attempting to pass her off as white. Lena Horne's next film, *Thousands Cheer* (1943), was what she called her first big, all-star musical, and the beginning of a long line of movies where she was pasted to a pillar to sing. "They didn't make me into a maid," she has said, "but they didn't make me into anything else either. I became a butterfly pinned to a column singing away in Movieland."

Henceforth, like Hazel Scott, Lena Horne came on as herself. She was always elegantly and sensuously dressed. She did her bit, then vanished. She was also displayed as a sex object—what could have been more suggestive than draping this exquisite black woman around a white marble column? When Lena Horne finally played her two big starring roles, the sex-object syndrome (actually nothing more than the tragic mulatto without the tragedy) was carried a step further by casting her as exotic sirens. But to everyone's surprise—and perhaps to the credit of Lena Horne—she always proved herself too much the lady to be believable as the slut. Indeed her Georgia Brown in *Cabin in the Sky* was more a tease than anything else, and her startling freshness and untainted wholesome beauty in this film and in *Stormy Weather* made her an object of contemplation rather than one of possession.

I Dood It, Swing Fever (1943), *Broadway Rhythm of 1944, Two Girls and a Sailor* (1944), *Ziegfeld Follies* (1944), *Till the Clouds Roll By* (1946), *Words and Music* (1948), and *Duchess of Idaho* (1950) were other pillar pictures. In all these films, Lena Horne looked lovely as ever, but she never seemed to be enjoying herself. She came across as aloof and remote. Yet curiously, it was this very aloofness and artistic detachment that added to her allure and mystery.

Toward the end of the 1940s, Lena Horne had trouble with her studio. In her autobiography, *Lena,* the actress reports that relations with MGM were never very friendly once she became involved with the white musician Lennie Hayton, whom she later married. Then, too, Horne became more selective about the roles she wanted to play. For a time, MGM made it difficult for her to get nightclub assignments. When the studio remade *Show Boat* in 1951, Lena Horne pleaded for the role of Julie, the mulatto. But the part went to Ava Gardner. Later in 1953 when MGM cast *Bright Road*, their first "serious" black film of the 1950s, Horne was bypassed for the lead, which went to Dorothy Dandridge. Later she lost *Carmen Jones* to the same actress. In the early 1950s, too, she was listed in Red Channels, and consequently was blacklisted from television and some radio appearances. Because of her friendship with Paul Robeson and her interest in the Council for African Affairs, she was resented by many conservatives in the entertainment industry. For a while it looked as if the legendary beauty's star were on the descent. But Lena Horne worked her way back into the mainstream, returning to the studio that had once shunned her for another pillar stint in *Meet Me in Las Vegas* (1956), then triumphing on Broadway in *Jamaica*. In the 1960s, she came back strong with concert and stage performances, then finally a movie role—as Richard Widmark's mistress in *Death of a Gunfighter* (1969). In the film she was a unique admixture of middle-class haughtiness and down-home, nitty-gritty daredevilment. Today, however, Lena Horne is still thought of as *the* black leading lady of the war era. As such, she starred in the period's two big all-black spectacles: *Cabin in the Sky* and *Stormy Weather*, both released in 1943, both taking the entertainer syndrome to its apex.

Cabin in the Sky

MGM's *Cabin in the Sky* was based on a successful Broadway show that had starred Ethel Waters, Dooley Wilson, and the Katherine Dunham dance troupe. It had long sat on MGM's shelves, since all-Negro productions were still financial risks. But once the studio finally gave the go-ahead signal to producer Arthur Freed, they went all the way, and their all-Negro musical—the first in nearly fourteen years—was launched with tremendous fanfare.

Ethel Waters was signed to repeat her role as the good wife, Petunia. Eddie Anderson was cast in the lead male role. And the studio's black-beauty-in-residence, Lena Horne, was set to portray the temptress Georgia Brown. Vincente Minnelli was assigned to direct. To it he brought his sensitive, sometimes airless style, one nonetheless appropriate for the story. A handsome sepia-tone surface was employed effectively, and the film had the studio-made period glow MGM prided itself on.

A light and ingratiating fantasy, *Cabin in the Sky* told the story of Little Joe Jackson, a harmless little colored man who enjoys shooting craps and raising a bit of cain. He is married to a decent God-fearing woman, Petunia, who worries plenty about him. But neither Joe nor Petunia knows of the battle between the general of heaven and Lucifer, Jr. of hell for the rights to Jackson's soul.

To win his victim, Lucifer, Jr., throws everything—including a winning sweepstakes ticket and the temptress Georgia Brown—Little Joe's way. But, in the end, Petunia's prayers save him, and together the two are able to walk to their cabin in the sky.

The plot, characterizations, and naïve sentiments of *Cabin in the Sky* now seem passé. No doubt the film's world was remote even in 1943. But what gave it charm was the wit and innocence the director and actors poured into it. As for the actors, it was not as important what they did as who was doing it. The film was advertised as an all-star production. For once not even the MGM publicity department could be accused of luring an audience under false pretenses. Just about everybody was in it.

Rex Ingram, in several roles, stood out as an immaculately gleaming debbil. Oscar Polk played Deacon and Fleetfoot. Butterfly McQueen was Lily, the pious I-told-you-so. Ruby Dandridge, the mother of Dorothy and a popular actress in her own right, appeared as a mammy. John "Bubbles" Sublett of the Buck and Bubbles team did a virtuoso stick-and-staircase dance sequence. Duke Ellington played his rousing and raunchy rendition of "Shine." Newcomer Kenneth Spencer, then just fresh from a serious role in *Bataan* (1943), was so impressive as heaven's general that he was touted as a new Robeson. Included also were Willie Best, Mantan Moreland, and Louis Armstrong, all at their incredible coon best. Rochester and Horne stopped the show with their "Life Is Full of Consequences." And Ethel Waters, who had temper tantrums throughout the filming, was beautifully restrained. When she sang "Happiness Is a Thing Called Joe," the fantasy world of *Cabin in the Sky* vanished and the reality of a strong, heartfelt experience entered. "The main thing," wrote one reviewer, "is that Ethel Waters is on hand, for there are songs to be sung . . . and in that respect, she is incomparable."

Impressive as the cast was, *Time* magazine commented perceptively: "Like many star-filled pictures, this one never really shows off its crowded heavens. The Negroes are apparently regarded less as artists (despite their very high potential of artistry) than as picturesque, Sambo-style entertainers." Indirectly, *Time* referred to the blackface fixation that affected many of the players. The entertainers often did sink into old-style darktown-strutter style.

In subject matter, *Cabin in the Sky* resembled earlier black films. Again Negroes were removed from the daily routine of real American life and placed in a remote idealized world. As in the past, the exotic features of black existence were played up. There was the familiar theme of the Good Colored Boy who leaves at home the Christian Good Woman to take up with the Bad Black

ABOVE: *Cabin in the Sky* (1943) and the eternal triangle in black musicals: Lena as the bad black girl; Eddie Anderson as the good colored boy; Ethel Waters as the long-suffering Christian woman.

LEFT: Lena Horne and Fats Waller in *Stormy Weather* (1943).

Girl. And once more, as in *Green Pastures,* ersatz Negro folk culture was passed off as the real thing.

Apparent as the distortions of *Cabin in the Sky* were, the picture received favorable notices. *The New York Post* commented: "It's a spirited and charming fable which Vincente Minnelli has directed with great gusto and delicious abandon." *The New York Times* said: "*Cabin in the Sky* is a beautiful entertainment . . . sparkling and completely satisfying . . . by turn an inspiring expression of a simple people's faith in the hereafter and a spicy slice of their zest for earthly pleasures." Apparently by 1943 this false image of American Negroes had been so thoroughly ingrained in the psyches of moviegoers that, had the movie been made straight, it would have been considered an unbelievable portrait of Negroes.

Stormy Weather

Those Negro entertainers who did not appear in *Cabin in the Sky* had a second chance for glory in the all-black production of *Stormy Weather* (1943). Directed by Andrew Stone and released by Twentieth Century–Fox, the film was a thinly veiled dramatization of the life of Bill Robinson, who starred in it with Lena Horne. The cast also included the jazz musician Fats Waller, the comic Flournoy Miller, the Cotton Club singer Ada Brown, the acrobatic dancing team known as the Nicholas Brothers, the anthropologically oriented Katherine Dunham dancers, and the phenomenal hi-de-ho man, Cab Calloway.

Stormy Weather was not the undiluted fantasy its predecessor had been, but it was not without its aura of unreality. The musical was a cavalcade, a revue of Negro entertainment from 1918 to 1943, seen through the eyes of its star, Robinson, and told in a series of entertainment sketches with Horne singing, Cab clowning, and Bojangles tapping. In between the musical shenanigans was the usual backstage drama in which two entertainers—Robinson and Horne—fall in love, break up, and then fall back in love again in an extravagant grand finale. The plot did not amount to much and was shamelessly illogical, but fortunately there were some good songs and some wonderfully diverting performances. Fats Waller and Ada Brown provided spicy renditions of "Ain't Misbehavin' " and "That Ain't Right." Dooley Wilson did not have a chance really to sing, but he proved thoroughly ingratiating as the quick-witted, smooth-talking Gabriel. Cab Calloway, splendidly arrayed in a zoot suit ten times too large for him and with hair falling onto his face, displayed appropriate razzmatazz. Bill Robinson, although far from being the great dancer he had been in his prime, hoofed with agility and precision in his riverboat sequence. Most spectacularly, the Nicholas Brothers, noted for their somersaults, flips, and twirls, actually spiraled beyond and around the movie, framing the film with their fierce energy. Their great style more than compensated for the movie's lack of substance. Finally, Lena Horne, so tightly controlled in her acting that she appeared to be the biggest black bourgeois phony the movies had ever seen, managed somehow to be perfect as Selina. In her important scene, when she sang the title song, "Stormy Weather," Lena Horne's beauty and melancholy brought depth to the lyrics. The song was a hit, went on to establish her reputation in Europe, and was ever afterward associated with her.

Stormy Weather may not have been the best movie of the year, but audiences of 1943 would have wanted it to be no different. The film represented wartime escapist entertainment at its peak. Curiously, in its own naïve way, it attempted also to break away from stereotyped situations and characterizations. Proudly announcing how the movie had avoided the use of the standard crapshooters and no-accounts, producer William Le Baron explained how one line of dialogue was eventually cut. When a character was asked where he got his new suit, his reply had been, "I won it in a crap game." This touch might now seem hopelessly naïve, especially because *Stormy Weather* was really no major departure from any stereotype tradition. Still, by the very nature of its all-black cast, *Stormy Weather*—and *Cabin in the Sky,* too—was an exception to the rules of 1940s moviemaking. Each showcased the entertainer syndrome at its slick best. In the South, where all-Negro films were usually shunned, these two reached the all-black movie houses, and black audiences greeted them enthusiastically. They were also shown at army camps (where Lena Horne was a great favorite) and abroad. Ironically, although neither was what Hollywood called a box-office success, each found an audience.

Bits and Pieces of Black Action

The entertainment syndrome endured a bit past the mid-1940s. Ultimately it wore itself thin and died. But before its demise, the syndrome had some sparkling and unforgettable moments when black faces appeared, parading their wares, showcasing their talents, and invigorating wartime films with some exciting black action.

The Nicholas Brothers, Harold and Fayard, captivated audiences' with their stylized acrobatics and proved themselves the

The entertainment era's greatest dancers: the Nicholas Brothers.

greatest dance team ever to work in American movies. Their first film was *Big Broadcast of 1936*. In the war era, they appeared in *Down Argentine Way* (1940), *Sun Valley Serenade* (1941), *The Great American Broadcast* (1941), *Orchestra Wives* (1942), *Carolina Blues* (1944), and Vincente Minnelli's *The Pirate* (1948). As they flipped and leap-frogged, even a casual observer could see that all dancers, including Fred Astaire, had picked up steps, routines, and distinctive rhythmic quirks from this unusual team.

Another distinctive black dance team that was to prove successful and influential was the Katherine Dunham company. The attractive founder and leader was an anthropologist and lecturer with a Ph.D. During her student days, Dunham had lived among isolated maroon people in Jamaica. She carefully analyzed their rituals and primitive dance rhythms, and later incorporated their movements into her choreography for dances done to swing music. The company was spotlighted in *Star-Spangled Rhythm* (1942) —in which Dunham and Rochester danced an extravagant tribal jitterbug. Dunham was the choreographer on several other Hollywood films, and in *Casbah* (1948) she played a dramatic role. After a brief hiatus from moviemaking, she returned in the 1950s to portray Silvana Mangano's dancing teacher in Robert Rossen's *Mambo* (1955). In the same era, her pupils Eartha Kitt and Marlon Brando made names on their own.

Still another interesting and offbeat performing group was the Hall Johnson Choir. Considered by many the greatest choral company in the country, this group had first sung its stoic spirituals in *The Green Pastures, Lost Horizon* (1937), and *Way Down South* (1939). In the 1940s they worked in *Swanee River* (1940), *Lady for a Night* (1941), and *Tales of Manhattan*.

Other 1940s products featured individual Negro performers. Duke Ellington appeared in *Reveille with Beverly* (1943). *The Hit Parade of 1943* showcased Dorothy Dandridge with Count Basie's band, while *Pillow to Post* (1945) featured a lively duet between Dandridge and Louis Armstrong. Cab Calloway worked in *Sensations of 1945*. The same year Warner Brothers released a startling all-black jazz documentary *Jammin' the Blues*. Directed by Gjon Mili, this moody, well-textured short featured Marie Bryant (singing "On the Sunny Side of the Street" in a way in which it has never been sung since), Lester Young, and a host of other prominent jazz artists. Ben Carter, one of the most rigidly stereotyped and at times most embarrassing black actors to work in American movies, played the crusty old John-Henry in the Judy Garland musical *The Harvey Girls* (1946). Otto Preminger's *Centennial Summer* (1946) featured Broadway star Avon Long in an 1876 saloon number. Pearl Bailey made her motion-picture debut singing "Tired" in *Variety Girl* (1947). Later she appeared in *Isn't It Romantic* (1948). And *New Orleans* (1947) not only gave Louis Armstrong another chance to play his horn but provided Billie Holiday with her second opportunity to work in the movies. Previously she had appeared in the obscure short *Symphony in Black*.

An independently produced, all-black, three-reel musical, *Ebony Parade* (1947), starred Count Basie, Cab Calloway, June Richmond, the Mills Brothers, and Dorothy Dandridge, then a newcomer. The picture was promoted by the black press, but it ended as a great disappointment. It was technically and artistically inferior to the Hollywood musicals. And the black community's hopes of cashing in on the entertainment vogue sweeping the country went down the drain. But there were consolations as more and more blacks appeared in major industry productions.

All in all the entertainers were having a grand old time, but the quality of their work and their films seriously declined. Their overexposure and exploitation became obvious at the end of World War II. There were literally scores of other films with Negro dancers and singers, far too many, far too random, to permit specific discussion. It is hard, too, to pin down the exact time when the entertainment syndrome had had its day and had lost its appeal to the mass audience. But in many respects, a picture which spelled the ultimate end to the syndrome was Walt Disney's *Song of the South* in 1946. It provided a sad last look at the servant syndrome, too.

Song of the South

Stylistically, *Song of the South* was a great novelty. It was a live-action spectacle with clever animated sequences interspersed throughout. But its theme, that of the pastoral Old South, was familiar terrain. It took place on an Atlanta plantation where contented servants toiled joyously in magnificently photographed Technicolor work fields. Hattie McDaniel was the family mammy. James Baskette portrayed dear old Uncle Remus, a character glowing with sunshine and joy. In his spare time, Uncle Remus sings as animated bluebirds and butterflies whiz past. And his greatest delight is telling wondrous stories to the dear little white massa. Everything's just zip-a-dee-doo-dah.

Had the film been made in 1929, audiences might have excused it as merely naïve and innocent. But in 1946 *Song of the South* was a corruptive piece of Old South propaganda put together to make money. Even the actors seemed weighted down, entrapped in the mud of the money minds who wanted none of the diversions or perversities that had distinguished the servants of the 1930s and the entertainers of the early 1940s. Instead they sought only a plasticized sense of order.

James Baskette, in the role Rex Ingram had turned down, presented Uncle Remus as the paragon of contentment and domesticity. His storytelling was skillful and slick. Yet the one virtue of the Joel Chandler Harris tales, on which the movie was based, was that, although they distorted the black plantation experience, at least they revealed the moral insights of Uncle Remus. His gift had been to transliterate the social framework of his own community into animal adventures. In the movie the animated Br'er Rabbit and Br'er Fox were a delight, an example of clever animation. But their escapades were a showcase for the Disney speciality rather than any comment on the old Negro character's philosophical outlook.

Song of the South did yield its producers a profit. But the movie was criticized by both black and white reviewers. The Manhattan Council of the National Negro Congress called on the people of Harlem to "run the picture out of the area," then out of New York State. The NAACP joined the criticism, insisting that the movie gave "an impression of an idyllic master-slave relationship which is a distortion of the fact."

Song of the South glaringly signaled the demise of the Negro as fanciful entertainer or comic servant. The towering eccentric billboard figures had at last been cut down to cheap comic book size. Neither the songs nor the servants had worked. Afterward Hollywood ignored them both.

THE NEW NEGROES: AN INTERIM

Between the entertainers and the problem people, there was an interim period in American motion pictures, during which the New Negroes came into being. The New Negroes were an outgrowth of the social spirit of the day, and the following article from *The New York Times*, February 1943, indicates just how and why they came about.

Two major studios, Metro-Goldwyn-Mayer and Twentieth Century–Fox, in producing pictures with all-Negro casts, are following the desires of Washington in making such films at this time. Decisions to produce the pictures, it is stated, followed official expression that the Administration felt that its program for increased employment of Negro citizens in certain heretofore restricted fields of industry would be helped by a general distribution of important pictures in which Negroes played a major part.

The *Times* article underlined the new attitude that began to emerge during America's troubled war years. The nation had but recently recovered from a Depression that had unearthed social ills and injustices. Now the United States was threatened by the rise of fascism in Europe. Simultaneously, the nation was reminded by vocal civil rights groups of the bigotry and racial discrimination still operating in America's industries and even in its armed forces. At this time many Americans underwent their first pangs of guilt. Many people experienced a "liberal" urge to right old wrongs. Often the old wrongs were corrected in a patronizing or condescending manner, but significant social changes did come about. Pressured by A. Philip Randolph's proposed March on Washington in 1941, President Roosevelt issued Executive Order 8802, which forbade racial and religious discrimination in war industries. Under heavy criticism, the War Department had formed the first Army Air Corps squad for Negro cadets. Later the government pushed for integration in all areas. Soon the motion-picture industry, in tune with this new spirit, offered more movie roles to blacks. The new opportunities benefited the entertainers while paving the way for the emergence of sympathetic Negro character roles in feature films. Generally, these New Negro characters were used for social statements, and they often paid homage to the democratic way of life. In fact, however, the New Negroes were not entirely "new."

Sympathetic Negro characters had appeared in American movies before the 1940s, but there had been very few. The talkie era's first such character was the black Dr. Marchand in John Ford's *Arrowsmith* (1931). Played by Clarence Brooks, Marchand stood straight and confident as he introduced himself as a graduate of Howard University's Medical School. Surely this was the movies' first *professional* black character. Marchand became a hero when he helped star Ronald Colman fight the plague sweeping through the West Indies. He offered the white man the chance to experiment with a new serum on the island's black natives. "And if you succeed," said Marchand, "it will be a privilege for *my* people to have served the world." Few viewers forgot Brooks's characterization or his extraordinary self-containment.

One year later another sympathetic Negro made a brief appearance in Mervyn LeRoy's attack on penal institutions, *I Am a Fugitive from a Chain Gang* (1932). When hero Paul Muni escaped from the inhumane chain gang, he was aided by a massive Negro prisoner. Later director LeRoy employed another sympathetic black man in *They Won't Forget* (1937). In this film a Negro janitor, Tump Redwine (Clinton Rosemond), discovers the body of a murdered white girl and is forced to undergo a brutal interrogation by the small town's racist police force. LeRoy used the janitor not only to point up racial injustices committed daily by ordinary folks but, because of the janitor's innocence, as a symbol of all the oppressed, exploited peoples of the world. In addition to *Arrowsmith* and the LeRoy features, the films of Paul Robeson throughout the 1930s had centered on "noble" black characters. But there were not enough of these sympathetic Negroes to constitute a trend. Nor were they representative of standard policy for the handling of black characters. In the early and middle 1940s, there were, in retrospect, not many more sympathetic black roles. But there were enough. And audiences noticed the intelligent, socially significant New Negroes who appeared in a number of important dramas.

The lanky and emaciated actor Leigh Whipper was cast in a trio of sympathetic New Negro roles. Lewis Milestone's *Of Mice and Men* (1940) found him as Crooks, the crippled, battered old man who aids the film's derelict heroes, George and Lennie. In William Wellman's *Ox-Bow Incident* (1943), Whipper portrayed the somber Negro preacher Sparks. The film dealt with three men wrongly accused of a crime and lynched for it by an unruly mob. Throughout the movie Whipper's weary, weathered Sparks stands up to the angry mob, pleading for mercy. In a curiously moving sequence just after the hanging, he falls on his knees singing, "You got to walk that lonesome valley. . . ." Later Whipper worked in scores of vintage 1940s movies, often portraying relatively dignified servants or farmhands. With the exception of his work as Haile Selassie in Michael Curtiz's *Mission to Moscow* (1943), none, however, was to be as successful or important as these first two early performances.

Another black actor to give an impressive performance in a serious role was newcomer Ernest Anderson. Featured with Bette Davis, George Brent, Olivia de Havilland, and Hattie McDaniel in John Huston's *In This Our Life* (1942), Anderson portrayed an intelligent young law student arrested on hit-and-run charges. He maintains his dignity despite much badgering, until the real driver —Bette Davis—admits her guilt. Anderson's performance and the film's racial theme proved the only commendable things in an otherwise dull and ordinary motion picture. "This last . . . is the one exceptional component of the film—this brief but frank allusion to racial discrimination," wrote critic Bosley Crowther. "And it is presented in a realistic manner uncommon to Hollywood by the depiction of the Negro as an educated and comprehending character. . . . Ernest Anderson is remarkably good as the Negro boy." Remarkable as Anderson was, he made only two other films, *Deep Is the Well* in 1951 and *3 for Bedroom C* in 1952.

While *In This Our Life* presented the intelligent New Negro in civilian life, the 1943 films, *Bataan, Crash Dive,* and *Sahara* spotlighted the New Negro in the military. By 1941, Benjamin O. Davis had already been appointed brigadier general, becoming the first Negro general in the history of the United States armed forces. Consequently, by 1943 the film industry had no qualms about playing up black military heroism. *Bataan* featured Kenneth Spencer as a black demolitions expert. Not only does Spencer's Wesley Eeps lead the company's prayer services for their dead captain, but he later saves a white soldier from walking into enemy gunfire. Finally he dies heroically with the other men—all white—in his patrol. Similarly, the war film *Crash Dive* featured Ben Carter as Oliver Cromwell Jones, a character modeled on Dorie Miller, the Negro messman on the USS *Arizona* who manned a machine gun during the Pearl Harbor attack and downed four enemy planes. In the British import *Sahara* Rex Ingram was a magnificent Sudanese soldier, engendering audience affection as he heroically killed a Nazi and then sacrificed his own life in the name of the free world! And the government filmed *The Negro Soldier* (1944) and *The Negro Sailor* (1945), both hymns of praise for the wonderful work the nation's "colored boys" were contributing to the war effort.

Related to the military films but with far broader implications was Alfred Hitchcock's *Lifeboat* (1944). The film was about a group of Americans holed up in a battered lifeboat after their passenger freighter is torpedoed by the Germans. All the passengers symbolize specific elements in a full democratic society. A black steward, pensive and inarticulate, represents America's vast second-class citizenry. "Hey, Charcoal," the steward is greeted by Tallulah Bankhead. But when it is revealed that "Charcoal" has saved the life of a drowning white woman and her child, he becomes "Joe" and takes on heroic dimensions. The role was played with somber dignity and intelligence by Canada Lee, the Broadway actor previously acclaimed for his work in the Orson Welles production of *Native Son.*

From the Hitchcock picture, Canada Lee moved on to other sympathetic New Negro appearances. Robert Rossen's *Body and Soul* (1947) cast him again in the heroic mold when he portrayed a boxing champion, first defeated by a white man (John Garfield), then signed on as his former opponent's trainer, and ultimately revealed (like the faithful tom servants of old) as the new champ's only friend. *The New York Times* in reviewing the film said:

> It is Canada Lee who brings to focus the horrible pathos of the cruelly exploited prize-fighter. As a Negro ex-champion who is meanly shoved aside, until one night he finally dies slugging in a deserted ring, he shows through great dignity and reticence the full measure of his inarticulate scorn for the greed of shrewder men who have enslaved him, sapped his strength, and then tossed him out to die. The inclusion of this portrait is one of the finer things in the film.

Later in his career, Canada Lee appeared in *Lost Boundaries* (1949) and most memorably in *Cry, the Beloved Country* (1952). He remains one of those strange cinematic character presences who brought quiet strength and sensitivity to all their roles.

Possibly the most popular of the New Negroes was a shy little colored man who sat at a piano and sang "As Time Goes By" in Michael Curtiz's *Casablanca* (1942). The song became a national anthem for lovers and loners; the movie a box-office favorite, and the character Sam a byword for the friendly, congenial type of Negro everyone still cherished. Slick and smooth as actor Dooley Wilson was, his Sam was little more than an updated combination of faithful servant and entertainer. "Play it, Sam," Humphrey Bogart says, and Wilson goes into action. But the easygoing camaraderie between him and the film's star was without the normal racial barriers. It struck very close at what can only be termed the movies' *huckfinn fixation*.

The essential scenario for the exploration of the huckfinn fixation is quite simple: A good white man opposes the corruption and pretenses of the dominant white culture. In rejecting society, he (like Huck Finn) takes up with an outcast. The other man (like Nigger Jim) is a trusty black who never competes with the white man and who serves as a reliable ego padder. Traditionally, darkness and mystery have been attached to the American Negro, and it appears as if the white hero grows in stature from his association with the dusty black. Blacks seem to possess the soul the white man searches for. The huckfinn fixation, although treated superficially, had already run through the two film versions of the Twain classic in 1931 and 1939 (as it was to appear later—superficially again—in the 1960 version). It had popped up even in a typical 1930s product such as *Judge Priest*. Obviously, star Will Rogers could relax with servant Stepin Fetchit because the latter was not caught up in any phony social etiquette.

In *Casablanca* Bogart was the cynical, soured rebel, and it was appropriate that in rebelling against society's trumped-up phoniness, he should enjoy the friendship of a black man, someone equally undermined by the system. As the black man plays "As Time Goes By," Bogey is consumed by a sentimental longing for the past when the world seemed good and pure.

The huckfinn fixation perhaps represents the white liberal American's dream of lost innocence and freedom. To fit into society, one loses the "spirituality" the Negro is believed to thrive on. Regardless of its real meaning, the fixation made its way into other 1940s films. The screen adaptation of black novelist Frank Yerby's *Foxes of Harrow* (1947) starred Rex Harrison as a reckless, daredevil plantation owner who was most comfortable with his gambling cronies or his black slave, Achille (portrayed by former football star Kenny Washington). So close is Harrison to Achille that he wants the black man's son to become the personal manservant to his child. In a curiously bitter scene, Achille's wife, an African princess, drowns herself rather than live to see her child enslaved. In *Moonrise* (1948), Dane Clark as a young, restless community outcast, Danny, meets in the woods an old colored man, Mose (Rex Ingram). The two hunt, fish, hike, and live together until Mose discovers that Danny has killed a rich banker's son. He advises the white boy to go back and fight his outcast role. With such advice, Mose attempts giving the boy his manhood.

The huckfinn fixation, closely aligned to the master-servant syndrome yet with far deeper connotations, was represented in the 1950s with its great moments with Ethel Waters and Julie Harris in *The Member of the Wedding* (1952), with Sidney Poitier and John Cassavetes in *Edge of the City* (1957), with Poitier and Rock Hudson in *Something of Value* (1957), with Frank Sinatra and Sammy Davis, Jr., in occasional scenes from their clan pictures. In the 1960s, the tradition was upheld by Poitier and Rod Steiger in *In the Heat of the Night* (1967) and by Arlo Guthrie and his black college friend in *Alice's Restaurant* (1969). Though the fixation was to attain its full complexity in these later films and was eventually to be incorporated into standard television social dramas (such as the "Mod Squad" series), it was first innocently played with in 1942 in *Casablanca.*

Curiously, the most eloquent of the New Negro sentiment appeared not in an American movie but in Roberto Rossellini's Italian film *Paisan* (1948). In one episode of the film a black G.I. and an Italian shoeshine boy meet on the streets of Naples during World War II. The lonely G.I. takes to the child, but the boy hopes merely to steal the soldier's shoes once he sleeps. As the two talk, the weary G.I. reminisces, boasting of life back home. But when he looks into little Francisco's eyes, the black man is shamed and admits his home is no more than a dirty shack in Mississippi. As he speaks, the similarities between bombed-out Italy and the poverty-stricken South become apparent, and both the shoeshine boy and the G.I. are revealed as victims of a war and a system. "Don't go to sleep," the child warns his new friend, "for I will have to steal your combat shoes." In spite of the warning, the G.I. sleeps, and Francisco takes the shoes. The next day the soldier finds the child at his home place. But the black man is saddened by the horrible hopeless squalor and the boy's crippled grandfather. "Those are not my shoes," he says and drives off.

Paisan was followed by *The Quiet One* (1948), which had a commentary written by James Agee. It was a sensitive study of a lonely Negro boy, withdrawn and cynical, who is brought back through compassion and understanding. In a glowing review of the film, *The New York Times* wrote:

> Out of the tortured experiences of a 10-year-old Harlem Negro boy, cruelly rejected by his loved ones, . . . a new group of local filmmakers has fashioned a genuine masterpiece. His [director Sidney Meyers] handling of Donald Thompson, the Harlem youngster who plays the principal role, is a brilliant piece of directing, for he has got from this normal lad such attitudes and expressions as haunt the memory. In the shadows that drift across his countenance and in the very manner of his walk are mirrored the confusion and rebellion, the hope and relief of a tortured child.

Donald Thompson's fine performance remains one of the first intelligent treatments of the black child in American movies, a far cry from the pickaninny absurdities of Farina. A few years later another sensitive depiction of a black child was revealed in the work of young Philip Hepburn in *Bright Road* (1953), and in 1972 Kevin and Eric Hooks were to give effectively moving portrayals in *Sounder.* Today *Paisan* and *The Quiet One* stand out as perhaps the definitive statements on the New Negro. Others appeared in movies such as *The Lost Weekend* (1945), *Till the End of Time* (1946), and *Any Number Can Play* (1949), but the Agee and Rossellini vehicles sensitively characterized their black heroes without stress or strain.

The interim provided by the New Negroes was neither golden nor necessarily illuminating. Yet it was not without significance. For the New Negro characters demonstrated that blacks could be handled sympathetically without relying on the old types. Black characters could be made amusing or interesting without set "nigger" traits. Finally, it was apparent that this new kind of handling could contribute to the quality of serious and successful motion pictures. The New Negroes served as warm-up exercises, paving the way for the Negro as Leading Character, for the Negro Problem as Motion Picture Theme. After World War II, however, the New Negroes were not strong enough to meet the new audience demands.

THE PROBLEM PEOPLE

The postwar movie audience of the late 1940s was prosperous but not very relaxed. World War II had further complicated American lives, bringing into sharp relief basic political and social issues. For audiences that still had the terrorism of Hitler and Mussolini fresh on their minds, the old-time war call for solidarity was not muffled or toned down but heightened. Indeed, the 1930s concept of "equitable treatment for all" was finally extended so that the *all* included America's black people, too.

In films, the postwar audience demanded recognizable problems and issues, particularly on racial matters. The random self-indulgence and idealization of the old all-black spectacles now seemed remote. They were too diverting, too entertaining, too reflective of a corruptly innocent time when Hollywood had no conscience. American moviegoers now wanted to be pounded over their heads with facts, with guts, with realism. And they were willing to accept controversy. Thus the tone of American movies underwent its first stage of radical change.

In 1947, while answering the demand for facts and guts, Hollywood simultaneously satisfied the masochistic cravings of the postwar audience with the release of *Crossfire* and *Gentleman's Agreement.* Each focused on a subject that had once been taboo: racial discrimination. Both condemned anti-Semitism in America. Audiences and critics responded to the films favorably and indicated they were ready for more. The movies could go a step farther. And so finally by 1949, the audience expectations and demands, their quirks, their insecurities, and their guilt feelings created more surely than anything else a cycle of penetrating motion pictures that investigated the race problem in America. The Negroes of the films had their color stamped indelibly upon them, and they suffered, struggled, bled, yet endured. But as Hollywood had it, they always won their battles.

Home of the Brave and the Postwar Good Sensitive Negro

Home of the Brave (1949) launched the cycle of problem pictures. Independently produced by a thirty-five-year-old fledgling moviemaker, Stanley Kramer, directed by Mark Robson, and written by Carl Foreman, the picture went against all the accepted theories of Hollywood moviemaking. It was made on a low budget. It featured Frank Lovejoy, Steve Brodie, Lloyd Bridges, Jeff Corey, and newcomer James Edwards, none big-name stars. The subject matter was offbeat. As a successful Broadway play, Arthur Laurents' *Home of the Brave* had had an anti-Semitic theme. Its hero was a young Jewish soldier. Producer Kramer shrewdly substituted a Negro character for the Jewish protagonist. At the time a few major studios had already announced plans for "Negro tolerance" projects, but their properties were far from completion. Well aware that the first Negro tolerance picture released would garner the most publicity and reap the largest profits, Kramer swore his crew and cast to secrecy. His movie was filmed under the title *High Noon* (later used for another Kramer hit). When it opened, it took the entire film industry and the country by surprise.

Home of the Brave described, in a series of flashbacks, the emotional breakdown of a young Negro private, Peter Moss. As he undergoes examination by a sympathetic medical captain, Moss unravels his tale, revealing a number of racial incidents he endured while on a special five-man mission to a Japanese-held island. Repeatedly excluded and harassed, Moss had cracked up under the pressure. In the psychiatric sessions, it is revealed, however, that it was not the island experience alone that led to the soldier's disintegration. It is the American way of racism that has always forced the Mosses of the world "outside the human race."

"I told you I heard something in the middle of the night once," Moss tells the psychiatrist. "Some drunk across the hall from my aunt's yelling: 'Throw out the dirty niggers!' That was us. But I just turned over and went back to sleep. I was used to it by then. Sure I was ten. That's old for a pickaninny." Later he adds, "I learned that if you're colored, you stink. You're not like other people. You're—you're alone. You're something strange, different. . . . Well, you make us different, you rats."

Home of the Brave concluded on a conciliatory note. As Moss is about to leave the military hospital after his recovery, the easygoing white soldier Mingo approaches him. The war now over, Mingo plans to open a bar, and he asks Moss to become a partner. Genuinely touched, the Negro accepts, free of the past and equipped with a new philosophy for the future. "I am different," he says. "We all are. But underneath we're the same."

Today *Home of the Brave*'s optimistic ending may strike many as "rigged" and false. The ending lessens the impact of much that preceded it. Mingo's gesture is "noble" enough, yet it is believable only in the movies. There is even a tinge of white patronage because it is the white man offering his hand to the black man. No doubt *Home of the Brave* affected audiences in 1949 in the same way. But there was something decent about its optimism. No matter how much one rejects it intellectually (and the times would bear out this rejection), the bright ending had the type of fairy-tale idealism movie patrons thrived on. Audiences wanted to believe racial problems could be abolished if black and white simply took one another's hands, and here the movies reaffirmed that naïve wish. Thus it was no great surprise that patrons left the picture content that everything would work out. Even for black audiences, comparing the film's dialogue to Louise Beavers' "Please don't send me away, Miss Bee," Moss's words must have sounded like a black declaration of independence. In the end, *Home of the Brave* justified itself by meeting the requirements of its age.

The film was a solid commercial and critical success and was hailed as a Hollywood breakthrough in the presentation of racial discrimination as a central theme. *Time* magazine wrote: "[It] . . . has novelty, emotional wallop, and excitement that comes from wrestling with a real problem, rather than fencing with a cooked-up plot. . . . Even when it fumbles the statement of its message, the movie retains a sort of rough-and-ready strength." Surprisingly, even Southern movie critics liked the picture. *The Dallas Morning News* called it "brilliant," commenting that it "abashes the white man for both his habit of Negro prejudice and worse, his unconscious tactlessness." "Let no smug section of the nation think [the Negro Problem] is exclusively the South's baby," warned *The Memphis Commercial Appeal* in its review. "It belongs to us all." The movie played to full houses in major Southern cities such as Memphis, New Orleans, Chattanooga, Fort Worth, and Dallas.

Those connected with the film reaped the benefits. Producer Stanley Kramer became the high priest of the message-problem pictures of the 1950s and 1960s, spearheading with such films as *The Defiant Ones* (1958), *Pressure Point* (1962), and *Guess Who's Coming to Dinner* (1967). Mark Robson directed a series of successful melodramas. Carl Foreman emerged as a top scenarist. Black actor James Edwards went on to other starring roles. It looked as if he would become *the* black leading man in American movies of the 1950s. Unfortunately, Edwards' career was cut short just as it was beginning to flourish. James Edwards now remains one of those misplaced personages of the movies. He was a fine actor, but he was ahead of his time.

Born in Muncie, Indiana, Edwards studied speech and drama at Indiana and Northwestern universities, and served as a first lieutenant during World War II. He appeared in several Broadway productions before winning recognition as the hero of *Deep Are the Roots*, a long-running drama about a Southern household during the war years. He migrated to Hollywood and landed a role as a butler in *Manhandled* in 1944. There followed much later an important supporting role as the sensitive black prize fighter in Robert Wise's *The Set-Up* (1949). After *Home of the Brave*, he was cast in *The Steel Helmet* (1950) as a patriotic black American soldier, quick to defend America rationally and to put down the "Commies." In *Lights Out* (1952) he appeared as a blind soldier befriending a bigoted blind white military man. When the white soldier learns his friend is a black man, he is guilt-ridden and frustrated. All the stupid, foolish years in which he has accepted and promoted racial discrimination are suddenly brought into focus. At the end of the film, the white man has learned the meaning of tolerance and humanity from his black friend.

In these early films, Edwards presented a heightened portrait of the postwar American Negro. He is sensitive. He is intelligent. He is articulate. He is innately good. At times, he seems little more than a dressed-up tom. But as a prerogative reserved only for the postwar freed black man, he is capable of choosing to fight his white opponents (although often he chooses not to). Most important, though, Edwards' postwar Negro was the screen's first black hero (with the possible exception of Robeson) governed by a code of fundamental decency, courage, and compassion. Throughout his films, he stands tall and detached. He can easily pounce on his white friend, but his code of decency prohibits this move. Instead he waits patiently, ready to aid the white man when the time comes. Always he lies in wait for acceptance. The code first displayed by Edwards as well as his reasoned goodness and his middle-class qualities were later lifted almost intact to establish the Sidney Poitier star personality in the 1950s.

Impressive as Edwards' early performances were, he did not develop into a star. In the ambivalent late 1940s and the apathetic early 1950s, racial tolerance as a theme was fashionable but Negro actors were not. A nervousness and sexual ambiguity alienated him from white movie audiences. Sexy black men were never very popular in American motion pictures. In his features, Edwards was rendered sexless because he seldom had a love interest. Yet his sexuality was still evident—even in the way he walked. He smiled, not in the boyish or romantic way of a Sidney Poitier, but in a tentative and lewdly suggestive manner. Always his eyes looked straight ahead, burning with passion and resentment. His nerves seemed to be as taut and tense as his muscles. He was attractive and aggressive, and there was a distinctive nervous charge in his voice. He seemed dangerous. The very first of the Good Sensitive Postwar Negroes scared his public, and for that reason he was denied movie stardom.

Edwards' career underwent its great decline in the mid-1950s. Like Paul Robeson, he had refused to testify before the House Un-American Activities Committee, and his career suffered because of it. In 1952, he lost an important role in *Red Ball Express* to the up-and-coming—and safe—Sidney Poitier. His subsequent appearances in *The Member of the Wedding, The Caine Mutiny* (1954), *Innocents in Paris* (1955), *The Phoenix City Story* (1955), *The Killing* (1956), *Battle Hymn* (1957), *Men in War* (1957), *African Manhunt* (1957), *Fraulein* (1958), *Tarzan's Fight for Life* (1958), *Pork Chop Hill* (1959), *The Manchurian Candidate* (1962), and *The Sandpiper* (1965) were decent supporting roles but seldom significant ones. His last appearance before his death in 1970 in *Patton* was entirely forgettable.

Lost Boundaries' Tragic Mulattoes

Louis de Rochemont's *Lost Boundaries* (1949) was the second of the problem pictures. Alfred L. Werker directed the film, which was based on a *Reader's Digest* true account of a New England Negro family that had lived as whites for twenty years. Producer de Rochemont took his crew and his cast of unknowns to Portsmouth, New Hampshire, where he shot on location, using community residents in small roles and bringing his film in on a shoestring budget of $600,000. Thus *Lost Boundaries* was made to seem starkly realistic with almost a documentary flavor.

The film struck at the deep-rooted prejudice of the American small town. When Scott Carter, a handsome light-skinned Negro doctor, is unable to find employment at Negro hospitals (where he is rejected because he looks too white) or white hospitals (where he is rejected because he admits to being a Negro), he moves with his fair-skinned wife to a staid New England community. There they merely stop telling people what they are. The Carters win the friendship and respect of their neighbors, quietly rear a son and daughter, and participate actively in community affairs. The years pass without incident. But ultimately Carter's great patriotism proves to be his undoing. He enlists in the Navy as a commissioned officer and is warmly accepted until a naval investigation uncovers his Negro heritage. "Failure to meet physical qualifications," is the Navy's explanation for his rejection. Suddenly, the past years are brought into the present. The Carters are compelled to "confess." "Why didn't you tell me I was Negro!" cries son Howie upon hearing the news. Thereafter he leaves home to search for his "cultural roots" on the streets of Harlem. Daughter Shelly remains confused. As for the good, principled people of the community, once they learn the awful truth they turn against their former friends. Not until a special sermon on tolerance is delivered by the town's white minister do the townspeople, shamefaced and guilt-ridden, extend their hands again to their friends.

Dramatically, *Lost Boundaries* was without the didacticism of *Home of the Brave*, and its events flowed more naturally. Its sequence of the troubled Howie wandering through a circus-style Harlem was melodramatic and overdone, but its quiet moments more than compensated. "They've been saying your folks are Negroes," says Shelly's boy friend, pleading as he speaks that she will tell him the rumors are untrue. "Did they say anything *bad* about us?" she asks in one of the film's finest moments.

Lost Boundaries received glowing reviews. *Time* called it "not only a first-class social document, but also a profoundly moving film." Bosley Crowther commented in *The New York Times:* "One of the many bitter aspects of racism in our land—the in-between isolation of the Negro who tries to 'pass' as white—is exposed with extraordinary courage, understanding and dramatic power in the new film titled 'Lost Boundaries.' . . . Viewed as emotional entertainment, as social enlightenment or both, it is one of the most effective pictures that we are likely to have this year." In the South, reactions were diverse and divided. Although banned in Atlanta ("Contrary to the public good," said its movie censor), the picture met with success in Norfolk, Miami, Richmond, Houston, Louisville, Raleigh, San Antonio, and some twenty-five smaller Southern towns.

Despite its success, *Lost Boundaries* was weakened by its compromises. In 1949, the Carter family appeared to be a new "relevant" fixture on the screen. But actually its characters were the old-time tragic mulattoes. By dealing with such characters and such a remote problem as "passing," the movie, like most Hollywood productions, had created a dream situation, an isolated fan-

Mel Ferrer and Beatrice Pearson as the tragic, tragic mulattoes who marry and then leave the black community to pass for white in *Lost Boundaries* (1949).

tasy world no more real than those of the all-black musicals. And the film further compromised itself by casting white actors in the leading roles of the suffering blacks. Here it fell in line with a long list of productions which cast whites in important Negro roles to insure audience identification and box-office success. The film versions of *Show Boat* in 1929 and 1936 had featured white actresses as the doomed mulatto Julie. (The 1951 version was to repeat the casting procedure; so, too, did the 1959 version of *Imitation of Life*, in which a Jewish actress portrayed the rebellious black daughter.) Likewise all the films about *Cleopatra* from Theda Bara's to Claudette Colbert's to Vivien Leigh's, right up to Elizabeth Taylor's in 1963, used lily-white actresses to portray the "dark queen of the Nile." *Lost Boundaries* was cast with whites for the same reasons its predecessors were. The idea underlying the deluxe gloss was how awful it is that these good white people should have their lives ruined simply because of Negro blood. White audiences could readily extend their sympathy to these fair-skinned blacks because, as played by Mel Ferrer and Beatrice Pearson, they were literally no different from themselves. The audience could not fail to spot the intolerance heaped upon them.

Lost Boundaries' final compromise was that while it quickly pointed up the hypocrisy of the white townspeople, it failed to hit at them with a wallop. The whites' viciousness was understated at a time when it should have been emphatic. The light-skinned Negroes appeared to have wronged the town by keeping such a secret, and the guilt was placed on their shoulders, making the blacks the tragic characters. Curiously, this and the other compromises of *Lost Boundaries* were repeated in the next problem picture.

Pinky's Tragic Mulatto and Its Strong Black Woman

In 1949 Twentieth Century–Fox contributed *Pinky* to the cycle of problem pictures. Produced by Darryl F. Zanuck and directed by Elia Kazan, it starred Jeanne Crain, Ethel Waters, and Ethel Barrymore with William Lundigan, Frederick O'Neal, and Nina Mae McKinney in supporting roles. The feature was a slickly put together product. Its clearly defined black and white photography, its carefully composed scenes and its theatrical sets aided director Kazan in fashioning an insulated unreal world. The movie shifted the emphasis to an area more closely associated with racial hostilities: the Deep South. It explored other new turf, too. Not only was *Pinky* the first feature to deal with an interracial romance, but in the grandiose performance of Ethel Waters it presented the archetypal strong-black-woman character.

The film's plot is straightforward. A fair-skinned Negro nurse, Pinky, revisits the South after having passed for white in the North. She is depressed by the life she returns to—the squalor of her home, the daily threats and insults. She is attacked by a knife-carrying black woman. Later she is arrested by the police, who have come to her defense only to turn against her once they learn she is not white. She is followed and chased by two drunken thugs. "She's the whitest dinge I ever seen," one says, laughing. Pinky plans to return north to her white fiancé and her life as a white woman in a free society. But her hard-working grandmother saddles her with an obligation to care for an old aristocratic white woman, Miss Em. The woman is now impoverished and near death, but her pride and arrogance epitomize to Pinky the South's racist code. The twist of the story is that while caring for this crusty old woman (Ethel Barrymore), the mulatto attains maturity and stature. "Nobody deserves respect as long as she pretends she's something she isn't," the woman tells her. And Pinky realizes that if she returns north and passes for white—something she isn't—she can never have self-respect. When Miss Em dies, leaving her decaying mansion to Pinky, the girl fights to keep the property. She painfully comes to understand responsibility and justice. "Tom, you can change your name," Pinky tells her white fiancé after winning her property suit. "I wonder if you can change what you are. . . . I'm a Negro. I can't forget it. I can't deny it. . . . You can't love without pride." She ends her romance, opting to remain in the South and work with her people. In the movie's final and memorable shot, Pinky stands before Miss Em's mansion, which is now converted into a black nursing clinic. She is content because she has pride in her race. Yet Pinky is aware that she has sacrificed personal happiness. And so, as is true of all tragic mulattoes, Pinky ends as a wiser woman but one not completely fulfilled.

As a motion picture *Pinky* also ended not completely fulfilled. The reviews were conflicting. *Newsweek* glowed: "Elia Kazan . . . here does an admirable job of blending a courageous approach to racism and the strictly emotional factors of Pinky's personal history." But *The Daily Worker*, noting that Pinky "finds herself" through the aid of Miss Em, called the film a deception which insisted that "the solution to its [Negro] problems will come from the white ruling class and that they will be rewarded individually by the measure of simple goodness, not by organization or political struggle."

The Daily Worker pointed up but one of the compromises that diluted *Pinky*'s power. There were others. In *Quality*, the novel by Cid Ricketts Sumner on which it was based, Pinky won her courtroom case, but the Ku Klux Klan burned down Miss Em's house in retaliation. That ending was far more honest than the optimistic everything's-gonna-work-out-fine tone at the film's end, when a group of cute ebony nurses are seen laughing in the converted hospital.

But the film's greatest compromise was casting white actress Jeanne Crain in the lead role. More than any other film in which a white has played a black role, *Pinky* typified the movie industry's methods of grasping audience identification. In a number of scenes, Ethel Waters as Granny, the typical Negro domestic, is shown washing, ironing, or performing other menial chores. No one expected any more from her, and audiences were neither surprised nor outraged by her behavior. But when Jeanne Crain's Pinky was forced to take in washing to earn money for her lawyer's fees—as she stood over a scrubbing board with the carefully placed studio sweat rolling off her perfect porcelain-white face—white audiences were automatically shocked and manipulated so that they sympathized with this lovely white girl compelled to work like a "nigger." To Kazan's credit, that scene came across as intended, and by the time Jeanne Crain entered the courtroom, movie patrons of 1949 felt she had been through enough to earn winning the case. Likewise the insults and threats she underwent seemed twice as menacing because they were committed against a white actress. And by the same token, her "interracial" romance with actor William Lundigan upset no one because, in actuality, it was no such thing at all. (Still the pair were not permitted to marry.) Jeanne Crain as Pinky made a far more successful movie but a far less honest one, too.

Compromises aside, where *Pinky* shone through with brilliance was in Ethel Waters' moving portrayal of Granny. She is an old laundress, known to the townspeople as Aunt Dicey, who cannot even read. But she burns with humanity. In the Philip Dunne–Dudley Nichols screenplay the character was a combination tom and mammy, a further elaboration on Aunt Delilah of *Imitation of Life*. But Ethel Waters' great gift as an actress was that regardless of the script or character or the contrivance of the movie itself, she exhibited ambiguities and contradictions that seemed to come from her own personal experience. Unlike previous screen mammies, she was never emotionally one-sided, neither all Christian resignation (like Louise Beavers) nor all rage and indignation (like Hattie McDaniel). In *Pinky*, her great humanity bursts through as she is viewed washing the filth from the clothes of the town's whites in order to send money north to her granddaughter. Her

RIGHT: Black shoulders were made to cry on. So Jeanne Crain learns from Ethel Waters in *Pinky* (1949).

BELOW: *Intruder in the Dust* (1949) starred Juano Hernandez as the defiant, aristocratic Lucas Beauchamp. Hernandez' performance remains one of the strongest black male portraits in film history. At right, David Brian.

humanity is further revealed as the single member of the town whose sympathy extends to the rich cranky white lady up in the Big House.

As she appears in the courtroom wearing an absurd black hat or as she sits on her rocker on the broken-down porch describing her feelings for the dead woman and expressing her gratitude for the clothes and shoes Miss Em has left her, Ethel Waters' character is not the old tom trying to ingratiate in order to save his position. Rather she is a strong woman concerned with all humanity and dedicated to her own sense of truth and loyalty. Yet her character is complex enough to reveal another side of her personality: she can explode and revel in righteous anger. When she learns that her granddaughter has passed for white, she commands that the girl fall, fall, fall to her knees and repent. "That's a sin before God, and you know it. . . . Denying yourself like Peter denied Jesus. Get down. Ask the Lord to forgive you." Later she adds, "I worked hard to give you an education. If they done educated the heart out of you, then all I did was wrong. Now go up there to Miss Em or I'm going to whip the living daylights out of you!" To her credit as a remarkable actress, Ethel Waters played the scene as no other black actress could have done without ever seeming ludicrous, her voice so large and her strength so apparent that no one dared laugh at the lines. And thus she lifted her character from the pages of the script and transformed Granny into a heroic figure. In *Pinky* she made the archetypal strong black woman a figure that transcended the stereotype of her role. So forceful was her presentation that she won an Academy Award nomination for best supporting actress of 1949. Her performance spelled the death of the one-sided mammy figure.

Intruder in the Dust and the Defiantly Proud Black Man

MGM brought a close to the 1940s' cycle of problem pictures in 1949 with Clarence Brown's adaptation of William Faulkner's *Intruder in the Dust.* Considered by many the finest of the quartet of problem dramas, the movie remains one of the more faithful and intelligent of the Faulkner screen adaptations. It also introduced actor Juano Hernandez, whose performance and extraordinary presence still rank above that of almost any other black actor to appear in an American movie.

Like the first two problem pictures, *Intruder in the Dust* strove for realistic effects. Director Brown made his film without the big-studio machinery to which he was accustomed, taking his cast and crew from Hollywood to Oxford, Mississippi, to shoot most of his movie. More than five hundred townspeople of Oxford, including some hundred and twenty blacks, gladly worked as extras. Brown's great pains paid off, for his film captured not only the character of one massively impressive black man but the character —savage and venomous—inherent in one "typical" small American town.

Intruder in the Dust was many things—a melodrama, a detective story, a murder mystery, a condemnation of mob rule. But mainly it was a subtle study of a fearless and proud black man, Lucas Beauchamp. When he is accused of killing a white man, the tensions of his Southern townspeople mount. "He won't need a lawyer. He won't even need an undertaker," an angry mob shouts. But Lucas Beauchamp is on trial for more than murder. For Beauchamp, confident, aristocratic, and "insufferable," is a black man who—through his independence—has dared to act like a white, and the townsmen want him cut down to size. Beauchamp turns to a teen-age white boy, Chick. The summer before, during a hunting trip, Chick was saved from drowning by the black man, who literally lifted him from the sea, taking the boy to his home, offering him food and shelter. Because of the rigid racial-social codes of the South, the boy feels compelled to repay Lucas for the rescue. But the man refuses payment for an act of human compassion. Afterward the boy feels guilty. He owes something to a nigger. Now Lucas enlists Chick's aid, acting on an old Negro saying: If you want anything "out of the ordinary" accomplished, set women and children to working on it. Ultimately it is through Chick (the child) and an old spinster schoolteacher (the woman) that the out of the ordinary is accomplished, and Beauchamp is found innocent of the crime.

But most startling is the fact that not once does the black man bend. Not once does he stoop to prove he is as good as a white man. That's something only a man who does think he is inferior would do. And Lucas Beauchamp has no doubts about his equality. When it is revealed that Beauchamp has known the identity of the real murderer but kept it secret throughout his prison ordeal, he is asked by the white lawyer, "Why didn't you tell the truth when you were in jail?" "Would you have believed me?" Beauchamp replies bitterly. And the lawyer (as well as the townspeople) realizes, "He wasn't in trouble. *We* were in trouble."

Tough-minded and complex, *Intruder in the Dust* unearthed, among a number of things, a somber piece of Americana: a black man on trial has little chance for justice in our country, said the film, more than twenty years before such statements were fashionable. For the most part, the movie received excellent notices. Yet because it appeared at the end of the problem picture cycle it was overlooked and did not fare as well commercially as its predecessors. But *Intruder in the Dust* did bring well-deserved attention to its star, Juano Hernandez. Because of it he remains one of the great black male movie symbols. He might also qualify as another of our great black victims.

Hernandez came to the screen after a varied and sometimes hazardous career as a circus performer, vaudeville trouper, and radio actor. Born in 1901, he was the son of a Puerto Rican seaman. Self-educated and always self-assured, he spent a childhood in Brazil singing and performing acrobatics on the streets to raise pennies for food. Later he worked in a Cuban circus as a tumbler, strong man, acrobat, singer, and boxer. In America, he appeared in vaudeville. He worked in the chorus of the 1927 stage production of *Show Boat*, had engagements at the Cotton Club, and then scored in *Blackbirds*. But his biggest success came on radio, where for many years he was the only Negro actor consistently used for all kinds of roles. He portrayed everything from Mandrake the Magician to Benito Mussolini, Haile Selassie, and Chiang Kai-shek on the "Cavalcade of America" show.

Intruder in the Dust was Juano Hernandez's first film. He proved to be its greatest asset and virtue. His physical presence, like Robeson's, was towering. With massive shoulders, large hypnotic eyes, and jawbones that looked as if they were chiseled from granite, he loomed larger than the film. In Hernandez's first scene, director Brown shrewdly photographed him from his feet upward —from his massive boots to his iron-jawed face—so that the audience sensed the growing stature of the man. Hernandez played his character with skill and insolence. He strode through the film with a haughty arrogance that made him seem like a wise, many-faceted version of Hattie McDaniel. "The stance and magnificent integrity," wrote *The New York Times*, "that Mr. Hernandez displays in his carriage, his manner and expression, with never a flinch in his great self-command, is the bulwark of all the deep compassion and ironic comment in the film." Not surprisingly, when the Oscars and The New York Film Critics' Awards were passed out, Juano Hernandez was overlooked. But he did receive two foreign acting awards for his portrayal.

In Hollywood, Hernandez found steady employment, and his career showed great promise. The western *Stars in My Crown* (1950) featured him once more as a Negro falsely accused of murder. "And Juano Hernandez," wrote *Newsweek*, "again puts quiet dignity into his rendition of a colored man nearly hanged by some of his white neighbors." *Young Man with a Horn* (1950) costarred him opposite Kirk Douglas as a sympathetic jazz musician. *The Breaking Point* (1950), a dramatization of Hemingway's *To Have and Have Not*, starred him as the tough and stanchly honest fishing-boat partner of the wayward John Garfield. When Garfield becomes involved with gangsters, the mighty Hernandez tells him he must go straight. "Juano Hernandez," wrote Bosley Crowther, "is quietly magnificient as Harry Morgan's helper and friend. As a matter of fact, the suggestion of comradeship and trust that is achieved through the character played by Mr. Hernandez, and the pathos created by his death, is not only a fine evidence of racial feeling, but it is one of the most moving factors in the film." The film's director, Michael Curtiz, added: "Hernandez is the 'new Negro' in our movies. Now we have a dignified, intelligent, *big* man." In 1955 he appeared in *Trial*, an explosive courtroom drama in which he portrayed a judge determined to give a Mexican boy a fair trial, and *Kiss Me Deadly.*

In all these early appearances, Juano Hernandez presented a compelling, invigorating figure. He was the single black actor in the movies who appeared not to fight the dominant culture, not to be buried under by it, not to have been scarred by it. Whereas James Edwards (and later Sidney Poitier) presented sensitive, easily bruised, slightly confused young men, Hernandez was always the confident, archly independent strong black man. Hernandez in films was always the separatist, always the withdrawn, defiant individualist. He was perhaps the movies' Stokely Carmichael figure, arriving on the scene at a most unexpected time, proclaiming his own brand of black power, completely scornful of the petty rules of the white world.

Sadly, Hernandez seems to have lost out precisely because of his black assurance. An early Stokely Carmichael was not what audiences of the 1950s wanted to see in the movies. His career, as perhaps is now to be expected for a serious black actor, took a downward turn in the mid-1950s. In subsequent films, his roles were slight and vaporous, and audiences watched him floundering to invest his characters with significance. As the religiously fanatic father in *St. Louis Blues* (1958), he was much too good and involved for this B movie. Because of the mediocrity of most the other actors, Hernandez's talents seemed out of place. In *Something of Value* (1957), Sidney Poitier was the star, and Hernandez was reduced to the role of an African chieftain. When he appeared in a supporting role in *The Pawnbroker* (1965), critic Pauline Kael wrote: "The great old Juano Hernandez, as the man who wants to talk, gives the single most moving performance I saw in 1965." As a man whose spirit has visibly been crushed, a misplaced person seemingly coming from nowhere and then going back, mumbling and fumbling and pathetic and lost, Hernandez was nothing short of brilliant. But the performance failed to resurrect his career. In *The Reivers* (1969), as the black patriarch, Uncle Possum, his dignity was ever present, but the physical man had begun to decay. By the time of Sidney Poitier's *They Call Me MISTER Tibbs* (1970), Juano Hernandez, as a toothless morally decayed janitor, had become a joke to a new generation unaware that without his earlier work there perhaps would not have been a Poitier.

Juano Hernandez and the cycle of problem pictures appropriately ended the schizophrenic 1940s. As well as anything else happening in the arts—on the stage or in fiction or poetry or even politics—these movies indicated that America's racial problems could no longer be kept in the background. In many respects, the problem pictures set the tone and pace for the new films of the 1950s and early 1960s, and although the problem pictures themselves were compromised and in some ways as confused as their age, they signaled a coming of age of the racial theme in American motion pictures; ground for intelligent statements on the black experience in the movies had at long last been broken. Today they appear as the calm before the racial storm. But after them, never would the black character be so obviously exploited and demeaned as in the previous eras.

The 1950s: Black Stars

Ethel Waters sways her massive shoulders as she sings "His Eye Is on the Sparrow," and suddenly, becomes—for a new generation —its great earth-mother figure. . . . Dorothy Dandridge, first as Carmen, then as Margot, later as Bess, acts her heart out, wins her Oscar nomination, and emerges on screen and off as the living embodiment of the tragic mulatto. . . . Sidney Poitier enters the era shyly as a young unknown in No Way Out, *only to close the decade as one of the most important leading men—black or white —in the movies. . . . Writer Richard Wright, baseball player Jackie Robinson, boxer Jersey Joe Walcott, tennis champ Althea Gibson, football player Woody Strode, trumpeter Louis Armstrong, crooner Nat "King" Cole, songstress Eartha Kitt, comedienne Pearl Bailey, jazz stylist Ella Fitzgerald, and calypso artist Harry Belafonte invade the movies and go "dramatic." . . . And problem pictures continue, alternately engaging and alienating their audiences.*

It was the 1950s, an era to be remembered as apathetic and sleepy-eyed, vulgar and hypocritical, grandiose, spectacular, and tasteless. Yet the Eisenhower age was one of change and turbulence, a decade that encompassed an array of incongruities: McCarthy in the Senate, troops in Korea, a Nobel Peace Prize for

Ralph Bunche in Sweden, the National Guard in Cicero and Chicago, the Supreme Court Decision of 1954, Marian Anderson at the Met, Emmett Till lynched in Mississippi, bus boycotts (later bombings) in Montgomery, the rise of Martin Luther King, sit-ins in Oklahoma, federal troops in Arkansas.

The 1950s' social-political whirl penetrated the motion-picture industry, which like the rest of the country, had to undergo change. Already the industry had lost some of its best talents because of blacklisting. Slowly, too, the look of the American feature film was altered, no longer stamped with the big-studio gloss but marked now by the individual signature of the independent director or producer. Television sets had come into homes across the nation and when box-office attendance, after its great boom in the war years, tapered off drastically the film industry offered the giant wide screens—Cinerama, CinemaScope, VistaVision, 3-D— as a desperate means of holding the audience. Likewise the industry picked up bold themes in part to lure the television audience away from home and in part as a realistic reflection of the growing chaos in the streets of America and in the psyches of its citizens. Gone almost entirely was the magical, romantic, bigger-than-life daydream quality of the old movies as independent filmmakers brought to the public not only more problem pictures but "message" pictures, "serious" pictures, "thoughtful" pictures, "studious" pictures, and "controversial" pictures, all interchangeable but carrying different labels.

For black actors this era of silent change was important. The great gains of the late 1940s were continued in the 1950s with the emergence of distinct black personalities who, through their own idiosyncrasies, invigorated the Negro Lead Character and the Negro Theme. Almost immediately three diverse black personalities stood out prominently, and they were to remain so throughout the decade, making the greatest breakthrough for the black actor in American motion pictures. Sidney Poitier, Dorothy Dandridge, and Ethel Waters transformed the history of blacks in films from a study of pictures or parts or personalities to one of star dimensions.

As already seen, in the early days of moviemaking black actors were rigidly consigned to mythic types. Through the push and power of their personalities, some actors had created great pop figures. Everything in Hollywood was a game, they knew, and they did not expect to be taken very seriously. Movie audiences loved and laughed at these great comic strip characters. They left theaters having enjoyed themselves but with little reason to think twice about what they had seen. No one ever cared what Bill

Robinson was really thinking as he danced up the staircases with Shirley Temple. Nor did anyone give a second thought to how Hattie McDaniel must have felt as she ripped the bandana from her head after a particularly humiliating scene.

Occasionally, with black actors such as Stepin Fetchit or Lena Horne or Paul Robeson, because their off-screen exploits paralleled their on-screen images and because they were publicized by their studios, audiences felt they had some insight into the person on celluloid. But still unlike the important white stars—such as Garbo and Gable— the old black actors were not monolithic figures. They did not symbolize disparate elements of their audience's personalities. They were not able to affect lives dramatically or touch on the mass imagination. Indeed, the moviegoing public was not yet prepared to be swept off its feet by the intrigues of a colored personality.

But in the 1950s Poitier, Dandridge, and Waters reached out and affected the imagination of the mass audience. Patrons believed in them. Often because of their private lives or because of a strongly rooted image, the trio overpowered the films in which they appeared. Moreover, in this strange psychoanalytic age when audiences started dissecting not only their own inner selves but those of their movies and movie stars as well, when patrons went to see black performers not for mere entertainment but for a comment on the black experience, these three performers became popular because of what they represented to moviegoers. Like all great stars, they were aesthetic beings in themselves. To contemplate Waters' humanity or Dandridge's beauty or Poitier's code of decency was worth the price of admission, and the three made a slight dent at the place Hollywood has traditionally cherished most: the box office.

Ethel Waters: Earth Mother for an Alienated Age

Ethel Waters was the first of the three to win mass audience approval. She had been around for a long time, and her life and career were a tale of disorder and much early sorrow. Growing up in Chester, Pennsylvania, she had stolen food to eat, run errands for whores, been a lookout for pimps and underworld figures. At thirteen she was married. At fourteen she was separated. At fifteen she was a chambermaid and laundress at a Philadelphia hotel where she earned $4.75 a week. Then almost miraculously she rose from poverty to international acclaim, first in the cellars and cafés where she was billed as "Sweet Mama Stringbean" and later on the stage in such successful productions as *Africana, Blackbirds of 1930, Rhapsody in Black, As Thousands Cheer, At Home Abroad, Mamba's Daughters,* and *Cabin in the Sky.*

Ethel Waters later reached a whole new audience with her impressive film work. But suddenly her spiraling career fell flat in the mid-1940s. Overwork, exhaustion, exploitation, and personal unhappiness had made her "difficult" and chronically suspicious of everyone. Her outbursts on the set of *Cabin in the Sky* remain a part of Hollywood legend. Subsequently there was a six-year period of unemployment in the film capital, and by 1948, when Darryl Zanuck asked her to test for Granny in *Pinky,* Ethel Waters was almost at the point of begging for a role. Her Granny was an old typed vehicle but she got mileage out of it, and her career swung back into full gear. Today, because of her appearances in such films as *Cairo* (1942), *Tales of Manhattan, Cabin in the Sky, Stage Door Canteen* (1943), and *Pinky,* many still think of Ethel Waters as an exclusively 1940s figure. It was during this period that, singlehanded, she brought a new style and substance to the time-worn mammy. But as significant a figure as she was in the 1940s, it was in the Eisenhower era, in the film version of Carson McCullers' play *The Member of the Wedding,* that she scored her greatest screen triumph and an overwhelming personal victory.

The Member of the Wedding was more than simply a movie. It was in two very important respects a motion-picture event. Foremost, it marked the first time a black actress was used to carry a major-studio white production. Secondly, the movie was another comeback for Ethel Waters. Her autobiography *His Eye Is on the Sparrow* had recently been published and was a best seller. In it, she told all the lurid details of her life—the fights, the lovers, the marriages, the career troubles. Curiously, instead of alienating her audience, the turbulent events in the autobiography convinced patrons that Ethel Waters, who had always portrayed long-suffering women, was indeed the characters she played. Moreover, audiences knew Ethel Waters had truly suffered. Now patrons rooted for her to succeed—to triumph. When *The Member of the Wedding* finally opened, audiences got just that.

The Stanley Kramer–Fred Zinnemann feature was a serious, oddly structured film for 1952 American moviegoers. It starred the original Broadway cast. It had little plot, and focused instead on the interactions of three outcasts: Frankie Adams (played by Julie Harris), a twelve-year-old motherless girl entering adolescence and wanting desperately to belong; John-Henry (Brandon de Wilde), Frankie's six-year-old sickly cousin-playmate; and the weathered and beaten family cook, Berenice. In the course of the film, Berenice is revealed as the guiding spirit in the children's

Even in the 1950s, black shoulders were still made to cry on. In *The Member of the Wedding* (1952) Julie Harris goes to Ethel Waters for comfort.

solitary lives. She is cook, housekeeper, protectress, reprimander, adviser, and confidante. "Come on. Let us play a three-hand game of bridge," says Berenice as she and the children sit in the kitchen. "Play the King, John-Henry," she tells the boy when he is about to cheat at their bridge game. "You know you got to play the rules of the game." In these quiet or sometimes turbulent moments among the three, author Carson McCullers' great lyricism was apparent as much as her theme of human loneliness and alienation. "We go round trying one thing. Then another. Yet we're still caught," Berenice tells young Frankie. At another time, in her most moving monologue, she explains to the two children the fragmented blind alleys of her life. "He was the first man I ever loved. Therefore I had to go and copy myself forever after and what I did was to marry off little pieces of Ludi whenever I run across them. It was my misfortune that they all turned out to be the wrong pieces." She comforts the two and helps them grow from her experiences. She sings to them "His Eye Is on the Sparrow." The film is resolved with Frankie grown and over that aching period of adolescence. Berenice stands alone in the kitchen of the house. She is leaving to work elsewhere, and we understand that her talents as an earth mother, to nourish and comprehend, are needed in a new household.

The Member of the Wedding was a critical success, but reports of its strange plotlessness and unconventional characters scared off many viewers. Others found them baffling. But Ethel Waters, the actress and the human being, was praised by everyone, even by those who did not like the film. Berenice was a perfect role for her, and there were obvious parallels between the seamy, confused tragic life of the movie's heroine and the legends about the entertainer. In the film version of *The Member of the Wedding*, the role was so well written and the character so well etched that Waters at long last had the material for a bravura performance. In her hands, every line, even a seemingly unadorned statement, was delivered with a warmth and irony that went beyond the script. "Can't bid," she said during the card game. "Never have a hand these days." "All my life I been wanting things I ain't been getting," she uttered plaintively. Ultimately, because *The Member of the Wedding*, with its skinny tomboy heroine and its pint-sized bespectacled leading man, was so unlike the typical Saturday evening movie fare, audiences tended to accept Ethel Waters and her life rather than the lives portrayed in the film. She emerged now as more than just a representative of the long-suffering, strong black woman. She was a great "serious" popular myth come true. For black audiences, Ethel Waters was the personification of the black spirit they believed had prevailed during the hard times of slavery, and they felt she brought dignity and wisdom to the race. For the mass white audience, Ethel Waters spoke to an inner spirit of a paranoid and emotionally paralyzed generation that longed for some sign of heroism. Movie stardom itself has often been based on a thin line between actress and myth, and with this performance Ethel Waters became a genuine movie star. Her personality, rather than her character or her movie, had grasped the public imagination, and thus the history of the Negro in American films gained a new perspective.

But if Ethel Waters altered black film history, she was perhaps the last to know about it. For in spite of her impressive perform- ance, she curiously became in the mid-1950s a victim of audience indifference. From *The Member of the Wedding* she went on to important Broadway appearances. There was also the successful television series "Beulah." Then new troubles arose: income-tax evasion and other debts. Finally, her debts and problems mounted so high that she was forced to make an excruciatingly painful appearance on the television quiz show "Break the $250,000 Bank." The great actress stood before millions in their homes trying to win money to pay her taxes. Surprisingly, audiences took her plight in stride. There was neither outrage nor great sadness. In a frightening way, Ethel Waters' public sorrow and humiliation were considered fitting for the tough endurable mythic figure who had always shown America that she could prevail, even under the most trying situations. When her next film, *The Sound and the Fury* (1959), was released, Twentieth Century–Fox's publicity de- partment announced that "everybody's favorite," indeed "Ameri- ca's favorite," Ethel Waters, was back. As Dilsey, the "indomitable skeleton," the part Faulkner himself might have written for her, Waters again acted the strong black woman in grand style. The movie at first looked promising, with a cast that included Yul Brynner, Joanne Woodward, and Margaret Leighton. But the ac- tors floundered in one mess of a script, and Waters fought to stay afloat. It was her last film of the decade.

The 1950s ended with Ethel Waters having appeared in but two motion pictures. But for this anemic, insecure age, one scared of its own shadow and terrified of taking risks, she was an echo of the past. Ethel Waters seemed to be some noble part of our heritage that was quickly becoming extinct. In a period of mass uniformity, she was the individualist foolish enough to assert herself yet strong enough to pay for the consequences. In the end, her image—the myth she lived out—loomed larger than life over the decade. When viewers saw Lorraine Hansberry's *A Raisin in the Sun* on

Broadway in 1959, they left theaters asking why Ethel Waters had not played the strong mother, Lena Younger. Indeed, it has always been conjectured that Hansberry patterned the character after Waters.

Dorothy Dandridge: Apotheosis of the Mulatto

Dorothy Dandridge was the second of the black stars. Before the apathetic Eisenhower age ended, she had infused it with her great intensity and risen as its most successful black leading lady. For a period that prided itself on appearances, hers was a startling presence. She was a great beauty. Her eyes were dark and vibrant, her hair long and silky, her features sharply defined. And she had the rich golden skin tone that had always fascinated movie audiences, black and white. Moreover, she was a distinctive personality, schizophrenic, maddening, euphoric, and self-destructive. Before her Nina Mae McKinney had displayed uncontrolled raunchiness. Fredi Washington had symbolized intellectualized despair, and Lena Horne had acquired a large following through her reserve and middle-class aloofness. On occasion, Dorothy Dandridge exhibited all the characteristics of her screen predecessors, but most important to her appeal was her fragility and her desperate determination to survive. In a way never before demonstrated by a black personality, she used her own incongruities and self-contradictions to capture and extend the mass imagination. Her life and career were vigorously reported on by the white and black press. At times she seemed to bask in her own publicity, and it was obvious that she took pains to create an image, to package it, and then to market it for mass consumption.

The irony that overshadowed Dorothy Dandridge's career was that although the image she marketed appeared to be contemporary and daring, at heart it was based on an old and classic type, the tragic mulatto. In her important films Dorothy Dandridge portrayed doomed, unfulfilled women. Nervous and vulnerable, they always battled with the duality of their personalities. As such, they answered the demands of their times. Dorothy Dandridge's characters brought to a dispirited nuclear age a razor-sharp sense of desperation that cut through the bleak monotony of the day. Eventually—and here lay the final irony—she may have been forced to live out a screen image that destroyed her.

Dorothy Dandridge came to films after a lengthy and arduous career as a stage entertainer. The daughter of a Cleveland minister and a comedienne-actress named Ruby, she performed as a child with her older sister Vivian in a vaudeville act billed as "The

Dorothy Dandridge: the 1950s' definitive tragic mulatto.

Wonder Kids." At fifteen she and Vivian along with another black girl appeared as the Dandridge Sisters, touring the country with the Jimmy Lunceford band. At sixteen, Dorothy Dandridge performed at the Cotton Club, where she met Harold Nicholas of the dancing Nicholas Brothers. She married him and bore him a daughter. Later the pair divorced. Throughout the 1940s, she worked in nightclubs as well as in a string of films such as *Lady from Louisiana* (1941), *Bahama Passage* (1942), *Drums of the Congo* (1942), *Ebony Parade,* and *The Hit Parade of 1943.*

In the early 1950s, a trio of low-budget movies in which she played "good girl" roles served as springboards for Dorothy Dandridge's rise. The first, *Tarzan's Perils* (1951), was typical jungle fare with one twist. In a crucial episode, Dandridge, as a kidnaped African princess, was tied to the stakes by a warlike tribal leader. As she lay with legs sprawled apart, heaving and turning to break loose, it was apparent that never before had the black woman been so erotically and obviously used as a sex object. From the way Lex Barker's Tarzan eyed the sumptuous Dandridge, it was obvious, too, that for once Tarzan's mind was not on Jane or Boy or Cheetah!

In Columbia's *The Harlem Globetrotters* (1951), Dandridge was cast as a sympathetic young wife trying to keep a decent husband from going bad. She had little more to do than look lovely. MGM's 1953 all-black *Bright Road*, followed, giving Dorothy Dandridge her first starring role. As a grade-school teacher working to reach an unhappy wayward student, she was cast opposite child actor Philip Hepburn and a shy newcomer named Harry Belafonte. Here she revealed a soft, radiant, melancholic quality. "Her work in MGM's *See How They Run* [the title was changed upon release] projects sultry Dorothy Dandridge into the enviable role of Hollywood's No. 1 female star," wrote *Ebony. Life* magazine also ran a special article on the film, spotlighting its leading lady. Thus by 1953, the momentum for Dandridge's career was well under way. Had she continued playing such nice-girl roles, her career might have been entirely lackluster. But Dorothy Dandridge learned early that there were better things ahead on the other side of virtue.

Carmen Jones was the celebrated movie that established her as the definitive tragic mulatto. It also contains the definitive Dandridge mulatto performance. The legend of how director Otto Preminger first decided to cast Dandridge for the lead in his film reads like a press agent's dream tale, but it appears to be true. Initially, Preminger had thought her too sleek and sophisticated for the role of a whore. But he underestimated the talent and determination of the actress. When it appeared as if she had lost the role altogether, Dorothy Dandridge completely redid her appearance and style. She taught herself a Southern dialect. She mastered wildly uninhibited body movements. She shrewdly exploited her own nervous tension. With her new image perfected, she tossed her hair about her head, made up her eyes darkly, dressed herself in a sheer low-cut blouse and a long, tight skirt, and then audaciously strutted into Preminger's office. Vivacious, sportive, alluring yet somehow haunted and vulnerable, Dorothy Dandridge was the living embodiment of the director's Carmen. The role was given to her.

Carmen Jones, released in 1954, was the 1950s' most lavish, most publicized, and most successful all-black spectacle. If audiences truly yearned for relief from the tedium and routine of their lives, surely this was perfect pop entertainment. Based on Bizet's comic-strip opera *Carmen*, it cleverly transformed the opera's colorful Spanish cigarette girl into Carmen Jones, a sexy black factory worker in the South. Her foil is a Good Colored Boy, Joe, portrayed by Harry Belafonte. Carmen lures him into deserting the army, goes with him to a sleazy Chicago hotel where they evade the law, then deserts him for a prize fighter, and finally is strangled by him for her unfaithfulness.

The plot and the characters of *Carmen Jones* were pop creations, and the film relied on the stock situations: hair-pulling fights between black females, the inevitable barroom brawl, the exaggerated dialects, the animalistic passions and furies of the leads. Old-style *kitsch*, it was made impressive nonetheless by its director's exuberant style and its cast's great élan. Everyone seemed to be there to have a good time. Diahann Carroll had a small decorative role as one of Carmen's good-time girl friends. Olga James portrayed the submissive Cindy Lou. Brock Peters snarled gloriously as the villainous Sergeant Brown. Joe Adams as prize fighter Husky Miller was such an overtly sexual performer that audiences could understand why he never went far in films. White audiences still found sexually assertive black males hard to accept. Pearl Bailey was an open delight as she belted out a rousing "Beat Out That Rhythm on a Drum." But Dandridge's Carmen dominated the production. On the one hand, cool, calculating, and perfectly confident, on the other, reckless and insecure, she is animalistic and elemental. When pursued by Belafonte, she kicks, she screams, she claws, she bites, and at one point, she crawls on all fours. Belafonte must tie her hands and feet to prevent her from escaping. Here again Dorothy Dandridge was the jungle queen tied to the stakes. But her performance was curiously detached.

Scenes from the 1950s' most lavish all-black musical, *Carmen Jones* (1954).
ABOVE: Joe Adams (left) and Harry Belafonte vie for the attentions of Dandridge.
BELOW: *Carmen Jones*'s three good-time gals are out for a night on the town: Pearl
Bailey, Dandridge, and Diahann Carroll.

Certainly, audiences knew that here was a woman who was acting. But the sheer theatricality, the relish she poured into her role, made audiences forget the incongruities of the plot and instead delight in Preminger's black fairy tale and this extravagant, high-strung bumblebee. "Looka here, baby," she seemed to say, "it ain't real, but I am!"

"The range between the two parts [*Carmen Jones* and *Bright Road*] suggests that she is one of the outstanding dramatic actresses of the screen." wrote *Newsweek.* "Of all the divas of grand opera—from Emma Calvé of the 90s to Risë Stevens—who have decorated the title role of *Carmen* and have in turn been made famous by it, none was ever so decorative or will reach nationwide fame so quickly as the sultry young lady . . . on *Life's* cover this week," wrote the editors of *Life* when Dorothy Dandridge became the first black ever to grace its cover.

Carmen Jones made Dandridge a star. Her performance earned her an Oscar nomination as best actress of the year. Although she lost the award to Grace Kelly, no black performer had ever before been nominated for a leading actor award. (Hattie McDaniel's award and Ethel Waters' nomination were for best supporting actress.) Afterward the first rushing whirl of publicity closed in on her. *Paris-Match* and *Ebony* ran cover stories on her. A score of other publications, from *Time* to *Confidential,* carried feature articles about her. Dorothy Dandridge was reported on, probed, studied, dissected, discussed, scrutinized, and surveyed. There were incredible rumors and stories about her that yet live on in Hollywood, tales about her retarded daughter, her "hidden" son, her white father, and, in keeping with the image gradually growing about her, of her white lovers. She was said to be involved with everyone in Hollywood from Tyrone Power to Otto Preminger to Peter Lawford to Michael Rennie to Abby Mann to Arthur Loew, Jr. What with the publicity and gossip, Dorothy Dandridge now seemed a star of the first magnitude.

But despite the great fanfare and recognition after her triumph in 1954, Dorothy Dandridge sadly discoverd there was no place for her to go. Bigotry and bias still had their place in Hollywood. Very few film offers came her way. Those that did were little more than variations on Carmen. Always she was to be cast as exotic, self-destructive women.

Just such a character was Dandridge's Margot in Robert Rossen's *Island in the Sun (1957).* Here she was cast in the first of her interracial-love roles. Today some might think it totally unimportant that Dorothy Dandridge was the first black woman ever to be held in the arms of a white man in an American movie. Yet, because she was permitted to bring integrated love to the mass audience in an age about to erupt in chaos over the issue of integration, she remains a socially significant figure in this film. It was a testament to her importance as a star that Twentieth Century–Fox risked featuring her opposite white actor John Justin. But, significant as the move was, *Island in the Sun* was marred by compromises. Even its producer, Darryl F. Zanuck, has admitted not liking the finished film because of them. Because of its theme of miscegenation, *Island in the Sun* was controversial even during the shooting. Before its release, some theater owners (mostly Southern) threatened to boycott it. The South Carolina legislature even considered passing a bill to fine any movie house that showed the film $5000. That bill was never passed, but the threats had their effect. Cautious steps were taken to avoid too much controversy. In the movie, Dandridge and Justin held hands and danced together, but little else happened. "The one scene I objected to seriously was the one in the summerhouse where John confesses his love for me," Dandridge later said. "We had to fight to say the word *love.*" Throughout the film, Dandridge seemed tense and strained, and audiences associated that nervousness with the character rather than the actress. As patrons watched Dandridge and Justin waltz together, surely they thought how lovely the pair looked and how happy they could have been if only the jittery, sad-eyed beauty weren't *colored*. She had everything else going for her! Surprisingly, as controversial as some thought the miscegenation theme to be, it attracted movie audiences. *Island in the Sun* was made for $2,250,000 and grossed $8 million.

That same audience reaction, however—pity for the poor racially "tainted" beauty on screen—seemed built into the subsequent Dandridge features, *The Decks Ran Red* (1958), *Tamango* (1959), and *Malaga* (1962). All were filmed abroad. Like Paul Robeson, Dorothy Dandridge fled this country, hoping to find in Europe an opportunity to play diversified, untyped characters. But she too encountered only disillusionment and repeated compromises.

Tamango cast her as an exotic savage loved by a white ship captain (Curt Jurgens). Two versions, one French, the other English, of all the love scenes were filmed. Then because of the interracial love theme no major American company would distribute the picture, and it failed. *The Decks Ran Red* fared a little better. In this tempestuous tale of a ship mutiny, Dandridge was surrounded by a trio of handsome white actors, James Mason, Stuart Whitman, and Broderick Crawford. As all three furtively undressed her with their eyes, it was apparent that had she not been

ABOVE: Dorothy Dandridge as the exotic island girl in *Tamango* (1959) with Curt Jurgens cautiously eying her. LEFT: *Porgy and Bess* (1959), the last of the extravagant all-black musicals, with Sammy Davis, Jr., Dandridge, and Sidney Poitier.

black she would have ended up in the arms of one or the other before the picture's conclusion. In *Malaga,* Edmund Purdom and Trevor Howard were her leading men. As a girl torn between two loves, Dandridge was peculiarly remote and melancholy. So immersed was she in despondency that her performance at times seemed separate from the rest of the movie. Here Dandridge was fully stripped of the fire and passion that dominated her Carmen. Instead she appeared at her most vulnerable. What weighed her down was not so much her character's dejection as her own. "No one knew what her nationality was to be in the picture," her manager, Earl Mills, later reported. "The problem as to whether Trevor Howard should kiss her on the screen was called ridiculous. This was Dorothy's most frustrating acting experience by far."

Curiously, the important aspect of these three European movies (as well as *Island in the Sun*) was that Dorothy Dandridge was bringing her own personal disappointments and frustrations to her characters. Audiences responded to the sadness on screen as if it were a logical part of the story, rather than the result of an outside force. Perhaps they told themselves that the reason Dorothy Dandridge—this exquisite black love goddess—was unfulfilled was because of that drop of Negro blood. It was wrecking her chances for fulfillment. And indeed, for Dorothy Dandridge, on screen and off, the tragic flaw was her color.

Dandridge's last important American film was *Porgy and Bess* in 1959. As Catfish Row's torrid Bess, she put her star qualities on brilliant display. Designer Irene Sharaff's long tight skirts and dark wide-brim hats made Dandridge a stunning creation. As she walked through the theatrical sets of the film, she was Dorothy Dandridge. Even star performers Pearl Bailey and Sammy Davis, Jr., failed to take the screen from her. Costar Sidney Poitier was literally dwarfed. Again Dandridge portrayed the woman at odds with society, again the Bad Black Girl trying to go right, again the tragic heroine who ends up leaving the good Porgy to wander up No'th to Harlem with Sportin' Life. Dandridge's performance was not so much an acting job as a personality one, but it earned her the Foreign Press Award as best actress in a musical.

The rest of Dorothy Dandridge's career was a sad story. She appeared in but two more pictures. Producers and directors seemed unable to think of her in any terms but that of the exotic, doomed mulatto, and already by the late 1950s and early 1960s the mulatto figure was dated. There was talk of starring her in *Cleopatra*, but the plans fell through. Off-screen she was beset by a number of personal conflicts. In many respects, she epitomized the confused, unsatisfied movie star dominated by the publicity and life style that informed her screen image. She was openly seen with white actors. And the stories circulated that she was attracted to white men only. On the set of one film in which she worked opposite a very dark black actor, she underwent a minor trauma, it was said, because she did not want his black hands to touch her. In the late 1950s her marriage to the silver-haired white restaurateur Jack Dennison seemed to confirm suspicions that Dorothy Dandridge had fallen victim to acting out her screen life in private. In 1962 her troubles were heightened when after her divorce from Dennison she found herself bankrupt. There were no movie jobs, few club offers, and only occasional television appearances. Dorothy Dandridge found herself a has-been, an anachronism unwanted in a new Hollywood. Slowly, it was rumored, she drifted into alcohol, pills, and self-destructive love affairs. Then in 1965, at the age of forty-one, Dorothy Dandridge was found dead, the victim of an overdose of anti-depression pills. In the end, Dorothy Dandridge completely lived out and apotheosized the role she was always best at, the doomed tragic mulatto, trapped because of her color, unable to fulfill herself as either a complete black or a complete white.

Sidney Poitier: Hero for an Integrationist Age

Sidney Poitier was the 1950s' third black star. His career proved more substantial, professionally and personally, than those of his predecessors. Poitier came to the movies almost accidently. Born in Nassau in 1927, the youngest of eight children, he had lived in Miami before coming to New York in the 1940s. With no thought of a film career, he worked in New York at odd jobs as a dockhand, dishwasher, chicken plucker, and bus boy. One day while thumbing through the *The New York Times,* he stumbled on an ad for actors at the American Negro Theater. He auditioned—with disastrous results. But soon he became determined to be a successful actor. After minor stage roles and some road tours, Sidney Poitier came to films and just about took over.

Poitier's ascension to stardom in the mid-1950s was no accident. There were three important reasons why he succeeded and won an audience at a time when other black actors such as Hernandez and Edwards were losing out. Foremost was the fact that in this integrationist age Poitier was the model integrationist hero. In all his films he was educated and intelligent. He spoke proper English, dressed conservatively, and had the best of table manners. For the mass white audience, Sidney Poitier was a black man who had met their standards. His characters were tame; never did they act impulsively, nor were they threats to the system. They were amenable and pliant. And finally they were non-funky, almost sexless and sterile. In short, they were the perfect dream for white liberals anxious to have a colored man in for lunch or dinner.

Poitier was also acceptable for black audiences. He was the paragon of black middle-class values and virtues. American Negroes were still migrating north and were gradually increasing their political power. The rising middle classes and the power (limited as it might have seemed) of their money supported Poitier. Black America was still trying to meet white standards and ape white manners, and he became a hero for their cause. He was neither crude nor loud, and, most important, he did not carry any ghetto cultural baggage with him. No dialect. No shuffling. No African cultural past. And he was almost totally devoid of rhythm. In short, he was the complete antithesis of all the black buffoons who had appeared before in American movies. This was one smart and refined young Negro, and middle-class America, both black and white, treasured him.

But the second reason for Poitier's ascension was that in many respects his characters were still the old type that America had always cherished. They were mild-mannered toms, throwbacks to the humanized Christian servants of the 1930s. When insulted or badgered, the Poitier character stood by and took it. He knew the white world meant him no real harm. He differed from the old servants only in that he was governed by a code of decency, duty, and moral intelligence. There were times in his films when he screamed out in rage at the injustices of a racist white society. But reason always dictated his actions, along with love for his fellow man. Most important, he did not use his goodness only as a means of saving a position. Past good Negroes in the movies, notably Bill Robinson, were usually concerned about pleasing the master in order not to be booted out of the Big House. But Poitier did not care about the Big House. Nor did his goodness issue from some blind spot of Christian faith (as with his screen "mother" Louise Beavers.) He acted as he did because an overriding intelligence demanded that his characters be humane.

Finally, Poitier became a star because of his talent. He may have played the old tom dressed up with modern intelligence and reason, but he dignified the figure. Always on display was the actor's sensitivity and strength. One can trace in all the Poitier features of the 1950s the qualities that made him a national favorite. Interestingly, the evolution of the Poitier screen personality was swift. In his first film, *No Way Out* (1950), audiences saw all the qualities that would make Poitier characters

ABOVE: In the tradition of the dying slave, the good Poitier character sacrifices himself for his white friend John Cassavetes in *Edge of the City* (1957).
BELOW: Later, Poitier performs the same ritual for his white friend Tony Curtis in *The Defiant Ones* (1958). Distorted as both pictures might now appear, they were crucial in the emergence of Sidney Poitier as a full-fledged star in the late 1950s.

so "laudable" for the rest of the decade.

Joseph Mankiewicz's *No Way Out* launched not only Poitier's career but the cycle of problem pictures in the 1950s. Literate and sophisticated, the movie spotlighted the race riots that had broken out after World War II, at the same time presenting a sensitive portrait of the educated Negro. The plot centers on a young Negro doctor, Luther Brooks, at a large metropolitan hospital. When two white hoodlums are wounded during an attempted robbery, Brooks tends the pair. One of the men dies. The other then accuses Brooks of murder. Thereafter the young doctor is embroiled in controversy, and he fights to prove his innocence. When the remaining white hoodlum organizes a group of racist friends to attack the ghetto area, the city verges on a major race riot. By a lucky stroke of Hollywood imagination, Brooks proves his innocence through an autopsy, and equilibrium returns to the city.

With its crisp and quick-witted dialogue, *No Way Out* to some degree captured the mood of postwar America and summed up its repressed racial hostilities. Likewise its Negro characters were walking exponents of the postwar black doctrines of racial integration and *overprove*. "You got 'em. All A's," the doctor's wife tells him. "No wonder you're tired. Even I'm a little tired. Cleaning up after parties. Eating leftovers. One day off a week to be with my husband. To be a woman. . . . We've been a long time getting here. We're tired, but we're here, honey. We can be happy. We've got a right to be."

No Way Out garnered critical praise. *The New York Times* called it "a harsh, outspoken picture with implications that will keep you thinking about it long after leaving the theater." But strong, original, and honestly stated as the movie was, it failed to win a large audience. The public was already weary of the Negro-struggle film, perhaps because the struggles of previous cinematic Negroes such as the mulattoes Pinky and Carter had been so hokey and superficial. From its advertising campaign, *No Way Out* must have seemed only one more in the lot.

What distinguished the picture was Sidney Poitier. As Brooks, he had the archetypal modern integrationist tom role. He was a brilliant young doctor whose achievements—the all A's, the correct diagnosis—summed up the equal-by-being-superior philosophy. He was handsome. He stood straight, spoke well, and never trod on anybody's toes. He was a man who could be reasoned with. He and his wife represented the average middle-class black aspirants trying to make it. But he never made a move against the dominant white culture. Instead he nourished it. In one scene, after having been shot by the white hoodlum, Poitier struggles to save that man's life. In a purely Christian way, he forgives his opponent, saying: "Don't you think I'd like to put the rest of these bullets through his head? I can't . . . because I've got to live too. . . . He's sick. . . . He's crazy . . . but I can't kill a man just because he hates me." What red-blooded all-American white audiences in this Eisenhower age of normalcy could not have liked this self-sacrificing, all-giving black man? What integrationist-aspiring black audience would not be proud of this model of black respectability? Poitier was clearly a man for all races.

When one thinks of how much of Luther Brooks was to remain with actor Poitier, he is tempted to ask if scriptwriters Mankiewicz and Lesser Samuels should not be credited with creating the most important black actor in the history of American motion pictures. Obviously, what they did create was the character, the screen persona that Poitier was to popularize and capitalize on. In the early days, Poitier no more molded his image than did Stepin Fetchit; he lived out Hollywood's fantasies of the American black man.

The actor's second film was Zoltan Korda's 1952 adaptation of Alan Paton's South African drama, *Cry, the Beloved Country*. The feature starred Canada Lee as an old village priest journeying to Johannesburg in search of a son gone astray. In the city, where he is saddened by the poverty and filth and bewildered by the racism, he is aided in his search by a young priest played by Poitier. The movie made an ultimate plea for racial harmony and conciliation. Canada Lee had the finest role of his career. Poitier was a supporting player, but he brought good humor and a relaxed gregariousness to his priest. Moreover, the young Poitier was there to help a battered old man no one else in Johannesburg had the time for, and the humanity of his character (in keeping with his heroic code) merely added to the momentum of his career.

His next two films, *Red Ball Express* (1952) with Jeff Chandler and *Go, Man, Go* (1953) with the Harlem Globetrotters, cast Poitier in conventional bland supporting roles. *Red Ball Express*, a military adventure tale, did provide audiences with glimpses of one of Poitier's great prerogatives as a postwar freed black man, the emotional explosion. "Look, *boy*, where I come from you don't give orders. You take 'em," a racist soldier shouts when Poitier asks for a cup of coffee. But Poitier jumps upon him with passion and regains any lost dignity. Young black audiences loved him for it. Here at long last was a sane black man, free and strong enough to shout back to whitey.

Shouting back was very much a part of *The Blackboard Jungle* (1955). In this harrowing exposé of American high schools Poitier was costarred with Glenn Ford, Anne Francis, and Vic Morrow. He portrays Gregory Miller, an intelligent, complex student who fears that in the outside world there will be no place for a second-class citizen to take the lead. He hounds and torments white teacher Ford, who represents the oppressive system. He snarls, acts tough, and displays his virility more effectively than in any other film. "Come on! Go ahead! Hit me!" he yells to Ford. Here the disaffiliated young of the 1950s saw a man with a choice. He didn't have to take anything. Even before it was fashionable, he was bucking the corroding system. Yet at the same time, Poitier's Miller was an easily hurt, sensitive young man forced to live outside society. He was the classic loner of the 1950s, much like Marlon Brando and James Dean. And young audiences understood his loneliness, his confusion, and his entrapment because it was a comment on their own in the Eisenhower age. At *The Blackboard Jungle*'s conclusion, when he aids teacher Ford against a student with a switchblade, some of his earlier impact is diminished, but his code of decency is reaffirmed, and Poitier's Miller becomes a hero for young and old.

During the next four years Sidney Poitier worked in six motion pictures. In *Something of Value* (1957), with Rock Hudson, *Band of Angels* (1957), with Clark Gable and Yvonne De Carlo, and *The Mark of the Hawk* (1958) with Eartha Kitt and Juano Hernandez, he was an unlikely amalgam of *The Blackboard Jungle*'s Gregory Miller and *No Way Out*'s Luther Brooks. Sullen, angry, quick-tempered, and headstrong, he rebelled in many of these films, occasionally playing a modernized version of the black brute. (In the movies, most black men politically militant or merely politically motivated are simplified by the scenarists into the unreasonable, animalistic brutes of old.) But always, as if to save Poitier's image and the scriptwriter's white supremacist neck, the features concluded with Poitier's goodness and humanity reasserted, and once more audiences discovered him to be on the side of the angels. In this four-year period, the archetypal Poitier roles—the two that remain among the finest in his gallery of characters— were as Tommy Tyler in *Edge of the City* (1957) and as Noah Cullen in *The Defiant Ones* (1958).

The David Susskind–Martin Ritt production *Edge of the City* was an adaptation by Robert Alan Aurthur of his own television drama "A Man Is Ten Feet Tall," in which Poitier had already appeared. The story is about two men, a white and a black. In a true gesture of integrationist harmony, railroad worker Tommy Tyler befriends a wayward and confused army deserter (John Cassavetes). The story has a twist because for once it was the black man extending his hand to the white. Poitier helps the white man find a job, and then as his greatest manifestation of friendship invites him home to meet his wife (Ruby Dee) and have dinner. A Christlike figure, he stands for conscience and humaneness. But he is destroyed by his kindness and loyalty. During an argument with a fellow white worker in which Poitier defends Cassavetes, a fight breaks out. Poitier is winning. But he begs his white opponent to quit. When he turns to walk away, the white man stabs him in the back. Poitier dies in Cassavetes' arms.

Poitier's role won him great favor with the critics. *The New York Herald Tribune* called his black man one of deceptive simplicity. "With his quick smile and exhilarating talk," wrote the reviewer, "he can cajole the boy out of deep gloom. With a joke he can stop an ugly fight before it begins. But underneath he is a man of serious faith and deep strength, and when it's time for him to listen sympathetically or to say something important, he is the finest kind of friend." After *Edge of the City,* no moviegoer in America had any doubts about Poitier's talents. Nor did any fail to see what he represented. He was fast becoming a national symbol of brotherly love.

Oddly, when viewed today, the incongruities and disparities ignored by the audience of 1957 are blatantly apparent. Poitier's character falls into the tradition of the dying slave content that he has well served the massa. His loyalty to the white Cassavetes destroys him just as much as the old slave's steadfastness kept him in shackles. In this case, writer Aurthur smooths over the black man's death by having the white Cassavetes hunt down the killer.

Curiously, *Edge of the City* also revealed Sidney Poitier as a colorless black. So immersed is he in white standards that there is little ethnic juice in his blood. The dinner scene between Poitier, his wife, and their white friends is not an interracial summit meeting because there are no cultural gaps. Nor are there any cultural bridges to cross. All four are decent American citizens. Poitier also seems sexless in this movie. In previous features, scriptwriters were sure to keep Poitier's sexuality well hidden. He seldom had a serious movie romance. In those films in which he was married, it was generally to a sweet homebody type who seemed devoid of sexual passion. Dots Johnson had played this part in *No Way Out.* In *Edge of the City* it was Ruby Dee. She now remains the model movie mate for Poitier. (They have appeared in five films together.) An intense and talented actress, Ruby Dee is known for deft performances as unfulfilled, timid, troubled women. Certainly in *Edge of the City,* as she smiles sweetly at Poitier or proves how understanding and sensitive she is, audiences must have found the two a well-scrubbed sexless pair. One can understand why later militant patrons would view them both as sterile products of a decadent, materialistic Western culture. It should be noted that in one of their next films together, *A Raisin in the Sun* (1961), they effectively portrayed a couple with bedroom blues. Poitier's romantic apathy just about drives Dee up the wall in this film, and it is one reason why she wants to abort their expected child.

In the 1960s, Sidney Poitier's sexual neutralization became embarrassingly apparent, particularly when Hollywood provided romantic interest for him, albeit in a compromised manner. In *The Long Ships* (1964), when as a villainous Moor he kidnaps a beautiful white woman, he has been made to take a year's vow of celibacy. Therefore Poitier's sexual impulses remain safely suppressed. In *A Patch of Blue* (1965) he has a brief screen kiss with a blind white girl (Elizabeth Hartman). Everyone knows there is a romance developing between the two, but at the movie's end, rather than assert himself and bed the girl, he dutifully ships her off to a school for the blind. And in the notorious *Guess Who's Coming to Dinner* (1967) he wins the hand of a white girl in marriage, but they are a peculiarly unromantic couple who are seen kissing but once in the film, and the audience views this passionate event through a cabdriver's rear-view mirror. Later, in *They Call Me MISTER Tibbs* (1970), Poitier was finally cast opposite a vibrant, overtly sexual black woman, Barbara McNair. But audiences were openly baffled at seeing this beauty made up (with hair neatly groomed and clothes nicely dull and "tasteful") to look like Ruby Dee! Poitier's sexuality was still a problem for Hollywood moviemakers, and the attempts to keep him cool were so obvious that he seemed ludicrous. In the 1950s, however, audiences accepted the neutrality and rather respected him for it.

The Defiant Ones was Sidney Poitier's most important film of the decade. In it he played Noah Cullen, a black convict handcuffed to a white (Tony Curtis) as the two escape the law. Neither man likes the other. But before the picture ends, something akin to love has developed. For, once they have been unchained, the good Poitier comes to the rescue of Curtis, not out of necessity but out of brotherly love. Again he sacrifices himself, this time not with his death but his freedom, all for the sake of his white friend. In this film, one of his biggest hits, Poitier alienated a certain segment of the audience. When he saved his honky brother, he was jeered at in ghetto theaters. Black audiences were consciously aware for the first time of the great tomism inherent in the Poitier character, indeed in the Poitier image. Stanley Kramer's drama had glossed over the real issues and bleached out its black hero. Yet to Poitier's credit, his power as an actor demanded that the role and the film be taken seriously, and the jeers were somewhat muffled when he received an Oscar nomination for best actor of the year.

Porgy and Bess was Poitier's last film of the 1950s. The movie portrayed blacks as the singing, dancing, clowning darkies of old. Poitier accepted the role of Porgy only after much pressuring, and, although his performance was engaging, he seemed out of place. Here it was 1959. There was Martin Luther King. There were sit-ins, demonstrations, and boycotts. And what was America's black idol doing? There he stood singing, "I got plenty of nothin', and nothin's plenty for me."

In retrospect, it can be said that all the Poitier films of the 1950s were important and significant. Because they were all made to please a mass white audience at a time when the main topic of conversation was school desegregation, today their messages may seem rigged or naïve. But they retain a certain raw-edged bite and vigor. Audiences still respond to the actor's sophistication and charm, to his range and distinctly heroic quality. In the 1960s, Hollywood belittled and dehumanized Poitier's great human spirit by making it vulgarly superhuman. He became SuperSidney the Superstar, and he was depicted as too faithful a servant, the famous Poitier code then a mask for bourgeois complacency and sterility. But in the 1950s his work shone brightly. For black and white Americans he was a marvelous reason for going to the movies. And whether an integrationist or a separatist age likes it or not, Sidney Poitier's movie characters in the 1950s singlehandedly made audiences believe things would work out, that they were worth working out. It was still just a beautiful dream, but often that's what great movies and careers are all about.

Black Odds and Ends

Although the major black films of the 1950s featured Dandridge or Poitier, the era could also boast of a few offbeat and intriguing black cinematic diversities. Film biographies of two black athletes and one black composer were ghetto favorites. And audiences also enjoyed watching some of the beautiful blunders made by nonactors—athletes, musicians, singers, comedians, and one highly respected novelist—in serious dramatic roles. Minor problem pictures appeared, and there were some new variations on the old tragic mulatto theme.

The dramatization of Richard Wright's *Native Son* (1951) was one of the era's earliest problem pictures and also one of its first casualties. For some ten years since its publication, *Native Son* had been black America's proudest literary achievement. The story of the rebellious and angry ghetto youth, Bigger Thomas, who finds his *raison d'être* in two violent crimes, deeply affected black people who could identify with his quest for identity. Wright's work had visual power and sweep, and the dialogue was tense and dramatic. The writer himself had long hoped to see his novel filmed. When no Hollywood company would finance the project, he went to foreign financiers. But *Native Son* proved a fiasco, ill conceived and technically poor. Wright had authored the screenplay, which faithfully followed the novel, but key scenes and character details were missing. Filmed in Argentina, the movie lacked the sense of place essential for its story. Audiences felt neither the oppressiveness of the system nor that of its setting, Chicago. The actors did not help matters. Jean Wallace was rather stiff as the white girl accidentally murdered by Bigger, while newcomer Gloria Madison was perhaps too fluid as the black girl, Bessie. *Native Son*'s greatest liability was Richard Wright himself, who starred as the seventeen-year-old Bigger. At the time, Wright was fifty. Too old, too fat, too weary, too middle class, and too successful and sophisticated, Richard Wright was thoroughly implausible in the role of a tortured deprived youth. The time is ripe now, however, for a remake of his classic.

Another nonactor who acted in the 1950s was Jackie Robinson. The Dodger's star baseball player portrayed himself in *The Jackie Robinson Story* (1950), an inexpensive and quickly produced movie tracing the ball player's slow, steady rise. The movie also had a slow, steady rise before its filming. When Robinson had testified against Paul Robeson before the House Un-American Activities Committee he endeared himself to red-troubled white America. No studio could have objected to filming a low-budget version of his life. Yet two studios turned the project down because the promoters of the picture refused to film the story with a white man teaching Robinson how to be a great ball player. Self-reliant Negro heroes were still unfashionable. *The Jackie Robinson Story* was finally filmed by Eagle-Lion Studios for about fifty thousand dollars. A throwback to the race-achievement pictures of the black independents, the movie was too busy making viewers appreciate the hero's "credits to the race" to let them relax and enjoy a good story. In the end, it lacked drama and direction, plodding along on its star's name. Still it is doubtful if anyone has forgotten Joel Fluellen's sensitive portrayal of Jackie's college-educated, Olympic-winning brother, who works as a street cleaner. Nor could anyone fail to be charmed by Ruby Dee's bright appearance as the dedicated wife. There was Louise Beavers, too, large and lone-some as the champ's hard-working ma. And, finally, there was Jackie Robinson as Jackie Robinson. "Mr. Robinson," wrote *The New York Times*, "doing that rare thing of playing himself in the picture's leading role, displays a calm assurance and composure that might be envied by many a Hollywood star." Although few patrons were as enthusiastic about Robinson's performance (many thought him wooden), almost everyone agreed that during the action shots on the diamond Jackie Robinson was nothing short of fantastic.

Boxer Joe Louis was the subject but not the star of *The Joe Louis Story* (1953), a chronicle that recaptured highlights of a two-decade career, opening in 1934 and ending with the bout with Marciano. The movie starred Coley Wallace as the champ. James Edwards (with head shaved clean) was cast as trainer Jack Black-burn, and Hilda Simms (the original Anna Lucasta of the stage) played Joe's wife. Unfortunately, the picture failed to reach a large audience. But many a ghetto kid was to cherish it.

Jersey Joe Walcott, Althea Gibson, and Woody Strode were other athletes who went dramatic in the 1950s. Boxer Wolcott was appropriately cast as a fight trainer in *The Harder They Fall* (1956) with Humphrey Bogart. Tennis champ Gibson portrayed Constance Towers' maid in John Ford's Civil War epic *The Horse Soldiers* (1959). Controversy arose over Gibson's role; civil rights groups protested that it was a step backward and much too undig-nified for an Olympic champion to be cast as a servant. But the organization that should have complained was the Screen Actors Guild, for Althea Gibson was hardly anyone's idea of an actress.

Former Los Angeles Rams football player Woody Strode made the most successful transition from sports hero to movie personal-ity. With his magnificent physique and spectacular style—quick eyes that flash and dart malevolently, gleaming white teeth fixed in a broad smile, and biceps and triceps that he was quick to flex —Strode became the movies most notable black muscleman, ap-pearing in adventure stories and spectacles. *Androcles and the Lion* (1952) featured him as the lion in close-ups. On the television series "Mandrake the Magician," he appeared as the enormous Moroccan bodyguard of the comic-strip hero. Other Strode films of the 1950s included *The Gambler From Natchez* (1954), *The Ten Commandments* (1956), *Tarzan's Fight for Life* (1958), and *Pork Chop Hill*. With nothing to do but be blankly beautiful, Woody Strode always seemed but one more elegant period piece pro-vided by an imaginative set designer.

Strode had his most serious (and best) role in John Ford's *Ser-*

geant Rutledge (1960). The film also marked an important step in the evolution of the racial consciousness of director Ford. Previously, Ford, in his depiction of blacks, had gone from one extreme to another. On one hand, his *Arrowsmith* had been startling and ahead of its time in its humane and sensitive depiction of the black Dr. Marchand. On the other hand, his films *Judge Priest* and *Steamboat 'Round the Bend* had followed the accepted notions of their time. Each had demeaned and exploited Stepin Fetchit. In 1949, after conflicts with Ethel Waters over her interpretation of the character Granny in *Pinky*, Ford had been taken off the picture by producer Darryl F. Zanuck. "It was a professional difference of opinion," Zanuck later said. "Ford's Negroes were like Aunt Jemima caricatures." Then in 1959 the director was criticized for his handling of Althea Gibson in *The Horse Soldiers*. But *Sergeant Rutledge* seemed an apology for all his past racial indiscretions, and he attempted to present the Negro as a dignified and noble figure. Unfortunately, the picture itself did not succeed in the way Ford might have wanted, and Woody Strode's performance was the only aspect of the movie fully appreciated by the critics. Here Strode portrayed a Negro soldier on trial for double murder and the rape of a white girl. "*Sergeant Rutledge* may not add up to Mr. Ford's finest hour," wrote the *New York Times* reviewer, "but it certainly is Mr. Strode's." Throughout the film, as he is badgered and hounded, Strode maintains his integrity and his composure. At the film's conclusion his heroism is not only confirmed but his innocence is discovered too. Because of what most critics considered impressive work (seen today, Woody Strode comes across as very wooden), a whole new career appeared to be opening up for Woody Strode. But Ford's epic was an exception to the general run of movies Strode worked in. In subsequent films such as *Spartacus* (1960), *The Last Voyage* (1960), *The Sins of Rachel Cade* (1961), *Two Rode Together* (1961), *The Man Who Shot Liberty Valence* (1962), *The Professionals* (1967), and *Shalako* (1968), Woody Strode found himself again bare-chested with muscles bulging and teeth gleaming. Later he starred in *Black Jesus* (1971) and *Black Rodeo* (1972).

William Marshall was the 1950s' other physically overpowering black man. Although he was not an athlete, he looked like one; he stood six feet tall and weighed two hundred and twenty-five pounds. His appearance in *Lydia Bailey* in 1952 was memorable not so much because of his acting as due to his particular character. The movie was about Toussaint L'Ouverture's Haitian revolt at the end of the eighteenth century. Marshall was cast as a strong, and domineering islander. His costumes exposed and exploited his massive body. The studio sweat glistened on him. As he paraded his assortment of eight wives, it was apparent that here stood a man of prodigious strength and passionate desires. If audiences had any doubts about either the strength or the desires, they promptly forgot them when Marshall's character's name was revealed. He was called King Dick. Not too much irony or subtlety there. Clearly, William Marshall, like Woody Strode, was the 1950s version of the black buck. Marshall's other important role during the decade was as King Glycon in the spectacle *Demetrius and the Gladiators* (1953). Later he appeared in *Something of Value* (1957), *The Boston Strangler* (1968), and a string of other films, many of them forgettable. His career later renewed itself when he starred as a black vampire in the black horror film *Blacula* (1972).

The athletes-gone-dramatic were joined by the entertainers-gone-serious. Even in an old-style film such as *The Benny Goodman Story* (1955), in which a performer like Lionel Hampton portrayed his entertaining self, the musician also had the opportunity to reveal himself as a serious, thoughtful person. In *The Strip* (1951) and *High Society* (1956), Louis Armstrong was bugle-blowing Louis. But in *Glory Alley* (1952), he portrayed Shadow Johnson, a good-humored bartender. Someone cracked that with this performance "de shadow done returned." Armstrong had a chance for some intensified tomming as he tried untangling the love problems of the film's stars, Ralph Meeker and Leslie Caron. But as could be expected, old Satchmo came off best in the musical interludes. *The New York Times* wrote: "Every now and then, Louis Armstrong sticks his broad, beaming face into the frame and sings or blasts a bit on his trumpet. That makes the only sense in the whole film."

Ella Fitzgerald, too, was better when she forgot her dramatics. In *Let No Man Write My Epitaph* (1959) she portrayed a washed-out drug-addicted blues singer. Somehow her bluesy life never seemed very blue, and Ella looked mighty healthy for such a sick chick. She was much more at home when she appeared as herself in *Pete Kelly's Blues* (1955) and *St. Louis Blues*.

Big-name singing stars who went dramatic with more flourish but just as little success were Nat "King" Cole and Eartha Kitt. For a time, it looked as if Cole would be promoted into a black leading man. When he sang background music in a number of 1950s films such as *The Blue Gardenia* (1953), *Small Town Girl* (1953), and *Istanbul* (1957), Cole epitomized black cool. But cast as a French

Foreign Legionnaire in *China Gate* (1957) he played the part a little too hotly and lost his bearings.

Cole's big picture of the 1950s was the all-black *St. Louis Blues*, a highly fictionalized biography of the black jazz composer W. C. Handy. Here he was teamed with an array of talented black performers—Eartha Kitt, Cab Calloway, Pearl Bailey, Ruby Dee, Juano Hernandez, Mahalia Jackson, and Ella Fitzgerald. Modestly budgeted but heavily promoted by the black press, *St. Louis Blues* looked like a winner at first. Unfortunately, however, neither the film nor its cast came off very well. Mahalia Jackson used her powerful voice effectively and Pearl Bailey supplied some much-needed gusto, but they were not enough to save this routine, implausible melodrama. Worst of all, Cole proved the least interesting of all the cast. Thin and anemic and much too suave and courteous, Cole seemed out of place, and it was apparent that he lacked the strength and range to carry the picture. The following year he worked in *The Night of the Quarter Moon* (1959), but the studios lost all hope of transforming him into a leading man.

St. Louis Blues' other casualty was Eartha Kitt. On the stage, Eartha Kitt had been a marvel of wicked insouciance. Vain, naughty, obdurate, and teasing, she purred and pouted and won a vast following. Eartha Kitt epitomized the exotic black woman born to be bedded. The songstress had the polish and the playful wit and intelligence to make herself a highly prized sex object. For café society she represented the ultimate kept woman. Only a man with a large expense account could afford her. Only a man with a certain *savoir faire* could excite her. In films, however, Eartha Kitt proved much too distinctive and unusual to please the mass audience. In *New Faces of 1952*, she was an engaging novelty. Because patrons did not have to see a great deal of her, she was tolerated. But in her starring roles in *St. Louis Blues, The Mark of the Hawk*, and her most spectacular flop, the all-black *Anna Lucasta* (1958), she alienated her audience. She had been noted for her "cat" songs, but in these films she looked and sounded like a cat. A terribly affected and studied actress with too many self-conscious kinks and quirks and in need of a strong director to break down the defenses she had built up for herself, Eartha Kitt had an arch independence and what some saw as an underlying bitchiness that antagonized filmgoers. Physically, she lacked the conventional good looks that could make an audience take an interest in her no matter what she did. Easily intimidated audiences may have found her demonic and dangerous. In 1965, she returned to films after a lengthy absence for a rather solid performance in *Synanon*. But the picture failed, and Eartha Kitt went back to her nightclub appearances and her cat songs.

The two most successful entertainers-gone-dramatic were Pearl Bailey and Harry Belafonte. Yet neither was to live up quite to audience expectations. Both performed best before a live audience, where they could improvise or play on a mood or sustain a tone. Bailey's movie roles offered her greater flexibility than did those of Belafonte, and becauser her characters were such zany, uninhibited types she fared better.

In Pearl Bailey, moviegoers saw a brief return of the wisecracking, manipulative black woman Hattie McDaniel had popularized in the 1930s. As the good-time girl Frankie in *Carmen Jones*, as the audacious, clever maid Gussie in *That Certain Feeling* (1956), as the vivacious aunt in *St. Louis Blues*, and as the cynical Maria in *Porgy and Bess*, Pearl Bailey could be counted on to be sassy, sensible, and inventive. She was not taken in by sham, and never in her lifetime was anybody going to pull the wool over her eyes. Yet, independent and sure-footed as she was, Bailey was never pure cantankerous mammy. There was a streak of gentleness to her, and at times she was the cheerful aunt jemima who might rousingly speak her mind but who at heart meant no one any harm. Her distinguishing characteristic throughout her career was her astounding vivacity. Often her energies seemed too broad and outlandish for a medium that requires subtety and restraint. Who could forget how she lifted *Porgy and Bess* from its idealized, insulated world? As the shrewd, perceptive Maria she presented audiences with a chatty presence who could not abide idealization or falsification. If anything, her performance uncovered the shallowness and dishonesty of the stereotype figures that dominated the production. Pearl Bailey was genuine.

Pearl Bailey's most serious and offbeat role in the decade (a role in which the director tried getting her out of the mammy-jemima type and wedging her into the Ethel Waters strong-black-woman category) was as the boozed-out, Bessie Smith–type blues singer in *All the Fine Young Cannibals* (1960). She aids a young white musician (Robert Wagner) in his rise to jazz fame. The pair openly live together, but the script dishonestly tries to make their relationship platonic. Bailey was so blatantly miscast that audiences probably wished it were a platonic affair. She was too flamboyant, too self-aware, too full of common sense and sheer curiosity to be credible as the self-pitying, self-destructive entertainer.

After *All the Fine Young Cannibals*, there was a long absence from the movies for Pearl Bailey. In between she made nightclub appearances and had great success on Broadway in *Hello, Dolly*. Later she was signed to star in her own television series, and then moviegoers saw her return to films for the role of Maria in *The Landlord* (1970).

"From the top of his head right down to that white shirt, he's the most beautiful man I ever set eyes on," Diahann Carroll once said of Harry Belafonte. In the 1950s, those were the sentiments of American females, white and black. So handsome and slick a black dude was Belafonte that he seemed a born movie star, a natural new-style romantic hero. Hollywood capitalized on his looks and his sexuality, yet at the same time, in film after film, it appeared that the motion-picture industry feared them. Belafonte was usually cast in good-guy roles where his island-boy sensuality could be made safely antiseptic. And Belafonte himself lacked the gutsy style to break through the Mr. Clean roles and put forth the sexual raunchiness Hollywood secretly valued him for. Obviously, he fell into the black buck category. Even at that he could have been tolerable and at least a diversion from Poitier's noble tom characters. But if a black buck is not going to be daring or flashy or uninhibitedly sexy, then what good is he? That's just the question moviegoers asked themselves as they watched the even-tempered, mild-mannered Belafonte.

His first film, *Bright Road,* cast him as the understanding elementary school principal who pines for schoolteacher Dorothy Dandridge. But he lacks the security to make his move, hardly a believable predicament for a handsome leading man. In *Carmen Jones,* Belafonte's Joe was obviously no match for the movie's spitfire heroine. His naïveté and antiseptic air were in keeping with the plot and the character, but Belafonte's own shortcomings as an actor were evident. Once audiences had looked over his face and body and after the camera had finished playing up to him, there was little else to engage the viewer. If anything, Harry Belafonte had proved that looks alone (without passion or humor) mean very little.

The political potboiler *Island in the Sun* (1957) provided the actor with his meatiest character. He played David Boyeur, a political upstart, an island boy turned radical, a man of strong political and sexual drives. Not only does he take the election right out of the hands of the rich white candidate, but he woos and captivates an aristocratic white matron, Marvis. In the person of Belafonte, Boyeur is a nice, decent colored chap trying to do right but forced to play bad. Politically and emotionally, he is too phlegmatic and polite to be credible as a revolutionary. Nothing seems locked up within him. Even his voice lacks variety and strength. But worst of all, as Marvis' black buck, he proves to be little more than the model male hustler. He has a great come-on, but surely audiences wanted to accuse him of false advertising. All Marvis (and an expectant audience) got from this rebel-rouser was a limp handshake. Although one could blame Boyeur's inhibition on the scriptwriters, Harry Belafonte as an actor failed to look either passionate or even remotely interested in white actress Joan Fontaine. Instead he seemed to stand by merely to pay homage to her as a white woman. As a result, no one cared about him. Or his career.

In 1959 with *Odds Against Tomorrow* and *The World, the Flesh, and the Devil*, Harry Belafonte handled himself decently enough. But he still lacked conviction and humor. On the whole, his venture into motion pictures was a disappointment in the 1950s. Eleanor Roosevelt had said he could mesmerize audiences in concert halls, and on stage Belafonte did have a way of projecting oddly melancholy moods or strong gutsy rhythms. But in the movies he was strangely bland and innocuous. Surprisingly, just when everyone was about ready to write Belafonte off as a screen performer, the actor returned to the movies after an eleven-year absence. In the 1970 production of *The Angel Levine* he gave a decent but uninspired performance opposite Zero Mostel. Then in *Buck and the Preacher*, Belafonte turned in a wonderfully developed and stylized performance. Cast as a Bible-totin', pistol-whippin', tooth-decaying ornery backwoods preacher, he used the full reserves of his personality. No longer was he simply Mr. Beautiful Black America; now Harry Belafonte had discovered in himself, at forty-four, a rough-and-ready, gutsy quality that had vitality and delighted audiences. *Buck and the Preacher* almost made up for all his past screen work.

In the 1950s, the tragic mulatto seemed in for a massive resurrection, and a number of white actresses had opportunities to bemoan a mixed fate. The 1951 version of *Show Boat* featured Ava Gardner as the mulatto Julie. In *Band of Angels* Yvonne De Carlo portrayed a Kentucky-bred belle who is sold into slavery when it is learned her mother was a Negress! But because actress De Carlo is not black at all, the film's hero (Clark Gable) first buys her, then falls in love with her. If a movie mulatto is really white, her chances for happiness are usually better. In the World War II melodrama *Kings Go Forth* (1958) Natalie Wood portrayed a beautiful French girl pursued by infantrymen Tony Curtis and Frank Sinatra. When word leaks out that her father was an American Negro she is deserted by both men. She attempts suicide but recovers and in the end transforms her family's posh villa into a hostel for war orphans, those just as deprived of love as herself. Luckily, Natalie Wood is really white. Therefore Frank Sinatra can return (minus an arm lost in combat) to ask forgiveness—a broken man for a broken woman.

Natalie Wood was most blessed. Other heroines were not. Julie London has a horrendously rough time in *Night of the Quarter Moon* (1959). When she weds a wealthy San Francisco lad (John Barrymore), Julie London informs him that she is a quadroon. No matter, he says. When the couple arrives in San Francisco, however, the young man's family does everything it can to dissolve the marriage. But Julie London's problems were nothing compared to those of the mulatto in *Raintree County* (1959). In this drama a Civil War Southern belle (Elizabeth Taylor) is driven to a frenzy merely because she *thinks* she is part Negro. First she is carted off to a mental institution; later she is found dead under the raintree. Of course, Taylor is revealed as being all white, but the movie shows how awful just the thought of black blood can be.

By far, the 1950's greatest mulatto was the heroine Sarah Jane in Douglas Sirk's remake of *Imitation of Life* in 1959. Version two's Sarah Jane is no happier than the original's Peola. Nor is her mama Annie (Juanita Moore) any more content about her daughter's "affliction" than was Louise Beavers. Not only is Sarah Jane severely beaten by a white boy friend (stunned by the "discovery"), but she is so wretched that she drives herself to self-degradation by becoming a singer in a sleazy red-light district. The film concludes with her return to her dead mama, weeping over the casket and again causing a flood of tears in movie theaters. White actress Susan Kohner was a sinister but convincing Sarah Jane, and Juanita Moore, as Annie, was effective enough to earn an Academy Award nomination for best supporting actress. From this role, Moore went on to a series of minor forgettable roles in *Walk on the Wild Side* (1962), *The Singing Nun* (1966), *Rosie* (1967), and *Uptight*.

The remake of *Imitation of Life* was successful at the box office, revealing that audiences could still respond to the old corn. It also gave birth to a number of similar films in the early 1960s, most notably *I Passed for White* (1960). Here white actress Sonya Wilde portrays a fair-skinned Negro lass who migrates north, where, to no one's surprise, she passes for white. Everything seems fine as she settles down with a white husband. But then her child is born and in terror she screams to the nurse, "Is the baby black?" No, the baby is not black. But word is soon out that his mama is. And thus tragic consequences finally catch up with the doomed mulatto.

In a final look at the 1950s, *Deep Is the Well* and *The Last Angry Man* (1959) should be mentioned. The former was little more than a low-budget potboiler about a small town almost ready for a race riot. Trite as the movie was, it accurately and graphically depicted the violence that American cities and small towns would later experience. *The Last Angry Man* was not as violent in subject matter or tone. An old-style sentimental problem picture about a kindly white doctor, it remains of interest chiefly because of Paul Muni's moving performance and the gallery of new black faces it introduced: Claudia McNeil, Cicely Tyson, Godfrey Cambridge, and Billy Dee Williams. Each was to go on to some critical or commercial success in subsequent decades.

The products and personalities of the Eisenhower age may now seem as ludicrous or irrelevant as those of earlier decades. But the era has to go on record as a self-consciously and self-righteously sincere period in which racial issues were confronted and dealt with in relatively honest terms, at least with as much integrity as the film industry was capable of giving. Films still ended happily, and if any black anger—such as that expressed in Poitier's emotional outbursts—popped up in movies, its impact was lessened by the picture's conclusion, when all difficulties and problems were resolved. Perhaps the tidying-up process was the major shortcoming of this decade's films. Movies such as *Edge of the City, Island in the Sun,* and *The Defiant Ones* failed to record black anger and anguish realistically. They naïvely announced that integration would solve our problems. Other films such as *Carmen Jones, St. Louis Blues, Anna Lucasta,* and *Porgy and Bess* returned to idealized, fake black worlds.

By 1959 America was approaching a social upheaval, a new period in which racism would be revealed as a national sickness, in which the doctrine of integration would be uncovered as too simple an answer to so complex a situation, and in which the American black man would assert himself culturally to articulate the rage he had suppressed through the years. That great social and political change—and its impact on Hollywood films—would render obsolete much of the work of the black stars and personalities of the 1950s and would usher in a totally new type of black film and even a new type of black star.

The 1960s: Problem People into Militants

7

Sidney Poitier, Ruby Dee, Claudia McNeil, and Diana Sands star in A Raisin in the Sun *as a Chicago ghetto family couped up in an inferno of a three-room apartment. . . . Shirley Knight is the Great White American Bitch and Al Freeman, Jr., is the Good Black Boy she leads to death in* Dutchman. *. . . De New South replaces de massa's ole plantation as Beah Richards, Robert Hooks, and Diahann Carroll whoop it up in* Hurry Sundown. *. . . An idealistic white girl arrives home in the affluent suburbs carrying Mr. Perfect Negro on her arm—who else but Sidney Poitier—as she announces* Guess Who's Coming to Dinner. *. . . Jim Brown makes his way through westerns, prison yarns, and adventure tales to become a box-office favorite and a challenger to the old way of black movie herodom. . . . Raymond St. Jacques leads a conclave of black revolutionaries armed with guns and slogans in* Uptight. *. . . Ossie Davis and Dionne Warwick are the stoic slaves who take over the Big House in* Slaves. *. . . The Learning Tree spotlights a young black boy growing up in Kansas in the 1920s and dramatically confronting the violence and self-destructiveness that are a part of this period. . . . Putney Swope showcases a troupe of high-flung, far-out jive-ass niggers storming through an advertising agency and out to get whitey.*

Turbulent, guarded, and paranoid—that was the steaming 1960s when the streets and then the screens exploded with anger and insolence. The nature of the times catapulted the movies' problem people of old into militants of new. No longer were sad-eyed black people trying to prove their worth in order to fit into white worlds. No longer were submissive, patient Negroes pleading for acceptance. Instead, the headstrong militants appeared. Black hearts were still broken, and black lives were still ruined. But with the militants, black rage, black anger, and black power began their maddening stomp, overturning the old placid way and lifting eyebrows as they introduced to America the deep-seated bitterness so long ignored.

Politically, the 1960s may prove the most important decade in the twentieth century for black Americans. An era of great change, the beginning of a transition period of which we have yet to see the end, it started with sit-ins, boycotts, and marches and ended with riots, demonstrations, and a series of horrifying assassinations. In 1960, Negroes were quietly asking for their rights. By 1969, blacks were demanding them. The decade moved from the traditional goal of cultural and academic assimilation to one of almost absolute separatism and the evolution of a black cultural aesthetic.

The movies of the period reflected the great transition. They were a mixture of old and new. It was almost exclusively a period of so-called significant films rather than great personalities. Sidney Poitier was still the top black box-office draw in the country, but at times even his movies overpowered him as a performer. For the most part, his features dealt with familiar aspects of integration and succeeded critically and commercially. Yet they seemed out of place in this separatist age, and they found competition from a number of motion pictures removed from the mainstream of American moviemaking. These films, in which the evolving militants were first to appear, presented a world heretofore ignored on the American screen—ghettos, whores, hustlers, addicts, pimps, and pushers, a world of racist sickness, of oppression, of black despair and rage. These new movies studied poverty, interracial marriages, the state of being black and finding fulfillment in the narrow confines determined by a hostile white world. As the era progressed—and as social pressures mounted—the first steps in the evolution of a new black film began with the appearance of black scriptwriters, providing films with startling dialogue and realistic characters. Later the evolution was just about completed with the appearance of America's first major black movie director. Ultimately, the new black film advanced in two directions. One approach was serious, lyrical, and poetic. The other was farcical, high-spirited, and flashy.

Steps Forward

Take a Giant Step (1960), an amalgam of old and new, launched the new decade. Rock 'n' roll singer Johnny Nash starred as a black boy approaching manhood, full of unanswered questions and stifled by the white environment in which he must function. Ruby Dee made an offbeat appearance as a housekeeper who helps Johnny out with some of his questions about sex. Appearing as Johnny's middle-class mother was Beah Richards. Frederick O'-Neal portrayed the singer's father. O'Neal had already appeared in a number of stage productions and had worked in *Pinky, Something of Value,* and *Anna Lucasta.* Later he became a footnote in theatrical history when he was elected the first black president of Actor's Equity. *Take a Giant Step* had little in the way of performances or direction to distinguish it. Its chief virtue was that black playwright Louis Peterson had adapted the movie from his successful off-Broadway play. Black screenwriters were a rarity in Hollywood. One only regrets that Peterson's venture did not fare better.

The film adaptation of Lorraine Hansberry's *A Raisin in the Sun* (1961) proved more successful. Directed by Daniel Petrie and produced by David Susskind, the film was a disorganized integrationist drama. Still it contained enough unusual twists and insights to move audiences. Set in a tiny Southside Chicago apartment, *A Raisin in the Sun* examined the Younger family. For years, matriarch Lena Younger has dreamed of getting out of the flat she shares with her son Walter, his wife Ruth, their child Travis, and her daughter Beneatha. Her deliverance comes in the form of a ten-thousand-dollar insurance policy left to her by her husband. With the money, Lena Younger will buy a house in the integrated suburbs. As she makes her plans and dreams her dream, the personal problems of each member of the household clash with those of the others. Author Hansberry captured the tension of blacks enduring lives of violent desperation, and she hit with unerring exactness on a number of things never dealt with before in the movies. Her drama took the average filmgoer into the grime and grit of the ghetto. It exposed the matriarchal set-up in black homes and examined the emasculation of the black male by a hostile white society. Hansberry framed her work with the gentle humor and wisdom a race of people had developed out of their heartache and anguish. *A Raisin in the Sun*'s message may seem dated today,

RIGHT: In 1951 Jackie Robinson temporarily left the baseball field for the movies, but he didn't forget to carry his glove along with him. Here he appears with Ruby Dee in *The Jackie Robinson Story.*
BELOW: The grime and grit of the ghetto as never seen before: *Raisin in the Sun* (1961), with Sidney Poitier, Ruby Dee, Claudia McNeil, and Diana Sands.

but even though the film celebrated integration and ultimately paid homage to the America of free enterprise and materialism, it mirrored a timeless sense of oppression and despair, and it contained performances that, if at times overblown, were often rich and effective.

As the restless, wayward son Walter, Sidney Poitier gave one of his most exciting performances, heightened because his character was so different from the established Poitier image. "I open and close car doors all day long. I drive a man around in his limousine and I say, 'Yes, sir,'" he cried. "Mama, that ain't no kind of a job ... that ain't nothing at all." His Walter was a deeply troubled man with whom black audiences could identify.

Newcomer Diana Sands portrayed the screwball, intellectual sister Beneatha. Hers was a witty and winning characterization. As she screamed out in comic-pathetic rage that there was no God, she revealed herself as a magnetic, compelling actress. Diana Sands ushered in the contemporary, untyped intelligent black woman. She was neither mammy nor mulatto. After *A Raisin in the Sun* she made an appearance in an entirely forgettable film titled *An Affair of the Skin* (1963). But later she was very successful in such stage productions as *The Owl and the Pussycat, Blues for Mr. Charlie,* and *Phaedra.* She returned to films in the 1970s with a sensitive performance as the black girl made pregnant by the white boy in *The Landlord* (1970). Somber, slightly hoarse, near tears but not about to break down, Diana Sands managed, amid heavy dramatics, to impart a comic, lighthearted side to her character. Following *The Landlord,* the actress worked in *Doctors' Wives* (1971). Here, even in a sudsy, exploitative soap opera, she proved that talent could transcend material. No doubt her most complex screen role was in the bizarre, dramatically uneven *Georgia, Georgia* (1972). With a screenplay by Maya Angelou, the film cast Diana Sands as a successful but emotionally driven American pop singer travelling abroad. Although her performance was not wholly satisfying, it was compelling nonetheless.

Generally, Claudia McNeil received glowing notices for her work in *A Raisin in the Sun. Time* magazine did cattily remark, however, that she often came across "like a mean old man in a wig." And it has to be admitted that the news magazine had its point. Seen today, McNeil seems grossly like the mammy of Hattie McDaniel vintage, but without the humor and spontaneity. She had the power but not the pathos required, and her work was most effective when she was hooting, yelling, and reprimanding.

Surprisingly, the one performance in *A Raisin in the Sun* that retains its full intensity is Ruby Dee's Ruth. As the wife who agonizes over cleaning someone else's home and then returns to find she has none of her own, Ruby Dee proved successful with a difficult character. She also showed that if given the chance she could do complex and delicately shaded work. Before *A Raisin in the Sun*, Ruby Dee had run through the perfect wife-girl-friend bit to the point where she was—as one newspaper called her— "the Negro June Allyson." In films such as *No Way Out; The Jackie Robinson Story; Go, Man, Go; Edge of the City; Virgin Island* (1960); and *Take a Giant Step*, she was either pleasantly understanding or sincerely forgiving. Although she occasionally rose above her material—her breakdown after Poitier's death in *Edge of the City* was extremely powerful—even in her good work, Ruby Dee never seemed a complete person. She appeared to be the typical woman born to be hurt. Everything about her suggested frustration and pain. Her voice trembled and broke. There were deep shadows under her eyes. She looked thin, anemic, weak, and terribly underfed and unloved. She always seemed to force a smile while standing by nervously and accepting whatever her men might throw her way. Often, because her performances were as inhibited and keyed up as her characters, she seemed limited in range as an actress, and audiences longed to see her break loose. But in *A Raisin in the Sun*, Ruby Dee forged her inhibitions, her anemia, and her repressed and taut ache to convey beautifully the most searing kind of black torment. The rest of the cast exploded with obvious rage, but Ruby Dee's tension, in contrast, was all the more immediate because it was so well controlled. *A Raisin in the Sun* must have been a liberating force for the actress; afterward she temporarily broke the mold of her frustrated heroines with appearances as a prostitute in *The Balcony* (1963) and as the pig-tailed pickaninny in *Gone Are the Days* (1964). Neither film was successful, and soon Ruby Dee was back in the old mold in *The Incident* (1967), another of her better performances where she again *used* her inhibitions, and *Uptight* (1969). Later, in *Buck and the Preacher*, Rudy Dee, like Harry Belafonte, gave an admirable performance. As Sidney Poitier's long-suffering wife, a woman simply hoping to escape racist America and live her life without having to fight battles, she delivered a moving monologue. The role might be classified as a typical Ruby Dee understanding-endurable-sensitive-wife character, but that seemed a bit beside the point here. The important thing was that she played her role so well.

The integrationist theme of *A Raisin in the Sun* also informed Roger and Gene Corman's cheaply made *The Intruder* (1963). Centering on a mysterious white man who enters a small Southern town and sets off racial animosities resulting in bombings, burnings, and night rides of the Klan, the film had neither aesthetic nor great social significance. But *The Intruder* did go into something still very much on the nation's mind: school desegregation and the hysteria growing out of it. Moreover, the film revealed that the racial theme and pro-civil-rights issues were acceptable enough to infiltrate the American B movie.

Black Art Films

During the first half of the 1960s, a quartet of inexpensively but sensitively made motion pictures offered grimly realistic and cynical looks at black America. *Shadows* (1961), *The Cool World* (1963), *One Potato, Two Potato* (1964), and *Nothing But a Man* (1964), all apparently not made only for commercial reasons, presented "art-house style" depictions of America's racial problems. Audiences viewed black protagonists demanding a chance to fulfill themselves on their own terms without having to live up to white standards. Behind their placid exteriors, there shone the evolving great militant spirit.

John Cassavetes' *Shadows* picked up the old tragic mulatto theme and turned it inside out. Here a black girl who looks white falls in love with a white man. She neglects to tell him she is black not because of any shame. She simply believes it unimportant. By the picture's end (and after the white man has rejected her upon discovering her racial heritage), the girl has learned that in America such problems are never unimportant. Filmed in *cinema vérité* style, *Shadows* unearthed squarely and honestly the hazards of an interracial romance.

By 1963, most movie patrons were accustomed to reading about the Freedom Riders in the South and the various protest activities of Martin Luther King. Civil rights involvement was becoming respectable, and the great white liberal movement was in full swing. But not even the liberals—and surely not the majority of the moviegoing public—were acquainted with the world Shirley Clarke's camera probed in *The Cool World*. Here the camera focused on previously unexplored turf—Harlem. Based on Warren Miller's novel, the film showed the plight of a fifteen-year-old ghetto victim, Duke, and his gang, the Pythons. Duke searches for a gun, the great power symbol that will assure him of his leadership and help him defeat the rival gang, the Wolves. In between the search for the gun, director Clarke presents a disciplined and realistic portrait of Harlem as Divine Hell. The Pythons trade comic books for marijuana, share their gangland whore, drink booze, snatch purses, storm the city streets in anger, in boredom, in utter hopelessness. At the same time, Clarke turns her camera to other faces of the city: an out-of-state high-school class touring New York, viewing all of Fifth Avenue but oblivious to the blood on the sidewalks of 125th Street and Lenox Avenue.

An honest and difficult film, *The Cool World* was produced by Frederick Wiseman (now known for his brilliant documentaries on hospitals and high schools) and features a number of impressive performers, some of whom, like Gloria Foster and Clarence Williams III, would be heard from again before the decade ended. Shirley Clarke was co-author of the script along with Carl Lee (the son of actor Canada Lee), who also played Priest. Here again a perceptive black writer was able to bring new insights to a filmic exploration of the black experience. Four years after *The Cool World*, Shirley Clarke returned to a treatment of a black subject with *Portrait of Jason* (1967), a devastating documentary study of a black male prostitute.

Sam Weston and Larry Peerce's *One Potato, Two Potato* was the screen's first study of an interracial marriage. (Other features had dealt with interracial romances; there is a difference.) The film centered on a custody battle between a divorced white couple for their young daughter. Previously, when the woman had been deserted by her husband, she had met and fallen in love with a black man. Against opposition mainly from his family, the two married, taking her child by the previous marriage to live with them. Despite social pressures, their marriage is working, and the black husband's parents have developed a deep feeling for their daughter-in-law and her little girl. But when the former husband learns of his daughter's whereabouts, he initiates a court battle to take the child away. He wins his suit, and the film concludes with his driving off with the confused child.

Skillfully photographed in Painesville, Ohio, *One Potato, Two Potato* was a somber film, its approach restrained and decent, its direction adroit. Its modest success (along with the critical interest in *Shadows*) surely led the way for such major-studio studies of the interracial marriage-romance in *A Patch of Blue* and *Guess Who's Coming to Dinner*. All its performances were well handled. Barbara Barrie deserved her Cannes Film Festival Award as best actress for her portrayal of the wife. Robert Earl Jones (the father of James) and Vinnie Carroll played the hostile black parents ultimately unable not to love the little girl. But *One Potato, Two Potato*'s chief virtue was Bernie Hamilton's charming portrayal of the Negro husband. For a number of years, Hamilton had been working on and off in films, appearing in *The Jackie Robinson*

Story, Let No Man Write My Epitaph (1960), *The Young One* (1961), and *The Devil at Four O'Clock* (1961). But never before had he a role he could do anything with. Here in *One Potato, Two Potato* he presented a portrait of a decent and intelligent black man without glamorizing or idealizing the character. Later he appeared in *Synanon* and *The Swimmer* (1968).

That same quality of screen honesty shone through Ivan Dixon's fine performance in *Nothing But a Man*. The film itself was as neatly restrained as the actor. It dealt with a black railroad laborer, Duff Anderson, living in the Deep South. When he marries an attractive schoolteacher (Abbey Lincoln), the film records the pressures in his home and outside it which nearly crush the pair. Duff's independence from his white bosses marks him as a target for their racism. Fired from one job after another, taunted and hounded, he eventually takes out his frustrations on his wife. He leaves her and sets out on a black odyssey that carries him to Birmingham, where he visits his self-destructive alcoholic father. There he sees a man dying with nothing, denied even his manhood. Deeply affected, Duff returns to his wife, taking his own illegitimate son with him, and attempts to re-establish the relationship.

Shot in distinct black and white, quiet in tone, notable for its subtlety, *Nothing But a Man* told its deep, dark tale simply. The film owes much of its power to its performers. Julius Harris portrayed the alcoholoic father. Although director Michael Roemer never points a finger at racist white America for Harris's condition, and although Harris never cries out in self-pity as a victimized black man, the implications are there nonetheless. As the understanding wife, jazz vocalist Abbey Lincoln (in her acting debut) provides appropriate strength and passion. It is one of the warmest black female characterizations of the decade. The other impressive female performance in *Nothing But a Man* is that of Gloria Foster. She had already revealed herself in *The Cool World* as an introspective actress of great power. Here cast as the stoic mistress of Julius Harris, Foster is a marvel of intensified pain. Fine as that performance is, she has made few film appearances since then. With her marriage to Clarence Williams III, of television's "Mod Squad" series, she moved to California from New York, where she had had great success in off-Broadway productions. In California she made many television guest shots, With astounding skill, she managed even on the tritest of shows to be convincing and to present herself as a totally contemporary black woman. Her style is the most naturalistic of any black actress in American pictures. Foster's subsequent films included *The*

ABOVE: The interracial marriage comes to the screen—Barbara Barrie and Bernie Hamilton in *One Potato, Two Potato*.

BELOW: Brock Peters, who emerged in the 1960s as the era's most prominent black brute figure.

Comedians (1967), *The Angel Levine,* and *Man and Boy* (1972).

Moving as the other actors were, *Nothing But a Man* marked a personal triumph for actor Ivan Dixon. A black performer of great skill, Dixon had previously appeared in scattered empty roles in films such as *Something of Value* and *Porgy and Bess* and in a few television programs. As the African beau of Diana Sands in *A Raisin in the Sun,* he had a fleeting opportunity to show his mettle, but it did little to advance his career. Today *Nothing But a Man* remains his finest work. His Duff was a fitting precursor to the militant spirits about to burst on the scene. His character's quarrel was not only with his white oppressors but with those blacks who permit oppression. Dixon affected his audience without relying on histrionics. Both he and Bernie Hamilton ushered in a new style of black sexuality in the 1960s. Through the way they walked, through the way they eyed and held women, these two actors let audiences know they were sensitive, tortured men as well as sensual ones. Unfortunately, neither actor was to work steadily in movies. Dixon later appeared in a thankless role in *Patch of Blue.* In 1972, he directed Robert Hooks in *Trouble Man.*

A Step Backward: Ossie Davis and *Gone Are the Days*

Whereas the art-house films attempted to present untyped black characters, the 1964 film adaptation of Ossie Davis' play *Purlie Victorious* carried audiences back to the old stereotype figures. Retitled *Gone Are the Days,* the movie centered on a fast-talking, coon con-man minister, Purlie, whose ambition is to convert a battered barn (the property of a stanch Southern aristocrat) into an integrated church. He enlists as many as he can in his community—the local mammy and the local tom and the local pickaninny and the local white liberal—to aid him in his plan. In the end, Purlie gets his church. As a film *Gone Are the Days* was humorless and dismal. Had Ossie Davis not been associated with it, the picture would hardly be worth mentioning.

By 1964, Ossie Davis had already acquired a following, composed mainly of white liberals and members of the black bourgeoisie. Through sheer push and panache, he had promoted himself into the leading-man category, replacing Poitier on stage in *A Raisin in the Sun* and then winning decent reviews for his work in *Purlie Victorious.* In motion pictures, Davis met with moderate success. He gave competent though hardly inspiring performances in such features as *No Way Out, The Cardinal* (1963), and *Shock Treatment* (1964). Later he was to appear in *The Hill* (1965), *The Scalphunters* (1968), and most notoriously in *Slaves* (1969).

It was evident that Davis lacked the range and variety for big, important starring roles. But there was a place for Davis in the film world. He was usually cast as a stoic, relatively dignified tom. He was an educated Negro priest in one film, a Latin scholar of sorts in another. Like Poitier, he was a model integrationist hero: intelligent, reasonable, reliable, and well-mannered. But Davis's toms were not very likable and they lacked charisma. Their only distinguishing characteristic was that they were masochists of the first degree. If any reactionary white audience wanted to see a black man get his due, an Ossie Davis film was the thing to see. In *The Cardinal* (1963), Davis, the great liberal delight, portrayed a Southern priest journeying to Rome to cry out against discrimination in the Catholic church. Practically everyone in the theater knew the journey would be of no avail. Almost anyone could have predicted that retaliation would be taken against this outspoken black man. Consequently, when the gentle and well-bred Davis was brutally attacked by the Ku Klux Klan, no audience member was terribly surprised—or upset. Admirable or heroic as Davis's character was, he had been asking for trouble. The same was true of his kind-hearted tom character in *Slaves*. Here again Ossie Davis was brutally beaten, and once more through his stoicism, he seemed to encourage his own abuse and mistreatment. Regardless, in all his films, whether cast as pure masochist or near-masochist (as was the case with *The Scalphunters*), Ossie Davis proved interesting in bits and pieces. But he was far from being overwhelming.

As an actor, so, too, as a writer. Ossie Davis's *Gone Are the Days* proved mildly diverting in bits and pieces, namely in the idea behind the work. But as a whole the movie was far from the great farce its author envisioned. Davis believed American audiences, black and white, were sophisticated enough in the early 1960s to enjoy the old stereotypes and laugh at their exaggerations. Therefore he cluttered his work with types, clichés, and platitudes. Unfortunately, his actors played their roles as if their characters were to be taken seriously. Godfrey Cambridge's tom was static and emotionally anemic. Beah Richards' mammy was intolerable. Davis himself was a crackerjack coon dazzling with his razzmatazz but ultimately too one-dimensional. Ruby Dee turned up surprisingly as an uninhibited pickaninny named Lutiebelle, and, surprisingly too, she was the only funny character in the picture. *Gone Are the Days* was a prodigious failure. Ossie Davis's pure stereotypes had not worked, and he may have pined over their failure —but not for long. Later his idea that audiences were removed enough from the stereotypes to respond to them if they were exuberantly presented was proven true with the enormous success of the Broadway musical *Purlie* (based on *Purlie Victorious*) and the Davis-directed movie *Cotton Comes to Harlem* (1970). If anything, *Gone Are the Days* was the first step in the evolution of the new-style all-black movie.

Along the Road, in Harlem, and on the Subway

The far-fetched efforts of Ossie Davis were followed by the serious approaches of the so-called little pictures *Black Like Me* (1964), *The Pawnbroker* (1965), and *Dutchman* (1967). *Black Like Me*, based on John Howard Griffin's bestselling book, reversed Hollywood's great theme of passing the color line. Playing the author, who actually performed this social experiment, James Whitmore, as a white man, undergoes a special chemical treatment to darken his skin. Then he hitchhikes across the South passing as a Negro. During his travels in a black man's America, the white man witnesses the cruelty and hatred that infest the land. He is shoved on buses, chased by white hoodlums, abused by employers, refused employment, questioned about his sex life, and repeatedly subjected to humiliation.

Critics of *Black Like Me* still view it as merely another example of the white man slumming at a black man's expense. Others have seen it as a continuation of the tragic mulatto theme and nothing more. (Indeed, the film's thesis was that here was a white man being treated so shamelessly simply because his skin was darkened.) But the more relevant fact was that, crude and shoddy as this B movie was, it was an earnest attempt to confront and expose racism in America.

The production's earnestness was greatly aided by the engaging work of a line-up of new black faces. Al Freeman, Jr., appeared briefly as a quick-tempered 1950s-style sit-inner. As Mr. Educated Negro, Roscoe Lee Browne provided an appropriate insolent and neurotic flair that went a little deeper than his written role. He was a stage actor with only one previous screen credit—in Shirley Clarke's *The Connection* (1960). Some of his mannered theatrics did not work to full effect. But he introduced in this film a new type of black character of which he would be the chief exponent and which would be more fully developed in his subsequent films *Uptight* and *The Liberation of L. B. Jones* (1970). His characters were cynical, lost, sterile toms, products of a decadent black bourgeoisie. Perhaps his were the most realistic toms ever presented in American films. Having sold out, they have profited economically, but they have lost their self-respect and always seem to be verging on emotional breakdowns. Browne's most likable role, an exception to his lost tom characters, was as the dapper, cane-carrying dandy in *The Comedians* (1967). *Black Like Me* also introduced a slender and surprisingly pleasant Raymond St. Jacques, as a middle-class black businessman, and the delightful Thelma Oliver, as a black girl who talks too much although she tries her best not to. Both also appeared in *The Pawnbroker.*

Sidney Lumet's *The Pawnbroker* did not have a black theme, but the picture was set in Harlem, and it prominently featured a number of black actors. Like the film's disillusioned Jewish hero, the blacks were inhabitants (sometimes victims; other times, predators) of a world that daily assaults and dehumanizes them. Thelma Oliver was moving and resonant as the broken-spirited black girl ready to sell everything, including herself, to save her lover. Oliver's black whore was a beautifully defined and individualized figure, a creature as comic as she was sad. In a minor role, Raymond St. Jacques proved adequate—no more, no less. On the other hand, Juano Hernandez was excellent in his role.

Although he was not the most impressive black actor in the picture, Brock Peters nonetheless merited close attention. He was cast as a sinister hood terriorizing the Jewish pawnbroker. For Peters, the role as the tough was nothing new. His previous performances as Sergeant Brown in *Carmen Jones* and as Crown in *Porgy and Bess* had been personifications of the classic black brute. Brock Peters was pitch black (that was enough to frighten any white audience) and without the healthy good looks of a Poitier or a Belafonte. He perfected a vicious snarl and as he malevolently eyed the other characters in his films he suggested uncontrolled violence. Finally, when he pounced upon his opponents, he was the incarnation of unbridled brutality. Even when cast later as the homosexual West Indian Johnny in the British film *The L-Shaped Room* (1963) or as the emasculated farmhand on trial for rape in *To Kill a Mockingbird* (1962), his characterizations had raw edge and bitter power. In *The Pawnbroker*, Peters was in top brute form. Belligerent, hostile, and downright nasty, he played his part well, but it was apparent that he was playing a type and doing little more. He continued in this tradition with his black supremacist work in *The Incident* (1967) and later in *The McMasters* (1970).

When adapted for the screen, LeRoi Jones' one-act play *Dutchman* was expanded to fifty-five minutes. Directed by Anthony Harvey in England, *Dutchman* was a grim little parable, beginning with a subway ride and ending with a nightmarish dance of death. On a new York subway train, a psychotic white woman,

Lula, meets a respectable middle-class black man, Clay. By the time the ride has ended, Lula has stabbed Clay to death before a trainload of passive passengers and is well on her way to doing in a second black victim. By its conclusion, too, *Dutchman*, better than any other piece of dramatic writing of the decade, articulated the options left open to a black man in white America: either he can survive by joining the ranks of the black bourgeoisie (those apers of white manners who are doomed to lives without their manhood) or he can lash out at the dominant culture and run the risk of being chopped down. Jones's thesis was not particularly pleasant. Nor was the film. But they worked dazzlingly.

Dutchman owed most of its power to its high-charged theatrical dialogue and the acid performances of Al Freeman, Jr., and Shirley Knight. Today this is still Freeman's best screen performance, and his character is typical of the sort he played during the 1960s. His Clay is a number of things. For the first three-fourths of the picture he is the educated tom, a "civilized" Negro who quietly turns the other cheek. In the last quarter, Freeman violently explodes, asserting himself as he protests the injustices and atrocities black Americans live with daily. Clearly, Freeman's Clay is a middle-class creation. But he is a radicalized one. Not content to be intellectually stagnant, he is transformed into a forceful militant. In *Dutchman* and his other films *Black Like Me, The Troublemaker* (1964), *The Detective* (1968), *Finian's Rainbow* (1968), and *The Lost Man* (1969), Al Freeman, despite the fact that he played supporting roles, emerged as the movies' best black spokesman on militancy and intellectualized hostility. Never were his characters portrayed as the typical black brutes (as most movie militants were to be depicted). Each of his performances was so well thought out and so expertly tempered that his emotional outbursts were never just uncontrolled hatred. Instead they were explanations of why black America had so much pent-up anger. For this reason, Freeman's work still outshines that of many name actors of the period.

Way Down in de New Ole South with Tom-Tom, Miss Bronze Barbie Doll, and Ms. Militant Mammy

Otto Preminger's *Hurry Sundown* (1967) was the first major, big-budget, star-studded motion picture to center on the militant spirit of the mid-1960s and the black revolt. Preminger based his film on K. B. Gilden's sprawling, best-selling novel about the post–World War II New South. He shot his movie in Baton Rouge, Louisiana (where crew and cast were often threatened by the Ku Klux Klan), and he lined up an impressive roster of actors: Michael

Caine, Jane Fonda, John Philip Law, Faye Dunaway, Burgess Meredith, and the black actors Robert Hooks, Diahann Carroll, Rex Ingram, and Beah Richards.

Hurry Sundown was, in many respects, a summation of almost every Southern white and black cliché the movies had ever relied on. The Southern Belle, the Simon-Legree massa, the white idiot child, the faithful mammy, the white Liberal, the New Educated Black Woman (a la Pinky), the New Good Sensitive Negro, the Corrupt Old White Bigot, the Po' White Trash—all had their place in this drama. The plot was complicated and circuitous. A corrupt simon-legreeish Michael Caine wants to make an important land deal, selling property belonging to his wife (Jane Fonda). But he also needs that of his wife's cousin Rad (po' white trash portrayed by John Philip Law) and his wife's mammy (Beah Richards) to complete the transaction. Through much wheeling and dealing, with many heated passions and bed scenes in between, Caine is able to persuade Fonda to take her mammy's land. "That old woman was my mammy," she protests at first, "and she loved me. There was a time when she was the only one in this whole world I knew loved me. And I *cain't* go against her!" But, of course, she does. Still, before Caine knows it, the po' white trash cousin Rad (who's a war veteran) has joined with the mammy's uppity militant son Reeve (also a war veteran, portrayed by Hooks) to keep their property and to work it together. Theirs represents the new postwar spirit, that of integration, and Preminger implies that this spirit will defeat their common enemy, the white supremacist.

The film builds to two heady climaxes. The first is in a courtroom session at which a white bigoted judge (Burgess Meredith) presides. Before the session ends, Diahann Carroll has chased Fonda into a white ladies' room, has berated her for sticking by a man who means her no good, and has brought about such a drastic transformation that Fonda marches back into the courtroom and demands that the proceedings be stopped. She drops her case. Black Reeve and white Rad are victorious. Or so they think. For during the second climax, greedy Caine has dynamited Rad's farm. But the movie's liberalized conclusion announces that the postwar integrationist spirit will not be destroyed so easily. Black Reeve and his black church-and-farm friends march with white Rad to help him rebuild his farm. Throughout a black chorus sings dat dey don't mind de sufferin' cause de sundown's a comin'. And thus we see the dawn of a new South.

Preposterous as *Hurry Sundown* may sound, it remains a key pop work of the 1960s, and it contains some intense, if at times outlandish, performances by its black players. Screen newcomer

Robert Hooks portrays Reeve, the World War II veteran returning home to fight another battle. He accepts insults and humiliations until he can take no more, then joins forces with his white friend. Hooks' character was to symbolize a new type of militancy in tune with the outspokeness of a Stokely Carmichael. But in actuality he is little more than the postwar Negro figure of the 1940s, a sort of pepped-up James Edwards. He is a tom's tom, pliable and decent, and the character is made redeemable only because of the actor's personal charm and healthy good looks. If *Hurry Sundown* did nothing else, however, it revealed that with the right roles Robert Hooks could have developed into a black matinee idol.

Diahann Carroll plays the part of the pretty schoolteacher Vivien. It is a role she was perfect for, but perhaps for all the wrong reasons. It seemed as if Diahann Carroll had been grooming herself throughout her career for this role as the post-integrated black woman. In her first films, *Carmen Jones* and *Porgy and Bess*, Carroll was cast as a pleasing, unadorned pickaninny. She was pretty and pert but hardly glamorous. She was slightly sensual but far from seductive. All in all Diahann Carroll came across as the nice, innocent girl next door. But in the 1960s, this engaging naïveté was lost; Diahann Carroll's film style underwent a drastic change. (The image she presented in nightclub and television appearances and on Broadway in *No Strings* underwent the same change.) It was in *Paris Blues* in 1961 that she first emerged as a plasticized, middle-class Negro lady type. ("I'm acceptable . . .," she explained years later in a magazine interview. "I'm a black woman with a white image. I'm as close as they can get to having the best of both worlds. The audience can accept me. . . . I don't scare them." Truer words were never spoken.) Here she portrayed an American girl off to learn about life and love in France. Her best friend is a white girl, played by Joanne Woodward, and it is obvious that culturally and philosophically the two are of the same world, except perhaps that Woodward exhibits a bit more spunk and spontaneity.

Black leading ladies had always been cast close to the white ideal, but always, of course, even in the cases of Lena Horne and Dorothy Dandridge, there was some trace of the ethnic experience, something "cullid" about them that black audiences could identify with. In *Paris Blues*, however, Diahann Carroll came closer in speech, dress, mannerism, looks, and life style to the great white ideal than any black actress before her. But more disturbing (or perhaps enlightening) was that she revealed how sterile and shallow such an ideal was. On the screen, not one hair was out of place. Not one word was mispronounced. There was not one false blink of the eyes. So perfectly planned and calculated was she that Diahann Carroll seemed more an automation—some exquisite bronze Barbie Doll—than a leading lady. For politically sensitive black audiences, Diahann Carroll represented one more dehydrated and lifeless accruement of a decadent capitalist society. And curiously the elegant sterility may explain her magnetism.

In *Hurry Sundown,* that sterility and decadence were a bit out of place, but with it Carroll gave her definite bronze Barbie Doll performance. Here she portrayed an outspoken, educated black woman just returned from the North. Her character was to be horrified and indignant over segregation yet bright and resourceful enough to work her way around difficult situations. Curiously Carroll seemed more bored by the racism in the picture—or amused—than irritated. She is obviously a woman accustomed to getting what she wants, one who really doesn't have any great feelings of discrimination. She knows oppression only on a superficial level. The scene in which she follows Jane Fonda into the white ladies' room and slaps her face seems somewhat ludicrous. In the first place, Carroll looks as white as Fonda—and acts it, too. So why the fuss over her entering the white ladies' room? Secondly, Carroll's pleas for her rights are almost laughable because she seems too far removed from the harsh black experience to fully understand it. Perhaps for this reason, though, her work has a certain daffy effectiveness. She herself clearly symbolizes the post-integrated black woman. Her color will never make her feel shame, and she is to be respected for that. But she has entered a free society at the expense of her own individuality. She has adopted so many white values that she has lost her own soul.

This type of black woman—and some of the decadence she acquires by fully accepting the values of the dominant culture—could have been fascinating if properly handled. Later William Wyler toyed with it in *The Liberation of L. B. Jones* (1970). But he unwisely cast his picture with a black whore type (Lola Falana) rather than a black decadent middle-class lady figure. This type of character is one that the movies, even black fiction and poetry, have yet to deal with. But if ever it is dealt with, Diahann Carroll could be the actress to represent it best in American movies. Regardless, she came close after *Hurry Sundown* in parts of *The Split* (1968) and most notably with her successfully packaged Doris-Day-in-blackface character in the television series "Julia."

Beah Richards, as Mammy Rose, came off better than any other black actor in *Hurry Sundown,* presenting to audiences a middle-class mammy in revolt. Previously Richards had appeared in movies such as *Take a Giant Step, The Miracle Worker* (1962), and *Gone*

Are the Days. Later she appeared as the mother in *Guess Who's Coming to Dinner.* In all these films—and even in *In the Heat of the Night* (1967) in which she was uncharacteristically cast as a whore—Beah Richards was always the paragon of black respectability—at least at first glance. One always imagined her wearing white gloves and having a bridge party to attend. But unlike the middle-class Diahann Carroll, Richards has a humorous side, and emerged as the prim little black lady whom audiences secretly loved to hate. There had never been anyone quite like her before. She was so soft-spoken and genteel (notably later in *Guess Who's Coming to Dinner*) that audiences knew she had to be acting. Beah Richards just did not look like the typical middle-class black woman. For one thing, she was very dark and had "Negroid" features. Almost always middle-class black characters, on screen as off, were thought of as being light-skinned—as close in complexion to whites as they were in their life styles. For another thing, she looked hard and "evil," as if she would bite back in a minute if anyone dared step on her toes. She looked as if she had been raised in a ghetto, and that if she wore white gloves she was only putting on airs. There was something definitely "cullid" about her, and audiences just wanted her to drop the middle-class sweetness and phoniness and scream out in black rage. In *Hurry Sundown,* Beah Richards was once again cast as the sweet, lovable, pious, well-spoken, pliant black woman. But this time, audiences saw the obviously fake middle-class black lady break loose.

Made up to look at least two-hundred and fifty years old, with a head of hair that looks like a cotton patch, Richards' character, Mammy Rose, was at first the essence of the Louise Beavers type of submissive, cheerful domestic. "Sometimes, Rose," says white actress Fonda, "I think you just about invented love." The proper, intelligent, polite Mammy Rose smiles. But within a few minutes when she is asked to give up her property, she collapses with a heart-attack. Then, like a pepped-up, enraged version of Ethel Waters, she cries out to her son, "I was wrong. . . . I was a white folks' nigger. I was. . . . You got to fight. . . . Swear to it. . . . You'll know at the end you won't have this agony. This taste of bitterness and gall. In these last minutes, you know what I feel most of all. Anger. And hateful. Not so much of them but for what they done to me. . . . And myself for helping them to do it. . . . I truly grieve for the sorry thing that has been my life." In the context of the film, the scene is comic. No one acquires that much insight in five minutes. But at the movies anything can happen. And, most important, because actress Richards was finally saying the lines it looked as if she should have been crying out throughout this picture (and perhaps her previous ones), the sentiments appeared real. The middle-class mammy had dropped the airs and become real. The audience forgot the rest of the film and picked out those parts it held closest. And Beah Richards came off as a heroine of sorts.

Beah Richards' success in *Hurry Sundown* epitomized the things that went into making this particular movie a success with black audiences. Like Richards' character, the film dealt with issues, questions, even taboos that were on everyone's mind. And in dealing with these the film spelled everything out without attempting ambiguity or nuance. "If we want to make it better," said Robert Hooks's Reeve, "we gotta make it better. Nobody's going to do it for us." Coming from Hooks's tom, the words were ridiculous. But they summed up the mood and the attitude (simplified, of course) of militants in the 1960s. Consequently, the audience forgot about the character saying the lines and instead responded to the lines themselves. "On your feet," said a white judge when he found Diahann Carroll sitting in his office. "What has come over you people? Have you no sense of decorum? Isn't there a trace of respect left in any of you?" Later the same judge asks during a courtroom procedure, "Are you aware of how extraordinary it is for a white man to come into my court to represent a black boy?" "Well," replies the white lawyer, "no more than it was for my daddy to present me a negra half-brother!" "Don't rattle your skeletons in my face!" the judge commands.

But *Hurry Sundown* rattled everyone's skeleton in everyone else's face. It presented archetypal scenes and characters that audiences associated with the South, with bigots, with liberals, and with touchy racial situations. Although it was cluttered with clichés and misrepresentations, *Hurry Sundown* was directed as one big glorious comic strip with pop scene after pop scene, and thus it succeeded on a primal level as a popularization of current events. Eventually, because of its inadvertent satire and parody, the movie pointed a new direction for the handling of the Negro problem. It led the way to the pure satire and madness and the intentional use of stereotypes and clichés found in *Putney Swope* (1969) and *Cotton Comes to Harlem.*

A *Man Called Adam* and the Son of Sunshine Sammy

At the same time Preminger's rambunctiously absurd effort appeared, movie viewers were also presented with a psychodrama, *A Man Called Adam* (1966). The film starred Sammy Davis, Jr., with Cicely Tyson, Peter Lawford, and Ossie Davis. Except for

Tyson's sensitive and intelligent work as the ingenue, the acting and direction were pedestrian at best. In fact, the only saving grace of this tawdry film about a disturbed and difficult jazz musician wallowing in self-pity was that it unintentionally revealed the funkiness and confused, misplaced anger then felt on American street corners. The feature seemed to have a certain oppressive centered-in-the-ghetto air about it (perhaps because it was such an inexpensive film and because its producers shrewdly distributed it in ghetto areas), and certainly the idea of a jazz film itself appealed to black audiences. So, too, did the idea of a new black heel of an antihero. (This idea was later successfully picked up in 1971 with *Sweet Sweetback's Baadasssss Song* and *Shaft*.) But the movie's great failing was what the producers had thought was its great asset: Sammy Davis, Jr. Had he been a better equipped actor, the character at least might have succeeded.

Throughout the late 1950s and early 1960s Sammy Davis, Jr., had had a spectacularly lackluster film career. He always received featured billing in movies. Because he had been an entertainer nearly all his life, beginning as a tot with his father in the Will Mastin Trio, the black press sentimentally gave him good coverage. Audiences had been conditioned to think of him as a show-business legend. Yet his actual film performances were far from outstanding. His first film of the 1950s, *The Benny Goodman Story*, was hardly memorable. In his next feature, *Anna Lucasta*, he and Eartha Kitt were billed as "the entertainment world's most electrifying pair." Yet there was little electricity to the coupling. As the hard-as-nails sailor boy friend Davis was miscast and totally unconvincing, clearly lacking the physical presence and personality for a lead role. Afterward there came his most publicized appearance, as the flashy, jive-ass nigger Sportin' Life in *Porgy and Bess*. Here he seemed more at home, but the Gershwin music was more interesting than the character. At times, too, Davis came across like a shrimp trying to act like a big fish. The secret to playing the coon Sportin' Life was to be rowdy and outrageous but to do it with the greatest of ease. Sammy Davis, Jr., seemed to be trying too hard.

In the features that dominated his career, the clan movies in which he costarred with Frank Sinatra, Dean Martin, and Peter Lawford, he alienated black movie patrons because he was too much the coon-pickaninny figure. On the surface the clan pictures were egalitarian affairs; underneath they rotted from white patronizing and hypocrisy. In *Ocean's Eleven* (1960), Davis portrayed the agreeable lackey sidekick. In an era in which token niggers were popping up in offices throughout America, he became the "showcase nigger" for the white stars. To maintain such a privileged position, Davis underwent much abuse in his films. At the conclusion of *Robin and the 7 Hoods*, when Davis, Dean Martin, and Frank Sinatra were all dressed as Santa Clauses, the racial joke of a ludicrous black Santa was at Davis's expense. In that same film it was apparent that Sinatra ordered him about as he never did the white actors. When he shouted for Davis to cut out the nonsense, it was no different from Will Rogers threatening to give Stepin Fetchit a kick in the pants in the 1930s (except that in the earlier pictures there was no pretense of equality).

In *Sergeants 3* (1962), in which he was actually cast as a diligently faithful coon servant, the movie tried prettifying the situation by making him a hero. But in Davis's work there was too much exaggeration, too much playing up to whitey for him to satisfy black audiences. He wanted desperately to please, and as he scampered about on his missions in the film he was curiously reminiscent of Harold Lloyd's little black sidekick Sunshine Sammy. With *A Man Called Adam* Sammy Davis, Jr., may have wanted to redeem himself. But he was dramatically unprepared for the role, and he failed terribly in the scenes in which he whined or broke down in pathos. Later he returned to his comic coon figures when he co-starred with Peter Lawford in *Salt and Pepper* (1968) and its sequel *One More Time* (1970). As he portrayed Lawford's loyal man-Friday, Sammy Davis, Jr., was a regrettably embarrassing figure with little spunk or artistry.

Super Sidney of the 1960s

Sammy Davis, Jr., did not make it as a leading man, but audiences did not seem to mind. They simply stuck by their old reliable leading man now transformed into a superhero, Sidney Poitier. By 1967, the year Poitier's biggest hit of the decade, *Guess Who's Coming to Dinner*, was released, the actor had already ascended to the ranks of superstardom. It was evident that he had no rivals. His screen personality was still that of the intelligent, kindhearted black man, and his code had remained intact throughout a series of alternatively entertaining and dull motion pictures. *Paris Blues* had supplied the heretofore sexless leading man with some romance in the form of Diahann Carroll, but the pair's moments on screen were torpid. *All the Young Men* (1960) and *Pressure Point* had proven disappointing, and not even the drawing power of the Poitier name could save them. Likewise *The Long Ships* had failed to make him a romanticized villain.

But just then when the career of an ordinary screen presence might have disintegrated, there had appeared the wildly successful *Lilies of the Field* (1963). Under Ralph Nelson's direction Poitier starred as the easygoing Homer Smith, an ex-G.I. who stumbles across a group of refugee nuns in the Arizona desert. They hope to build a chapel, and they see him as their savior. Before Homer knows it, he has begun work on the chapel, and is devoting all his time to it, and has even taken a part-time job to earn money to buy additional materials. Charming but light, *Lilies of the Field* offered Sidney Poitier an opportunity to flex his muscles and be the ingratiating and dependable character he was so good at portraying. It earned him an Academy Award, thus making him the first black man to win one. His career soared to undreamed-of heights afterward.

Paradoxically, while *Lilies of the Field* won Poitier an even larger following, it revealed more of the cracks in the great idol's armor. In the 1944 production of *Since You Went Away*, Hattie McDaniel had portrayed a long-time loyal servant to Claudette Colbert's family. When they saw her taking a part-time evening factory job to help the war-stricken family through their financial difficulties, black audiences laughed at Hattie McDaniel. Even in 1944, her character's obvious tom quality seemed ludicrous. Twenty years later, when Poitier took a similar part-time job for similar reasons—to help the white nuns—it seemed to black audiences, if not to white, that he was now leading the black character back in his place as a faithful servant. Worst of all, his character was not a pop figure who could be laughed at, but something deadly serious.

After his Oscar, Poitier was made even "nicer" by Hollywood scenarists, and it appeared as if he were going along with the program. In *The Slender Thread* (1965) with Anne Bancroft he became the black savior of the crazed white woman who had taken an overdose of pills; in *A Patch of Blue* the seeing-eye dog for a poor blind white girl; in *Duel at Diablo* (1966) a conventional cowboy; in *To Sir, with Love* (1967) a schoolteacher oddly representative of the system that the old Poitier of *The Blackboard Jungle* had rebelled against. Most of the Poitier features of the 1960s were solid entertainment vehicles. They pleased audiences but failed to satisfy them completely because the social significance and political implications of the 1950s Poitier features were lacking, and a surprisingly mannered ideal black man, so far above the masses who loved him, was emerging. *Guess Who's Coming to Dinner* paid homage to that new superblackman, and, while it was enormously successful, it was the one that jolted Sidney Poitier as he sat on his throne.

Directed by Stanley Kramer, *Guess Who's Coming to Dinner* was really an innocuous film. Poitier starred with Katharine Hepburn, Spencer Tracy, Katharine Houghton, Beah Richards, and Roy Glenn, Jr., in a story that tackled the touchy subject of interracial marriage. A white girl comes home to mother and dad in the suburbs with a tall handsome black man whom she wants to marry. Everybody goes into a dither, but of course, in the end, after a major summit meeting of both the bride's and the groom's parents, everything is worked out.

Guess Who's Coming to Dinner was pure 1949 claptrap done up in 1940s high-gloss MGM style. By concentrating on nice decent people entangled in personal heartaches, director Kramer diverted the audience from any real issues. In fact, there were no issues. There stood monolithic Poitier, charming, good-looking, mannerly, and brilliant, a candidate for the Nobel Prize. Who could refuse him for a son-in-law? Large audiences, taken in by the picture's clever advertising campaign and its star packaging, turned the picture into a tremendous commercial success. It was received well critically, too, and Beah Richards even received an Oscar nomination as best supporting actress for her pallid performance. But the movie proved the last of the explicitly integrationist message pictures. And the newspaper and magazine articles by black and white attacking Poitier and Kramer flowed after its release. The now legendary feature article that denounced Poitier characters as too limited and unrealistic to continue having much force, was run in *The New York Times* under the title: "Why Does White America Love Sidney Poitier So?" "Civil Rights is one thing," maid Isabelle Sanford had said in *Guess Who's Coming to Dinner*, "but this here is another." That no doubt will remain the final comment on the film and Poitier's role in it.

Sidney Poitier's next films were the big hits *In the Heat of the Night* and *For Love of Ivy* (1968). The former was an adventure tale about a Negro police officer investigating a Southern murder case. During the process of solving the crime, he comes face to face with racism. But, true to the new superdynamics of Sir Sidney, he not only uncovers the murderer's identity but also wins the admiration and friendship of a bigoted officer (Rod Steiger). Along the way he performs enough physical highjinks to rival James Bond. *For Love of Ivy* was a Doris Day–Rock Hudson romantic comedy done in blackface. A faithful servant (Abbey Lincoln) announces she will leave the family that has employed her for years. They do everything to persuade her to stay, even offering her a trip to Africa! Finally, the family's hip teen-age son

The picture that made a mint but was the last of the old-style integrationist dramas: *Guess Who's Coming to Dinner* (1967) with Katharine Hepburn, Katharine Houghton, and Poitier.

decides Ivy needs a lover. He tricks local stud Poitier into romancing the maid. The two fall in love and have a big sexless sex scene, and everything turns out just right. Despite the corn, *For Love of Ivy* distinguished itself because it offered the first love scene between blacks in a popular movie. Otherwise, it seemed hopelessly out of time and tune, and leading man Poitier seemed almost obsolete. A sign of the fickleness of movie audience tastes is that this film looks much better today. Abbey Lincoln's charm has not diminished, and the romantic ease and agility of the film now are apparently coming back into vogue.

What remains the most intriguing aspect of the 1960s, particularly the mid-to-late 1960s, is the rapidity with which attitudes, outlooks, and opinions changed. In dealing with racial situations, moviemakers had been accustomed to moving in cautious steps, in tune with the cadence of the mass audience. During the Johnson era, however, Hollywood appeared to lose track of the speed with which the mind of the mass audience was moving. By 1966 Martin Luther King's philosophy of nonviolence was just about dead, although only a few years earlier he had been the unchallenged spokesman for black America. Yet the film industry was still coasting along on the King attitudes. Malcolm X had been assassinated. Stokely Carmichael had arrived. H. Rap Brown had said violence was as natural in America as apple pie. Watts, Detroit, Harlem, South Philadelphia, Cleveland, and Washington, D.C., had exploded with riots. The President's National Advisory Commission had reported that America was "moving toward two societies, one black, one white, separate and unequal." And yet the industry continued with its brotherly-love everything's-going-to-be-dandy escapist movies, assuming that audiences would still believe in them. But the new audience was exposed to much more. Television familiarized people with incredible scenes of blood and brutality in their own living rooms. Added to the physical brutality was a new interest and awareness of the black experience. It was becoming "chic" and "hip" to understand the black man's style, even to speak in his jazzed-up dialect. By the end of the 1960s, the motion-picture industry caught up, jumping on the bandwagon before it even knew what was really happening. As a consequence, there appeared two new phenomena. One was the final evolution of a new kind of black film. The other, which actually came first, was the extraordinary rise of an actor named Jim Brown.

Jim Brown: Black Buck Hero for a Separatist Age

He came to the movies in the mid-1960s after a phenomenal college and professional career as an all-star football player. When he decided to switch careers, the news certainly must have seemed a joke to movie executives, to football commissioners, indeed even to film audiences. But Jim Brown had the last laugh on virtually everyone. He arrived in motion pictures at a time when the mass black audience was in desperate need of him. Even though he was to be nothing more than the black buck of old, he answered—because of his unique charisma and astounding physical presence—the need for a viable black-power sex figure.

Before Jim Brown, the black leading man had been physically self-sufficient, but never overpowering. Robeson and on occasion Rex Ingram came close to it, but generally their films were realistic ones, not pop pictures, and therefore they could not overstep reasonable bounds of strength. Jim Brown suggested violence and power, a dash and daring never before exhibited by a black male. On a physical basis alone, he was impressive. He stood six feet, two inches, weighed well over two hundred pounds, and had a forty-five inch chest. Brown had been acclaimed as the most powerful and elusive running back in the history of professional football. Off the field he made headlines when he was arrested for allegedly throwing a girl off a balcony and a full-grown man over a car. All of these added to the Brown mystique. He was big. He was black. He was outspoken. He was baaaddddd. In films, Jim Brown simply played the big, black, baaadddd nigger parts it seemed he was born to play. The fact that he lacked enough talent to play them did not much matter.

In his first features, the western *Rio Chonchos* (1964) and the graphic war drama *The Dirty Dozen* (1967), he was wisely cast as men forced to operate in worlds where they were motivated by their physical strength rather than their sensitivities. Brown had ample opportunities to show his stuff, notably in *The Dirty Dozen*, with astounding vigor and occasionally with what seemed like overzealous sadism.

The first films established Brown as a rugged, insensitive yet surprisingly sincere and dependable adventurer. He made his way through a series of similar rough-and-ready exploits in subsequent films: *Dark of the Sun* (1968), *The Split, Kenner* (1968), *100 Rifles* (1968), *Ice Station Zebra* (1968), *Riot* (1969), *The Grasshopper* (1970), *Tick . . . Tick . . . Tick* (1970), and *El Condor* (1970). Jim Brown was always a bold man, decisive, anxious for action, and completely confident of his own power. Males relished the situa-

Tough, arrogant, and a master of machismo, actor Jim Brown emerged in the late 1960s as the perfect black hero for a separatist age.

tions in which he was cast and his skill in getting out of them while keeping his cool. Young black children in the ghetto liked him because he was a black man who could shove back to whitey the violence whitey had originally dealt out. And women responded to him because his intense sexuality was closely related to his power. Directors were quick to show him with his chest bare, with his thick legs exposed. The blackness of his skin and his sheer physicality took audiences back to the myth of the black man as a pure creature of astounding sexual prowess.

Another reason for Brown's success with females (notably white ones) was his apparent lack of sensitivity. When he took Raquel Welch to bed in *100 Rifles*, it was evident that his character lacked the tenderness and humanity which in the past had always redeemed the most violent of movie heroes in the eyes of female fans. Consequently, the main thing women could respond to in Jim Brown was his beautiful physical being. Surprisingly, there were not many black women among his fans. His lack of feeling and passion made him seem just as sterile as certain white adventure heroes. On the other hand, Brown's characterizations may have won him a certain homosexual following. One scene in his prison drama, *Riot*, seems to have been inserted not only to shock the sensibilities of the mass audience but also to titillate some of the homosexual patrons. In the film Brown is approached by a white prisoner who begs to spend the night with him. As Brown's character remains aloof and implausibly untouched, the homosexual's passion merely grows. Brown's low-keyed, understated sadism obviously turns him on.

The most interesting aspect of Jim Brown's characters in the 1960s was that their strength was always used to work with the dominant white culture rather than against it. Whites applauded him and gave him their stamp of approval because he aided them. Thus in *The Dirty Dozen* his violence was directed against enemy troops. In *Riot*, it is directed against the corrupt white warden and in aid of mistreated prisoners, white and black. In *Dark of the Sun*, his strength united with that of white mercenaries trying to rid an African nation of revolutionary simbas. Jim Brown's brute force, if not properly guided, would be blind and indiscriminate and too much of a threat to white males in the audience; thus he could never be cast as a politically militant black man.

Regardless, Jim Brown proved himself an exciting new presence in American motion pictures. He starred in almost nothing but B movies. Yet they succeeded because of him, seeming to subordinate themselves to his presence. Curiously, although patrons did not go to see Jim Brown movies for their social significance, the

Brown vehicles carried some political weight simply because there was a black man up there on the screen, raising cain, strutting like a glorious prima donna, and sure to let everyone know that he could not care less whether he was liked or not. And he seemed to be avenging all those earlier black males who had to bow and kowtow. Jim Brown was a hero for a distinctly separatist age, and he proved in the separatist late 1960s that he was the right actor at the right time in the right place. His following dwindled somewhat when audiences saw through the transparency of his buck heroes, but Jim Brown's one-dimensional comic book adventurers led the way for the proud and physically overbearing characterization of boxer Jack Johnson that James Earl Jones brought brilliantly to life in 1970 in *The Great White Hope.* And surely the Brown characters were precursors of the independent, arrogantly aggressive buck-pimp heroes that dominated black movies during the first years of the 1970s.

The New-Style Black Film

The 1960s' most curious phenomenon, the new-style black film, made its way onto American screens with the 1969 appearance of the movies *Uptight, Slaves, The Learning Tree, The Lost Man,* and *Putney Swope.* Each conformed to a broader type of film then rising in popularity, the let's-hate-ugly-corrupt-America motion picture. All were indictments of the system. Each focused on some aspect of the new black militancy, often applauding separatism. Significantly, too, most of these films had blacks working behind the cameras as well as in front.

Jules Dassin's *Uptight* was the first American movie to spotlight black revolutionaries and the separatist movement. Set in the Hough ghetto area of Cleveland shortly after the assassination of Martin Luther King, the film takes up the theme of nonviolence. Nonviolence died with King in Memphis, declare the dashiki-clad revolutionary protagonists as they arm themselves with guns and slogans. When one of the group's leaders is turned into the police by a fellow member of the organization, the militants track down and assassinate the informant. Little else happens in the film.

Most considered *Uptight* a major disappointment. Audiences had waited anxiously for a film that would dramatize the chaos of the streets. On the surface, with its trappings—the ghetto, the beards, the beads, the afros, the armaments—the film looked contemporary, but underneath it was compromised and dishonest, revealing its white director's inability to see a black story from a black point of view. Preachy and didactic, Dassin's movie was based on John Ford's 1935 film *The Informer*. Dassin and his black screenwriters, Ruby Dee and Julian Mayfield, had substituted black revolutionaries for the Irish rebels of the Ford drama. But by this substitution, the trio exposed their failure to grasp the complexities that distinguish the new black movement from any other in the history of Western man. Moreover, their characters lacked commitment and passion, and as they stormed about the streets of Cleveland they emerged as little more than one-dimensional, pent-up black brutes. In fact, if *Uptight* made any statement at all, it was that blacks were effectual only at wiping out one of their own. Never did audiences see a heated black-white confrontation. In this respect, *Uptight* resembled Griffith's *The Birth of a Nation*, in which the renegade brute slaves failed to erect their great black state and succeeded only in flogging a member of their own race.

But the most disturbing aspect of *Uptight* was its actors. Individual militant performances could have invigorated the platitudes, the didacticism, and the brute stereotypes. But Dassin, almost as if to undercut the black movement itself, cast his picture with dull American actors. As the black whore, Ruby Dee still touched audiences with her vaguely pathetic smile, but she lacked the range to play the part successfully. Writer Julian Mayfield should have stuck to the books; portraying the alcoholic informer Tank Williams, he was little more than a walking vacuum.

Uptight's greatest liability was Raymond St. Jacques. Before his appearance in the Dassin feature, St. Jacques had been building up a following. Audiences, ignoring his uncharacteristically agreeable portrayals in *Black Like Me* and *The Green Berets* (1968), had been attracted to the shrewd and insolent air he exhibited in minor roles in such 1965 films as *Mr. Moses, The Pawnbroker,* and *Mr. Buddwing*. The crowning point of his career had come with his performance as the sadistic captain of the Haitian police in *The Comedians* (1967). Here he had used his deep, resonant voice splendidly, and his menacing *sang-froid* had conveyed appropriate hostility and aggression; as he strutted about in his dark glasses or shoved Lillian Gish onto the pavement, Raymond St. Jacques was the incarnation of militant anger. Thereafter he was touted as the new revolutionary hero. But the touting proved premature.

When next cast as the hard-as-nails, no-nonsense convict in the adaptation of Chester Himes's *If He Hollers, Let Him Go* (1968), Raymond St. Jacques had his first starring role, but he was not strong or interesting enough to carry the picture throughout. Some of his defects were quite apparent, too. His voice was still resonant but unvaried. At times his delivery was dry as a biscuit and his monosyllabic grunts and groans made him sound as if he were suffering from cinematic constipation; one hoped he would find the bathroom before the movie ended. In *Uptight,* in a role for which he was physically perfect because he resembled so much the real revolutionary H. Rap Brown, the underlying lack of charisma in St. Jacques's personality was used by director Dassin not only to undercut but to deglamorize the black militant spirit by presenting so unpassionate and uninspiring a leader. At best, his work could be called competent, but it was not enough to charge the movie with the vitality it needed. Later, in *Cotton Comes to Harlem, Come Back Charleston Blue* (1972), *Cool Breeze* (1972), and *The Final Comedown* (1972) St. Jacques proved more successful in roles that demanded less.

Radicalized plantation slaves were the protagonists of Herbert Biberman's *Slaves.* Through this undercover remake of *Uncle Tom's Cabin,* director Biberman hoped to draw an analogy between the brutal America of the past and the violent America of the 1960s. But the analogy was uncalled for because it was already so vividly self-evident, and surely if anything was superfluous in 1969 it was a rehash of the Stowe novel. As it turned out, *Slaves* relied on stock characters and episodes: the inhuman slave auction; the sadistic white master; the beautiful mulatto mistress in the Big House; the kindly, loyal black manservant. Actor Ossie Davis was in standard masochistic tom form. Newcomer Barbara Ann Teer provided the picture with its only genuine moments of anguish and pain. As the slave wife about to see her man sold to another plantation, her cry, "It just ain't fair, it just ain't fair," was urgent and real but still not enough to elevate a film already weighed down by a poor script and a melodramatic, heavy-handed piece of direction. Finally, as the master's black mistress, Dionne Warwick was—to put it kindly—preposterous. But like Jackie Robinson when he had made his film debut, she was great in the action shots as she roamed drunkenly through the plantation singing, singing, singing 'bout slavery.

Black novelist John O. Killens was employed as one of *Slaves'* scriptwriters. Killens had turned in professional work with his screenplay for *Odds Against Tomorrow,* but here he seemed overwhelmed by a white director's demands. In one interesting scene the corrupt slave master (Stephen Boyd) relates the rich history and accomplishments of African tribes to his white friends. Because the achievements are indeed real, the scene has a startling impact. Surely, Killens had something to do with writing it. But ultimately the achievements are turned against them and are used by the film as one further assertion of white power. For, rich and productive as the African tribes were, the almighty white man, as usual, conquered them.

Uptight and *Slaves* were moderately successful. False and hollow as they were, the films offered black audiences recognizable images. Here at least were products that acknowledged the violence and cruelty of the white American way of life. Black audiences accepted them but with the hope that something better might come along.

Gordon Parks's *The Learning Tree* was something better, although it was not to meet with as much success as its predecessors. In 1963 Parks, a distinguished black photographer for *Life* magazine, had added another entry to an impressive list of credits when his autobiographical novel *The Learning Tree* was published and widely praised. When Warner Brothers signed him to adapt his book for the screen, Parks became the first black man to direct a major American movie. With a cast that included young Kyle Johnson, Alex Clarke, Mira Waters, Estelle Evans, Dana Elcar, and the fine character actor Joel Fluellen, Parks shot his movie in his home town, Fort Scott, Kansas.

The Learning Tree was a nostalgic evocation of a period and a place seemingly remote in 1969. It records the events in Parks's childhood in Kansas during the 1920s. At first glance it is an innocent time when the picture's hero, Newt, can do cartwheels in a field of flowers or steal apples from a vineyard with his buddies. But it is also an age polluted by violence and racism. A creek where Newt swims suddenly turns red from the blood of a black man senselessly shot by a bigoted white sheriff. In an old country barn a white man is mercilessly beaten to death by a black. In the town courtroom, that same black man flees an angry group of townspeople and blows out his brains before they have a chance to do it for him. On second glance, Newt's age is not so remote from the late 1960s after all. "Some of the people," the hero's mother tells him, "are good and some of them are bad—just like the fruit on a tree . . . think of it like that till the day you die—let it be your learnin' tree."

Simply and sensitively, Gordon Parks's film presents a boy who is black but not tortured by his blackness. He is like other boys, no matter what the color or place or time. Yet he is not colorless. Nor indistinct. He knows what it is to be told to leave a restaurant, to be advised that college is not for colored boys. He knows violence and cruelty. But unlike other black characters in the late 1960s (most notably the brute protagonists of *Uptight* and *Slaves*), he does not suffer consciously. Nor does he cheaply parade his discontent. Parks's hero, played beautifully by Kyle Johnson, observes the world. Bruised by it, he learns from it nonetheless.

As good as it was, *The Learning Tree* did rely on a number of clichés. But to director Parks's credit, he presented them with such feeling as to render them new, and he resensitized his audiences so that they experienced again the pain of being told to leave a restaurant because of their color. In the end he restored the clichés' original meanings, and his film remains a lyrical and eloquent statement on the black experience in America.

The Sidney Poitier vehicle *The Lost Man* seemed in many respects a successor to *Uptight*. Based also on an old movie (*Odd Man Out*, 1947) about the Irish Revolution, its transatlantic substitution of blacks for Irish rebels failed to be dramatically convincing or coherent. Black militants prepare to overtake a city (Philadelphia) through an "infallible" payroll robbery. Amid decaying brownstones and deserted, littered lots, Poitier stands lean and pure as ever. Outfitted with dark glasses as he raps with the brothers, he is not the out-and-out tom of old, but he is not the radicalized brute the movie wants him to be either. Flat and pretentious, *The Lost Man* failed at the box office, and the trumped-up romance between the black hero and the white society girl almost set ghetto theaters aflame with indignation. In this separatist age, such white-black alliances were clearly out of place.

Robert Downey's *Putney Swope* closed the decade and was the first of the new black films to take a farcical look at black America. The film was part parody, part put-down, part satire—of stereotypes, power manipulations on Madison Avenue, capitalism, and the various hang-ups infesting the American way of life. Downey achieved his end by reversing the racial scales.

Putney Swope's plot is simple. A black token figure in an advertising agency is accidentally elected chairman of the board. "I'm not going to rock the boat," Putney announces upon his election. "I am going to sink it!" Thereafter in one superbly edited sequence the board of directors is no longer the line of pole-faced white cadavers, corrupt and hungry for money and power. It has been replaced by a new vital black staff equipped with dashikis and afros, later with guns and munitions. The agency changes its name to Truth and Soul, Inc., and it sets out to shake up the sensibilities of just about everyone.

By the time the film ends Putney and company have sunk the boat and at the same time revealed blacks to be just as corrupt and power-hungry as whites. Their black Establishment (best symbolized by Mrs. Swope berating and hounding her scrawny white maid) proves no better than its white predecessor. White has been turned black and black turned white, and everybody is made ugly.

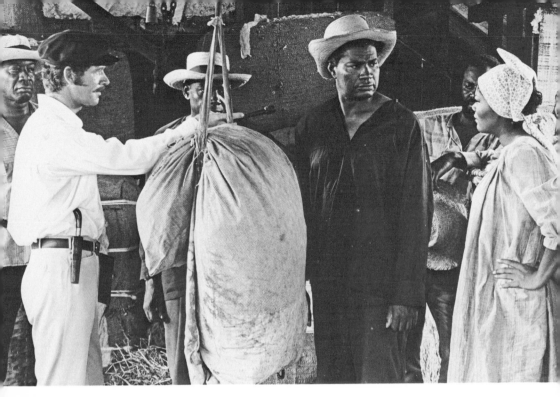

ABOVE: An undercover remake of *Uncle Tom's Cabin* passed as a "new style black film": *Slaves* (1969), with Stephen Boyd as the wicked massa, Ossie Davis as the stoic, masochistic slave, and Dionne Warwick as that mysterious black gal livin' up there in de massa's Big House.

BELOW: The trials and tribulations of a decadent middle-class black couple (Lola Falana and Roscoe Lee Browne) were sensationalized and distorted in *The Liberation of L. B. Jones.* (1970).

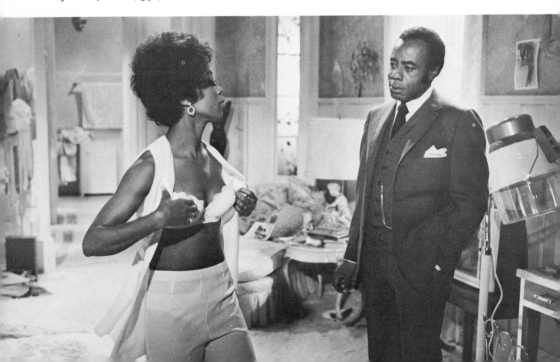

In reviewing *Putney Swope*, Arthur Knight of *Saturday Review* said the film "just goes to show what might happen should blacks ever get control of the power structure in this country." In actuality, *Putney Swope* was merely what Mr. Knight, Mr. Downey, and others thought would happen in America should black citizens attain economic or political control. To substantiate his view, director Downey relied on the misconceptions and myths about blacks that had pervaded and polluted white America for so long. The blacks of *Putney Swope* were depicted as supercharged athletes, as high-powered sexual beings, as loud-mouth do-nothings. Instead of picking at any genuine black follies to prove his point, the director chose to satirize the lies, myths, clichés, exaggerations. For some, *Putney Swope* is an entertaining film. But for others, it is a work admirably filmed in segments but horribly distorted with black brutes and bucks and exotic whores that hark back to the days of D. W. Griffith.

Putney Swope and the other new black films of the late 1960s may today seem like historical pieces and not very powerful stuff. But they do reveal the manner in which films were being used almost explicitly to make political statements. The new motion picture makers—for whatever reasons—wanted their products to take a stand on current social, political, and even economic issues. Statement-making continued and ultimately the new black films of this period proved to be merely the genesis of a new style and a new attitude on what movies should be all about. It was in the next decade, however, that the new black film fully evolved.

Epilogue: 1970 Onward

What can we say about a film history that carries us from the submissive stoicism of Tom in Edwin S. Porter's *Uncle Tom's Cabin* to the equally submissive stoicism of the Sidney Poitier characters in *Lilies of the Field* and *In the Heat of the Night?* What are we to think when some morning we see on television the notorious pranks of a slow-witted shuffling Stepin Fetchit and then the same evening we visit a local movie house and view the demeaning shenanigans of a dim-witted, shifty character played by Sammy Davis, Jr.? How are black Americans to react when they read about the supernigger highjinks of Griffith's blackfaced baddies in *The Birth of a Nation* and then endure similar highjinks in contemporary movies like *Putney Swope* and *Cotton Comes to Harlem?* When we compare the actors of the past with those of the present or when we contrast the movies of yesteryear with those of today, I think all of us ask ourselves despairingly just how far American movies have progressed in the past half-century in recording the black experience accurately or sensitively. In some ways it does not look as if we have progressed at all. We are tolerant of the demeaning stereotypes of yesterday because we can understand the social forces then at work. But that does not mean we should continue accepting such stereotypes, particularly now in an age of "heightened" black consciousness.

In the early 1970s our black films often still use degrading myths and clichés as well as the five basic stereotypes to define the black experience. Curiously, at a time when interest in black films has never been higher and when black studies programs across the country are about to incorporate film courses in their curricula, American black movies remain distorted and far from satisfying. New movies that claim to interpret the black American's way of life are often disappointing. Some, without their own awareness, seem to justify exploitation just as much as a movie like *The Green Pastures* justified white condescension and patronizing of blacks.

Ossie Davis's rowdy production *Cotton Comes to Harlem* opened the new decade. For years the black intelligentsia had sworn that were blacks able to write, direct, and control their own films there would be more integrity on screen. On occasion, even crafty old Oscar Micheaux had unintentionally proven the intellectuals right. But Davis failed to give his audience any insights into the black experience. His film with its idealized all-black world (not too remote from those of the all-black musicals) took place in the ghetto and presented a crew of congenial coons, toms, and black whores. Its plot was a standard-thriller cops-and-robbers type, and it offered a picturesque glimpse of Harlem—still depicted as that exotic playground. *Cotton Comes to Harlem* was immensely successful. Structurally and thematically it followed in the farcical vien of *Putney Swope* and *Gone Are the Days.* It studiously played up not only to black fantasies on a black world order but to white fantasies of a black world full of harmless stereotypes. The great irony of *Cotton Comes to Harlem,* and part of the reason it proved mindlessly entertaining, was that its audiences, at least black ones, were a step ahead of the director and knew the stereotypes to be just that. After so many dreary television programs on the "race problem" and after a flood of newly published pseudo-relevant black literature, black audiences were content to sit back and laugh for a change. And so the audience triumphed over the picture. Later director Davis picked up a serious theme with his adaptation of Wole Soyinka's *Kongi's Harvest.* But he proved out of his element as he wrestled with sophisticated and subtle political problems. Shortly after *Cotton Comes to Harlem's* success, however, there appeared a sequel *Come Back Charleston Blue* (1972). This film, like its predecessor, was based on a novel by Chester Himes. The sequel was not directed by Davis. Instead television director Mark Warren piloted the project.

William Wyler's *The Liberation of L. B. Jones* drew moderate attention. Lola Falana as a middle-class sepia slut generated some excitement, but not for long. *The New York Times* referred to Falana as a "black Harlow," but at a time when there was a great movement among blacks to elevate the image of the black woman —to remove her from the exotic sex object creation—Falana's leaden portrayal of a time-worn false character, the black whore, only irritated black audiences. In the end, the only redeeming qualities of the film were Roscoe Lee Browne's effective suffering bourgeois tom character and Yaphet Kotto's triumphant insolence as a radicalized young black man who throws an old white racist into a hay chopper to atone for the sins of ugly white America.

The adaptation of William Faulkner's *The Reivers* (1969) was innocent fluff and mildly entertaining. Backing up Steve McQueen's roguish hero was Rupert Crosse's comic and fairly individualized performance as a black slickster. With only one previous screen performance, in Cassavetes' *Shadows,* Crosse proved effective enough in his role to earn an Academy Award nomination as best supporting actor. It was the first time a black actor had ever been nominated in that category.

Later James Earl Jones won an Academy nomination as best actor for his work in *The Great White Hope* (1970). Jones's previous screen work included roles in *Dr. Strangelove* (1963), *The Comedians,* and *End of the Road* (1969). On stage he had appeared spectacularly in *Othello* and the Broadway version of *The Great White Hope.* The movie version of this play, although static and stagey, offered Jones a chance to display his capacity for monumental agony. Often his character looked as if it would slip into the old black buck category, but the actor's smooth intelligence saved him. Later he scored another triumph in *The Man* (1972). As a black politician who becomes the first black President of the United States, Jones made an otherwise dense movie something worth seeing.

One of the new era's biggest hits was *Sweet Sweetback's Baadasssss Song,* the third feature of black director Melvin Van Peebles. The director's first effort, the European-made *The Story of a Three-Day Pass* (1967, based on his novel), about an interracial love affair, received a lukewarm reception by American critics and audiences. His second film, *Watermelon Man,* received elaborate publicity but was no great success either; its greatest distinction is that it now ranks as the classic tragic mulatto movie of the early separatist 1970s. Godfrey Cambridge stoically portrayed (in white-face) a white insurance man who was transformed overnight into a *Negro.* His wife deserts him, and he suffers an identity crisis—black blood has made his life wretched and intolerable. *Watermelon Man* dramatized a great white fantasy/nightmare (and perhaps marginally a great black fantasy about whites)—that of mysteriously losing lily-whiteness and turning coal black. The film's theme was banal but harmless. Yet, as a motion picture that supposedly addressed itself to the black experience, it seemed remote. Moreover, it was filmed in the style of a mid-1940s domestic comedy, and consequently failed to reach a large audience. But with *Sweet Sweetback's Baadasssss Song* director Van Peebles, who also wrote the script, as he had for his other movies, discov-

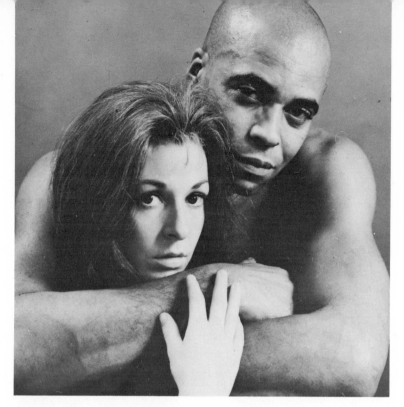

ABOVE: In the early 1970s, James Earl Jones (here with Jane Alexander) repeated his sensational stage role as the boxer Jack Jefferson in the movie *The Great White Hope.* He won an Oscar nomination for his performance. BELOW: Melvin Van Peebles, star and the director of the controversial black film *Sweet Sweetback's Baadasssss Song* (1971).

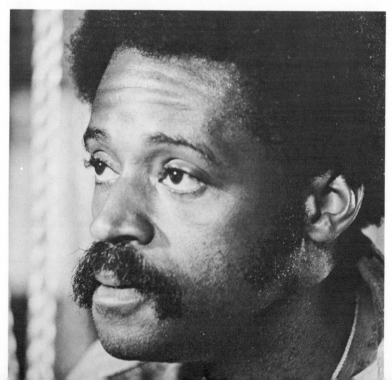

ered not only his audience but his style and subject.

The film centers on a cool-as-a-cucumber black stud, Sweetback, who hacks two bigoted policemen to shreds with a pair of handcuffs and then after a series of wild sexual adventures and chase sequences manages to escape the law. The film ends with the message: "A BAADASSSSS NIGGER IS COMING BACK TO COLLECT SOME DUES." The fact that a black man triumphs over the corrupt white Establishment appealed not only to the mass black audience (which flocked to it) but to the white one as well. *Sweet Sweetback's Baadasssss Song* was a commercial success, and it gave birth to a series of imitations. So carried away by the film's daredevil hero were black ghetto teen-agers that many left the theaters mimicking the "Sweetback saunter" as they walked the streets. (Ironically, these saunters are reminiscent of the way bootblacks and bus boys imitated the Stepin Fetchit shuffle in the 1930s.) The movie was widely reported on by the white press and hotly debated in the black community.

"There is a certain grim white humor," wrote Lerone Bennett in *Ebony*, "in the fact that the black marches and demonstrations of the '60s reached artistic fulfillment in the '70s with Flip Wilson's Geraldine and Melvin Van Peebles' Sweetback, two provocative and ultimately insidious reincarnations of all the Sapphires and Studs of yesteryear." Bennett's article attacked the film as trivial and tasteless and labeled it a negative classic "because it is an obligatory step for anyone who wants to go further and make the first revolutionary black film."

Much of the black intellectual community seemed to feel the movie failed as black art. During this period of obvious social flux, of a moral awakening of black America's consciousness, and particularly of the development of a black cultural aesthetic insisting that black art give the black community some political and social direction, *Sweet Sweetback's Baadasssss Song* seemed to offer not direction but a daydream of triumph. At heart, its hero was the familiar brutal black buck. In many respects the picture fed on white hysteria and paranoia.

But Van Peebles' movie will no doubt remain of great historical importance because it played on a new reactionary philosophy prevalent in the late 1960s and early 1970s. In the 1960s, in rejecting the black bourgeoisie that had aided and abetted white America through its attempts at cultural assimilation, the new rising militant black classes came to identify blackness with the degrading conditions imposed on black America by white America. In reaction to this, they sought to glamorize poverty and the ghetto. To be really black one had to suffer, suffer, suffer. No longer was it despicable that human beings had to live in tenements with rats, roaches, and filth. Instead such an existence was viewed as "ennobling." With the glamorization of the ghetto, there also came the elevation of the pimp as folk hero. Van Peebles played up to this new black sensibility, and his film was the first to glorify the pimp. It failed, however, to explain the social conditions that had made the pimp such an important figure. At the same time, the movie debased the black woman (perhaps unintentionally), depicting her as nothing other than a whore. To director-writer Van Peebles, however, the black-woman-as-whore, the pimp-as-hero, and even the ghetto-as-noble-jungle were all a part of his romanticized conception of a black world order. His film remains a striking social document on the nature and the attitudes of the new era. More important, however, in its own way, *Sweet Sweetback's Baadasssss Song* revealed through music and movement a communal spirit —call it tribal if you will—existent in black America alone. Throughout the movie, hero Sweetback is aided by members of the black community wherever he goes, and surely, at the movie's conclusion, it is the community that has contributed to the individual's triumph as much as the man himself. No matter what the opinion on this movie, it seems destined to become legendary, and its flamboyant, outspoken director has already emerged as a folk hero of sorts.

Another film glorifying the pimp-heel hero but with far less significance was Gordon Parks's *Shaft*. It starred newcomer Richard Roundtree as a cynical, rebellious black detective. His pimp type lives in an elegant book-lined Village duplex, dresses in expensive leather coats and pants, and is confident enough to down every white cat in sight. Bullets almost bounce off his chest; if one does hit him, it never causes any real pain. And Shaft is a whiz with the ladies. "Hotter than Bond. Cooler than Bullitt," read the advertisement. Vulgar, shallow, and crudely done, *Shaft* distinguished itself mainly by having the best musical score of the year. Isaac Hayes's sensual, moody background music added to the texture of the film, and Hayes himself earned an Academy Award for it. *Shaft* was so successful commercially that it was followed in 1972 by a sequel, *Shaft's Big Score*.

Another unrealistic tale of a black man putting down the Man was *Black Jesus*. Although far from important, the movie offered Woody Strode another opportunity to give an impressive performance. "It was a thrill yesterday to see the name of this exceptionally fine Negro actor elevated to solo star billing, after propping up many a film for years," wrote Howard Thompson in *The New York Times*. "Mr. Strode, with his keen lidded eyes and strong, gaunt face, does a perfectly respectable job of portraying an imprisoned, tortured and executed visionary leader in an African country. His gentle spirit of nonviolence and agonized endurance under pressure are painfully real. The rest is not." Unmemorable as *Black Jesus* was, the film was a money-maker, and its reviews added to the myth that Woody Strode was a great actor. This movie's success, however, along with that of *Cotton Comes to Harlem, Sweet Sweetback's Baadasssss Song,* and *Shaft,* was an indication of a black movie boom in the early 1970s.

Two offbeat films of the new decade were *Right On* (1971) and *Soul to Soul* (1971). The former was a hard-driving, rhythmic spoken blues concert, a poetry recitation on a New York rooftop by the Original Last Poets. *Soul to Soul* recorded a black rock concert in Africa, where Ike and Tina Turner, Roberta Flack, Wilson Pickett, and others took soul back to "where it all began." Following these films was an array of "black" movies: *Honky* (which centered on an interracial love affair and starred Brenda Sykes), *Brother John, The Organization,* and *The Bus Is Coming* (all 1971), plus *Soul Soldier* (a 1972 release featuring athlete Rafer Johnson), *Georgia, Georgia, Buck and the Preacher, Black Rodeo, Cool Breeze, Top of the Heap, The Final Comedown, Blacula, The Legend of Nigger Charley, Slaughter, Melinda, Trouble Man,* and *Blackenstein* (all 1972). There also appeared documentaries on such black political figures as Angela Davis, Fred Hampton, and Malcolm X. All in all the early 1970s at least proved that there was a new audience for black films.

Of this new crop, the more successful critically were *Buck and the Preacher, Super Fly, Lady Sings the Blues* (1972), and *Sounder.* Each drew a sizable audience and was passionately discussed by members of the black community. One of the more pleasant surprises of the new decade, *Buck and the Preacher,* was directed by Sidney Poitier and starred him with Harry Belafonte and Ruby Dee. Rousing, adventurous, nicely comic at times (often because of Belafonte's high-spirited performance), a level-headed popularization of black history, the movie was first-rate entertainment. It centered on an obscure part of history, the period following the Civil War when freed slaves were tracked down by sadistic bounty hunters and forced to return to unofficial slavery in the South. Realistically, the movie spotlighted white violence directed at the freed slaves. It ended on a note of triumph, with the blacks defeating their white opponents. Some might complain that the conclusion of *Buck and the Preacher* obviously played up to the fantasies and wishes of its black audience, but the picture was so decently acted and consistently intelligent throughout that such a complaint here seems invalid. Unlike the buck-pimp fantasies, this one does no harm. Poitier and Belafonte play the leads, an incongruous pair who outsmart the crew of bounty hunters. At first it looked as if both actors were doing penance for some of their other films and as if *Buck and the Preacher* would be a slow-witted, sermonizing, unspontaneous motion picture. But soon it became evident that the leads of this black western were viable black folk heroes. Despite the title, neither actor was the old-style buck creation. In fact, the entire picture went against the popular buck vein that was then sweeping the film industry.

One final word about Poitier. Here the fine American actor attempts to redeem himself and re-establish his roots with the black community. His performance is hardly among his more demanding or compelling ones. Indeed, throughout he seems taciturn, withdrawn, almost as if he were afraid to move, to *act*. The Poitier code—of intelligence, decency, humanity, and loyalty—is intact. But here that code is used to please black America, not white. His character not only questions the inhumane white system and his white oppressors, but also takes direct action against them. With Sidney Poitier, Belafonte, and little sturdy Ruby Dee riding triumphantly through the plains, it seems like a homecoming for the trio. Black audiences openly screamed out in joy, and *Buck and the Preacher* emerged as a solid hit with the community.

A film at the opposite end of *Buck and the Preacher* was the corruptive *Super Fly.* Independently produced by Sig Shore and financed by a group of black businessmen, this film met with great financial success—as well as vehement controversy. Its hero, a Harlem cocaine dealer, drew adverse criticism from various parts of the black community, some areas going so far as to ban the picture. Many consider the movie a glorification of the pusher-hero, and, although producer and star have both denied such charges, it has to be admitted that the hero, Priest, does cut a dashing figure. Dressed in long, sweeping coats and large wide-brimmed hats, Ron O'Neal is a romanticized version of the Harlem pimp. His character clearly falls into the buck category. This is more than evident during a bathtub sequence when Priest and his woman make love. Curiously, the love scene in this black film as well as those in *Melinda, Slaughter, Shaft,* and other new films, fail to fit in with the structure of the picture as a whole. Instead it seems as if this sex scene (much more graphic and lingering than any such scene found in a white film) had been inserted simply to play on the legends of blacks' high-powered sexuality. Sex that fits in is one thing. Gratuitous sex scenes are another. At the end of *Super Fly,* the hero triumphs over the system, defeats his white oppressors, and is able to leave the cocaine business with a hefty bankroll to boot. Directed by Gordon Parks, Jr., *Super Fly* is a black fantasy picture almost devoid of any humanity or reflection. Technically, it is adequate. Perhaps the power of the film (and, distorted as it was, it did have a certain raw vigor) lies in Curtis Mayfield's sensual, driving music. Then, too, some of the film's allure must be credited to actor O'Neal's performance. Or perhaps his lack of it. Drawing on his own personality and mystique to fill in the gaps in the script, O'Neal presents an arrogant, enigmatic street hustler who is careful not to reveal too much about himself. O'Neal seems to hide parts of himself from the camera, and what is hidden arouses interest.

While Ron O'Neal's character held things back, Diana Ross as Billie Holiday pushed everything forward. In *Lady Sings the Blues*, a Motown/Paramount production, the former lead singer of the Supremes made an impressive screen debut. The picture itself emerged almost overnight as a historic event. For the first time, black movie patrons had the chance to see a full-fledged black romantic melodrama. Often the film resorted to clichés found in many 1940s movies, stories of show-biz folk rising from rags to riches, then bringing about their own sorry downfall. In many respects, the movie was not at all representative of jazz stylist Billie Holiday's stormy, trouble-filled life. In her autobiography, Billie Holiday had related incident upon incident in which she was discriminated against and publicly hurt and humiliated. Certainly, great pain and sorrow in her life were heightened by racial conditions in America. This film had offered Hollywood a chance to really make a statement on a legendary black woman's life. But, except for a lynching episode and another dealing with the Klan, there were few other comments on the bigoted racial situation. Moreover, events in the Holiday life—working in a brothel as a teen-ager and struggling for success—were treated humorously. On the other hand, for those not familiar with the real subject matter of *Lady Sings the Blues* (and evidently many patrons were not), the picture was vastly entertaining. Richard Pryor proved delightful (although occasionally uncontrollable) as the good-humored piano player. Diana Ross and Billy Dee Williams emerged as a perfect love pair. In one particularly engaging nightclub sequence shortly after the two characters have met, the actress and actor were permitted to improvise the scene. The improvisation worked splendidly and is a wonderful moment in the history of black cinema. Although Diana Ross is never really credible as Billie Holiday, she does beautiful work by playing herself. Charming, intelligent, and vivacious, her performance is solid and often invigorating. She is exciting to watch. As for Williams, who has been around in the entertainment business for some time, he sets female hearts to fluttering with his smooth and debonair portrayal of Louis McKay.

Another performer finally able to reach a large audience after being around for some time was Cicely Tyson. In *Sounder,* the actress found the role she had been preparing for throughout her career. In previous films such as *A Man Called Adam, The Comedians,* and *The Heart Is a Lonely Hunter,* and on the television series "East Side, West Side," she had acquired a small but dedicated group of fans. Always her characters were infused with intelligence and sophistication. In *Sounder,* as Rebecca, the Louisiana sharecropper's wife, she was what critic Pauline Kael called "the first great black heroine on the screen." Kael added, "Her Rebecca was worth waiting for. She is visually extraordinary. Her cry as she runs down the road toward her husband, returning from prison, is a phenomenon—something even the most fabled actresses might not have dared." Unlike Diana Ross in *Lady Sings the Blues,* who gives a star performance in which she projects her own personality rather than that of a character, Cicely Tyson firmly embodies a guarded and tough yet supremely delicate black woman. The other performances in the film, those of Kevin Hooks (the son of actor Robert), Paul Winfield, and Janet MacLachlan were likewise impressive.

Sounder itself is an intensely warm and winning motion picture. Directed by Martin Ritt, it centers on sharecroppers in the South during the 1930s. A number of white critics have praised the film, hailing it as a welcome relief from the sadistic and exploitative qualities of the buck movies. Perhaps an unmentioned reason for the white critical establishment's acceptance of this picture was that once again blacks are pictured as dignified but quiet and *restrained* folks. There are no contemporary black Americans caught up in the cities and forced to deal with urban problems. In some respects, the movie harks back to a past portrait of film Negroes.

But it has to be said that the picture is indeed lovely and moving. It also marks the evolution of the black family drama in movies. King Vidor's *Hallelujah* had centered on a rural black family of sharecroppers in the South, a tightly knit, cohesive social unit. Idealized and romanticized, that family was indestructible. *Hallelujah* presented the black family at its best but not entirely in a realistic way. Later, *Imitation of Life* had dealt with urban blacks. The family, represented by Aunt Delilah and Peola, became victims of social pressures beyond their control—racist, capitalistic, oppressive white America ripping this family asunder as Peola rejected her mother in search of the almightly American Dream. *Pinky*'s theme paralled that of *Imitation of Life*, except that the family—Pinky and Granny—were re-united once Pinky rejected white America. And films such as *Anna Lucasta* and most notably *A Raisin in the Sun* had revealed the black family in overwhelming conflict with itself. Because of the tightness and congestion of the city (and the system), members of the black family took their problems out on one another and stayed at each other's throats. With *The Learning Tree* the black family was presented in relatively honest terms, although at times director Gordon Parks had idealized the unit. Once again we had a harmonious rural family group. Finally, *Sounder* picked up many of the things toyed with before and amalgamated them to create a rich and fully realized portrait of the black family in America. Although the blacks in *Sounder* must contend with a hostile white world which does strain the relations between members of the family, they remain nonetheless a sturdy, unyielding unit. The problems that arise are never overstated, and, although the family has difficulties, there are none of the histrionic outpourings that characterized earlier portraits of the black family.

The new era also gave exposure to other new black actors and actresses. Robert Hooks gave an intelligent although mannered performance in *Last of the Mobile Hot Shots* (1970). The comedian Godfrey Cambridge, who had been around for a long time and had worked in such movies as *Gone Are the Days, Bye Bye Braverman* (1968), and *The President's Analyst* (1968), had leading roles in *Watermelon Man, Cotton Comes to Harlem*, and *Come Back Charleston Blue*. Though Cambridge is as black as tar, he has to be singled out as one of the few black actors in the history of movies who seemed without any ethnic background whatsoever. He appeared more like a Jewish comic than a black one. On the other hand, Moses Gunn offered strong (although excruciatingly stylized) performances as black hoods in *WUSA* (1970), *Shaft*, and *Shaft's Big Score*, and also in supporting roles in *Eagle in a Cage* (1972) and *The Hot Rock* (1972). Newcomer Judy Pace (the sister of singer Jean), having appeared successfully on television's "Peyton Place" series, worked in *Three in the Attic* (1968) and *Cotton Comes to Harlem*. Although her performances were anything but exciting, Pace received good coverage from the black press and went from her movie roles to a leading part in the television series "The Young Lawyers." An impressive new serious actress was Emily Yancy, whose charm and relaxed sensuality enhanced segments of Otto Preminger's *Tell Me That You Love Me, Junie Moon*

(1970) and *Cotton Comes to Harlem.* Another exciting newcomer was Glenna Forster-Jones, who appeared splendidly in *Joanna* (1968) and *Leo the Last* (1970). Also new to the movies was former football player Fred Williamson, who made his debut in *Tell Me That You Love Me, Junie Moon* and went on to appear in Ingo Preminger's *M*A*S*H* (1970). Later he costarred as Diahann Carroll's boy friend on the "Julia" television series. Slick, affable, and debonair, Williamson was not the world's greatest new actor, but he was one of its more personable ones. His most important role of the new decade was as the star of *The Legend of Nigger Charley.*

Certainly the most spectacular new black presence in the early 1970s was Calvin Lockhart. With his well-defined features and clear mahogany skin, Lockhart seemed the contender for black star of the early period simply on the basis of his looks. Born in 1934 in the Bahamas and the youngest of eight children, he made his reputation as the black stud in the import *Joanna.* Afterward he appeared in *Myra Breckinridge* (1970), *Halls of Anger* (1970), *Cotton Comes to Harlem,* and *Leo the Last.* Then before anyone knew it he had acquired such a following that he was being pitted against Poitier as the most important new black actor on the scene. "The question of Poitier's obsolescence," wrote Vincent Canby in *The New York Times,* "is prompted by the emergence of major new black actors like . . . Calvin Lockhart who, in three recent films, has been able to play everything from a dedicated school teacher *(Halls of Anger)* to a bogus preacher promoting a back-to-Africa swindle *(Cotton Comes to Harlem),* and a perennially precious acting student *(Myra Breckinridge)* who dusts his hair with sequins."

By means of his wit and intelligence and *savoir-faire,* Lockhart brought to his screen characters a quickness, an agility of mind and spirit, and a contemporary sensitivity never before expressed by a black actor. His portrayal of the ghetto man-of-the-people in *Leo the Last* remains the best defined and most individualized version of this type yet presented in a movie. In one scene he burns with anger when he believes his girl has prostituted herself. In another he is lighthearted and clever as he lets a pigeon loose in a grocery store, causing terror as patrons run about screaming while he steals a chicken for dinner. But his character has complexity and diversity, and he is never the one-dimensional posing and posturing type of militant that had already been exploited in television programs and movies such as *Uptight* and *The Lost Man.* With the arrival of Calvin Lockhart, American audiences saw an untyped embodiment of the contemporary militant experience.

Curiously, in 1972, one of Lockhart's most successful films had one of his least effective performances. As the narcissistic disc jockey Frankie J. Parker in Hugh Robertson's *Melinda*, Lockhart seemed all razzle-dazzle, all surface. True, he portrayed a superficial character, but the fact is that he played him superficially. In fairness to Lockhart, it must be noted that the real failings were those of the script. Lonne Elder III, who had done fine work with his treatment for *Sounder*, had, no doubt, run into studio problems with *Melinda*. So, too, had black director Robertson. Previously, he had proven himself an exceptional film editor when he worked on such productions as *Midnight Cowboy* (1969) and *Shaft*. Members of the black community anxiously looked forward to his first directorial job. But Robertson and Elder both have said they had repeated battles with their studio on just how the movie should be done. Actress Rosalind Cash also battled, demanding certain scenes to establish her character in the film as something other than a black whore. Cash must have won some of her battles, because her work in the film is the best thing it has to offer. Previously, Cash had appeared in *The Omega Man* (1971) and *The New Centurions* (1972). Here, in *Melinda*, notably during the sequence in the bank when her character explodes in rage, Rosalind Cash emerges as an important black actress.

Calvin Lockhart's characters, and those in such films as *Buck and the Preacher, Lady Sings the Blues,* and *Sounder,* remain, for the most part, the exception to the rule of black moviemaking in the early 1970s. Most blacks in American motion pictures of this period were still depicted as subhuman, unbalanced, undisciplined, childlike mental inferiors. Even though audiences were sometimes taken in by the beards, the beads, and the attitudinizing, there was seldom a sense of the texture of people's lives. Van Peebles' rough-tough cream puff of a militant stud and Roundtree's big black spade of a detective were no more real than the servants of the 1930s or the entertainers of the 1940s. Their worlds were just as idealized and patently false as those of the past.

Now, having viewed American black film history in its sixty-eight-year span, one might ask exactly what goes into the making of a decent, humane black film. Exactly what should the new black artists give to their audiences? There are no definite outlines for what should be done, but from our knowledge of the past we do have an idea of the possibilities, the potentialities, of a new black cinema. From a glimpse of black cinema outside the United States we can also get an idea of how it can be developed and enriched in America.

If one compares any American black film of the late 1960s and early 1970s with the movies of the Senegalese filmmaker Ousmane Sembène it is obvious that intelligence and sensitivity can be brought to black films by a black director, and that it can be done without relying on types or clichés. The Sembène movies released in this country have all been relentlessly depressing, but they flowed rhythmically and naturally from their director's own distinctly black sensibility. In the somber *Borom Saret,* in the distressingly cerebral *Mandabi,* and in the masterpiece of suicidal despair, *Black Girl,* Sembène creates characters victimized not only by white hypocrisies and injustices but by black ones as well. In more ways than one his people are trapped by their color. Yet he never uses the cheap trick of exploiting their suffering or despair. His characters never sell their agony to audiences along with the popcorn as characters in American films had often done. Nor are they pictured as unrealistically triumphing over hostile forces. Often, as in *Black Girl,* the Sembène character emerges as a victor only because of his own awareness. And most important, the Sembène character functions in a social system not glamorized but rightfully depicted as corrupt, oppressive, and dehumanized.

In many ways, Sembène's bleak films point the way for American moviemakers. That is not to say that American filmmakers should adopt his view of existence as painful and utterly futile. But they must express their views with the same integrity and the same attempt to extend the consciousness of the audience. If there are to be such things as "black films," the black actors, the directors, the writers, the producers, and the technicians who are at last being given the chance to work must articulate the contemporary black man's mind, his point of view, his aspirations and goals. The black filmmaker must come to terms with the world he lives in, whether it be 125th Street and Lenox Avenue or an integrated suburb that is nothing more than a prison. Black films can liberate us from illusions, black and white, and in freeing us they can give us vision and truth. It is a tremendous responsibility, much greater than that placed on ordinary white moviemakers. But the dignity of the American black man has traditionally lain in his ability to face reality no matter how senseless it may seem and then, if he is lucky, to alter that reality. Black movies, like many of the new black dance companies and a few of the new black poets, must help their audiences, the community, to continue to see reality.

The enormous response of the black audience in the 1970s has shown that blacks expect more from their films and are eager for material worthy of their expectations. Perhaps tomorrow some exciting new black director will give us not the great black American film but at least a good one in which the new black consciousness is combined with some of the rich spontaneity and charisma of the old-style black performers. Perhaps we will get a remake of *Native Son* with a young Poitier to do the kind of role Sidney Poitier himself never had a chance to do. Perhaps we will have a Dorothy Dandridge who will not have to play or live out the tragic mulatto role and end by sacrificing herself. Perhaps we will have a Louise Beavers who will explore the black religious experience without having to rely on exploitative sentimentality. Perhaps we will get a magical comic-tragic little actor who will touch, amuse, and rouse us consistently as Rochester and Mantan Moreland were permitted to do intermittently. Perhaps we will have an actor with the talent of Stepin Fetchit, who will be able to "sweep a nation off its feet" through his art without having to demean himself. Perhaps ultimately American movies will wake up and be invigorated by black cinema the way poetry was by black poets and the way sports were by black athletes and the way music was by black composers, musicians, and performers. Perhaps we will get our American Sembène, or better still perhaps Sembène will come here and film for us.

No one knows what the future holds. We only know that the black man's past entitles him to a better future. And we know that black actors can transcend even base material. And now we can only hope that new dazzling black lights will emerge on the screen (and behind it) to capture and extend our imaginations as good performers and good movies should.

INDEX

INDEX

(Page numbers in italics refer to illustrations)

Act of Murder, An (1948), 56

Adams, Joe, 169, *170*

Adventures of Huckleberry Finn, The (1939, 1960), 70, 140. *See also: Huckleberry Finn* (1931)

Affair of the Skin, An (1963), 198

Affectionately Yours (1941), 93

Africana (stage), 161

African Manhunt (1957), 147

Agee, James, 125, 142

A-Haunting We Will Go (1942), 72

Alexander, Jane, *233*

Ali, Muhammad, 44

Alice Adams (1935), 83–84, 85

Alice's Restaurant (1969), 141

All God's Chillun Got Wings (stage), 25, 94

All the Fine Young Cannibals (1960), 67, 189

All the Young Men (1960), 215

"Amos 'n' Andy" (television series), 72, 102, 107

Anderson, Eddie "Rochester," vii, viii, 35, 37, 69, 77–82, *78*, 92, 97, 99, 102, 117, 119, 128, 129, *130*, 134, 244

Anderson, Ernest, 138–39

Anderson, Marian, 160

Anderson, Myrtle, 69

Androcles and the Lion (1952), 185

Angel Levine, The (1970), 191, 204

Angelou, Maya, 198

Animal Crackers (1930), 37–38

Annabelle's Affairs (1931), 63

Anna Lucasta (1958), 15, 71, 188, 193, 196,

Anna Lucasta (cont'd.) 214, 240

Anna Lucasta (stage), 185

Another Face (1935), 83

Any Number Can Play (1949), 142

Armstrong, Louis, 71, 75–77, *76*, 117, 119, 121, 129, 134, 135, 159, *187*

Arrowsmith (1931), 137, 138, 186

Artists and Models (1937), 75

Astaire, Fred, 48, 134

As Thousands Cheer (stage), 162

At Home Abroad (stage), 162

Atlantic City (1945), 75

"Aunt Jemima," *120*

Aurthur, Robert Alan, 180, 181

Autry, Gene, 109

Bahama Passage (1942), 168

Bailey, Pearl, 135, 159, 169, *170*, 174, 188, 189

Baker, Josephine, 33

Balcony, The (1963), 199

Bancroft, Anne, 216

Band of Angels (1957), 180, 191

Bankhead, Tallulah, 139

Bara, Theda, 150

Bargain with Bullets, 109

Barker, Lex, 168

Barrie, Barbara, 201, *203*

Barrymore, Ethel, 150, 151

Barrymore, John, 192

Barrymore, Lionel, 47, 48

Basie, Count, 117, 134, 135

Baskette, James, 135–36
Bataan (1943), 129, 139
Battle Hymn (1957), 147
Baxter, Warner, 54
Beard, Stymie, 7, 21–23
Beavers, Louise, 35, 37, 45–46, 57, 58, 59,
   60, 62–67, 65, 77, 83, 86, 102, 109, 145, 152,
   176, 185, 192, 212, 244
Belafonte, Harry, 30, 124–25, 159, 168, 169,
   170, 189, 190–91, 199, 207, 236, 237
Belle of the Nineties (1934), 45, 46, 119
Belle of the Yukon (1944), 186
Bend of the River (1952), 44
Bennett, Lerone, 234
Benny, Jack, 35, 75, 77–81, 92, 97
Benny Goodman Story, The (1955), 187, 214
Berry Brothers, 127
Best, Willie "Sleep 'n' Eat," 35, 46, 50, 51,
   52, 71–72, 73, 74, 129
Betrayal, The (1947), 110, 111, 116
"Beulah" (television series), 66, 165
Beware (1946), 108
Biberman, Herbert, 225
Big Broadcast, 121
Big Broadcast of 1936 (1936), 48, 134
Big Parade, The (1925), 26
Big Timers (1946), 108
Bill Cracks Down (1939), 79
Birth of a Nation, The (1915), xi, 4, 10–18
   passim, 11, 20, 24, 26, 101, 102–103, 224, 230
Birth of a Race, The 103
Birth of the Blues (1941), 82
Birthright (1924), 111, 115
Biscuit Eater, The (1940), 38
Blackbirds (stage), 31, 48, 125, 156
Blackbirds of 1930 (stage), 161–62
Blackboard Jungle, The (1955), 179–80, 216
Black Boy (stage), 60, 94
Blackenstein (1972), 236
Black Girl (1960), 243
Black Jesus (1971), 186, 235–36
Black King, The (1932), 108
Black Like Me (1964), 206, 207, 208, 224
Black Magic (1932), 111
Black Rodeo (1972), 186, 236
Black Sherlock Holmes, 105
Blacula (1972), 187, 236
Blonde Venus (1932), 83
Blood of Jesus, The, 108
Blue Gardenia, The (1953), 121, 187
Blues for Mr. Charlie (stage), 198
Body and Soul (1924), 99, 111

Body and Soul (1947), 139–40
Bogart, Humphrey, 140–41, 185
Bojangles, *see* Robinson, Bill
Bombshell (1933), 63
Borderline (1928), 95
Borom Saret (1963), 243
Boston Strangler, The (1968), 187
Boyd, Stephen, 225, 228
Brando, Marlon, 134, 180
"Break the $250,000 Bank" (television show),
   165
Breen, Bobby, 56
Breezing Home (1937), 72
Brent, George, 138
Brewster's Millions (1945), 82
Bride Walks Out, The (1936), 84
Bridges, Lloyd, 144
Bright Road (1953), 127, 142, 168, 171, 190
Broadway Bill (1934), 13, 53–54, 56
Broadway Melody, 121
Broadway Rhythm (1945), 82
Broadway Rhythm of 1944 (1944), 124, 127
Brodie, Steve, 144
Broken Chains (c. 1916), 16
Broken Strings (1940), 56, 108
Bronze Buckeroo (1938), 108–109
Brooks, Clarence, 108, 137
Brooks, Lucius, 109
Brother John (1971), 236
Brown, Ada, 131
Brown, Clarence, 154–55, 156
Brown, Everett, 92
Brown, H. Rap, 219, 224
Brown, Jim, x, 4, 194, 219, 220–23, 221
Brown Buddies (stage), 48
Browne, Roscoe Lee, 206–207, 228, 231
Browser, Aubrey, 105
Brute, The (1920), 111
Bryant, Marie, 134
Brynner, Yul, 165
Buck and Bubbles, 129
Buck and the Preacher (1972), 56, 191, 199,
   236–37, 242
Buck Benny Rides Again (1940), 80
Buckwheat, 7, 21–23
Buell, Jed, 108
Bunche, Ralph, 160
Bundle of Blues (1933), 119
Burden of Race, The, 105
Burns, Tommy, 17
Bus Is Coming, The (1971), 236
Bye Bye Braverman (1968), 240

Cabin in the Cotton (1932), 54
Cabin in the Sky (1943), 31, 69, 70, 72, 74, 75, 81–82, 93, 117, 127, 128–31, *130*, 131, 162
Cabin in the Sky (stage), 162
Caine, Michael, 208–209
Caine Mutiny, The (1954), 147
Cairo (1942), 162
Call of His People, The, 103–105
Calloway, Cab, 62, 119, 121, 131–32, 134, 135, 188
Calvé, Emma, 171
Cambridge, Godfrey, 193, 205, 232, 240
Canby, Vincent, 241
Can This Be Dixie (1936), 84
Capra, Frank, 53–54, 56
Cardinal, The (1963), 204, 205
Carmen (Bizet opera), 169, 171
Carmen Jones (1954), vii, 30, 33, 128, 168–71, *170*, 174, 189, 190, 193, 207, 210
Carmichael, Hoagy, viii
Carmichael, Stokely, 157, 210, 219
Carolina (1934), 42, 54
Carolina Blues (1944), 134
Caron, Leslie, 187
Carroll, Diahann, 169, *170*, 190, 194, 209, 210–11, 212, 213, 215, 241
Carroll, Vinnie, 201
Carter, Ben, 56, *87*, 134, 139
Casablanca (1942), viii, 140–41
Casbah (1948), 134
Case of Mrs. Wingate, The (Oscar Micheaux novel), 110
Cash, Rosalind, 242
Cassavetes, John, 141, *177*, 180, 181, 200, 232
"Cavalcade of America" (radio program), 156
Centennial Summer (1946), 134
Certain Smile, A (1958), 121
Chandler, Jeff, 179
Charlie Chan in Egypt (1935), 74
Chase, Charlie, 24
Chester, Slick, 114
Chicken Thief (1910–11), 8
China Gate (1957), 188
China Seas (1935), 85
Chinese Cat, The (1944), 74
Chinese Ring, The (1947), 74
Clansman, The (novel; Thomas Dixon), 10
Clark, Dane, 141
Clarke, Alex, 226
Clarke, Shirley, 200–201, 206
Cleopatra (1963), 150, 174
Cochran, Gifford, 99

Cohen, Octavus Roy, 105–107
Colbert, Claudette, 57, 59, 62, 150, 216
Cole, Nat "King," 121, 159, 187–88
Colman, Ronald, 137
Come Back Charleston Blue (1972), 225, 231, 240
Comedians, The (1967), 204, 207, 224, 232, 239
Comic, The (1969), 75
Condor, El (1970), 220
Confederate Spy (c. 1910), 6
Congo Maisie (1940), 69
Connection, The (1960), 206
Connelly, Marc, 67, 68
Connor, Edgar, 38
Cool Breeze (1972), 225, 236
Cool World, The (1963), 200–201, 202
Coon Town Suffragettes (c. 1914), 9
Cooper, Ralph, 109
Corey, Jeff, 144
Corman, Roger and Gene, 199–200
Cotton Comes to Harlem (1970), 206, 213, 225, 230, 231, 236, 240, 241
Count of Monte Cristo, The (1934), 54
County Chairman, The (1935), 42
Crain, Jeanne, 150, 152, *153*
Crash Dive (1943), 139
Crawford, Broderick, 172
Crimson Fog (1932), 105
Cripps, Thomas, 105
Crosby, Bing, 56, 75, *76*
Crosse, Rupert, 232
Crossfire (1947), 143
Crowther, Bosley, 44, 138–39, 148, 157
Cry, the Beloved Country (1952), 140, 179
Cukor, George, 63
Curley McDimple (stage), viii, 94
Curtis, Tony, *177*, 182, 191
Curtiz, Michael, 138, 140, 157

Daly, William Robert, 6
Dandridge, Dorothy, vii, x-xi, xii, 4, 30, 33, 128, 129, 134, 135, 159, 160, 161, 166–75, *167*, *170*, *173*, *183*, 190, 210, 244
Dandridge, Ruby, 129, 166
Dandridge, Vivian, x-xi, xiii, 166–68
Daniels, Bebe, 48
Dark Manhattan (1937), 109
Dark of the Sun (1968), 220, 222
Dark Sands (1938), 97
Darktown Jubilee (1914), 102
Darktown Revue (1931), 111
Dassin, Jules, 223–24, 225

Daughter of Shanghai (1937), 69
Daughter of the Congo (1930), 111, *113*, 115
David Harum (1934), 41–42
Davis, Angela, 236
Davis, Benjamin O., 139
Davis, Bette, 79, 81, 138
Davis, Ossie, vii, 59, 194, 204–206, 215, 225, *228*, 231
Davis, Sammy, Jr., 4, 25, 31, 118, 141, *173*, *174*, 213, 214–15, 230
De Carlo, Yvonne, 180, 191
de Havilland, Olivia, 138
de Rochemont, Louis, 147
de Wilde, Brandon, 162
Dean, James, 180
Death of a Gunfighter (1969), 128
Debt, The (1912), 9
Deceit (1921), 111, 115
Decks Ran Red, The (1958), 172–73
Dee, Ruby, vii, xii, 59, 181, 182, 184–85, 188, 194, 196, *197*, 198–99, 205, 224, 236, 237
Deep Are the Roots (stage), 146
Deep Is the Well (1951), 139, 193
Defiant Ones, The (1958), 145, *177*, 180, 182–83, 193
DeKnight, Fannie Belle, 31
Demetrius and the Gladiators (1953),
Dennison, Jack, 175
Detective, The (1968), 208
Devil at Four O'Clock, The (1961), 202
Dietrich, Marlene, 83
Dimples (1936), 43, 46
Dirigible (1931), 54
Dirty Dozen, The (1967), 220, 222
Disney, Walt, 135
Divorce in the Family (1932), 63
Dixiana (1930), 48
Dixon, Ivan, xii, 202–204
Dixon, Thomas, 10
Doctor Rhythm (1938), 75
Dr. Strangelove (1963), 232
Doctors' Wives (1971), 198
Doolittle, Hilda, 95
Douglas, Kirk, 157
Down Argentine Way (1940), 134
Downey, Robert, 227, 228
Drums of the Congo (1942), 69, 168
Drums of the Jungle (1935), 62
DuBarry Was a Lady (1943), 66
Duchess of Idaho (1950), 127
Duel at Diablo (1966), 216
Duel in the Sun (1947), 66, 93
Duke Is Tops, The, 109

Dunaway, Faye, 209
Dunbar, Paul Laurence, 105
Dungeon, The (1922), 111, 115
Dunham, Katherine, 128, 131, 134
Dunne, Philip, 152
Durante, Jimmy, 41
Dusky Village, The (1932), 105
Dutchman (1967), 194, 206, 207–208

Eagle in a Cage (1972), 240
"East Side, West Side" (television series), 239
Easy Money, 105
Easy Street (1928), 111
Ebony Parade (1947), 108, 135, 168
Edge of the City (1957), 141, *177*, 180–82, 193, 199
Edison, Thomas Alva, 7, 8
Edwards, James, xi, 144, 145–47, 157, 175, 185, 210
Elcar, Dana, 226
Elder, Lonne, III, 242
Ellington, Duke, 62, 117, 119, 121, 129, 134
Elmer Gantry (1960), 71
Emperor Jones, The (1933), xi, 60, 70, 98–99, 108
Emperor Jones, The (stage), 94, 119
End of the Road (1969), 232
Evans, Estelle, 226
Every Day's a Holiday (1935), 119
Ex-Flame (1931), 75
Exile, The (1931), 110, 111

Facts of Life, The (1961), 67
Falana, Lola, 15, 31, 211, *228*, 231
Farina. *See* Hoskins, Allen Clayton
Faulkner, William, 154, 165, 232
Ferrer, Mel, *149*, 150
Fetchit, Stepin, vii, viii, x, xii, 4, 8, 28, 34, 35, 38–44, *40*, 45, *46*, 53, *71*, *72*, 74, 75, 79, 83, 101, 102, 108, 119, 140, 161, 179, 186, 215, 230, 234, *244*
Fiddler, Jimmy, 64
Fields, W. C., 38, 79, 119
Final Comedown, The (1972), 225, 236
Finian's Rainbow (1968), 208
Fired Wife (1943), 70
First Baby, The (1936), 84
First Year, The (1926), 26
Fitzgerald, Ella, 159, 187, 188
Flack, Roberta, 236
Flowing Gold (1940), 186
Fluellen, Joel, 184, 226

Follow Your Heart (1936), 56
Fonda, Henry, 79
Fonda, Jane, 209, 212
Fontaine, Joan, 191
Fountaine, William, 31
Ford, Glenn, 180
Ford, John, 42, 44, 137, 185–86, 224
Foreman, Carl, 144, 145
For Love of Ivy (1968), 217–19
For Massa's Sake (1911), 6
Forster-Jones, Glenna, 241
Foster, Gloria, 201, 202–204
Foxes of Harrow (1947), 141
Fox Movietone Follies (1929), 41
Francis, Anne, 180
Fräulein (1958), 147
Frazier, E. Franklin, 109
Free and Equal (released 1925), 16, 24–25
Freed, Arthur, 128
Freeman, Al, Jr., 194, 206, 208
Freeman, Bee, *112, 114*
From Hell to Heaven (1933), 54
Frontier Scout (1938), 74

Gable, Clark, 85, *91,* 161, 180, 191
Garbo, Greta, 161
Gardner, Ava, 127, 191
Garfield, John, 139, 157
Garland, Judy, 134
Garvey, Marcus, 108
General Spanky (1936), 72
Gentle Julia (1936), 84
Gentleman's Agreement (1947), 143
Georgia, Georgia (1972), 198, 236
Gershwin, George, 117, 124, 214
Ghost Breakers, The (1940), 72
Ghost Talks, The (1929), 41
Gibson, Althea, 159, 185, 186
Gilden, K. B., 208
Gilpin, Charles, 102
Girl from Chicago, The (1933), 111
Girls Around Town (1931), 63
Gish, Lillian, 14, 20, 224
Glenn, Roy, Jr., 217
Glory Alley (1952), 75, 187
Go, Man, Go (1953), 179, 199
Goddard, Paulette, 72
Goddess, The (1958), 67
Go Down Death (1944), 108
God's Little Acre (1958), 71
God's Stepchildren (1937), 111, 114, 115
Going Places (1939), 75
Go into Your Dance (1935), 38

Goldberg, Jack and Dave, 108–109
Gold Diggers of 1933 (1933), 119
Gold West, The (1932), 83
Gone Are the Days (1964), 199, 204, 205–206,
211–12, 231, 240
Gone with the Wind (1939), viii, ix, 36, 54,
66, 86–94, *87, 91,* 94
Gonzales Mystery (1921), 111
Grant, Cary, 45, 66
Grasshopper, The (1970), 220
Gray, Harry, 31
Great American Broadcast, The (1941), 134
Greatest Thing in Life, The (1918), 20
Great White Hope, The (1970), 223, 232, *233*
Great White Hope, The (stage), 232
Green Berets, The (1968), 224
Green Pastures, The (1936), 8, 27, 34, 67–69,
70, 77, 79, 90, 131, 134, 231
Griffin, John Howard, 206
Griffith, D. W., 10–18 passim, 19, 20, 24, 26,
102–103, 224, 229, 230
Guess Who's Coming to Dinner (1967), 145,
182, 194, 201, 212, 215, 216, 217, *218*
Gunn, Moses, 240
Guthrie, Arlo, 141
Gwynn, Helen, 39

Hall, Mordaunt, 30
Hallelujah (1929), 26, 28–34, *32,* 107, 118, 239
Hallelujah, I'm a Bum (1933), 38
Hall Johnson Choir, 134
Halls of Anger (1970), 241
Hamilton, Bernie, 201–202, *203,* 204
Hampton, Fred, 236
Hampton, Lionel, 117, 187
Handy, W. C., 188
Hansberry, Lorraine, 165–66, 196–98
Harder They Fall, The (1956), 185
Hardwicke, Sir Cedric, 97
Harlem after Midnight (1934), 111
Harlem Globetrotters, The (1951), 168
Harlem on the Prairie, 108
Harlem in Heaven, 108
Harlow, Jean, 34, 62, 63, 85
Harris, Edna Mae, 69
Harris, Joel Chandler, 136
Harris, Julie, 141, 162, *163*
Harris, Julius, 202
Harris, Phil, 79
Harris, Theresa, 81
Harrison, Rex, 141
Hartman, Elizabeth, 182
Harvey Girls, The (1946), 134

Hayes, Isaac, 235
Haynes, Daniel, 31, *32*
Hayton, Lennie, 127
Heart Is a Lonely Hunter, The (1968), 239
Hearts Divided (1936), 84
Hearts in Dixie (1929), 26, 27–28, 34, 53, 107, 118
Heat's On, The (1943), 124
Heaven Can Wait (1943), 56
Helldorado (1935), 43
Hello, Dolly (1968), 75
Hello, Dolly (stage), 189
Hemingway, Ernest, 150
Hepburn, Katharine, 84, 217, *218*
Hepburn, Philip, 142, 168
Hernandez, Juano, xi, *153*, 154–58, 175, 180, 188, 207
Hidden Hands, The (1943), 72
Hi-De-Ho (1935), 119
High Noon (1952), 144
High Society (1956), 75, 187
High Tension (1936), 84
Hill, The (1965), 204
Himes, Chester, 224, 231
His Eye Is on the Sparrow (Ethel Waters autobiography), 162
Hitchcock, Alfred, 139
Hit Parade (series), 121
Hit Parade of 1937, The (1937), 119
Hit Parade of 1943, The (1943), 134, 168
Holiday, Billie, 135, 238
Holman, Buddy, 105
Home of the Brave (1949), 144–46, 148
Home of the Brave (stage), 144
Homesteader, The (1919), 111
Homesteader, The (Oscar Micheaux novel), 110
Honky (1971), 236
Hooks, Eric, 142
Hooks, Kevin, 142, 239
Hooks, Robert, x, 194, 204, 209, 210, 213, 239, 240
Hooray for Love (1935), 48
Hope, Bob, 72
Horne, Lena, vii, x, xii, 31, 52, 81, 102, 109, 117, 121, 125–28, *126*, 129, *130*, 131, 132, 161, 166, 210
Horse Soldiers, The (1959), 185, 186
Hoskins, Allen Clayton (Farina), 7, 21–23, *22*, 142
Hot Mikado (stage), 52
Hot Rock, The (1972), 240
Houghton, Katharine, 217, *218*

Howard, Dorothy, 63–64
Howard, Trevor, 174
Huckleberry Finn (1931), 13, 53, 140: *see also: Adventures of Huckleberry Finn* (1939)
Howard, Gertrude, 45, 46
How Rastus Got His Turkey (c. 1910), 8
Hudson, Rochelle, 57
Hudson, Rock, 141, 180
Hughes, Langston, 37, 56
Hurry Sundown (1967), x, 15, 71, 194, 208–13
Hurst, Fannie, 57
Huston, John, 138

I Am a Fugitive from a Chain Gang (1932), 137–38
I Dood It (1943), 93, 124, 127
I Love a Bandleader (1945), 82
I Passed for White (1960), 192
I Take This Woman (1940), 72
Ice Stallion Zebra (1968), 220
If He Hollers, Let Him Go (1968), 224
I'm No Angel (1933), 45, 46
Imitation of Life (1934), 57–60, *58*, 62, 63–64, 67, 152, 239–40
In Humanity's Cause (c. 1913), 9
In Old Kentucky (1927), 26, 41, 48, 54
In Slavery Days (c. 1913), 9
In the Heat of the Night (1967), 141, 212, 217, 230
In This Our Life (1942), 138–39
Ince, Thomas, 24–25
Incident, The (1967), 199, 207
Informer, The (1935), 224
Ingram, Rex, x, 26, 69–71, 129, 136, 139, 141, 209, 220
Innocents in Paris (1955), 147
International House (1933), 119
Intruder, The (1963), 199–200
Intruder in the Dust (1949), *153*, 154–56
Irish Luck (1938), 74
Island in the Sun (1957), 171–72, 174, 190–91, 193
Isn't It Romantic (1948), 135
Istanbul (1957), 187
It Happened One Night (1934), 36
It's a Mad, Mad, Mad, Mad World (1963), 82

Jack London (1943), 66
Jackie Robinson Story, The (1950), 66, 184–85, *197*, 199, 201–202
Jackson, Mahalia, 188
Jade Mask, The (1945), 74
Jamaica (stage), 128

James, Olga, 169
Jammin' the Blues (1945), 134
Jam Session (1944), 75
Janie (1944), 92
Jasper Landry's Will (1923), 111
Jazz Hound, The, 105
Jazz Singer, The (1927), 26
Jeffrey, Herbert, 102, 108–109
Jezebel (1938), 54, 79, 81
Jitterbug Party (c. 1933), 119
Joanna (1968), 241
Joe Louis Story, The (1953), 185
Joe Palooka in the Knockout (1947), 56
Johnson, Dots, 181
Johnson, George, 103, 110
Johnson, Jack, 17, 223
Johnson, Kyle, 226–27
Johnson, Noble P., 26, 103, 110
Johnson, Rafer, 236
Jolson, Al, 26, 38, 119
Jones, James Earl, 201, 223, 232, *233*
Jones, LeRoi, 207
Jones, Robert Earl, 201
Jordan, Louis, 108
Judge Priest (1934), 42, 44, 45, 83, 118–19,
140, 186
"Julia" (television series), 211, 241
Jurgens, Curt, 172, *173*
Just Around the Corner (1938), 52
Justin, John, 172

Kael, Pauline, 157, 239
Kazan, Elia, 150, 151, 152
Keaton, Buster, 24
Keighley, William, 67
Kelly, Grace, 171
Kenner (1968), 220
Kentucky Kernals (1934), 71
Killens, John O., 225
Killing, The (1956), 147
King, Martin Luther, 160, 183, 200, 219, 223
King Kong (1933), 69–70
King of Kings (1927), 26
Kings Go Forth (1958), 191–92
King Solomon's Mines (1937), 97
Kiss Me Deadly (1955), 157
Kiss the Boys Good-Bye (1941), 82
Kitt, Eartha, 15, 134, 159, 180, 187, 188, 214
Knight, Arthur, 229
Knight, Shirley, 194, 208
Kohner, Susan, 192
Kongi's Harvest (1971), 231
Korda, Zoltan, 33, 95, 179

Kotto, Yaphet, 231–32
Kramer, Stanley, 144, 145, 162, 182, 217
Krimsky, John, 99

Lady by Choice (1934), 38
Lady for a Night (1941), 134
Lady from Louisiana (1941), 168
Lady Sings the Blues (1972), 236, 238–39,
242
Lady's from Kentucky, The (1938), 64
Lamour, Dorothy, 79
Landlord, The (1970), 190, 198
Lang, Fritz, 121
Last Angry Man, The (1959), 193
Last Gangster, The (1937), 64
Last of the Mobile Hot Shots (1970), x, 240
Last Parade (1931), 54
Last Voyage, The (1960), 186
Laurents, Arthur, 144
Law, John Philip, 209
Lawford, Peter, 213, 215
Le Baron, William, 132
Le Roy, Mervyn, 137–38
Learning Tree, The (1969), 30, 194, 223,
226–27, 240
Lee, Canada, 139–40, 179, 201
Lee, Carl, 201
Lee, Ed, 41
Legend of Nigger Charley, The (1972), 236,
241
Leigh, Vivien, *87*, 89, *91*, 150
Leighton, Margaret, 165
Lem Hawkin's Confession (1935), 111
Lena (Lena Horne autobiography), 127
Leo the Last (1970), 241
Leslie, Lew, 31, 125
Let No Man Write My Epitaph (1959), 187,
202
Levy, Robert, 103
Liberation of L. B. Jones, The (1970), 15, 31,
206, 211, *228*, 231–32
Life Goes On (1938), 64, 109
Lifeboat (1944), 139
Lights Out (1952), 146
Lilies of the Field (1963), 216, 230
Lincoln, Abbey, 202, 217–19
Lincoln's Dream (ind), 103
Little Colonel, The (1935), 13, 46, 47, 48, 83,
118
Little Men (1934), 83
Little Miss Marker (1934), 46
Little Rascals, The, see: Our Gang
Little Robinson Crusoe (1924), 26

Littlest Rebel, The (1935), 13, 46, 47, 48–52, 51, 54, 71
Lloyd, Harold, 21, 215
Lockhart, Calvin, 241
Lombard, Carole, 66
London, Julie, 192
Long, Avon, 134
Long, Walter, 4
Long Ships, The (1964), 182, 215
Lost Boundaries (1949), 140, 149–50, *149*
Lost Horizon (1937), 134
Lost in the Stratosphere (1934), 83
Lost Man, The (1969), 208, 223, 227, 241
Lost Weekend, The (1945), 142
Louis, Joe, 108, 185
Love in a Bungalow (1937), 64
Lovejoy, Frank, 144
Love Thy Neighbor (1940), 80, 81
Lowe, James B., 5, 6–7
L-Shaped Room, The (1963), 207
Lucas, Sam, 6
Lucky Ghost, 108
Lumet, Sidney, 207
Lunceford, Jimmy, 168
Lundigan, William, 150, 152
Lydia Bailey (1952), 186–87

Mabley, Moms, 102
McCullers, Carson, 162, 164
McDaniel, Hattie, vii-viii, ix, xii, 4, 9, 35, 37, 46, 47, 56, 66, 77, 82–89, *87*, 92–93, 99, 118, 135, 138, 152, 156, 161, 171, 189, 198, 216
McGarrity, Everett, 31
McKay, Louis, 239
McKinney, Nina Mae, 4, 31–34, *32*, *96*, 101, 102, 150, 166
MacLachlan, Janet, 239
MacMurray, Fred, 84
McMasters, The (1970), 207
McNair, Barbara, 182
McNeil, Claudia, 15, 193, 194, *197*, 198
McQueen, Butterfly, vii, viii, ix, 35, 66, 77, 89–90, *91*, 92, 93–94, 129
McQueen, Steve, 232
Made for Each Other (1939), 64–66
Madison, Gloria, 184
Mad Miss Manton, The (1938), 85–86
Make Way for Tomorrow (1937), 64
Malaga (1962), 172, 173
Malcolm X, 219, 236
Mamba's Daughters (stage), 62, 162
Mambo (1955), 134
Man, The (1972), 232

Man About Town (1939), 79, 81, 119
Man and Boy (1972), 204
Man Called Adam, A (1966), 213–14, 215, 239
"Man Is Ten Feet Tall, A" (television series), 180
Man Who Shot Liberty Valence, The (1962), 186
Man Who Would Be White, The (Aubrey Browser novel), 103–105
Manchurian Candidate, The (1962), 147
Mandabi (1969), 243
"Mandrake and the Magician" (television series), 185
Mangano, Silvana, 134
Manhandled (1944), 146
Manhattan Merry-Go-Round (1937), 119
Mankiewicz, Joseph, 178, 179
Marciano, Rocky, 185
Margie (1946), 92
Markham, Pigmeat, 102
Mark of the Hawk, The (1958), 180, 188
Marsh, Mae, 14n.
Marshall, William, 186–87
Martin, Dean, 214, 215
Marx, Groucho, 37–38
Maryland (1940), 56, 69, *87*, 92
M*A*S*H (1970), 241
Masher, The (1907), 8
Mason, James, 172
Masquerade (Oscar Micheaux novel), 110
Massey, Raymond, 7
Mathis, Johnny, 121
Mayfield, Curtis, 238
Mayfield, Julian, 224
Meanest Man in the World, The (1940),
Meeker, Ralph, 187
Meet Me in Las Vegas (1956), 128
Melinda (1972), 17, 236, 237, 242
Melody for Two (1939), 79
Melody Parade (1943), 74
Member of the Wedding, The (1952), 141, 147, 162–65, *163*
Member of the Wedding, The (stage), 162
Men in War (1957), 147
Meredith, Burgess, 209
Merrily We Live (1938), 72
Meyers, Sidney, 142
Micheaux, Oscar, 99, 101, 102, 109–16, 231
Midnight Cowboy (1969), 242
Mildred Pierce (1945), 93
Milestone, Lewis, 138
Mili, Gjon, 134
Miller, Dorie, 139

Miller, Flournoy, 134
Miller, Warren, 200
Millionaire (1927), 111
Mills, Earl, 174
Mills Brothers, 135
Minnelli, Vincente, 81–82, 125, 128, 131, 134
Miracle in Harlem (1947), 108
Miracle Worker, The (1962), 211
Mission to Moscow (1943), 138
Mississippi (1935), 38
Mr. Blandings Builds His Dream House
  (1948), 66
Mr. Buddwing (1965), 224
Mr. Moses (1965), 224
Mitchell, Margaret, 86
"Mod Squad" (television series), 141, 202
Monster Walks, The (1931), 71
Moonrise (1948), 70, 71, 141
Moore, Archie, 70
Moore, Juanita, 192
Moore, Tim, 72
Moreland, Mantan, x, 71, 72–75, *73*, 101, 102,
  108, 109, 129, 244
Morgan, Helen, 99
Morrow, Vic, 180
Morton, Edna, 105
Moses, Ethel, *113*, 114
Mostel, Zero, 191
Moten, Etta, 119
Muni, Paul, 137, 193
Murder on a Bridle Path (1936), 72
Murder on a Honeymoon (1935), 71
Murphy, Dudley, 34, 99
Muse, Clarence, x, xi, 13, 28, 53–56, *55*, 70,
  108
Music Is Magic (1935), 83
Myra Breckinridge (1970), 241

Nancy Drew, Trouble Shooter (1939), 72
Nash, Johnny, 196
Native Land (1942), 100
Native Son (1951), 183–84, 244
Native Son (stage), 139
Navigator, The (1924), 26
Negro in Films, The (Peter Noble book), ix
Negro Sailor, The (1945), 139
Negro Soldier, The (1944), 139
Negulesco, Jean, 121
Nelson, Ralph, 216
New Centurions, The (1972), 242
New Faces of 1952 (1952), 188
New Orleans (1947), 135
Next Time I Marry (1938), 74

Nicholas Brothers (Harold and Fayard), 131,
  132–34, *133*, 168
Nichols, Dudley, 152
Night Affair, The (1961), 125
Night of the Quarter Moon, The (1959), 188,
  192
No Strings (stage), 210
No Way Out (1950), 176–79, 180, 181, 199, 204
Noble, Peter, ix
Nothing But a Man (1964), 200, 202–204

Ocean's Eleven (1960), 214
Octoroon, The (c. 1913), 9
Odd Man Out (1947), 227
Odds Against Tomorrow (1959), 191, 225
Of Mice and Men (1940), 138
Oliver, Thelma, 207
Omega Man, The (1971), 242
On Such a Night (1937), 79
On the Avenue (1937), 43
On with the Show (1929), 43
O'Neal, Frederick, 150, 196
O'Neal, Ron, 237, 238
Once in a Lifetime (stage), 69
One Dark Night (1939), 74, 109
One Exciting Night (1922), 24
100 Rifles (1968), 220, 222
One Mile from Heaven (1937), 52, 62, 79
One More Spring (1935), 43
One More Time (1970), 215
One Potato, Two Potato (1964), 200, 201–202,
  203
O'Neill, Eugene, 25, 94, 98
Operator 13 (1934), 83
Orchestra Wives (1942), 134
Organization, The (1971), 236
Othello (stage), 94, 232
Our Colored Fighters (1918), 20
Our Gang (series), 7, 20–23
Our Hell Fighters (1918), 20
Ox-Bow Incident (1943), 138
Owl and the Pussycat, The (stage), 198

Pace, Jean, 240
Pace, Judy, 240
Paisan (1948), 141–42
Panama Hattie (1942), 125–27
Paris Blues (1961), 75, 210–11, 215
Parks, Gordon, 226–27, 235, 240
Parks, Gordon, Jr., 238
Patch of Blue, A (1965), 182, 201, 204, 216
Paton, Alan, 179
Patton (1970), 147

Pawnbroker, The (1965), 157–58, 206, 207, 224

Pearson, Beatrice, *149, 150*

Peck's Bad Boy with the Circus (1938), 64

Peerce, Larry, 201

Pennies from Heaven (1936), 75, 118–19

Pete Kelly's Blues (1955), 187

Peters, Brock, 169, *203*, 207

Peterson, Louis, 196

Petrie, Daniel, 196

"Peyton Place" (television series), 240

Phaedra (stage), 198

Phoenix City Story, The (1955), 147

Pickaninnies and Watermelon (1910–11), 8

Pickett, Wilson, 236

Pillow to Post (1945), 72, 75, 134

Pinky (1949), 33, 59, 62, 117, 150–54, *153*, 162, 186, 196

Pirate, The (1948), 134

Poitier, Sidney, vii, viii, x, xi, 4, 59, 97, 141, 146, 147, 157, 158, 159, 160, 161, *173*, 174, 175–83, *177*, 190, 193, 194, 195, *197*, 198, 199, 204, 205, 207, 215–19, *218*, 227, 230, 236, 237, 241, 244

Polk, Oscar, 69, 90–92, *112*, 129

Pollard, Bud, 108

Pollard, Harry, 6

Porgy (stage), 60, 69

Porgy and Bess (1959), 27, 31, 56, *173*, 174, 183, 189, 193, 204, 207, 210, 214

Pork Chop Hill (1959), 147, 185

Porter, Edwin S., 3, 4, 230

Portrait of Jason (1967), 201

Postal Inspector (1936), 84

Powell, Adam Clayton, 60, 125

Preminger, Ingo, 241

Preminger, Otto, viii, x, 30, 134–35, 168–69, 171, 208, 209, 213, 240

President's Analyst, The (1968), 240

Pressure Point (1962), 145, 215

Professionals, The (1967), 186

Proud Valley, The (1941), 97

Pryor, Richard, 238

Purdom, Edmund, 174

Purlie (stage), 206

Purlie Victorious (stage), 204, 206; *see also: Gone Are the Days*

Putney Swope (1969), 13, 194, 213, 223, 227–29, 230, 231

Quality (Cid Ricketts Sumner novel), 151–52

Quiet One, The (1948), 142

Racing Lady (1937), 72

Rainbow on the River (1936), 64, 79

Rain or Shine (1930), 54

Raintree County (1959), 192

Raisin in the Sun, A (1961), 16, 182, 194, 196–200, *197*, 204, 240

Raisin in the Sun, A (stage), 165–66, 204

Randolph, A. Philip, 137

Rapper, Irving, 124

Rastus and Chicken (1910–11), 8

Rastus in Zululand (1910–11), 8

Ratoff, Gregory, 122

Ray, Mona, 7

Raye, Martha, 75

Realization of the Negro's Dream, The, 103

Reap the Wild Wind (1942), 66

Rebecca of Sunnybrook Farm (1938), 52

Red Ball Express (1952), 147, 179

Red Dragon, The (1942), 74

Red Stallion (1947), 72

Reddick, Laurence, 15

Reed, George, 69

Reform School, 109

Reivers, The (1969), 158, 232

Return of Frank James (1940), 69

Reunion (1936), 84

Reveille with Beverly (1943), 134

Revenge of the Zombies (1943), 74

Rhapsody in Black (stage), 162

Rhapsody in Black and Blue (1932), 119

Rhapsody in Blue (1945), 124

Richards, Beah, 15, 194, 196, 205, 209, 211–13, 217

Richardson, Jack, 25

Richmond, June, 135

Riding High (1950), 56

Right On (1971), 236

Rio Chonchos (1964), 220

Riot (1969), 220, 222

Ritt, Martin, 180, 239

Ritter, Tex, 109

Roach, Hal, 7, 20–23, 24

Road Demon (1938), 52

Robertson, Hugh, 242

Robeson, Paul, xi, 25, 31, 33, 35, 60, 70, 94–100, *96*, 102, 119, 128, 129, 138, 146, 147, 156, 161, 172, 184, 220

Robin and the 7 Hoods (1964), 215

Robinson, Bill "Bojangles," vii, viii, 4, 13, 35, 37, 47–52, *49, 51*, 62, 75, 77, 79, 108, 119, 131–32, 160–61, 176

Robinson, Jackie, 66, 159, 184–85, *197*, 225

Robson, Mark, 144, 145
Rochester, *see:* Anderson, Eddie
Roemer, Michael, 202
Rogers, Will, *40,* 42, 48, 83, 140, 215
Roosevelt, Eleanor, 191
Rosemond, Clinton, 69, 138
Rosie (1967), 192
Ross, Diana, 238–39
Rossellini, Roberto, 141
Rossen, Robert, 134, 139, 171
Roundtree, Richard, 235, 242
Royal Romance, A (1930), 53
Rufus Jones for President (c. 1931), 118
Russell, Alice B., 110

Sahara (1943), 70, 71, 139
Sailor Takes a Wife, The (1945), 82
St. Jacques, Raymond, 194, 207, 224–25
St. Louis Blues (1929), 34, 118
St. Louis Blues (1958), 157, 187, 188, 189, 193
Salt and Pepper (1968), 215
Salute (1929), 44
Samuels, Lesser, 179
Sanders of the River (1935), 33, 95, 97
Sandpiper, The (1965), 147
Sandrich, Mark, 79
Sands, Diana, xii, 194, *197,* 198, 204
Santa Fe Trail (1940), 186
Saratoga (1937), 85
Sarong Girl (1943), 74
Sarris, Andrew, 37
Savini, Robert M., 108
Scalphunters, The (1968), 204, 205
Scandal Street (1938), 64
Scarlet Clue, The (1945), 74
Scar of Shame (1929), 107
Scott, Alma Long, 122
Scott, Emmet J., 101, 102–103
Scott, Hazel, xi, xii, 117, 121, 122–25, *123,* 127
Scott, R. Thomas, 122
See How They Run; see: Bright Road
Sergeant Rutledge (1960), 185–86
Secret Sorrow, 105
Secret Wilderness (1931), 54
Selznick, David O., 64–66, 86, 89, 93
Sembène, Ousmane, 243, 244
Sensations of 1945 (1945), 134
Sergeants 3 (1962), 215
Set-Up, The (1949), 146
Seven Chances (1925), 24
Shadow of a Doubt (1943), 56
Shadow of the Thin Man (1941), 66
Shadow over Chinatown (1946), 74

Shadows (1961), 200, 201, 232
Shaft (1971), 17, 214, 235, 236, 237, 240, 242
Shaft's Big Score (1972), 235, 240
Sharaff, Irene, 174
She Done Him Wrong (1933), 45, 63
Shock Treatment (1964), 204
Sholako (1968), 186
Shore, Sig, 237
Show Boat (1929), 41, 150
Show Boat (1936), 56, 84–85, 99, 150
Show Boat (1951), 127, 150, 191
Show Boat (stage), 31, 156
Show-Off, The (1946), 82
Shuffle Along (stage), 60
Sign of the Cross (1932), 69
Simms, Hilda, 185
Sinatra, Frank, 141, 191, 192, 214, 215
Since You Went Away (1944), 46, 66, 92, 93, 216
Singing Kid, The (1936), 119
Singing Nun, The (1966), 192
Singin' the Blues (stage), 60
Sins of Rachel Cade, The (1961), 186
Sirk, Douglas, 192
Skelton, Red, 124, 125
Skolsky, Sidney, 38–39
Slaughter (1972), 17, 236, 237
Slaves (1969), 194, 204, 205, 223, 225–26, *228*
Slender Thread, The (1965), 216
Small Town Girl (1935), 187
Smiling Ghost, The (1941), 72
Smith, Bessie, 34, 189
Smith, Mamie, 108
Snowden, Carolyn, 26
So Red the Rose (1935), 13, 54
Something of Value (1957), 141, 157, 180, 187, 196, 204
Something to Shout About (1943), 122
Son of Satan (1922), 111
Song of Freedom (1938), 95–97, 119
Song of the South (1946), 8, 92, 135–36
Sothern, Ann, 125
Soul Soldier (1972), 236
Soul to Soul (1971), 236
Sound and the Fury, The (1959), 165
Sounder (1972), 30, 142, 236, 239–40, 242
South of Dixie (1944), 74
Soyinka, Wole, 231.
Sparks, Ned, 57
Spartacus (1960), 186
Spencer, Kenneth, 129, 139
Spider's Web, The (1926), 111
Spirit of Youth, The (1937), 56, 108

Spitfire, The, 105
Spivey, Victoria, 31
Split, The (1968), 211, 220
Sport of the Gods, 105
Stage Door Canteen (1943), 162
Stahl, John, 57, 59
Stand Up and Cheer (1934), 41, 46, 119, *120*
Stanwyck, Barbara, 85–86
Star for the Night (1936), 84
Stars in My Crown (1950), 156
Star-Spangled Rhythm (1942), 82, 134
State Fair (1945), 186
Steamboat 'Round the Bend (1935), 42–43, 44, 45, 54, 186
Steel Helmet, The (1950), 146
Steiger, Rod, 141, 217
Sterne, Elaine, 103
Stevedore (stage), 69, 94
Stevens, George, 83, 84
Stevens, Rise, 171
Stewart, James, 44, 66
Stone, Andrew, 131
Stormy Weather (1943), xi, 52, 69, 127, 128, *130,* 131–32
Story of a Three-Day Pass, The (1967), 232
Story of Temple Drake, The (1933), 83
Stowe, Harriet Beecher, 6
Strip, The (1951), 187
Strode, Woody, 159, 185–86, 187, 235–36
Strong, Porter, 24
Stymie, *see:* Beard, Stymie
Sublett, John "Bubbles," 129
Sullavan, Margaret, 54–56
Sumner, Cid Ricketts, 152
Sun Shines Bright, The (1954), 44
Sun Valley Serenade (1941), 134
Sundown Trail (1931), 63
Sunshine Sammy, 7, 21, 215
Super Fly (1972), 17, 236, 237–38
Super Sleuth (1937), 72
Susskind, David, 180, 196
Swanee River (1940), 134
Sweet Sweetback's Baadasssss Song (1971), 16–17, 214, 232–35, 236
Swimmer, The (1968), 202
Swing Fever (1943), 127
Sykes, Brenda, 236
Symbol of the Unconquered (1920), 111
Symphony in Black (1935), 119, 135
Synanon (1965), 188, 202

Taboo (stage), 94
Take a Giant Step (1960), 196, 199, 211

Tales of Manhattan (1942), 56, 82, 99–100, 134, 162
Talk of the Town (1942), 70
Tall, Tan, and Terrific (1946), 108
Tamango (1959), 172, *173*
Tammy and the Bachelor (1957), 67
Tarzan's Fight for Life (1958), 147, 185
Tarzan's Peril (1951), 168
Taylor, Elizabeth, 150, 192
Taylor, Libby, 46
Teen-Age Rebel (1956), 67
Teer, Barbara Ann, 225
Tell Me That You Love Me, Junie Moon (1970), 240, 241
Temple, Shirley, 35, 45, 46–52, *49,* 161
Temptation (1936), 111, 115
Ten Commandments, The (1923), 26
Ten Commandments, The (1956), 185
Ten Minutes to Kill (1933), 111
Ten Minutes to Live (1932), 111
Ten Nights in a Barroom (1926), 107
Ten Pickaninnies (1904), 7
Thalberg, Irving, 33
Thank You, Jeeves (1936), 73
Thank Your Lucky Stars (1943), 72
That Certain Feeling (1956), 189
They Call Me MISTER Tibbs (1970), xi, 158, 182
They Won't Forget (1937), 138
Thief of Bagdad, The (1924), 26
Thief of Bagdad, The (1940), 70
36 Hours to Kill (1936), 43
Thompson, Donald, 142
Thompson, Howard, 235–36
Thousand and One Nights, A (1948), 70
Thousands Cheer (1943), 127
3 for Bedroom C (1952), 139
Three in the Attic (1968), 240
Three Men on a Horse (1937), 79
Tick . . . Tick . . . Tick (1970), 220
Till, Emmett, 160
Till the Clouds Roll By (1946), 127
Till the End of Time (1946), 142
To Have and Have Not (Ernest Hemingway novel), 157
To Kill a Mockingbird (1962), 207
To Sir, with Love (1967), 216
Todd, Mike, 52
Top of the Heap (1972), 236
Topper Returns (1941), 80
Topsy and Eva (1927), 8, 26
Towers, Constance, 185
Tracy, Spencer, 217

Trader Horn (1931), 69
Treacher, Arthur, *73*
Trial (1955), 157
Trooper K, 103
Troublemaker, The (1964), 208
Trouble Man (1972), 204, 236
Tucker, Lorenzo, x, 111–14, *112*
Turner, Ike and Tina, 236
Twentieth Century (1934), 36, 38
Two Girls and a Sailor (1944), 127
Two in Revolt (1936), 72
Two Rode Together (1961), 186
Two Smart People (1946), 56
Tyson, Cicely, 193, 213–14, 215, 239

Uncle Tom's Cabin (1903), 3, 17, 230
Uncle Tom's Cabin (1914), 6, 17
Uncle Tom's Cabin (1927), 5, 6–7, 63
Underworld (1936), 111, *112*, 115
Up Pops the Devil (1931), 71
Up the River (1938), 52
Uptight (1969), 13, 192, 194, 199, 206, 223–24, 225, 226, 227, 241

Valiant Is the Word for Carrie (1936), 84
Van Peebles, Melvin, 16–17, 232–35, *234*, 242
Vanishing Virginian, The (1941), 54
Variety Girl (1947), 135
Veiled Aristocrats (1932), 111
Vidor, King, x, 28, 29, 30, 31, 33, 54, 93, 239
Virginia (1941), 54
Virgin Island (1960), 199
Virgin of the Seminole, The (1922), 111
Vivacious Lady (1938), 72
von Sternberg, Josef, 83

Wages of Sin (1929), 111
Waiting for Godot (stage), 74–75
Wagner, Robert, 189
Walcott, Jersey Joe, 159, 185
Walk on the Wild Side (1962), 192
Walker, Leila, 103
Wallace, Coley, 185
Wallace, Jean, 184
Waller, Fats, *130*, 131
Warren, Mark, 231
Warwick, Dionne, 194, 225, *228*
Washington, Booker T., 101, 102
Washington, Fredi, 57, *58*, 59–62, *61*, 166
Washington, Isabelle, 60
Washington, Kenny, 141
Washington, Mildred, 28
Washington Merry-Go-Round (1933), 54

Watch on the Rhine (1943), 56
Watermelon Man (1970), 75, 232, 240
Waters, Ethel, 4, 31, 59, 62, 66, 99, 117, 118, 128, 129, *130*, 141, 150–51, 152–54, *153*, 159, 160, 161–66, *163*, 171, 186, 189, 212
Waters, Mira, 226
Watts, Richard, Jr., 33
Way Down South (1939), 56, 134
Welch, Raquel, 222
Welles, Orson, 139
Wellman, William, 138
Werker, Alfred L., 147
West, Mae, 9, 45–46, 62, 63, 66, 89, 119
West of the Pecos (1934), 71
Weston, Sam, 201
What Price Hollywood (1932), 63, 79
What's Buzzin' Cousin (1943), 81
Wheeler and Woolsey, 48
When Men Betray (1928), 111
Whipper, Leigh, 105, 138
Whispering Ghosts (1942), 72
White, Walter, 16, 99, 125
White Bondage (1937), 79
White Hunter (1936), 69
Whitman, Ernest, 69
Whitman, Stuart, 172
Whitmore, James, 206
Widmark, Richard, 128
Wilde, Sonya, 192
Will Mastin Trio, 214
William, Warren, 57
Williams, Bert, 25, 101, 102
Williams, Billy Dee, 193, 238–39
Williams, Clarence, III, 202
Williams, Spencer, 102, 108, 109
Williamson, Fred, 241
Wilson, Dooley, viii, 128, 131, 140
Wilson, Flip, 234
Wilson, Frank, 69
Wilson, Woodrow, 10
Wind from Nowhere, The (Oscar Micheaux novel), 110
Winfield, Paul, 239
Wings over Honolulu (1937), 64
Winner Take All (1933), 54
Wise, Robert, 146
Wiseman, Frederick, 201
Within Our Gates (1920), 111
Woman from Monte Carlo (1932), 54
Women, The (1939), 93
Wonder Bar (1934), 38
"Wonder Kids, The" (vaudeville act), 166–68
Wood, Natalie, 191–92

Woodward, Joanne, 165, 210
Wooing and Wedding of a Coon (1905), 8
Words and Music (1948), 127
World, the Flesh, and the Devil, The (1959), 191
World Moves On, The (1934), 41, 44
Wright, Richard, 159, 183–84
WUSA (1970), 240
Wyler, William, 79, 211, 231

Yancy, Emily, 240
Yerby, Frank, 141
You Can't Cheat an Honest Man (1939), 79

Young, Artie, 108–109
Young, Lester, 134
"Young Lawyers, The" (television series), 240
Young Man with a Horn (1950), 75, 156–57
Young One, The (1961), 202
Your Cheating Heart (1964), 71

Zanuck, Darryl F., 150, 162, 172, 186
Zanzibar (1940), 56
Zenobia (1939), 43
Ziegfeld Follies (1944), 127
Zinnemann, Fred, 162